N

Sensing Danger

A Raven & Sinclair Novel

Sensing Danger is a work of fiction. Names, places, and incidents either are products of the author's imagination or are used fictitiously.

Also by Wendy Vella

Historical Romances

Regency Rakes Series
Duchess By Chance
Rescued By A Viscount
Tempting Miss Allender

The Langley Sisters Series
Lady In Disguise
Lady In Demand
Lady In Distress
The Lady Plays Her Ace
The Lady Seals Her Fate

The Raven and Sinclair Series
Sensing Danger
Seeing Danger

Novellas

The Lords Of Night Street Series
Lord Gallant
Lord Valiant

Christmas Wishes

Stand Alone Titles
The Reluctant Countess

Contemporary Romances
The Lake Howling Series
A Promise Of Home
The Texan Meets His Match
How Sweet It Is
It Only Took You

Dedication

Nan Nan

I didn't realize my dream until you had left us, so this one is
for the best Nana a grandchild could ever ask for.
Funny, intelligent, you were strong and resilient and always
knew the right thing to say.
You loved us unconditionally and expected nothing in return,
and we miss you so very much.
There are Nan Nanisims in the family that will last for
generations to come.
You taught us to love and laugh, and had never ending
patience as you tried to teach me to knit.
We miss your meat pies and trifle; we miss the lessons you
continually taught.
Love you for ever and always, and promise to keep my top
button firmly done up!

xxx

PROLOGUE

It is said that when lowly Baron Sinclair saved the powerful Duke of Raven from certain death in 1335 by single-handedly killing the three men who attacked his carriage, King Edward III was grateful. Raven was a wise and sage counsel he had no wish to lose, therefore, he rewarded Sinclair with the land that sat at the base of Raven Mountain. Having shown himself capable of the duty, Baron Sinclair was now, in the eye of the King, to be the official protector of the Ravens.

Over the years the tale has changed and grown as many do. There were rumors of strange occurrences when a Sinclair saved a Raven in the years that followed. Unexplained occurrences that caused many to wonder what it was that the Sinclairs were hiding, but one thing that never changed was their unwavering duty in the task King Edward III had bestowed upon them.

To honor and protect the Raven family was the Sinclair family creed.

CHAPTER ONE

England 1818

"He's home you know, him up there in that bloody great castle. Two weeks and we've not had one sighting!"

Miss Eden Sinclair pretended to tug her earlobe and then forced the small plug of wax in tighter. Old Mrs. Radcliff tended toward yelling when she was excited, and Eden's hearing was excellent—in fact, beyond excellent, therefore she needed the protection the wax offered.

"The new Duke of Raven, do you mean? Is he in residence? It was my belief he hasn't lived there since he was a young boy, or so Devon said." Eden looked out the cottage's only window but could see nothing in the darkening sky. However, she felt the huge castle that dominated the landscape loom above them. The people of Crunston Cliff had lived under its shadow for hundreds of years, and most especially the Sinclair family.

Sensing she had a willing audience who was happy to indulge her favorite pastime of gossiping, Mrs. Radcliff attempted to straighten her stooped shoulders as she rocked back on the heels of her soft, worn leather boots.

"Well now, middle Sinclair," the old woman said, using the name most of the villagers did for Eden and her brother Cam, situated as they were below Devon and Essie Sinclair, and above Warrick, Somer, and Dorrie Sinclair. "You'd be right in stating that fact. The young Duke was driven from his home at ten years of age by that vile, perfidious father of his, and he never returned, even when the old Duke demanded he do so. In fact, he went away to war and has only now ventured home, nigh on eleven months after his father's death."

"Scandalous," Eden whispered with just the right amount of awe.

Mrs. Radcliff sucked on her bottom lip, which seemed to draw in the entire lower half of her face as she had no teeth.

"They say he's back to take a bride."

"She'll be one of those titled well-bred ladies who have fluttering eyelashes and white skin." Eden gathered her basket off the table. "He won't settle for just anyone."

"Rather it was you do you, middle Sinclair?"

"Not likely," she answered, moving around Mrs. Radcliff's small cottage, making sure everything was clean and the old lady's supper was laid out ready for her when Eden left. "I'd rather marry Elijah Barry."

"He's seventy!" Mrs. Radcliff cackled.

"Which should leave you in no doubt of my feelings regarding marrying the Duke, Mrs. Radcliff." Eden swung her cloak around her shoulders. "Not that he would propose to a Sinclair."

"Don't protest too much now, middle Sinclair, those words would taste mighty bitter if you had to eat them one day. Plus, there's that business between your families."

"What business?"

"You'll find out when you need to," the old lady said evasively, and Eden dismissed her words. Mrs. Radcliff tended to say things for effect.

"And remember, child, your father was a gentleman, so

there is no reason for you not to marry a Duke if it's your wish to do so." The old lady settled herself in her chair before the fire.

"Enough of this nonsense if you please, you're having far too much fun at my expense." Eden bent to kiss a wrinkled cheek. "And I must be away before someone comes looking for me."

"Lord! Look at the sky, 'tis close to full darkness, and you have to ride the cliffs to reach your home. Go now, before one of your brothers comes searching for you, and shame on me for keeping you so late."

"Dev will be looking after the others, and Cam... well, Cam could be anywhere," Eden added as she felt a weight settle in her chest.

"He'll come about, girl, don't you worry. He's just lost his way for a while."

"I hope you are right, Mrs. Radcliff. Because I for one am growing weary of his behavior."

"Go, girl, before you cannot see a foot in front of your face."

Eden laughed as Mrs. Radcliff made shooing gestures with her hands.

"Remember I am for London in two days with my family, but either Bertie or Josiah will visit with you until I return."

"And you remember to keep your skirts touching the floor and your drawers fastened." The old lady cackled. "And I want of full accounting of every minute upon your return, girl."

"Why, Mrs. Radcliff, I'm outraged at your words," Eden said, pretending to look indignant when she wanted to laugh. "And me an innocent too."

"Bah! No one can be innocent with brothers like yours."

Letting herself out of the little cottage Eden gave in to her laughter as she collected her horse from the small shed, and was still giggling as she set out for Oak's Knoll, the Sinclair home.

The weather was brisk in February anywhere in England, but as Crunston Cliff was situated on a windy ridge above the sea in Dorset, it was not often they had a warm night until summer was well advanced.

She trotted through the small village, where the shops were butted up to each other like a row of books wedged on a shelf. The paint was fresh, the windows clean, and Eden could never remember a time when Crunston Cliff hadn't looked just as it did this day. She could name each proprietor and their children, as she and her siblings had played with the residents of the small town for many years. This was her home, the only place she wanted to be. The thought of London made her shudder. Smelly and overcrowded, Eden knew she would loathe it.

Uncaring that in doing so she was more than likely incurring her brother's wrath, she urged her mount right instead of taking the left-hand fork that led to her home. Pulling out her earplugs, she tucked them down her bodice. Seconds later she was galloping along the cliff top.

"If this is to be our last night here, Atticus, then we will enjoy it as we see fit." The wind caught her words and threw them over her shoulder. The braid her sister had carefully tended was soon free as she bent low over her horse's neck, but Eden didn't care. If this was to be her last night of freedom, she'd be sure to make it a good one and to hell with her family's fury.

Both horse and rider were out of breath when she reined Atticus in at the end of the path. From here there was a sheer drop to the water on two sides. The roar of the sea was almost deafening as it buffeted the cliff below. The moon was bright tonight, allowing her to see the gulls that still hunted prey, and would do so until none could be found, their cries carrying on the breeze. She needed to remember this place when she felt stifled by the confines of London.

"Here we have solitude, Atticus."

Not many ventured this far along the cliffs, as it led nowhere, so Eden was surprised to hear the distant rumble of men's voices. Surprised, and annoyed that someone was about to disturb her. She was even more surprised that whoever it was had taken the route down Raven mountain and through the dense forest. They had a heavy foot, she thought as the sound of cracking wood reached her.

"Why do you suppose someone would take such a route in the dark, Atticus?"

The horse twitched its ears.

"Should we not kill him before we toss him in?"

Eden shook her head, unable to believe she had heard those words correctly.

"Seems a terrible way to die."

She had two choices: make a run for it, and gallop home hard before whoever belonged to those voices saw her, or wait until they left. Could she leave, knowing the men were intent on murder? As the thought entered her head, Eden was suddenly gripped by an urgency that drove the breath from her body. It had her moving to the narrow, winding path that led down the cliff. Inhaling, she took a deep breath and nudged Atticus over the edge. She had ridden it before, but not at night.

Don't think about what's below.

Wincing as she heard a rock dislodge and tumble to the sea, Eden did not release a breath until she had reached the wide ledge at the base of the cliff.

"Good boy." The hand she brushed over the warm neck shook.

"Our orders are to bind his hands and feet and throw him off the cliff. The man didn't say anything about killing him before we do."

"Seems a terrible way to die though."

Nudging Atticus deeper into the shadows, Eden tried to

make sense of what she had heard.

"He's unconscious anyways. Bloody big brute; there's no way we could have handled him awake."

Eden's heart started thumping hard in her chest as she slid from Atticus's back. Was she about to see a man thrown to his death? What should she do? The men were drawing closer and would soon be above her.

"He'll wake when he hits the water for sure."

Eden looked at the sea as she listened to the men talk. Wind brushed the surface, producing whitecaps and swirls of frothy water. Did she dare try and save the man? Could she, or would it be too dangerous to attempt? Sea spray peppered her face as it collided with the rocks.

"Bloody hell," she whispered into Atticus's warm neck as she tried to think rationally, which if she was honest had never been her strong suit. Dev would kill her for this.

Removing her cloak, Eden then pulled off her boots. Forcing the buttons through the holes, she quickly pulled off her dress next. Her chemise would offer her more freedom in the water, which she knew would be bloody frigid.

"Don't feel right does it?"

The men were directly above her now.

"What don't feel right?"

"Tossing a man into the water like he was a lump of rotten meat when he's still breathing. Especially this man."

"If we want to get paid, we do what we were told."

"But how's his lordship to know what we do? We could just leave him here bound like this."

Horrified at the discussion taking place above her, Eden prayed they did not kill the man first. Retrieving a dead body was not something she relished.

"Of course he'll know, you dunderhead! Especially when the man he thinks is dead suddenly appears before him unharmed.

He knows everything; wouldn't be surprised if he's watching us now."

Was it brave or stupid to contemplate saving the man? Was he a good person or bad? Did it make a difference; surely no one deserved to die in such a horrific way? Taking the knife she had strapped to her calf, she clamped it between her teeth.

If there is trouble to be found it is you who will find it, Eden.

With her eldest brother's words ringing in her head, Eden crouched on the rocks and then quietly crept forward. Taking the knife from her mouth, she drew in three deep, slow breaths before once again biting down on the blade. She then lowered herself over the edge and into the icy depths below. The cold squeezed her lungs and she struggled to breathe through her nose. Pushing off as the water sucked away from the rocks, Eden kicked hard to get as much distance as she could between herself and the jagged surface before the next wave came.

The going was tough and within minutes she was breathless, the cold sapping her strength.

How far would they throw him? What if she was too late and he died before she reached him, or what if she never reached him and died trying?

Her family often accused her of being overly dramatic, yet for once she had reason to be.

Fighting the currents, she swam until the cold numbed her limbs, and they grew too heavy to carry on. Drawing a shuddering breath Eden trod water and tried to battle the panic that clawed at her as she thought about her family.

I will see them again, she vowed silently.

Focusing on the cliffs, she listened to what the men above were saying.

"On three."

"What about four?"

"Why would it be four when it's always three?"

"Who made it three?"

"It's on bloody three and if you say one more word I'm tossing you in after him!"

At least the idiots had chosen not to murder the man first. She would take that small blessing as a good omen. She watched their silhouettes as they swung the unconscious man back and forward.

"One, two, three!"

Eden kept her eyes on his body as it flew through the air and then sucking in a deep breath she watched it hit the water a few feet from where she floated. Diving beneath the surface, using her arms and legs, she propelled herself deeper, following the body as it plummeted.

Eden was a good swimmer, her brothers had ensured that, yet as tightness began to crush her lungs, fear made her frantic to drag in air. Engulfed in terrifying darkness, panic choked her, making it harder to descend. Surging forward with another desperate kick she reached out and something brushed her fingers.

He was wriggling like an eel, his body thrashing for release. Grabbing one of his shoulders then using the man's body like a ladder, Eden struggled to climb down him to reach the ankles. Taking the knife from between her teeth she began to saw through the ropes. It was sharp, but they were moving downward fast and combined with her terror, it made the task almost impossible. Desperate now for air, Eden wrapped her legs around his waist, gripped him tight and sawed harder on the ropes. In seconds she had his feet free. Her lungs were shuddering and her head felt light as the man twisted, also desperate for air. They had to reach the surface quickly so she abandoned the idea of freeing his wrists and gripped the knife between her teeth once again. Grabbing his bound hands, Eden kicked upwards. Together their legs propelled them through the black waters until they broke the surface seconds later.

Eden felt some of her panic ease as she took the knife from her mouth, and gulped in a huge, breath. Wracking coughs came from the man as he tried to suck in air and spit water from his mouth. Looking to the top of the cliffs, she was relieved to see no sign of his captors.

"Quiet!"

He did as she asked, and she tracked the men to the edge of the forest.

"They are gone."

Eden could not make out the man's features, only hear the deep rasps of breath as he drew them into his body. "Y-your hands." Her teeth chattered from the cold. "I n-need to untie them." It took her several attempts but finally she had him freed.

"I— How did you—"

"W-we must reach the rocks." Eden cut off his words. "They may come back and see us, so we need to m-move fast."

"Yes." His words were hoarse as they both struck out for the cliffs. Their progress was slow, exhaustion making Eden's limbs leaden. Putting her head under the water and using her hands and feet she swam as fast as she could toward the rocks. When she came up for air, a wave hit her and she spat and spluttered for several seconds, losing her knife in the process.

"Kick!" he yelled.

Eden took a deep breath and swam with the last of her energy. Seconds later her hands touched the rocks.

"Th-thank you," the man rasped, gripping the rocks beside her. They both dragged in huge lungfuls of air. "I-I am not sure how or why you were there, but thank you for saving my life."

Eden's eyes stung from the salt water as she tried to look at him. He appeared big beside her, but she couldn't make out his features. She wondered what he had done to deserve tonight's fate and hoped he was not some horrid, nefarious man who had done evil deeds.

"Are you a good man?"

"What?"

"I-I need to know I have not saved a bad man." Although if she was honest, she probably would have, but suddenly it seemed important to know, which was possibly because she was feeling light-headed.

"No, I am not a bad man."

Eden believed the clipped words.

"We must get to safety." Looking to where Atticus waited for her above, she wondered how they would reach him. The combination of cold and exhaustion had sapped her strength, and surely the man fared little better.

"I-I cannot m-manage without your help, sir. W-we must climb up to my horse," she said, bracing herself as a wave threatened to drag her off. One arm wrapped around her waist, and she was pulled into the shelter of his arms.

"We will make it because I will let nothing happen to you." The deep words were whispered into her ear. "I owe you my life."

She felt a hand on her bottom then, and suddenly she was rising. Reaching the rocks, she scrambled to her knees and then reached down to pull him up behind her. He was a big man, and she had to lean backward and brace her feet. He collapsed beside her, breath heaving in and out of his lungs.

"J-just one more climb."

"Put your foot in my hands," he rasped.

"Let me help you first."

"Put your foot in my hands." This time the words held more strength.

Eden didn't argue, and soon she was again moving upward. He was getting weaker and it took several attempts before their combined efforts got him up beside her.

Hurrying to Atticus, she grabbed her cloak and wrapped it around the man. Reaching for her dress next, Eden quickly stepped into it. She did not try to lace it, and would have removed her chemise had the man not been here. Collecting her boots, she forced her damp stocking-clad feet into them.

"You need it more," he said, taking the cloak from his shoulders and wrapping it around her.

"No, I have my dress, you have nothing." She tried to push it back toward him, and then stopped as the sound of voices reached her once again from above.

"What is wrong?"

"Th-the men," she whispered, dragging him to the wall of rock behind them. "We must hide—they are c-coming."

Eden urged her stallion closer, so he stood before them with the cliff face at their backs. Arms reached for her, moving her right up against the horse.

"Be still now," he whispered.

Eden laid her cheek on Atticus's soft neck and nearly moaned as the heat seeped into her chilled body.

"Thank you." He whispered the words into her hair, his breath briefly warming her scalp. "I should be dead."

The words were fact and made her shiver. Had she not saved this man, he would never have woken to a new day. Never have loved or laughed again. She wondered if he had family. A wife or children?

"Of course he's bloody dead, how could he not be? Coming back was foolish, and I'm the biggest fool for letting you drag me with you."

Scared they would be found, Eden moved closer to the man, her face now wedged between his chest and the horse. One of his hands wrapped around her waist as the voices above drifted down to them. His breath was warm against her damp cheek, rapid puffs of air as he struggled to control the sound in the night air.

"He's dead I tell you!"

"Do you think we should go down to make sure?"

"Make sure of what, you idiot? How the hell could he have escaped? His hands and feet were bound, and we tossed him as far as we could. He'll be fish food now."

The man stiffened in anger, and Eden gripped the front of his shirt, fearing he may do something to alert the men to their presence.

"But I'm sure his lordship wants proof."

"And we're telling him we saw his body floating on the surface. Now unless he's suddenly sprouted gills and fins, Syd, he's dead, so come on. My belly aches, I'm so bloody hungry. Besides, his snootiness is probably sleeping between some wench's thighs by now. He usually has a different one each night, so I've been told."

Eden listened as the voices grew weaker, tracking them until they had left the area. Only then did she move, breaking free from the comfort of the stranger's arms.

"P-put your foot on my hands."

"You first," he said.

"No. I'm sure you are injured, whereas I am just c-cold."

Ignoring her, he picked her up and tossed her onto Atticus's back, and Eden heard his sharp hiss of pain. Then, using the rocks, he climbed up behind her.

"Home, Atticus." Eden urged the horse up the steep track as two large arms wrapped around her waist.

The ride was slow due to the loose ground underfoot and the narrow path. Eden stopped briefly at the top to listen. Hearing no noises, she urged Atticus into a gallop. It was a ride she had undertaken many times in her twenty-three years, but she knew that never again would she travel this path without memories of this night.

"Faster, boy!" Eden urged the stallion as her passenger slumped against her. Following the base of the mountain, she veered right and galloped hard. Minutes later she reached the Sinclair family home.

"W-we are safe now," she whispered, sliding to the ground when Atticus stopped. The man's legs were unsteady as she helped him down, and he now leaned heavily on her. Pushing open the worn front door, she started calling for her siblings as the man slumped against her.

CHAPTER TWO

"Where the bloody hell have you been, Eden? You should have been home hours ago!"

The eldest of the seven Sinclair siblings stalked through a door at the end of the hallway, his long legs closing the distance between them in seconds. Tall and dark, with a scowl that seemed perpetually etched on his handsome features lately, her big brother was the man she had turned to for support at a young age after realizing her father could offer her nothing but pain.

"Dear God, what has happened?"

He ran the remaining few feet as he realized she was not alone. He quickly took the weight of the man who was slumped at her side.

"He is unconscious, Dev. Please, we must help him."

"You are both wet, sister. What has happened?"

"I will explain, I promise, but first we must see to him."

"What madness has befallen us now?"

These words were from Cambridge Sinclair. The other middle Sinclair appeared beside her, reeking of ale and a woman's scent. She intercepted the sour look Dev gave his brother.

"Hurry, Cam, help us," Eden urged him.

He did not hesitate, as she'd known he wouldn't. He may be a drunken idiot, but family was important to him. Between them they carried the man into Dev's room and laid him on the bed, rolling him gently onto his side.

"Eden, what has happened?" These words were spoken by Essie, Eden's elder sister, who hurried to the bed.

"No time for explanations, Essie, we need blankets and hot water and bring your supplies. This man likely needs your help," Dev ordered. Eden fell against his side as he reached for her, giving her a brief hard hug.

"Are you hurt in any way, Eden?"

"No, I am well, but I need to explain—"

"Not now. I will have your tale but first, we must see to the man. But while we do, you can change out of your wet clothes, as your teeth are chattering."

"Yes, of c-course," Eden said.

"If you can manage it in your inebriated state, Cambridge, get some light over here, so we can tend this man," Dev snapped.

"I'm not inebriated!"

Eden knew what was coming. Her brothers fought constantly over Cam's behavior. "And now is not the t-time to start arguing, brothers."

She heard the snap of Dev's teeth, and Cam stalked away to get the lamp. He placed it on the table carefully, and then the brothers reached for the man, turning him gently onto his back.

"Christ, it's the Duke of Raven!"

"Are you sure?" Eden looked from Dev's shocked face down to the man.

His eyes were closed, black lashes forming crescents on his pale cheeks, dark hair damp and tousled. His face was made up of sharp edges and angles that were more pronounced as he lay motionless. Even leeched of color, it was a face that demanded a second look.

"Dev?" Eden accepted the blanket Cam wrapped around her before she looked at her eldest brother. His jaw was clenched, eyes fixed on the Duke with an unwavering intensity that he usually only reserved for disciplining his siblings.

"Did you rescue this man tonight, Eden?"

"Dev, let me—"

"Answer the question."

She nodded. Her brother seemed agitated and Eden sensed that her arriving on the doorstep with an unconscious man was not the entire cause. It took a great deal to unsettle the eldest Sinclair, but suddenly the tension in the room had become so thick it cloaked each of them. Dev's pupils had dilated, and both Essie and Cam were focused unwaveringly upon him.

"Dear Lord, so it's true!"

"What's true?" Eden whispered.

"I will tell you later." He shook his head. "First we must remove his wet clothes, and check for injuries."

Essie moved first, running from the room to collect her medical supplies.

"Go, Eden. You need to get warm, or Essie will have to tend you also."

"Yes, Dev."

"Thank God the others are in bed," Cam said, running a hand through his hair. "Having the unconscious Duke of Raven in the house would have set them twittering."

Eden agreed. The three youngest Sinclair's would have been beyond excited at having the man they had grown up hearing tales about so close.

With a final look at the Duke, Eden followed her sister. Once in the room she shared with Essie, she stripped off her clothes, dried her hair as best she could, and rubbed her body hard before slipping into her nightdress and thick dressing gown. Looking longingly at the bed, she could not remember a time she'd felt so tired. Exhaustion seemed to have turned her legs to jelly, and her arms felt heavy. She would sleep soon, she thought, slipping her feet into her slippers, but for now, she had a duke to see.

Dev stood watching from the foot of the bed while Essie was bent over him, studying the dark, angry bruise on his chest. His eyes were still closed and he lay so still she could believe him dead.

"His color is strong, so I don't fear for his life," Devon said. "Can you detect anything, Essie?"

Shaking her head, Essie stood up. "There are a few bumps and one of his ribs is cracked. He has obviously taken a thorough beating, but nothing life-threatening appears to be wrong with him. However, I think Eden should listen to his lungs and heart."

Flicking her hair over the opposite shoulder, Eden placed her ear on the Duke's bare chest. Ignoring the smooth planes and muscles beneath her cheek, she closed her eyes and focused. There were the usual sounds working in the body, but nothing irregular.

"Everything sounds as it should," she said, feeling breathless at the close contact with the Duke and not understanding why. Eden was surrounded by men, and none of them had ever made her breathless.

"Getting him warm is important now." Essie carried two flannel-wrapped bricks forward. Together she and Dev placed them beside the Duke's body then tucked the covers around him once more. "I have water heating and will make him a tonic to aid his healing, and if he has not woken soon, we will attempt to pour some down his throat."

"I do not doubt your skill, Essie, but do you think because he is a duke we should call a doctor?"

"No doctor, Dev, not yet," Eden said. "Let me tell you what

happened and then if he is not awake after that we will make a decision about the doctor."

"You come and get warm, Eden. I'm sure it will be a miracle if you don't take a chill from your adventures this evening. Imagine if you arrived in London with a bright red nose."

"I'm all right, Essie." Eden followed her siblings into the small parlor off the bedroom. She sank into Devon's large chair before the fire.

The Sinclairs had two servants, Josiah and Bertie Hemple, who had been with the family for years. Josiah's wife had passed and Bertie had never married. They were wonderful men who cared for the siblings as if they were their own.

"You're chilled through, Miss Eden." Bertie handed her a mug of tea while Josiah draped a blanket over her legs. The brothers then left the room.

Cam and Essie settled into seats, while Devon remained standing beside the fire, his large presence reminding Eden that now she would have to answer for her actions this night.

"Begin your story."

"We were taking a last run, Atticus and I, after leaving Mrs. Radcliffe's cottage."

"Yet you knew I would be unhappy with your choice. Especially knowing the danger the cliff pass presents at night."

"Let her speak, Dev."

Eden sent Essie a grateful nod before continuing. "I was just about to return home when the sound of voices reached me."

"Thank God you could hear them, at least that gave you time to get out of sight." Devon ran a hand over his face.

"Yes. To start with I had thought they were either drunken locals or a couple intent on a private tryst, but then I heard them talking about the Duke, and deciding if they were going to kill him before throwing him over the cliff."

"Christ!"

"Did you see who they were?" Cam asked.

"No, I was on the ledge underneath by then."

"Bloody hell!" This time it was Cam who cursed. "You rode that bloody beast down the cliffs at night?"

"I am sure that by the time I have finished my story, you will both have roared at me several more times, so perhaps you can wait till I finish," Eden snapped, relishing the bite of anger that was slowly replacing the numbing fear.

Both brothers glared but remained silent. Essie patted Eden's leg comfortingly and urged her to continue.

"I had already thrown off my boots and stripped to my chemise by the time they were directly above me."

"Why would you take such a risk for someone you did not know?"

Eden looked at Dev and remembered the urgency that had gripped her.

"I could not let him die like that, Dev, and neither would you have. But it was more than that." She tried to tell her siblings how she had felt. "Something drove me into that water. An urgency I have never felt before."

Dev made a sound deep in his throat.

"I slipped into the water and swam out as far as I could and waited." She told them how she had followed the Duke's body under the water, remembering the terror that had consumed her. "It was so dark, and I couldn't find him until in desperation I kicked my legs one last time before I had to surface, and my fingertips brushed his head."

"My God." Devon pushed off the mantel and stalked across the room, the breath hissing from his throat with each step.

"How the hell did you get him untied and out of the water without running out of air? Christ, Eden, you could have drowned and we wouldn't have known," Cam rasped.

"But I did not."

"Take that bloody horse off her and forbid her to leave the house, Dev."

"I intend to," the eldest Sinclair said, and for once her brothers were in agreement, even if it was against her.

"You will not take Atticus off me!"

"Finish your story, Eden; we will talk about the rest tomorrow."

Sending Cam a dark look, Eden continued, finishing with the Duke helping her up the cliffs to her horse.

"Well, I am proud of her." Essie gave her sister's hand a squeeze. "I do not condone riding along the cliffs in the dark, but in this instance she has saved a life and that I will rejoice in. Although I confess I too feel the terror of nearly losing her."

"And now I have something to tell you, and would ask that you hear me out before deciding I have lost my wits." Devon sank into the empty chair after delivering these ominous words. He suddenly looked every one of his thirty years. "Check our patient, Cam, then come and sit before the fire," he added.

"He sleeps." Cam slid to the floor minutes later, leaning back on his brother's chair.

They were so alike in appearance, her brothers, Eden thought. Yet they were as different as night is to day in personality. With the death of their parents Devon had retired from the army and returned home to take responsibility for his six siblings, a duty he took seriously. His family was his life and he would protect them with everything he had.

Cam loved his family just as passionately but allowed his brother to shoulder most of the burden for their welfare. He was a rake who drank heavily and kept company with any woman who would have him.

Consequently, the two older Sinclair brothers had an uneasy relationship. Both occasionally frequented London society, Devon only briefly and usually because he had business to attend, while Cam stayed until his funds ran out.

"Before I enlisted father told me of a story that his father had told him many years before. He believed it had been passed through generations of Sinclairs for centuries and thought it was time I heard it too. He asked me to tell you all when I felt the time was right… I believe now is that time."

Eden felt it again, that sense of urgency she had experienced earlier.

"It is believed, that hundreds of years ago one of our ancestors saved the Duke of Raven from certain death. It is believed by the Sinclairs, and possibly the Ravens, but as I have never asked one, I can neither confirm or deny this, that our gift was the result of this event and—"

"It is not a gift, it is a curse," Cam muttered.

"The Sinclairs became protectors of the Ravens from that day forth," Dev continued, ignoring his brother.

"Bloody hell!"

"My thoughts exactly," Dev said, acknowledging Cam. "Father said that his father had saved the current Duke's great-grandfather from a fire in the village. Apparently, the old Duke had a soft spot for fresh-baked bread and was often seen at the bakers. One day it caught fire and our grandfather pulled the Duke free."

"Can it be?" Essie whispered.

"Supposedly our ancestors were gifted this land by King Edward III in 1335 for our protection of the Ravens, who were—and still are—wealthy, titled, and owners of substantial lands throughout England. The Duke was one of King Edward's advisors and someone he respected greatly, hence the reward and the order for the Sinclairs to protect the Ravens."

"Do you have anything strong to drink in this room?"

Nodding, Devon pulled a bottle and glasses from a cupboard and handed them to his brother.

"If it has not been destroyed, supposedly there is a document King Edward III signed at the time, yet neither father nor our grandfather knew where it was. He believed that the Ravens have it stowed away somewhere in the castle."

Eden couldn't take it in. It all seemed so far-fetched, and yet they did live at the base of Raven Mountain, and they did have their heightened senses.

"I didn't think again of the tale until my unit was called to fight. He was there leading the Eleventh Hussars." Devon pointed to the wall behind which the Duke slept. "I asked about him, knowing he was the one who had grown up away from Raven Castle, yet also knowing that one day he would be the next Duke."

"Yes, he was sent away to school at a young age." Essie frowned as she recalled the facts. "He never came home, even in the holidays. Mother said she was surprised when the future Duke went into the army straight from school. She had been amazed that his father allowed it, as he had been ailing at the time and surely would not want his heir in danger."

"Miserable old bastard that he was," Cam muttered.

Nodding, Devon continued with his story. "His men said that as a leader he was unequaled, his every move carefully calculated, and his losses were minimal."

Eden watched her brother take a large swallow of brandy before continuing. It took a great deal to disturb the eldest Sinclair, yet there was no doubting that tonight he was disturbed—greatly.

"He was taller than most men and when he rode into battle, he always wore a red ribbon on his helmet so they could see him. Of course this made him a target, but it also made his men fight harder to protect him. One day on the battlefield for some reason I found myself next to him. He fought like five men. I have never seen a man wield a sword like him; he was tireless.

Our horses were side-by-side for a while and then I was drawn away in battle, and when I looked back, he was gone."

Eden saw the demons chase across her brother's face as he remembered the fighting. He did not speak about his days in the army often, yet she knew the memories plagued him.

"I still don't know why I did what I did, but something made me search for him. I became desperate, reckless in my need to reach him, almost as if I were possessed by something, very likely as Eden was tonight."

She caught and held her brother's eyes briefly.

"Finally, I found him wounded on the ground behind his horse."

"But surely you remembered Father's words and that was why you went after him?"

Shaking his head at Cam, Devon continued. "No, it wasn't until afterward that I remembered what I had been told."

"What happened then?" Cam urged his brother.

"When I got to him, his right arm was injured, and he was fighting with his left. I fought to get him free and then held out my hand; he took it, and I pulled him up behind me. I rode for his camp, desperate to get him to safety. It was all very strange," Devon added.

"Yes, that was how I felt tonight," Eden whispered. "As if I had the strength of three people and that I could not give up until I had saved the Duke."

Dev nodded.

"Did he see you in the battle, Dev? Did he know who had saved him?"

Devon shrugged at Cam's question. "In truth, I have no idea."

The silence that followed was loaded with tension as the four Sinclair siblings worked through what Devon had just said.

"And now Eden has saved him again," Essie whispered.

"You believe it, don't you?" Cam questioned.

Devon ran a hand through his hair. "I don't know. Once, with me, was perhaps a coincidence, but this, what Eden did tonight—risking her life and feeling the urgency I did, I just don't know."

"Did the tale say that it was always the Duke who was protected?"

"This is only hearsay, Essie, but I believe our great-great-grandmother saved the then Duke's youngest daughter."

"B-but he did not have our gifts?"

"Who?" Everyone turned to look at Eden as she spoke.

"F-father, he did not have a gift and he was a Sinclair."

"He did, actually. However, it was not as strong as ours. He could see," Dev said.

"We did not know that!" Essie looked indignant.

"He wanted it that way." Dev shrugged. "However, the important thing here is that someone is trying to kill the Duke, and he has only just arrived home from his last campaign to take up his rightful place at Raven Castle."

"And because we are supposed to care, we should do so?" Cam muttered. "As if I have time to protect a nobleman with an extremely large ego."

Their father had had the gift of sight but had hidden it from them. Eden could not quite take that in as around her, her siblings discussed what Dev had said. He had made her life torturous with his constant demands of her, and all the time he had carried a gift too. Bastard!

James woke with fear clawing his throat. He battled to breathe as water closed around him, filling his nose and mouth.

"You are safe, Raven. Easy now."

Blindly he sought the owner of that deep male voice. Reaching for the hand that touched his shoulder, he manacled it with his own, gripping the wrist tight.

"Come now, you are safe."

These words finally penetrated the fog of fear, and clarity soon followed. Where was his angel?

"The woman?" he rasped, remembering that without her he would have died tonight. She had risked her own life to somehow be in that water to save him. James shuddered as he remembered the panic. He had been helpless, and it had been many years since he'd felt that emotion.

"She too is safe."

A man came into focus above him. He was tall and dark haired, with serious green eyes. A shiver of awareness ran through James as he studied him.

"I am Lord Sinclair, and it was my sister Eden who saved you."

"She risked her life."

"Aye," the man said as James released him, and he could hear the anger in his voice at what his sister had done this night.

"Water," James croaked. He usually never let anyone help him. He relied on no one and had lived his life that way, yet when the large arm slipped behind his shoulders he was grateful for the support. He drank deeply from the cup, enjoying the cool liquid as it soothed his raw throat.

"It was an act of incredible bravery that some of the men of my acquaintance would be loath to undertake," James said when Sinclair once again lowered him to the pillows. "She risked her life to save me."

"It was an act of incredible stupidity."

He understood the anger the other man was feeling. He had a sister and would be equally as furious if she placed herself in danger. Yet without the woman's bravery he would be dead. Floating in the sea, his body unlikely ever to be seen again. His sister—No, he would not think about that now.

"And yet I will be forever grateful, Sinclair." James looked him in the eye. This man was familiar to him; even his name stirred something in his memory. Had they met in London? No, he would have remembered. James was bigger than most men, and Sinclair would come close to rivaling his height.

"You are safe here with us, Raven, you have nothing further to fear this day."

"Is your sister all right?"

"Aye. She took a fright, and is exhausted, but otherwise unharmed."

"I owe her a great deal."

"Sinclairs look after each other, Raven, therefore consider your debt discharged."

James looked at the man again. Something in his memory slipped into place. Sinclair—dear God, so it was true?

"Did you fight at Quatre-Bras?"

"Aye."

"So I also owe you my life?"

"I believe it is a family tradition."

James muttered under his breath before speaking. "I did not give any credence to that story when my grandfather told it to me, but now it seems I must."

"If it makes you feel better, my own joy upon hearing it was no greater than yours."

James grunted in acknowledgment of Sinclair's words and then winced as his ribs tugged viciously. "So I am currently residing at Oak's Knoll?"

The man nodded but remained silent.

"Twice," James hissed in disgust. "It seems I must place some belief in what I had thought an overdeveloped fable, and I am now indebted to two Sinclairs."

"You owe us nothing, as I have already stated." Lord Sinclair scowled, no happier than James with the conversation. "Have you any idea who wishes to dispose of you?" he asked, changing the subject.

"I'm sure there are many, but I cannot think which one would stoop to such measures as they did this night, and not here in Crunston Cliff, seeing as I have only just arrived."

"Well, as I have stated, you are safe here for now. Whoever tried to end your life very likely believes they succeeded."

"My sister will be worried if I am not there when she wakes in the morning," James said. "I must return home."

"I would advise against it, Raven."

James did not like people telling him what to do, especially this man, who supposedly was one of his protectors. He chafed at the knowledge that his grandfather's words may have been true, and not a story told to a child to intrigue him.

"Is he awake, Dev?"

James felt the air squeeze from his lungs as he looked at the owner of that voice.

CHAPTER THREE

She was exquisitely beautiful, and he knew it was her, his angel.

James watched Sinclair hold out his hand and the woman walk to his side. Not overly tall, she would reach his chin. A long dark braid hung over one shoulder and feathered brows arched over dove-gray eyes. Tilted slightly at the corners, they were framed with long curling lashes. Her teeth trapped her lower lip.

The jolt of awareness he felt looking at her made his fingers curl around the bedding. It was merely a reaction to what they had experienced and nothing more, James reasoned.

It was unfathomable that someone so small and delicate could have saved him. Dressed in that worn blue dressing gown, she did not look old enough nor strong enough to have saved him in the manner she had.

"Raven, this is my sister, Miss Eden Sinclair. It was she who rescued you."

Lord Sinclair wrapped an arm around his sister's shoulders and held her to his side, and James could see the close bond they obviously shared. His family had been cold and distant, in fact, he had never been close to anyone, although he would try for his little sister's sake.

"I am forever in your debt, Miss Sinclair. I will never be able to repay you for the risks you took on my behalf this night, but please allow me to try."

"I did what needed to be done, Duke, and as I have recently learned it is something of a family tradition, there is no need to feel indebted."

"I have just informed my siblings of what lies between our families, Raven," Sinclair said. "They were understandably unsettled by the revelations."

"I have known since my youth."

"Yet, until today you did not believe it?"

Her beauty was disturbing in its power, James thought as Eden Sinclair spoke. He could not stop looking at her; such was her allure. He wondered how many weak men she had ensnared with just a glance.

"The evidence is certainly proving hard to ignore."

"Yet, like us, I am sure you wish to."

James nodded. He had dismissed his grandfather's words, but then he had been six when he heard them.

"Are you sure you are unhurt, Miss Sinclair?" James said as he watched her yawn.

"Yes, thank you. The only aftereffect from the night's activities is tiredness. I shall feel more the thing in the morning."

James wondered how she could sound so dismissive when her actions could have resulted in her death this night. To have risked that for him was humbling, and extremely unsettling. He'd never had someone risk so much for him before. Well, that was not entirely true; her brother had done it also.

"Diving into a freezing ocean to save me is not something I can dismiss easily. Without you, I would now be dead."

"Yet I have told you to do so, Duke, so please do not give it another thought."

Her smile was small and tired, and James had the urge to pull Eden down on top of him and let her rest, which was ridiculous because James rarely had irresponsible urges; dukes could ill afford them.

"You cannot be serious? It is the only thing I will be able to think about for days to come, Miss Sinclair."

"I believe I am."

"I do not like to be beholden to people, and most especially because of something that happened hundreds of years ago, Miss Sinclair."

"Perhaps you could endeavor to stay out of danger then, Duke. It would certainly make both our lives easier," she said, still smiling.

"I don't believe it is a laughing matter, Miss Sinclair."

"You will forgive my sister, Raven," her brother said. "We Sinclairs tend to find humor in situations that others do not."

James had one six-year-old sister, and they did not tease or laugh with each other; in fact, they were barely acquainted, so the Sinclair siblings' obvious closeness was entirely out of his realm of understanding.

"We are not so rare, Dev." Eden Sinclair smiled up at her brother. "I'm sure the Duke knows how to laugh."

"No, I don't," James said before he could stop himself, and instantly felt like a fool. He fell back on what he did best: being a duke. "Furthermore, I have no time to lie here bandying words. My sister will wonder at my absence," he lied. In fact, his sister wished him to Hades.

"Are we bandying?" Eden looked from James up to her brother.

"We were, however, now we are about to explain to the Duke why he cannot leave alone, unprotected, in his current condition."

"Is he all right?"

James looked to the door once more.

"And here are two more Sinclairs for you to become

31

acquainted with, Raven. Both, I'm afraid, are given to bandying words and sudden bouts of unexplainable laughter also. With your permission, as there are many of us and we rarely stand on ceremony, I shall introduce you to them using their Christian names."

It was informal, but as he was lying on a bed in their house and couldn't bow or do more than nod, James agreed and reluctantly added, "My name is James." Who was he to stand on ceremony when he couldn't even stand?

"Cambridge and Essex," Sinclair said, pointing to the man and woman as they reached the bed. James sensed some tension between these two. "I am Devonshire, or rather Devon, and the three youngest Sinclairs are at present sleeping," he added.

"There are seven of you?" James said, bemused as his eyes moved over the siblings.

"Yes." Devon sighed.

"You're each named after a town or county?" James studied each Sinclair. He noted they all had black hair. However, Eden was the only one with gray eyes. The others shared the eldest Sinclair's green eyes.

"Yes, my parents liked to travel and wherever we were… um, conceived… we were named after that place."

James noted Devon wince as Cambridge spoke.

"So where did Eden come from?" he questioned, looking at her.

"Eden was the only one of us conceived here at Oak's Knoll, Duke," Essex said. "My mother always called her home the Garden of Eden, hence my sister's name."

"The Duke wishes to return home tonight," Eden said, no longer smiling. The conversation was obviously uncomfortable for her.

"I would not recommend that course of action, considering someone has just tried to dispatch you to the afterlife, Duke,"

Cambridge Sinclair said. "Your strength will be weakened by tonight's events. I suggest you stay here for a few days. Whoever tried to end your life believes they succeeded, so we do not want to alert them otherwise."

"And yet my sister will wake at 7:00 a.m. and I will be there," James said, his voice steady.

"'Tis folly, Duke. You are still injured and in such a weakened state you cannot hope to defend yourself," Eden added.

"I do not believe whoever attempted to kill me this evening will do so again the following day, Eden. And please call me James." For some reason, he wanted to hear his name on her lips.

"But—"

"Leave it, Eden, the Duke must be allowed to do as he pleases," Devon said. "However, if I may suggest that you leave early before the sun rises, then no one will see you. I would also ask you to stay out of danger until our return, Raven. There will not be a Sinclair on hand should you require one."

"You are leaving?" James said, ignoring the attempt at humor. His gaze lingered on Eden. There was something about the woman that drew his eyes, and he felt it was more than just her beauty.

"We are going to London for the season, Duke," Essex said.

By the downcast looks on the faces of the siblings, James guessed this was not something any of them were looking forward to.

"Is there a problem with my name?"

"Problem, Duke?" Cambridge Sinclair said.

"I have asked you to use it, yet you are not."

Silence greeted these words as the siblings looked at each other then back to him. Devon was silently allocated speaker.

"My mother told us your father was most insistent that he

33

be addressed only by his title."

James battled anger at the reference to his sire.

"I am not my father."

"But you are a duke, and a powerful one," Essex said.

"That has no bearing on you using my name." James wasn't sure why he was pursuing this matter when normally he liked the distance his title afforded him.

"It has when the closest we have come to such a lofty title is Dev."

The siblings laughed over Essex Sinclair's words.

"Where will you reside in London?" James asked, wondering why he cared.

"Our mother's sister is the Countess of Wynburg, James," Cambridge Sinclair said. "She wishes to sponsor Essex and Eden this season, but has expressed her wish that we all come to London to see her."

James may not have spent much time at Raven Castle, but he had made it his business, since returning, to find out every thing he could about the people and events that took place around his estate. His butler, who had been with the family since he was born, was a font of information.

He knew the Sinclairs lived in genteel poverty, and that the previous Baron Sinclair was not a well-liked man in the village. James was unsure how their circumstances now sat; he doubted the current Lord Sinclair was a spendthrift, yet did not know him well enough to know if that was fact.

"I'd like to offer you some compensation for your part in saving my life—twice," James said, although the words stuck in his throat. He didn't care if this… whatever the arrangement between their families was called, was indeed true, he would not be beholden to anyone. Therefore, he would do what needed to be done in his eyes to clear this debt.

"We do not need your money," Cambridge said.

"I would be honored to offer you my coach for the journey then—"

"Thank you for the offer, Raven, it is most generous, yet we are quite capable of getting ourselves to London," Devonshire Sinclair cut him off.

Pride was something James understood as he had his share; the eldest Sinclair, he noted, appeared no different.

"I too am making for London, Sinclair, and wished only for some company for my young sister, as I will be riding," James said, surprised that the words had come from his mouth. He had not intended to leave for London until next month and had definitely not planned to take Samantha with him. However, perhaps after tonight's events he and Samantha would be safer away from here.

"Oh that will be lovely for the twins, don't you think, Dev?" Eden rushed to say.

They were interesting to watch, these Sinclairs, the undertones and glances they gave each other. Almost as if they spoke another language, James thought as the eldest Sinclair glared at Eden.

"Twins?"

"Dorset and Somerset, our sisters, James," Essex Sinclair said.

James suddenly wanted his sister to be in the company of the Sinclairs as they journeyed to London. She was such a shy little girl, who rarely met anyone her own age, and with the Sinclairs she would be safe. They would make sure of it.

"I would be grateful for your protection, Sinclair. Not for myself, but for Samantha."

The siblings all looked at Devon, who in turn looked resigned.

"My sisters would be grateful for the company, Raven. I am sure you will also need a carriage, as your ribs will still be too painful to ride."

"I have two carriages; both will be here by midday two days from now," James snapped, his pride stinging somewhat. "I, however, will be riding."

"Of course, if that is your wish."

"It is."

"If I may suggest that we depart before the sun rises in the morning, Raven, so no one sees you leave. I would caution you to stay hidden in the castle until we leave the village and surrounding area, so those intent on killing you do not realize you are alive," Devon added. "Now we will all get some sleep and then Cam and I will rise by five, in time to have you home by seven."

James did not like anyone telling him what to do but saw that in this Sinclair was probably right. He also knew when he was outnumbered. He had no horse or carriage, and his ribs pulled viciously every time he so much as breathed. He would not make it home alone. It chafed to be at the mercy of another.

He drank from the cup filled with horrid-tasting liquid that Essex Sinclair forced on him. Eden then removed his pillows and lowered him to the bed.

"Sleep well, James, and know that you are safe," she said quietly as the other Sinclairs filed from the room.

"And you, Eden." James touched her hand simply because he needed to. "Thank you once again for what you did, although a mere thank-you seems inadequate."

"It will suffice." She smiled, and then she was gone. Closing his eyes, James let the exhaustion he had been battling finally take hold.

***

"This is really not necessary, Sinclair!"

Ignoring him, Devon and Cam rode with him wedged between them the following morning as they escorted James home. The hour was early, and the darkness was only just beginning to lift and awaken the new day.

"And I had thought my stubbornness unequaled," James muttered as he glared at the stern profiles of the two men flanking him.

He had slept deeply and now enjoyed the crisp bite in the morning air as it cleared his head. Above him, his home was slowly taking shape through the mists. The journey was not long, yet the climb up Raven Mountain was steep and winding, and his abused body protested several times, forcing a hiss from his lips that was not missed by either Sinclair. As they turned the final bend, James looked at the cliffs and then to the swirling seas below. This had never been his home, and yet something still pulled at him when he was here.

"'Tis a magnificent sight."

"Aye, it is," James acknowledged the younger Sinclair's words, his own sounding gruff as he dragged his eyes from the water that last night could have signaled his death.

"I still cannot believe your sister saved me in the manner she did, Sinclair."

"It is something that will haunt me for many years to come, Raven."

James grunted his acknowledgment.

"You did not tell us how you were abducted, James," Cam Sinclair said.

James allowed himself to think back to yesterday—Lord, was it only yesterday? "I was riding through the village, had reached the end, and they rode up beside me. I heard nothing, so their horses' hooves must have been muffled. Before I could fight back, they had pulled me to the ground and forced a cloth over my mouth. I remember nothing more."

The Sinclairs fell silent, mulling over his words while James returned to studying his castle.

His father had forced him from it many years ago, yet now that he had returned his love for the old building had resurfaced. He could see the crenellations where the armies of his ancestors had stood ready to defend the family. The Raven flag flew high, as it had for generations, fluttering in the gentle morning breeze. The crest was etched in his memory as his father had intended: the maroon color depicting patience yet victory in battle, three heraldic lions denoting bravery, strength, and valor, and lastly, the cross fitchée announcing his ancestors' unshakeable faith. James often laughed over the last; he had lost faith in his father when he was old enough to realize the man he was. The weak morning light cast the stone walls almost gold as he led the Sinclairs past the gatehouse and into the courtyard.

"Cambridge will stay at your side until you and your sister are ready to leave tomorrow, Raven," Devon said as they handed their reins to a groom.

"I do not need a bodyguard," James said as calmly as he could, and then winced as he dismounted, lowering himself gingerly to the floor.

"Just think of him as another set of eyes." Devon smiled, which annoyed the hell out of James. "He will watch the reactions of the people around you to see if anyone looks guilty enough to have trussed you like a goose and hurled you off a cliff for fish food."

"Are you mocking me?" James glared at the eldest Sinclair as the men walked into the castle. He wasn't used to being the brunt of someone's joke. Dukes were above that sort of thing; most often people wanted to please him but never had they ridiculed him.

"Just ensuring your survival," Devon added.

"I have servants for that."

"If you'll pardon my rudeness, they don't appear to be very good at it," Cam said, stopping inside the main entrance. "And we seem to have the history that suggests we are."

"I've never been inside here." Devon lifted his eyes to the ceilings.

Huge graceful arches of stone swept above them, each pillar anchored by intricately carved pieces of wood. It was imposing, and if you closed your eyes, as James often had as a child, you could almost imagine the knights of old here.

He watched the Sinclairs walk around in circles, taking in the carved staircase and surrounding walls adorned with armor and paintings.

"You've never visited here?" he queried.

Devon shook his head. "Your father was not overly fond of the Sinclairs. In fact, had it not been for the…." Shaking his hand around, Devon tried to find the right words.

"Curse," Cam supplied.

"Pledge," Devon added, ignoring his brother, "My father always believed he would have dropped boiling oil on top of Oak's Knoll."

"I apologize," James said curtly.

"The fault was not yours, Raven."

"I believe we have established you are not like your father," Cambridge added, walking to the wall that held rows of Raven ancestors all glaring down upon them.

James followed with his eyes; there was not one smiling face among them.

"I see where you get your scowl from, James."

Cambridge Sinclair, he had come to realize, was a man who liked to tease and torment those around him, and did so with extreme accuracy.

"I wonder where that document is?"

"Document?" James looked from Cambridge to Sinclair.

"I was told that there was a document somewhere from King Edward, stating the details of the pact and gift of land that

Oak's Knoll stands on. My father said it contained our supposed creed."

"Which is?" James raised a brow.

"To honor and protect the Ravens," Sinclair said. "No one has seen it, however."

"And you believe it is here?"

"Well,r it's not at Oak's Knoll because it is not overly large and with seven enquiring minds living there, it would have been unearthed by one of us by now."

James thought about the many rooms in his castle and decided he would have his staff search. If that document was here, he wanted it found. He wasn't sure why, or what he would do with it, but he'd decide on that matter when and if it was located.

"I shall leave you then." Devon Sinclair nodded to James, and then he was gone.

"You won't even know I am here, James," Cambridge Sinclair said, following him up the stairs.

"Somehow I doubt that," James drawled as the man gave one of his maids an exaggerated wink as she hurried passed.

CHAPTER FOUR

Three large carriages arrived at Oak's Knoll before the sun rose of the day they were due to leave. Dorrie and Essie were beside themselves with excitement at the prospect of a new friend, while Warwick was still moaning about being stuck in a carriage with three girls. The house was a hive of industry, with Dev barking last-minute orders and Josiah and Bertie carrying luggage to the front entrance.

"You will ride with us as often as you wish, Warwick, and when you can bear it no more, you can sit with your sisters and Essie." Eden held her smile as the youngest Sinclair brother dragged his feet toward the front door.

Eden then called to her little sisters, urging them downstairs so she could take them outside to meet the Duke's sister. She didn't want to see him again, because for the first time in her life a man had unsettled her, and Eden was not pleased it was the somber-faced Duke of Raven who had done so.

"I have packed your things, Cam, and left clean clothes and water if you want to change and wash before we leave," Eden said to her brother as he strolled through the front door.

"Excellent." Cam flashed her a smile before dropping a kiss on her cheek.

"Did you encounter any trouble?" Dev queried, joining them.

"No, he's a bloody cold fish though. I tried to converse with him upon several occasions, but he refused to talk. Even over our evening meal, he sat in stony silence. It was enough to give a man indigestion."

"The servants?"

Eden stood silently, listening to her brothers. She felt a frisson of fear that someone could finish what they had started the other night and hoped they got the Duke safely to London before those responsible realized he still lived.

"I don't think the ones I saw were involved in the attempt on his life; most didn't even look at him. In fact, only the butler spoke, and from what I gather he's been part of the castle since the current Duke was a babe," Cam said, rubbing the back of his neck. "And the little sister didn't lift her eyes from her feet when I was introduced to her, and then I never saw her again until this morning. She's a sweet little thing, and I look forward to our sisters befriending her, as she has surely been lonely up there in that bloody great monstrosity with him."

"I will tell you what I told your sisters," Dev said, looking serious. "Be on your guard, use your senses if you think it necessary to do so, but for Christ's sake don't alert the Duke. He'll have us tied to a stake in seconds."

"I would never do anything to harm this family and I hope you know that," Cam said quietly before he turned and climbed the stairs to his room.

"Perhaps if you go a little easier on him, he will not be a man hell bent on securing his own destruction."

"What?" Devon said, pulling his eyes from the top of the stairs to face Eden.

"He needs your guidance, Dev, not your continual censure."

"I do not have time to coddle him, Eden. This family is only just staying out of the poorhouse, and with a little help from him its turnaround would be hastened."

Sighing, Eden watched her elder brother stalk out the front door. Hopefully a change of scenery would help her brothers rekindle the close bond they'd once had, and if that didn't work, securing an eligible suitor with pots of money for Essie or herself would sort things out nicely.

"We are ready!"

Eden watched her little sisters come down the stairs. Even though the hour was early, they had made sure Essie and Eden dressed their hair exactly as they wished. Beneath their bonnets black ringlets bobbed and their green eyes sparkled with excitement. Eden sank into a curtsey as they reached the bottom, which produced a burst of giggles.

"Are you ready to meet the Duke's sister?"

"Yes!" they cried in unison.

Taking a hand of each, Eden led them out the door.

"Oooh, the carriages are grand, Eden, we will not be bumped about in those!" Dorrie gasped. "And there are three, not two."

They were indeed grand, Eden thought. Polished until they shone, even in the early morning light she could see they were the very finest money could buy. Bertie and Josiah were securing luggage, with help from the Duke's men. The Duke stood beside one of the carriages; the door was open and he had his head inside. Eden could hear his words clearly.

"The Sinclairs will not harm you, Samantha. Please come out and greet them."

Eden could hear the frustration in his voice as she and her sisters approached.

"Excuse me, James." Eden tapped one of his shoulders.

He pulled his head out of the carriage to glare at her, stepping slightly to the left, which gave her enough room to slip in front of him and tug her sisters inside the carriage behind her. Lamplight allowed her to see a small child. Sitting huddled in one corner, with her arms wrapped tightly around her knees, was the Duke's sister.

"Hello. Aren't brothers annoying? My name is Eden, and these are my sisters Dorrie and Somer."

Samantha looked nothing like her brother. She was slight and pale, and her big blue eyes were filled with tears. She was dressed in yards of ill-fitting gray fabric, her clothes seeming to wear her instead of the opposite.

"Hello, Samantha, I hope we can be friends," Somer said, climbing onto the seat beside her while Dorrie moved to stand before her.

"We have a basket of food with Josiah's favorite cherry cake, and books and toys for our journey. Do you know how to play chess?" Dorrie asked.

Eden watched as Samantha straightened in her seat. Her eyes grew rounder as they darted between the twins.

"Never mind, we'll teach you," both girls said at the same time and then giggled.

"They do that a lot," Eden said, "I'll leave you alone now so you can become acquainted while we finish the packing, ladies, and then we will begin our journey."

Backing out of the carriage, Eden heard her sisters chattering and smiled. Turning, she bumped straight into the Duke. He steadied her, then his hands fell away, leaving her with two large imprints of heat on her arms.

Two nights ago she had believed him handsome and nothing she saw changed that opinion. His strong, dark hawklike features were breathtaking. An angry purple bruise ran the length of his jaw, and one of his eyes was slightly bloodshot, yet even with these things he was still disturbing. Dressed in a black overcoat, he seemed even larger than he had in her brother's bed.

"Thank you."

The wealth of frustration in those two words tugged at Eden's heart.

"Change is always hard on the young. We just have to give them lots of love and support and in time they adjust."

Running a hand through his hair, the Duke winced and Eden suspected his ribs were still causing him pain. In fact, she imagined his body hurt all over, but of course, he would never admit that.

"The problem is we have only known each other such a short time, and she is still wary of me. I have no experience with young children, Eden. We are both struggling with the changes forced upon us."

Eden was confused—hadn't he said that Samantha was six years old? "I don't understand, James. Your sister is six years old. Have you not spent much time in her company?"

"My father did not tell me I had a sister, Eden. I found out after he died last year, and I instantly resigned my commission to travel here and be with Samantha."

"He must have been a terrible person to keep that information from you." How could anyone be that cruel?

"It is not a moment I like to remember. My only regret was that my father had passed away before I could confront him over the matter."

Eden saw the anger that still smoldered deep in the depths of his brown eyes.

"I understand your rage, James."

"I think not. You come from a family that obviously loves each other—"

"Appearances are not always what they seem."

"Meaning?"

Eden shook her head, wishing she'd kept her mouth shut. "I am sure given time you and your sister will form a strong relationship."

"I pray you are correct, yet given the distance between us I am not as optimistic as you."

"Children are resilient, James, it is adults that struggle to adjust to change."

His eyes lingered on her face before he looked away, and it was only then she was able to draw in a breath.

"Have you recovered fully from your plunge into the ocean, Eden?"

"I have, thank you. And you also? How do you fare after such a traumatic experience?"

"Very well, thank you."

The fatigue evident in his face contradicted these words. His ribs, Eden guessed, were aching every time he moved, and, like her, he had not slept well.

"If you are having trouble sleeping, Essie could mix up something to aid you."

"I need no help, thank you."

Men, Eden thought. Why could they just not admit they needed help? Her brothers were the same.

"Are you ready to leave, Raven?" Dev appeared at her side.

"Yes, thank you."

"Your face is very colorful this morning. How do your injuries feel?"

"I am more than capable of riding a horse, Sinclair, if that is your question."

"Pride comes before a fall, James," Cam said, joining them.

"Does every member of the Sinclair family use idioms to prove a point, like Cambridge?"

"I'm afraid so."

"Excellent," the Duke snapped. "I shall endeavor to keep conversations to a minimum in that case."

Eden watched the Duke's eyes travel between the three siblings. He looked bemused and irritated but merely nodded before stalking back toward the carriage.

"Perhaps for the sake of a harmonious journey, we shall not continually annoy the Duke, as he is not used to siblings or indeed Sinclairs."

"Now where would the fun be in that, sister?" Dev's eyes were on the Duke's rigid back.

"And I thought you my serious-minded stable elder brother," Eden muttered as she too left Cam and Dev to see if her sisters had everything they needed.

"The man takes himself far too seriously," she heard Dev say.

She was not about to divulge what she had learned about James and his sister only recently becoming aware of each other. Her brothers were good men; they would hopefully not do anything to outrage the Duke overly in the next few days.

"You can hold Lucy for the journey, Samantha, and I shall have Tibby and Dorrie can look after Bonny." She heard Somer's words as she arrived at the carriage behind the Duke.

"Well I'm glad that's settled," Eden said as she looked in the window, the Duke filling the doorway. Samantha seemed to have relaxed in the company of the twins and even offered a small smile when she was handed the doll made of rags.

"If you will step to one side please, James, Essie will join the girls inside. Here is our basket filled with wonderful things for the journey!" Dorrie clapped her hands and then pointed to where she wanted Essie to place it.

"Samantha, this is our eldest sister, Essex. She does not like to ride on horseback like the others, so will travel with us," Dorrie said.

"And she is the best reader, Samantha, she makes wonderful voices and is a whiz at chess," Somer added.

"There are so many of you." Samantha's voice was awed.

The Sinclair sisters all giggled at that. The Duke silently

followed the conversation between the little girls from his position in the doorway

"Seven in total." Essie smiled. "And I am very pleased to meet you, Samantha. We are going to be such friends by the end of our journey."

"Well, I will have to leave you ladies to your fun," Eden said, nudging the Duke to one side once more. She lifted her skirts to kneel on the carriage floor and give her little sisters a hug good-bye. Each planted a loud smacking kiss on her cheek. She took Samantha's hands in hers and gave them a small squeeze.

"Samantha, do you have need of Miss Billerson before we leave?"

Samantha tensed at her brother's gruff barked question. Did the man not know he was scaring Samantha? Good Lord, the girl was terrified of him, anyone could see that. The smile had fallen from the child's lips and her tiny hands clenched the doll close to her chest.

"No, Duke," Samantha whispered. "I have no need of Miss Billerson."

"That's silly, he's your brother so you should call him by his name, not his title, Samantha," Somer said, looking at the duke and completely unaffected by his dark scowl. "What is your name?

"James."

Eden could hear the surprise in his words. He was not used to being questioned by a child.

"Do you mind if your sister and my sisters call you James?"

She should intervene; it was wrong of Somer to be so presumptuous, but in this instance, she wondered if the informality may help the Duke and his sister in some small way. Eden decided to remain silent for now, as Essie was doing the same.

"I-it would be an honor, Miss Sinclair," the Duke said

bowing elegantly, which Eden was sure wasn't easy in a carriage doorway and with bruised ribs.

"There you see, Samantha, your brother wants to be called James. And, James, I am Somer and this is Dorrie, and I think you know Essie and Eden," Somer finished with a wide smile that no one but the Duke could resist.

"If you need me, Samantha, then just look out the window, I will be there."

His tone had softened, and Eden noted that Samantha had relaxed the grip she had on the doll. His words were telling to her. *If you need me, I will be there.* As he had not been in the past. It was obvious the man's guilt sat heavily on his shoulders, and he was desperately trying to make up for the neglect he had unintentionally inflicted upon his sister.

"I will call you at once if Samantha requires anything, James," Essie said, breaking the silence when Samantha did not reply. "And I am sure we can cope without your sister's companion for part of the journey at least, is that not right, ladies?"

The girls all nodded, Samantha vehemently.

Giving his sister one last look, his face once again composed, he nodded to Essie then held out his hand to Eden.

"Come, Eden, it is time to depart."

Eden took his hand and the contact traveled up her arm. Really, she must stop this; no man had ever had that effect on her, and she did not want to start with a duke, even if he was so handsome it made her teeth hurt. Pulling her hand free once she was clear of the carriage, she hurried to where her brothers waited.

"Good-bye." She hugged Bertie and Josiah and fought the tears of leaving them and the only home she had ever known. "We shall return to you soon."

"Enjoy every moment, Miss Eden," Josiah said, and she saw

that the brothers were battling tears also.

After several aborted attempts and cries of "Oh I forgot that!" the procession finally left Oak's Knoll.

"I find laughing helps, James," Cam said, "and then if that fails, a large swig of whiskey."

Ignoring Cam, the Duke took up his position beside Samantha's window. Warwick rode with Eden and chattered about anything and everything with all the enthusiasm that a seven-year-old boy could muster. Cam slouched in his saddle beside her while Devon took the lead. The Sinclairs waved to Josiah and Bertie for as long as they could see them, the twins leaning out the carriage windows and shouting their farewells.

"Enough now, girls," Dev said when he, like Eden, saw the Duke's expression turn thunderous.

"Yes, Dev," they parroted and withdrew back into the carriage.

"He takes himself very seriously," Cam whispered to Eden.

"I should imagine being a duke would come with serious responsibilities."

"True, yet the old Duke did not die until a year ago. Therefore he cannot have come into those responsibilities… What?" Cam queried as Eden started to giggle.

"Dorrie just told Samantha that if she wanted to make James laugh, she should tickle him."

"Christ, can you imagine anyone getting close enough to his snootiness to touch him?"

I can, Eden thought before she could stop herself. The man disturbed her and perhaps that was because she had never met another like him before. So arrogant and aloof, and yet she had glimpsed the vulnerable man beneath the stern facade. She could still feel his arms around her, the touch of his hand on her skin, and that would just not do, Eden reminded herself. This foolishness stopped right now because nothing could ever come of it, and what's more, she did not want it to.

Warwick moved between his siblings, but eventually as hunger took hold he succumbed to the carriage.

Eden had felt the Duke's eyes on her often, yet not once did he try to converse with any of the Sinclairs. Like a dark cloud he just rode silently behind them, yet she could no more ignore his presence than pluck the sun from the sky.

"You have to admire him, really. It would kill any one of us—with the exception of Dev maybe—to keep that quiet," Cam said then yawned loudly with his mouth wide open.

"Perhaps you could shut your mouth while doing that."

"I could, but then it wouldn't annoy you quite— What?" Cam whispered as Eden lifted a hand to stop him talking.

"What?" Dev said, moving to her other side.

Still holding the hand up, Eden did not speak, just listened. When she rode with her family she never wore earplugs, wanting to know if any danger lurked nearby. The usual sounds filled the air, the gentle hum of servants' conversation in the second carriage, the twitter of birds and rustle of leaves—yet there was something else. She heard it again, the snap of a twig. Eden sought the noise, yet it was still too far away.

Pointing left, she made the gesture of a branch snapping. Her brothers moved closer, their legs now touching, instantly alert. Eden watched Dev close his eyes briefly and when he reopened them his pupils were dilated. Cam lifted his chin and sniffed the air.

"Is there a problem?"

Shaking her head at the Duke as he drew near, Eden motioned for him to be quiet, which made his brows lower. People obviously did not shush dukes.

"I can see them," Dev said softly. "Three men mounted with guns. Tell us what you hear, Eden?"

"I smell spirits and foul body odor," Cam added.

"They are discussing how best to rob us."

CHAPTER FIVE

James looked around him as the Sinclairs conversed quietly. He could not hear each word, but understood that Eden believed there was a threat ahead of them. The road was not exceptionally wide, but he would still be able to see another carriage or horse approaching, yet he saw and heard nothing. To the left ran a paddock as far as the eye could see and to his right a row of trees.

"Where is this danger?"

Ignoring him, Eden moved slightly forward of the line they had formed, and his impulse was to pull her back if danger lurked. However, her brothers did not appear overly concerned with her movements, so he kept his thoughts to himself. From the corner of his eye, he noted Sinclair nudge his brother and look at James. What the hell was going on?

"And I repeat," James kept his voice low, "where lies the danger?"

"If you will be quiet please, James, I shall ascertain that very thing."

James couldn't believe she had just told him to be quiet. His eyes studied the rigid line of her spine, as he had done so many times today.

Her cloak was deep green with a wide ruffled hem, and it

fluttered behind her as a gentle breeze rustled the trees. He had watched the way she teased her brothers and cared for the youngest with firm gentleness. Two fat curls had escaped her straw bonnet and bounced on her spine as she rode. He had almost asked her to tuck them back inside, as his fascinated gaze had been drawn to them again and again. He wondered at their texture. Would they be like silk against his fingers? Cool or hot to the touch?

"They plan to ambush us as the first carriage draws near, Dev."

"Someone explain to me what the hell is going on?" James said.

"So we only have minutes, Eden, before they attack?" Sinclair said, ignoring him once more.

"Yes, they are preparing to do so now."

"How do you know that?" James asked Eden.

"I have good hearing."

"So do I, near perfect in fact."

"Now there's a surprise," Cam drawled.

"Yet I can hear nothing." James tightened his fingers on the reins so he wasn't tempted to strike the smug younger Sinclair.

"By the look of them, they should not present us too much trouble."

"I see nothing, Sinclair," James scanned the trees to his right.

"They smell of spirits."

"I can't smell anything, Cambridge," James growled, becoming frustrated that the Sinclairs were acting like he was not present when, if what they said was true, his sister's life could be in danger.

"If you will stay with the carriages, Raven, we will take care of this small problem and return shortly."

James actually shook his head to clear it. Had he just heard the eldest Sinclair correctly? Had he been dismissed like an errant schoolboy?

"If one of you doesn't start making sense in the next few seconds I will plant my fist in whoever is closest. Your sister is excluded from that, of course."

The siblings all turned to face him. Obviously unused to including anyone else in their conversations, they were surprised at his harsh words.

"We are about to be ambushed, James," Eden whispered. "And do not have time to discuss the matter. Therefore if you will stay with the carriages, my brothers and I will deal with this matter."

James stared at her and then the brothers. They were serious. Dear God, they were all mad! He had placed his sister's welfare in the hands of lunatics. However, if danger did indeed lurk around the bend now was not the time to discuss the matter further.

"My drivers are armed and can look after the carriages. I will have them surround all three, then I will return to assist you," James said steadily, once again making eye contact with the three siblings. He did not wait for their agreement, sure in the knowledge they would not defy his orders. He rode swiftly to the first carriage and began telling his men what he wanted from them.

James was stunned when he returned to find the Sinclairs gone. No one disobeyed him… ever! The most unruly of his soldiers had more discipline than this family. How could her brothers let Eden ride blindly into danger? She should be in the carriage safe with the others. Kicking his horse forward, he followed the Sinclair siblings. He would have several heated words to say to them when this was over.

He found them further up the road as he rounded a bend. Eden dared to throw him a frustrated look when he arrived. She placed a finger on her lips to quiet him. Quiet him, a bloody duke! Just as he was about to tell them what he thought of their behavior, the sound of voices drifted to him.

"I don't hear no carriages!"

The words were slightly slurred and James could smell the strong scent of spirits now. He wondered how Cam had done so from so far away, and how Eden had heard them. For that matter, how had Sinclair made out the shapes of whoever was beyond that tree line?

Moving forward, James attempted to take charge, but Eden grabbed his horse's reins and stopped it. Stunned that she would dare to do such a thing, James could only stare at her as she shook her head at him.

"They're coming, I tell you, I saw them miles back and circled round to get you and meet here. Three of 'em."

"Three carriages? May be some willing wenches amongst them."

James glared at Eden as the gruff voices reached them. Signaling with his hand that she return to the carriage, he followed it up with a glare. His gestures were wasted as she turned away to look at her brothers.

Sinclair signaled something James did not understand to Cam, then mouthed something to Eden that she seemingly understood. Before James could react to the fact they had not included him, yet again, Devon had urged his horse onto the road. Whistling a ditty, he headed toward the tree line the men were behind.

"What the hell is he doing?"

Cam shook his head at James and this time, it was he who placed a finger on his lips, and followed it up by tugging his ear, which James guessed meant he was supposed to listen.

"Stop. Where are the carriages?"

"I beg your pardon?" James heard Devon say politely to the gruff enquiry.

"There were three carriages on this road. Where are they?" someone demanded.

James had no idea how many men were waiting for them, but his first thought was to get Eden to safety again. He reached for her, intent on turning her horse around, but she pushed his hand aside and pulled a pistol from beneath her skirts, and then charged forward, followed by Cam. James followed seconds later when he had regained his wits.

"Halt or we shoot!" Cam shouted.

"Drop your weapons, gentlemen, if you please," James heard Sinclair say. He arrived to find three men with masks over the lower halves of their faces. All were on horseback.

"They tricked us!"

"Come now, trick? I believe outmaneuvered is the correct term," Cam said, riding forward to take the men's guns while Eden and Devon still held theirs trained on them.

"Bind their hands and feet, Cam, and we will leave them attached to a tree and alert the correct authorities… when we eventually find some."

"We could be out here for hours!" one of the men howled as Devon finished speaking. "We could be eaten by wild animals before they reach us."

"Imagine my horror"—Cam drawled as he pulled the first man from his horse and dragged him toward a tree—"at the possibility that you may have to suffer in any way when you were about to inflict terror upon my family."

"May I be of assistance?" James did not attempt to rein in the fury he felt as he joined Sinclair and Eden.

"If you will hold the front, Raven, I will assist my brother," Dev said, offering James his gun. James snapped his teeth together and pulled his own from his coat.

"Right then." The eldest Sinclair smiled as he slipped from his horse.

"I cannot believe you and your siblings would be so foolish as to ride into an ambush without first ascertaining how many men were involved and informing me of your plan," James said softly to Eden. He refused to give vent to his rage and roar like his head was telling him to. He was not his father.

"We are used to dealing with situations ourselves, James. Had we taken the time to explain things to you, we may have lost our advantage."

"I am not an idiot, madam, I can even understand basic instruction if spoken slowly enough," James snarled softly.

"I do believe that was sarcasm, James. You are not so very dissimilar to us as you seemed at first."

"Do not make a game of me, Eden, or you will very much regret it. I am a duke, and we are not a breed who enjoy being the butt of anyone's jokes, least of all a bloody Sinclair's!"

"Because we are beneath you?"

"I will not dignify that with an answer."

She was watching her brothers, not him, but James was running his eyes over the soft skin of her cheeks as color flooded them.

"Of course, forgive my rudeness, but I do not like to be threatened, even if it is by a duke." Her gray eyes were calm as she turned to face him, and James wasn't sure if he wanted to shake or ravage her.

With the men secured, the small party headed back to where the carriages waited. After soothing the children, servants, and Essie, they once again took to the road. This time James was in the lead, with Cam at the rear and Eden and Dev each taking a side of the carriage the children and Essie traveled in. He had no wish to look at any of them until his anger had cooled, or he feared he would say something everyone would regret.

"You're best to just spit it out, James. It can't be healthy to have all that angst roiling around inside a person." Cam's voice carried to him.

Devon coughed and Eden muffled a giggle. James, however,

growled softly and then ground his teeth. Neither action eased his spleen, so he spoke his mind.

"How dare you put your sisters and mine in danger!" James waited for the siblings to reach him. Each had left their position at his first word and now flanked him.

"They were never in any danger, Raven. In fact, my siblings and I did what we had to, to preempt just that," Devon added.

"You allowed your sister to ride into danger, Sinclair—a woman!"

"And therefore unable to protect herself, James?"

James turned at Eden's words; her face appeared calm yet her eyes were not. The laughter had gone to be replaced by an anger that suddenly seemed a match for his.

"I did not say that, Eden—"

"Come, James, we are all interested in what you have to say."

James swallowed. How had the conversation veered out of his control?

"Eden, it is our job to protect you, not plunge you recklessly into danger where—"

"I may break a fingernail, or perhaps my skirts would be dirtied?"

"If you will let me explain—"

"Dear Lord!" Eden gasped as if a sudden thought had occurred to her.

"What?" James looked up the road. Was there more trouble ahead?

"Imagine if I was all alone without one of my big male protectors and I had a stone in my slipper."

Cam was now laughing so hard he was snorting. Sinclair just smiled, but it was wide enough to expose his teeth.

"I wonder, James"—his name should not sound so sweet spilling from her lips, especially considering she'd spat it out through her teeth—"if you could locate my needlework." Eden looked around her as if it would magically appear.

"I did not mean to suggest you were unable to care for—"

Eden held up at hand to halt his words and once again, much to his surprise, he compiled. Her eyes flashed at him, cheeks flushed. She looked wild. A luscious wild virago, he thought, staring at her mouth. Hell, he wanted to close the distance and kiss her into silence.

"I understand your views, James, yet thankfully I have, for the most, forward-thinking brothers and do not have to adhere to them."

"Thank you, darling."

Ignoring Cam, she continued. "So perhaps for the remainder of this journey, you should endeavor to understand that I am different from the cosseted women of your acquaintance. Now if you will excuse me, my sister is calling me."

Before James could react she had turned away from him, and he was sure she muttered "addlepated fool."

Devon was still smiling, although he attempted to rein it in as James glared at him.

"A word of advice, Raven?"

"What."

"My sisters do not take direction kindly. It is best to guide them as one would a bad-tempered animal. They are headstrong, intelligent, and spirited, and I would have them no other way, though I beg you do not alert them to that fact."

"Sinclair, I would rather fall into a pit of venomous snakes than further acquaint myself with your siblings," James snarled rudely. He then rode back to the head of their little caravan and refused to feel any guilt over his words. They had been wrong to take such risks, and he would not allow them to do so again while he and his sister were keeping their company.

***

By the time the small inn came into view James's ribs were throbbing, he was exhausted, and more than ready to stop. However, he would rather have a tooth pulled than admit that to the Sinclairs. The remainder of the journey had been a long, quiet one, with the three other riders conversing occasionally but making no attempt to do so with him, as of course, he'd directed them to do. The problem was, he enjoyed listening to them and had even had a few things he'd wanted to add. Of course he hadn't, and knew it would not be appreciated. He was obviously more tired than he realized because usually he shied away from contact.

Darkness had fallen and the small building looked inviting to the weary travelers. Lights flickered in the windows and servants came out to take their horses.

James heard Eden groan as she dismounted, and then stretched her hands to the night sky, trying to ease some of the cricks hours in the saddle had left her with. The gesture was surprisingly graceful, and he found his eyes on those bloody curls once again. She then made her way to the carriage that held her siblings. He joined her seconds later.

"They are all asleep," Essie whispered when he reached the open door.

"Are you able to carry your sister inside with your sore ribs, James? She is asleep." Eden's words were as cool as the night air.

"Of course." James had never carried his sister anywhere—she never let him get close enough—but he wasn't telling Eden that.

A small chain was formed and Sinclair took Warwick, Cam, Dorrie, while Essie picked up Somer. Lastly, Eden handed him his little sister. Samantha slept deeply, her face relaxed in slumber. No fear clenched her features or clouded her eyes.

Christ, she looked sweet. He had to inhale around the lump in his throat.

"Is everything all right, James?"

Lifting his eyes from the sleeping child, he nodded to Eden. "She never lets me get this close to her." The words left his lips before he could stop them.

"She will." Eden ran a finger down Samantha's cheek. The girl wrinkled her nose then turned her face into her brother's chest. She had never turned to him, only away in fear.

"Come, we will get her settled for the night."

James did not think he could have spoken at that moment, so he simply followed Eden inside.

"There appears to be a problem, Raven. There is one extremely small room that has a single bed and a larger one with two. As you are the duke, the proprietor believes you should have the larger one, but as I'm sure you have no wish to share with—"

"I will take the small room," James snapped.

"No." Sinclair shook his head. "I could not allow it."

"Sinclair, I am tired, my body aches, and I have no wish to discuss the matter further. I will take the room, as I also have no wish to share with your brother, who I'm sure would spend the night annoying me, a pastime I have already gathered he much enjoys."

"It's not personal, Raven. He does that to his siblings as well."

"That does little to reassure me."

"If you are sure?"

"Yes." James nodded. He could sleep anywhere, and a small room did not bother him in the slightest; in fact, he was bloody insulted that Sinclair had even brought it up.

"You'll beg my pardon, your Grace, I did not realize there were so many of you."

61

James nodded to the proprietor. "'Tis of no mind, a bed is a bed."

"Very kind of you, Raven."

James only just refrained from striking Sinclair for his simpering tone, as he still held his sister.

While James's servants readied everything in their rooms and brought in the luggage, they were shepherded into a parlor where the comforting warmth from a blazing fire welcomed them. Lowering Samantha into a chair, James watched as she opened her eyes. Kneeling, he then untied the satin ribbons of her bonnet, his large fingers feeling awkward under her small chin.

"It is all right, Samantha, you fell asleep in the carriage and I carried you inside."

"Thank you, James."

He gave her a gentle smile that she tentatively returned, and he wondered how such a small gesture could make him feel fifteen feet tall. Perhaps because it was the first smile he had ever received from her. Swallowing the lump in his throat, he rose and looked at the Sinclairs. All the children had now woken.

Sinclair was carrying the youngest sibling on his shoulder and making the child chuckle as he whispered into his ear. Cam was doing something with a bundle of rags that James remembered was a doll, while one of the twins—which one was beyond him—was instructing him. Essie and Eden sat before the fire with the other twin draped across their laps, listening attentively to what she said. He had to admit they seemed to have a very strong bond, and he envied the comfort they obviously shared in each other's presence.

"Right, children upstairs for a wash before dinner, I can smell you all from here," Devon said, eliciting several loud comments of a teasing nature.

"Would you like to come up with us, Samantha?" Eden said, holding out one hand.

Nodding, Samantha slipped past James and took the offered hand. He couldn't blame her. James was half tempted to take it himself; such was the charm of the woman. Although she'd probably bite him if he tried.

After the women and children had left, silence settled around the three men. A servant entered bearing tankards of ale, which he distributed to them. Informing them that dinner would be served soon, he then withdrew.

"I fear we are about to receive another lecture, Cam," Sinclair drawled from his position near the fire. "I can feel the tension in the room."

James, who had been forming and discarding words the entire journey, trying to find a tactful way to say what needed to be said, saw red at the eldest Sinclair brother's cavalier attitude. He hadn't disputed Cam's request that they use informal names, yet his rank gave him the right to do so. He'd put up with their teasing and continual nettling of him, but no more. He would have his say now, and they would bloody listen. They may have saved him, and yes, their families had history, but enough was enough.

"I wish to reiterate that for the remainder of this journey my sister is not to be placed in danger, and I would hope you feel the same about your family."

"Excuse me, James, but you have no right to tell us how to protect our family."

Sinclair placed a hand on his brother's arm as Cam spoke. "He does not understand us, Cam, or for that matter, Eden."

"I understand what you did was foolhardy!"

"Eden can shoot better than any man I know, and always carries a pistol," Devon said slowly. "Essie's weapon of choice is a bow, and she is extremely accurate. I realized when I returned home that they must be able to protect themselves should their brothers not be near, so I undertook the task of training them."

A vision of a pistol strapped to Eden's soft thigh slipped into James's head. He forced it aside.

"She is a woman, and as such it is your job to protect her, not thrust her into danger. We should have turned the carriages around while we dealt with the threat. My sister was endangered, and that I will not tolerate."

Sinclair pinched his nose, a gesture James had seen several times in their short acquaintance and knew spoke of his frustration. Too bad, he was still bloody angry and they were going to feel the brunt of it.

"I would never put my family in danger, Raven, and if you say so again I will take it as a personal insult," Devon said softly. "My brother and I would lay down our lives for them, and it would be unwise of you to suggest otherwise."

"Are you threatening me, Sinclair?"

The two men stood toe to toe. Cam flanked his brother.

"If you wish to take it as such then that is your prerogative, Raven. But know this, the happiness and security of my family comes before anything else in my life."

"I understand we are something of an anomaly, James," Cam added, his voice now calm as he tried to ease the tension between the men. Suddenly he was the voice of reason, which James was sure he would find ironic when anger did not cloud his thoughts. "But I would ask you not to judge us and instead form an opinion on closer acquaintance."

Sinclair shot his brother a surprised look. "Such eloquence, brother."

"You must be rubbing off on me."

"That you are different is obvious, and I am aware of the debt I owe you, but I will not allow you to take further risks where my sister's safety is at stake," James said softly. "I hope you can understand that."

Sinclair did not reply as the children once again filed back into the room, but James could feel his anger because it matched his. London could not come soon enough as far as he was concerned. Then he could forget about the dark-haired sister with the soft gray eyes and lush body and her unusual family.

He had dismissed it at the time simply because he was concerned for Samantha's welfare, but now James wondered how they had heard and seen those men today intent on robbing them. He had detected nothing, yet these Sinclairs had. Unease stirred inside him. Where these people a danger to the Raven's or like history suggested, was their intention to protect he and Samantha? One thing he was certain of, was that he would be watching them closely from now on.

CHAPTER SIX

Eden had heard the argument taking place between her brothers and the Duke, but if she had not she would have felt the tension upon reentering the room with her sisters. Dev and the Duke were scowling, and Cam drew a finger around his neck as she looked at him.

His comments today had angered her, but that anger had cooled as she realized that he did not understand her or her family. How could he? Sometimes even she struggled to accept what they were capable of. To an outsider they would appear reckless, but in truth they had been in total control today, their senses had ensured that.

The problem was that the Duke, she was sure, had lived a solitary life that he no doubt controlled ruthlessly, and Eden imagined the women who had passed through his life had bowed to his every wish. Something that neither she nor Essie would ever do.

"Do you want a drink, Eden?"

"No thank you, Dev. I wish to talk with the Duke."

He looked wary at her words, but what she had to say to him could not wait, especially considering what she knew was taking place above them.

"Your sister's nanny would not allow her to come back

downstairs with us, James. In fact, she locked the door to Samantha's rooms and I heard her yelling at your sister." She hadn't actually heard her yelling, more a venomous hiss, but still, it would have terrified Samantha. "When I tried to enter the room, she would not allow it, and told me to go away. I would ask that you go upstairs and retrieve her at once."

"I am sure Miss Billerson knows what is best for my sister, Eden."

"In that I am afraid you are incorrect, Duke," Essie said. "She is a mean-spirited virago who has your sister completely cowed, and I have just spent five minutes trying with little success to get her open the door."

"Essie, calm down, love." Dev came forward to place an arm around her.

"'Tis true, Dev, Miss Billerson had Samantha in tears when she tore the doll from her earlier, and said the only fit place for it was the fire," Dorrie said.

"She is mean and has a mouth that does not know how to smile," Somer added.

Eden could see their words had shocked James.

"I am sure I would have heard had Samantha's nanny been mistreating her."

"From whom, James? Certainly not Miss Billerson, and as you said, Samantha is scared of you."

He winced as she spoke, and she hated causing anyone pain, but Eden knew this must be dealt with. She could not allow that sweet little girl to suffer any longer.

"Samantha told us that she is afraid of Miss Billerson because she makes her kneel on the cold floor to say her prayers for an hour five times a day. She calls Samantha the devil's spawn and says that it is her duty to rid her of the evil that is in her soul." Dorrie stepped in front of Eden to speak to the Duke, and Somer followed. "But she is not evil, James."

"When can we eat?"

"Soon, Warwick." Cam picked up his brother and moved closer to the fire. Dev followed, leaving the Duke alone with four angry Sinclair sisters.

"Surely I would have known." He said the words mostly to himself as he looked at each sister. Eden saw the exact moment he realized they were speaking the truth.

"Excuse me."

He rushed from the room and Eden followed. His long legs took the stairs two at a time, even though she knew the action must hurt his ribs. She lifted her skirts and tried to keep pace with him. Reaching the top, she pulled out her earplugs and heard Miss Billerson's nasty words.

"You must pray longer this evening to purge the evil influence of the heathen Sinclairs."

James did not stop at the door. Instead, dropping his shoulder, he charged at it. The door gave and slammed into the wall, and he stalked inside with Eden following.

She saw Samantha huddled on her knees praying beside the bed. Miss Billerson stood behind her with a switch in her hand, which she appeared to be using to poke Samantha.

"What is the meaning of this, your Grace!" Miss Billerson glared at Eden. "I cannot be expected to instruct your sister with these interferences. These Sinclair women are undermining what I have striven months to teach your sister."

"Have you ever struck my sister?"

Eden shivered at the words. His tone may have been soft but the thread of rage was evident to all in the room.

"Come to me, Samantha," Eden said softly as she saw the Duke's fists clench at his side. The little girl looked at her brother, then to Miss Billerson, before scrambling to her feet and running to Eden. Picking Samantha up, she held the shivering body close. "It's all right now, sweetheart."

"It is important to rid her of the evil influences." Miss Billerson's words now held a quiver.

"Answer the question."

She looked like a turkey as she gulped in several mouthfuls of air, but Eden felt no pity for the woman. She had tormented this poor child.

In two strides the Duke had the stick in his hands. Lifting it high, he drew his arm back.

"You cannot strike me, your Grace!"

Eden thrust Samantha to Essie, who had just entered the room. Stepping forward, she wrapped her fingers about James's raised arm.

"While I wish to see this woman punished as much as you, James, it will not help if you do so in front of your sister. Nor will you like how it makes you feel when you come to your senses." The muscles beneath her fingers were rigid, each one tensed and poised to strike.

"Lower the switch, James."

Eden saw the turmoil in his gaze as he slowly did as she asked. He then braced the wood between both hands and snapped it in front of the woman before throwing it at her feet.

"I cannot strike you, and do you know why, Miss Billerson?"

Shaking her head, the woman took a step backward.

"Because the blame is as much mine as yours."

Eden heard the self-loathing in his voice. He was blaming himself for Samantha's treatment at the hands of this woman, because in his eyes, he had neglected his sister himself.

"Had I taken more interest in my sister's welfare, she would not have suffered at your hands. Now pack your bags and leave this inn tonight."

"But where will I go?"

"I will send a servant and carriage to take you to the nearest town, and from there you are on your own."

"Your sister needs me, your Grace, she has an evil soul that must be purged," Miss Billerson pleaded.

"No!" James roared. "Never speak of my sister again. She is all that is pure and sweet and it is you who are filled with evil, you and that man who fathered her."

Eden watched him battle with the rage inside him.

"Now leave before I withdraw the offer of my carriage."

She watched the woman scurry from the room, and saw the foot Essie, her sweet gentle sister, stuck out to send Miss Billerson flying out the door to land in a heap outside.

"Oh dear, Samantha, look at silly Miss Billerson lying there on the floor."

The girl lifted her head from Essie's shoulder briefly before burrowing it back down.

"Take Samantha to our room please, Essie. James will come for her shortly."

Eden watched her sister leave, and then she was alone with the Duke. Angry, confused, and hurting, not unlike a wounded animal, he stood with his back to her, fists clenched, shoulders straight. She could hear the rasp of his breathing as he struggled to control his emotions. Moving forward, she placed her hand on his arm once more.

"James, please, she is gone now and Samantha will be all right, I promise you."

"I should have known!" The words sounded like they had been ripped from his chest. "We were thrust upon each other so suddenly. I-I thought I had done the right thing by getting a governess for her. She was so scared of me, every look and touch she would flinch, and I was helpless to know how to reach her."

"You will both begin to heal now."

He turned so suddenly Eden would have fallen backward if he had not steadied her. His hands gripped her arms, pulling her closer.

"He didn't tell me about her because he wanted to break her like he tried to do to me. That sweet little girl lived with that monster and I know exactly what he did to her, as he did it to me before I was forced to leave."

"Who, your father?" Eden whispered. He was looking at her but not really seeing, lost in the memories of his childhood.

"Yes, he destroyed everything he touched."

"I'm so sorry." Eden had had a father who tried to break her, but her siblings had kept her sane.

"Please, James, do not be too hard on yourself. The situation that was thrust upon you was not of your making and cannot have been easy on either you or Samantha. Sometimes things appear to be different than what they actually are. You did not know she was being mistreated by Miss Billerson, and your sister, for whatever reason, chose not to inform you."

"Samantha's care lies solely with me, Eden, and I have failed her. Therefore, it is I who am to blame."

"No!" Eden said, grasping the lapels on his jacket as he tried to brush past her.

"Yes!" He tried to ease her aside, his hands moving to her waist.

"And if you are to blame, what then? Will you chastise yourself and put more distance between you and your sister? Surely that can help no one."

"Eden, now is not the time for this conversation. I need to see Samantha and you need to go back to your family."

She placed one hand on his chest and wondered what was going on behind those eyes. They were suddenly shuttered—she could read nothing in the brown depths. Where before there had been rage, they were now blank.

"Please talk to your sister calmly, James. She needs your understanding and love—"

He shut her up by kissing her.

Eden was stunned. His lips were soft when she'd expected them to be hard, his hands on her back branding her through her clothing, and Eden felt weakness flood her veins. Following that was a need for more. The urgency she had experienced saving his life was back. She needed him to touch her, wrap his arms around her body and hold her close. She wanted to feel his skin, feel his hands on her body. Dear Lord, it was a kind of madness that filled her. As if she wanted to crawl inside this man and be part of him.

His mouth ravaged her lips; where one kiss stopped another started until Eden couldn't draw a rational thought into her head. Climbing to her toes, she threw her arms around his neck and held on. His chest was hard against her breasts, the pressure almost too painful to bear. She felt his lips nip her chin then move to her neck and a moan welled from deep inside her, her head dropping backward to allow him better access.

"No!"

Eden stumbled forward as the Duke wrenched himself away from her. "No," he said again, this time softly as his hands steadied her. "I cannot take advantage of you like this, not with your family below. I owe you too much to disrespect you like that."

"I-I do not understand?" Eden tried to focus on his words.

"I was angry, Eden, and needed an outlet for that anger. Unfortunately, you were it." He raked a hand through his hair, sending the dark waves in several directions.

Flinching, she took a step backward as his words doused the flames inside her.

"I used you and that is beneath me. I beg you to forgive me."

God, that hurt. He had felt none of the wondrous emotions that Eden had. He had used her to slake his rage, and nothing more.

"I understand." Eden lifted her chin. She would not show

this man how much his words had hurt her, but she felt a need to strike at him as he had her. "And I would appreciate it if you stuck to the original pact."

"Pact?" he queried as Eden walked to the door.

"Turn to me only when your life is threatened, Duke. We both know that this is all my family is good for in your eyes. After all, the proof is already laid out before you."

Eden would have smiled at the sound of his teeth clamping together if she were not biting her lip to stop herself from crying.

"Eden, let me—"

But she was already walking to the door, and once she had passed through it, she closed it quietly behind her. Head high, she continued to her room, where she put a smile on her face for Samantha. After hugging the little girl, she then moved behind the screen to change her clothes.

When James arrived, she had just finished. Essie greeted him, and then the sisters left the room, leaving the Raven siblings alone together.

Dev shot Eden a look as she stepped into the room, his brows lowering as he studied her face. He knew her better than anyone, and no matter how much she tried to hide how she was feeling, he would know. However, much to her relief, he chose not to question her.

The Sinclairs were their usual boisterous selves at the dinner table. Occasionally eyes strayed to the two empty seats, yet no one commented. James and his sister had as yet not returned. Beef stew and bread were brought to the table and they fell upon the meal like a pack of ravenous animals.

Dev tried to rein his siblings in but Eden suspected his hunger was as great as theirs, and soon he too was shoveling in large mouthfuls. She sat to his left and tried to eat, which was not easy as she had no appetite.

The Duke's kiss had been unexpected and that was why she was unsettled, Eden reasoned. Surely if she had received several such kisses she would realize just how unspectacular James's had been. Yes, Eden told herself, this was why she had reacted as she had, there was nothing to compare the experience with. Once she was in London she was sure to receive another kiss from someone, and would see instantly that James's kisses were in fact average, or even below average. Feeling much better about the entire incident, she was able to sit calmly as the door opened and in walked the Duke and his sister.

None of the Sinclairs commented on their reappearance, although by silent mutual consent they started using their table manners, and ate as if they were dining with the Royal Family.

James guided Samantha around the table. He watched one of the twins move to the next seat, thus leaving a space between them for his sister.

"Thank you, ladies." He held out the chair for Samantha and then pushed it closer to the table once she was seated. His little sister gave him a nod, her face serious.

"You're welcome, James," Dorrie or Somer said. He really must work out one from the other.

The only other empty seat was next to a twin and beside Warwick Sinclair, which was a new experience for James, as he had never shared a meal with children, and in all honesty was not particularly looking forward to the prospect. His father had believed children should be kept out of sight while the adults ate, and in this James had agreed; the Sinclairs apparently did not.

"Pass the potatoes to James, Warwick."

James had found Samantha with Essex and Eden. When he had entered the room, they had silently left. Essie had given him a gentle smile; her sister had ignored him, which was no more than he had deserved.

Crouching before his solemn-faced sister, he had then apologized to her. He had told her what he should have months ago—explained that he had not known of her existence until the death of their father, and that he had had no idea how to care for her, and that was why he employed Miss Billerson.

"I promise to do better now, Samantha, but you must trust me."

Her reply to his words had made him ill.

"Do you promise not to st-strike me if I say something you dislike?"

Her face had been clenched in fear and James had known how much those words had cost her.

"I will never hurt you, Samantha, I promise," he had vowed. She had looked at him for a long time and then just when James had believed she would not answer him she had nodded and taken the hand he held out to her. He had stayed there for several minutes, just clutching her small fingers until they both felt calmer. Only then had he stood and led her down to their evening meal.

Eden sat across from James, careful to look at everyone but him. She had changed into a gown of the palest lilac. Matching ribbons were threaded through the neckline, which settled on the top of her breasts, and he felt his body tighten as he remembered them pressed to his chest. Her hair was simply pulled together at her nape, yet the look was more alluring than any he had seen in society.

She was danger to James. Dangerous in a way that would make the wall he had built to protect himself crumble. Just pressing his lips to hers had created a fire inside him, and that told him to keep his distance from her in the future. James did not want to lose control; control was how he had survived. Control ensured his life was as it should be with no deviations.

He had said what he had to hurt her, to push her away from

him, and her reply had surprised him. She hadn't cried or cursed, just stated calmly that in the future she would be available to him only in the capacity of a rescuer. She had spirit, Miss Eden Sinclair, and were he a man wanting a spirited wife he would look no further, but he wasn't and never would be. James had no room in his life for anyone but Samantha from this day forth.

"I choose dessert!"

James was wrenched from his thoughts by the youngest Sinclair.

"Oh please, you always choose dessert. Can we not stretch our brains further than food?" Eden scoffed while winking at her youngest brother.

"Tartlets!" Warwick Sinclair cried, bouncing up and down in his seat.

James looked at the boy. Surely he was not asking too much to eat his meal with only the gentle hum of conversation, if indeed there must be conversation. And what the hell was he doing screaming out the word tartlets? He had not seemed unstable, yet surely this conversation indicated something was not as it should be inside his head. But then, considering his siblings….

"You cannot just cry tartlets. What kind?"

James swiveled in his chair to look at one of the twins, who was questioning her brother. What were they talking about? There were no tartlets on the table. Perhaps half of the Sinclairs were unbalanced but hid it well? Samantha just smiled and shook her head as he gave her a questioning look.

"Berry tartlets and the accompanying sentence must be in Latin."

"I'll take berry," Essex Sinclair said slowly. She appeared deep in thought.

"I'll take tartlets." Cambridge Sinclair laughed. "I've always been partial to tart… lets."

Devon Sinclair glowered at his brother then rolled his eyes when Cam poked out his tongue.

How the hell was James to digest his food with all this nonsense, whatever it was, going on around him? He could cope with a child calling him James—just—but this carry on was not good for his digestion.

"But Egbert roasts rodents year-round? You could not have done better than that?" Essie scoffed, she then added a sentence in faultless Latin.

Eden laughed as her sister poked out her tongue. It was a beautiful sound, rich and full and the smile reached her eyes. Why the hell did he have to notice things like that about her, and why was Essex quoting phrases that included rodents at the dinner table? James's head was beginning to ache. He wondered if he should leave the room and take his sister with him before the Sinclairs displayed more of their disturbing behavior.

"Tactfully Amelia Rose taught little Egbert toasting skills," Cambridge Sinclair said in a slow drawl, and then he too spoke in Latin. James could find no fault in his pronunciation either.

"Cam, that was wonderful."

"Thank you, sweeting." Cam blew the twin who spoke a kiss.

"Dare one enquire what is going on?" James asked when he could no longer stand being left in the dark. He liked to be in control at all times, and these Sinclairs had a way of wresting it from him. In fact, they showed absolutely no regard for his title or standing in society, which, he silently added, was far above theirs.

"Oh sorry, James, it was rude of us not to explain first." One of the twins said. "We play word games. Someone chooses two words. A short verse is then made up using the letters of the word. Once it has been spoken then it must be repeated in whatever language is selected. Obviously the sentences are not constructed the same way, or with the same letters. Take

Spanish for example deadly means mortal and—"

"Thank you, yes I understand your meaning, Miss…"

"Somerset," she said. "Dorset is shorter than I, and my teeth protrude further than hers, if you need a way to identify us."

"Thank you for the explanation, and the tips on identifying you from your sister, Miss Somerset. For a brief moment I wondered what my sister and I had strayed into," James said, managing a thin smile.

"Bedlam, Raven," Devon drawled. "But we like it that way."

James held the other man's eyes. The eldest Sinclair was angered and he had a hunch it was not just from their earlier discussion. Had Eden told him about their kiss?

"Each to their own, Sinclair."

"Greek gods," Cambridge Sinclair stated, then forked a large mouthful of meat into his mouth.

"You try, James," Somerset prompted.

Dear God, no!

"Go on, James." Samantha's gentle words made James swallow. How could he refuse her when she was actually talking to him, and using his name without his instigating the conversation.

"If it's too much for you, Raven…."

Glaring at Devon Sinclair, James said, "I'll take the word Greek and will repeat the phrase in Russian. I realize that no one will understand what I am saying, but—"

"I can," a high-pitched voice said to his left.

"You speak Russian, Miss Somerset?" James pinched the bridge of his nose hard. He wasn't sure if he was standing on his head or feet around these people.

"Do you believe because we are not overly plump in the pocket we are therefore unintelligent, James?" Eden said the words and if her glare became any more heated he would be torched where he sat.

"I do not judge people because they are born either rich or poor, Eden." Which was only partially true, he realized, and then he wondered when he'd become a snob. The look she gave him told James she did not believe a word he had spoken.

"And I'll take gods," Eden said, looking at James's left ear, "and I'll repeat in Spanish."

She would, the little shrew. He just bet she was bloody fluent in any language he chose to name. They were a very unusual family, these Sinclairs.

"Our mother had a fondness for languages, Raven, and passed it on to her children."

James nodded at Sinclair's words before he said, "Goddess Rhode eats eels kindly." He then added a sentence in Russian. He spoke several languages, but Russian was his favorite.

"Not bad for a first attempt." Cambridge Sinclair raised his glass to James. "Your pronunciation needs work, but we understood it."

Not bad? It was bloody brilliant, James thought, refusing to speak his thoughts out loud.

"Gaia observes deadly silence," Eden said.

She may be bloody beautiful but she was also damned annoying. James scowled as Eden spoke in soft flowing Spanish and then smiled at him, the gesture never reaching her eyes.

"And on that note, Warwick, Dorrie, and Somer, please finish your food as it is now time for you to retire," Devon said.

"What is the extra ingredient in this pie, Essie?" Warwick asked around a mouthful.

"Saffron," Essex said. "Would you like Eden and me to take Samantha with us, James? She can sleep with the girls if she wishes to. They will share one bed and we the other," she added.

James hadn't thought further than firing his sister's nanny, but of course his sister would need a companion until they reached London.

"I would be grateful, thank you, Essex. Are you happy with these arrangements, Samantha?" James helped his sister from her seat.

"Yes, thank you, James."

The Sinclair siblings hugged their elder brothers before retiring. Samantha nodded his way, and James understood theirs was a relationship that needed a great deal of time to help it grow into something comfortable before they freely gave hugs, if they ever would. He understood that, but still felt a dull ache in his chest as he watched his little sister leave the room.

After bidding the brothers good night, he followed, eager to find his bed as his body was now one large ache. Each abused muscle was stiff and sore and his head throbbed.

"Your room is most unpleasant, your Grace, and the mattress lumpy."

These words greeted James as he entered his room. His valet was a small bird of a man who had been with him for many years. They rubbed along together because neither had much to say, but he tended to fuss more than James liked.

"I shall survive, Brenton."

Stripping off his clothes, James washed and pulled on his dressing gown. He rarely slept in clothes, as he was a restless sleeper and they ended up trapped around his body, waking him. Tonight, however, he was to share the inn with the Sinclair's and had no wish to be roused suddenly in a naked state by one of them.

"You may leave now, thank you."

"It is my hope you are refreshed in the morning, your Grace."

James grunted good night, and then fell on the bed, groaning loudly as the pain of various aching body parts pulled viciously. Closing his eyes, he sighed. At last, some peace and quiet from those frustrating Sinclairs. Considering the events of the last few days, it was testament to his tiredness that he felt himself sinking into sleep.

The dreams came with ruthless intensity and had him thrashing around in the sheets. Water was dragging him under as he tried to breathe, tried to find enough air to fill his lungs. The terror of being bound and helpless swept over him once more.

"Sssh, James, 'tis all right."

He woke to the soft words and a hand on his shoulder. Reaching out, he grabbed the wrist, needing to feel anchored to something. Something or someone who would save him.

"You are safe now."

"Who are you?" His voice sounded rough and unused as he forced his gritty eyes open and looked to the shape beside his bed.

"It is Eden, James. You were calling out in your sleep, and I came to see if all was well. You were reliving the nightmare of being thrown in the water."

"Christ." James hissed out the word. He remembered now. He was back there again, under the water with his hands and feet bound as he struggled to free himself.

"It will take time, but the memory will ease, I promise. I shall have Essie mix herbs to soothe you while you sleep."

James felt Eden's hand on his head, brushing the hair back from his forehead. It was the softest touch, but he felt it everywhere.

"You should not be in here."

"I grew concerned when you did not stop shouting, and while you are not my favorite person today, I could not listen as you continued to suffer."

As his eyes adjusted he began to see her clearly. The silhouette of her lovely body clad in a nightdress as she bent over him made him ache to reach for her.

"I am very rarely anyone's favorite person."

"Now you are being modest, Duke," she said, mocking him. "I'm sure there are any number of women who find you quite favorable."

He snorted. "They find my title favorable."

"Yes, it is quite surprising how a homely man with a title can suddenly gain popularity."

"Are you calling me homely, Eden?" Why did he love talking with this woman? Why did his heart beat harder and he feel lighter when in her company?

"Have I dented your ego? Forgive me, it was unfair considering you have just surfaced from a nightmare." Her hand patted his shoulder. "I would like to add that in a very short amount of time I have no doubt that you will be Samantha's favorite person."

James doubted that, but kept those thoughts to himself. "If your brothers found you in here they would attempt to beat me to a pulp."

"But not succeed?"

James heard the amusement in her voice.

"Perhaps if the two of them tried, they may rough me up a bit."

"Then I shall leave before they do."

"How did you hear me when your room is on the next floor up?" He didn't want her to leave him to fall back into the terror.

"I-I was, ah, checking on Warwick."

She was lying, her hesitation told him that, and also, they both knew Warwick slept in the same room as her brothers. However, he did not want to challenge her because then she'd leave.

"I do not like to feel fear." The darkness allowed him to show this weakness.

"But fear is something we all experience, James, and it makes us stronger if we have lived and survived fear."

"It weakens you," James said, closing his eyes. Her hand was on his shoulder again. He wanted her to slip inside his robe and stroke his skin. Visions of pulling her onto his body had him hard.

"No, it does not, but now is not the time for that conversation. Sleep, and you shall feel better in the morning."

He grabbed her wrist as she lifted it from his body. Swinging his legs off the bed, he settled her between them.

"James, let me go."

"I can't."

"You must."

There was no strength in her words as he kissed the side of her jaw.

"What is it about you?" James said the words into her throat.

"I-I… it is what lies between our families." Her hands went to his shoulders, digging in to the material of his dressing gown.

He didn't speak, simply took her mouth beneath his and kissed her. It was soft and deep and James swore he felt something stir inside him.

"No." She said the word softly as she pulled out of his arms. "No." This time it was firmer. "I won't do this to myself or my family. There can be nothing between us, ever, therefore this will lead to my downfall, so it cannot happen again."

"No matter how much we wish it," James ended the sentence.

"Yes."

She stood there for a few seconds, her breathing harsh, then turned and walked away from him, closing the door softly behind her and leaving James aroused and angry with himself. Angry at his loss of control and the fact that he had once again disrespected Eden and her family. He knew better than to make advances to a young unmarried woman, yet he had done so with her and more than once.

He lay back on the bed and stared at the ceiling. The last thought that filtered through his head before he slept once again was that she had not denied wanting him, and James wished like hell she had.

CHAPTER SEVEN

Looking out of the carriage window as it rumbled through the streets toward the Wynburg town house, Eden realized London appeared to be everything she had expected. Noisy, smelly and overpopulated.

When they had stopped to change horses, she had decided to travel with her sisters and Samantha. Her brothers had shot her a confused look, as she always rode with them, but Eden did not elaborate because telling the truth was not an option. Especially as it concerned a certain dark-haired duke who with just a glance could make her heart flutter. Plus, every time she looked at James she was reminded of her foolish behavior.

Twice yesterday she had yielded to his kisses. Thrown herself at him, wrapped her arms around his neck, and urged him to take more of what she offered. It horrified her how wantonly she behaved around him. So she had decided from this day onward she would keep her distance from him, and that included riding alongside him.

He'd been polite, as had she, when they encountered each other at breakfast, but that was the last time they'd spoken, and she would make sure it would be the last for some time.

She'd woken during the night and pulled out her earplugs to hear him call out in his sleep. Eden knew he would battle the demons from the night she had saved him for some time to come. The memory was vivid for her also, and her life had not been in danger like his. She had quickly climbed out of bed before his cries escalated and gone to his room. Pausing briefly at his door, she'd pushed aside her doubt. He was hurting and needed someone, and she would be that person.

He had been thrashing about, arching off the mattress as he tried to free himself from the invisible bonds that held him down. He'd woken to her touch, and fool that she was, she'd stayed instead of leaving as soon as she knew he was all right.

What has become of me? Eden wondered. To crave a man's touch like she did the Duke's was foolhardy, but there was little she could do about it. It was as if an invisible thread pulled her toward him. Well, that thread was now severed, and Eden hoped they saw nothing of him in London.

"What if our aunt is mean and nasty and does not like us?" Somer's words pulled Eden from her thoughts.

"Now why would our aunt and uncle invite us to London, if they were mean?" Essie said, cuddling her close.

The four children had grown quiet as the miles passed. Change was always frightening for them, especially the youngest Sinclair siblings. After the deaths of their parents, Dev, Cam, Essie, and Eden had done their best to be both mother and father to them, yet no one could replace their mother's love. Their father's love had never been without conditions.

"Will we see each other again?"

Eden put her arm around Samantha; the little girl's whispered words tugged at her heart.

"Of course; in fact I think your brother's home is on the same street as our aunt's, so we will grow quite tired of each other."

"Really?" Eden felt her heart sink as she looked at Essie. "How do you know that?"

"James told me last night."

"There will be no other boys for me to play with." Warwick entered the conversation. The boy looked forlorn. He had stared out the window for the better part of today's journey, mourning the freedom and wide-open spaces he had left behind at Oak's Knoll.

Unlike most families, who longed for the excitement of city life, Eden's father had taught his children to loathe London. His favorite quote, which he had never failed to deliver to any child who expressed a wish to leave the family home, was "country air does not blacken the lungs and wither the muscles as it does in London." Of course, it seemed the late Lord Sinclair had been exempt from this particular statement, as he had spent much time here, usually gambling away their money.

"Rubbish! Now enough of this nonsense, we are all weary and after a good meal and night's sleep everything will look so much better," Eden stated, hoping she was right. "Furthermore, there will be many new and exciting things for you to do and see here. We shall have some wonderful adventures."

Eden saw her words were not having the desired effect, as her siblings all looked as depressed as she felt. How long she wondered, before they saw the familiar sight of their home once more.

James was looking forward to getting off his horse. His ribs pulled, not that he would tell a Sinclair that, and he wanted brandy and a soft chair. Eden had ignored him since they had greeted each other this morning. Her words had been cool, and her eyes had looked over his right shoulder. She had then completely ignored him, which should have been exactly what he wanted, yet perversely wasn't.

He was not himself around her. In fact Eden Sinclair had achieved what no one else had ever managed. She made him lose control, and that would never do. He would have taken her innocence in that dark room without a second thought last night, and that was a sobering thought. Without even trying she had twisted him in knots, and James could only imagine what would happen to him if she put her mind to seducing him. He shuddered at the thought. *Distance,* he reminded himself. *Keep your distance from her.*

He had been relieved when she had chosen to ride in the carriage; at least for the remainder of the journey he did not need to constantly battle his need to look at her.

It seemed without Eden riding beside them, the Sinclair brothers did not have much to converse about. James realized after spending a few hours observing them that they were not as comfortable with each other as he had first thought. Sinclair rode like a man who had been in the military, his brother slouched in his seat, stretched out like a yard of pump water. They looked alike, yet on short acquaintance he knew this was their only similarity.

Sinclair was head of the family and James had to acknowledge the man took his responsibilities seriously. He was constantly asking his siblings if they required anything. Dropping back to ride beside the carriage to check all was well. His little brother was usually draped across his lap, and he told him stories and pointed out things as the journey progressed. Cam, however, sang Warwick Sinclair naughty songs that the boy should not be hearing.

"Ah, the sweet scents of London," Cambridge said.

The late afternoon sun had brought out people from all stations of life. Peddlers, pickpockets, and peers, James thought.

"Duke."

"Lord Harlow." James tipped his hat to the elderly man trundling by on a large bay.

The noise was deafening and James usually loved the

distractions London offered. It was a place where life moved at a clip, however, this time he had Samantha with him, and it worried him that life in London may be overwhelming for her.

"I believe your aunt lives not far from my town house. We will stop there first if that suits you, Sinclair?"

"As you wish, Raven."

Gritting his teeth, James remained silent, just giving the brothers a stiff nod. Even when they uttered something as simple as "as you wish," he felt they were needling him. He'd never had a brother or even a close friend, and if this was how uncomfortable they made you feel, he was revising the opinions of his youth, when he had longed for just such a companion.

He knew this area well, having lived most of his life here. The houses were large, imposing, and spoke of the wealth their owners had. Had he a choice, he would have purchased a smaller house, but the Raven town house had been in his family for generations and he could not bring himself to sell it.

He and the brothers followed the carriages through a set of tall black gates, and swept into a circular courtyard. This was the residence of the Earl and Countess of Wynburg. Lady Wynburg had been a friend of his grandfather's and as such, knew more about James than was comfortable to his mind.

Four imposing pillars marked the front entrance of the large town house. There were plenty of colorful beds of flowers to soften the hard gray stone exterior, and windows gleamed on all floors. The Earl's coat of arms fluttered from a flag on the roof. It was imposing and yet welcoming.

Climbing from his horse, James could not quite swallow the grunt of protest as his ribs tugged against the sudden movement. Cam, who was next to him, shot him a look, but thankfully refrained from commenting. Handing the reins to a groom, he then went to the carriage to talk with Samantha.

"Hello, James."

"Miss Somerset," James said, taking her small hand in his as she appeared in the doorway and helping her from the carriage. James had not had much exposure to children in his life, well none actually, but he had come to like the three littlest Sinclairs. Unlike their elder siblings, they were open and honest, and more importantly, they had befriended his sister.

"Are you unwell, Somer?" Her sweet face was sad.

She shook her head then sighed. Tilting it back, she stared up at him.

"I want to go back to my home, James."

James had no call for excess emotions in his life. Laughter had its place, as did anger and sadness, but too much of it turned a man weak. However, looking into the solemn face before him he felt something uncomfortable stab at his chest.

"I had planned to take Samantha to Astley's Amphitheatre one evening, Somer, and had hoped you and your brothers and sisters would accompany us." *And I have no idea where those words came from.*

"Oh, James!" Somer squealed, she then threw herself at him, wrapping her arms around his waist and squeezing before he could stop her. Releasing him, she began to chatter to her siblings and Samantha with no sign of her previous sadness he noted.

"Dorrie, Warwick, did you hear? We will see Samantha soon because James is taking us to Astley's Amphitheatre!"

The other children all piled out of the carriage and formed a small circle, proceeding to talk over the top of each other, their good humor now apparently restored. James noticed even Samantha managed to get a word in.

"Nicely done," Essie said, climbing down next. "But you will have to follow through, James, as they will not relent in their quest to get to Astley's now you have mentioned it."

"They shall badger us from dawn till dusk now. There will

be no peace for any of us." These words came from Cam. "One thing you have yet to learn is that children never forget, James. Most especially when it is something they want. A word of caution, if I may," he added. "Never promise until you are sure you can follow through."

"I would not have said the words had I not intended to honor them, Cambridge."

"Just as well," he muttered.

Shaking his head, James wondered what the hell had possessed him to make such a promise to Somer. Maybe he was more tired than he realized.

He watched the gaggle of children make for the door, and turned to look for Eden, who as yet had not appeared. Looking inside the carriage, he noted she was gathering armfuls of bonnets and coats from the seats and floor.

"Can I assist you, Eden?"

His words demanded a response, and as he had come to realize, the Sinclairs may be loud and boisterous, but they were well-mannered. She really had the most remarkable eyes; in some lights the gray depths held a blue tint and in others green. At the moment they were flat and cold.

"No, thank you."

She slid along the seat toward the door, now inches from where he stood, looking at him with cool reserve that shattered the resistance he had told himself he must have when she was near. James knew she wanted him to step aside, just as he knew he should, yet he didn't. Call it idiocy or exhaustion, but he had carried the taste of her on his lips all day. Bracing his hands on the doorway so no one could view inside, he leaned in until his face was inches from her own.

"Open your mouth, Eden."

"Wh—"

He swallowed the sound her word made and the small shriek

that followed. His tongue swept inside her mouth, marauding and conquering. Her hands gripped the lapels of his jacket to steady herself and his fingers dug in to the carriage roof as he battled the urge to pull her closer. She tasted of the woman she was, spicy and alluring, and her response was instant. Arching toward him she sank into his kiss. Their tongues met, danced, and flitted away and James could feel his control begin to slip.

"Eden," he whispered as he eased back from their kiss. She kept her eyes closed, her breathing ragged like his own.

"I don't want you to ever do that again."

"Eden, I—"

"I am not to be toyed with," she whispered.

"Yes," he sighed. "I know that, but—"

"Please just go."

It was the please that had his feet moving. He did as she asked and called himself every kind of fool for once again playing with fire. He had no rights to that woman and yet he had still kissed her… again.

What has become of you?

James was disciplined; he did not give in to impulses or urges. Yet when she was near he was consumed by a madness to be with her, possess her, touch her, and it bloody well had to stop! He would get Samantha and leave before he could do anything else without thinking. Then he would stay away from Eden Sinclair.

"At last you have arrived!"

James had met the Earl of Wynburg often, as they frequented the same club. He was a jovial man who did not rattle on excessively and had a wise head on his shoulders, unlike his wife.

The small gale-force wind that was the Countess of Wynburg had picked up her skirts and was now running down the steps at a rapid pace.

Moving to the rear of the small group of Sinclairs that held his sister, James shot a quick look behind him. Eden had not emerged.

"My darling nieces and nephews, this is one of the happiest moments of my life!"

"James," Samantha said, slowly backing into his legs, "that woman's hair is the same color as a carrot."

Cam snuffled beside them. His eyes too were fixed on the woman approaching. James didn't think she was overly tall, however her hair—likened to the color of carrots—added at least a foot to her height. Styled in some elaborate fashion, it was festooned with ribbons, feathers and….

"Is that a bird in your hair, Aunt?"

"Oh you clever child!" Lady Wynburg cried, reaching Warwick first as he spoke and sweeping him into a fierce hug that the young boy was doing his level best to break free from.

She was not a nasty person, just a woman whose presence you always felt. She laughed and spoke louder than most, her gestures were flamboyant, and she was everything James would not choose in his future wife. The few times the Countess had singled him out she had made him feel uncomfortable. Her brown eyes would look into his own, almost as if she could read his every thought, she would then hug him, "because I have the right due to my close relationship with your late grandfather, Duke," she would say. And perhaps that more than any was the reason he avoided her, because she had known the only person James had loved.

"Aunt," Cambridge Sinclair said, stepping forward next with obvious reluctance.

The problem was she didn't just greet people with the touch of a hand, she enveloped them. James watched her go to each of her nieces and nephews and welcome them.

"Where is Eden?"

"Here I am, Aunt."

James watched Eden grip the bundle of clothes in her arms tight as her aunt hugged her. Awareness shot through him as she looked at him briefly over her aunt's shoulder, and then just as quickly looked away.

"Come, Samantha, make your good-byes," James said quickly as Lady Wynburg released Eden and turned his way.

"Duke!"

"Escape is impossible." Sinclair laughed as his aunt made her way to where James stood with Samantha in front of him like a shield.

"And who is this beautiful child?"

"May I present my sister to you, Lady Wynburg. Lady Samantha Raven."

It was the first time he had ever seen her speechless. Her eyes filled with tears and then she sank to her knees, right there in the street where anyone looking in the courtyard could see her, and hugged Samantha. More surprisingly, his sister accepted the gesture. Seconds later she once again stood before him.

"I had no idea of her existence, James, or I would have told you."

He could see the genuine distress in her brown eyes. She really was quite a striking woman; her skin was lined yet still soft and creamy and had always carried the faintest scent of lavender.

"I know you would have, Lady Wynburg. As I did not find out myself until after the death of my father, I am sure not many people were aware of Samantha's existence."

James grunted as she reached over Samantha's head and hauled him into her arms.

He did not fight it; indeed, the small boy who had always wanted such a hug even enjoyed it, yet he remained still the entire time. James was not used to hugs and kisses of a maternal type. He may have loved his grandfather, but the man had not comforted him with anything but words.

"Of course I know you live nearby Oak's Knoll, yet what has you travelling to London with my nephews and nieces," she said upon releasing him.

"Raven wished for company for his sister, and as I met him in the village one day, we discussed our travelling together."

James nodded to Sinclair as he spoke. They could not tell the woman the truth, as he had no wish for anyone to know about the attempt on his life.

"Excellent!" she cried loudly, making James wince. "Well then, we shall take tea."

"If I may decline, my lady. Samantha is tired after the journey and in need of rest," James said. He had no wish to spend more time in Eden's company.

"Very well, however I insist on you coming to tea one afternoon soon so I may become better acquainted with Samantha. And of course, I am sure she and the twins are now firm friends."

"Yes!" Somer cried. "And James has promised to take us all to Astley's."

"I did warn you," Cam drawled softly.

"That you did."

James said his good-byes and minutes later he was leaving the Sinclair family. He sat inside the carriage with his sister while she waved good-bye.

"Do you like the Sinclair family, Samantha?"

She gave him a small smile.

"Very much, they are happy."

He could read so much into those simple words. She wanted to be happy? She had never been happy? He was not a happy person? The possibilities were endless. But one thing James did know was that he would do everything in his power to make her happy.

CHAPTER EIGHT

The refreshed elder Sinclair sisters left their rooms the following morning to make their way to the breakfast parlor. They had been too tired last night to venture far. After ensuring their younger siblings were being entertained, surprisingly by their aunt, uncle, and several maids, all of whom had been gathered around the fire toasting crumpets in the nursery wing, Eden and Essex had eaten and then fallen back into bed, once again slipping into a deep slumber.

"Good morning. I am the butler, Pennyroll."

"Good morning, Pennyroll," Essex and Eden said in unison when he appeared before them as they entered the long hallway. He was tall with wide shoulders and wore an immaculate black suit with crisp white shirt. Thick and the color of newly fallen snow, his hair was swept back from the forehead. Round eyeglasses enhanced a pair of bright blue eyes.

"You have the bluest eyes I've ever seen, Pennyroll," Eden said, leaning closer. "In fact, I would go so far as saying they are more indigo, don't you think, Essie?"

The butler didn't flinch as the two young ladies peered into his eyes.

"I think you could be right, Eden. They really are beautiful, Pennyroll."

"My mother said they were wasted on a boy."

"Surely not," Essie laughed. "I should imagine you are quite a success with the ladies, Pennyroll."

The butler merely smiled then led them down to the breakfast room at a stately pace.

The house was grand in every way, from the plush carpets to the softly painted walls. Light spilled into the rooms from large windows offering views of gardens and parks. Mirrors and paintings hung in huge gilt frames.

"It is very grand, Eden."

"Yes it is, but also strangely comfortable don't you think?"

"Yes, not what I expected at all after father's descriptions of our aunt and uncle. I must admit to preconceived ideas of gold fittings and lavish surroundings," Essie said, looking at a large print of a house in the countryside surrounded by wildflowers.

"Perhaps not everything Father told us was true," Eden whispered as Pennyroll opened a door before them. The entire Sinclair family were seated, as were their aunt and uncle.

"Now we are all together!" their aunt cried as she saw her two nieces enter the breakfast parlor. Waving to the only empty chairs at the table, she urged them to take a seat.

"Good morning," the sisters said to the room.

"Eden!" Dorrie said, getting out of her chair and running to her sister. "We played games after you left last night."

"It sounds like I missed all the fun," Eden said, replacing Dorrie in her seat and giving Warwick and Somer kisses.

"Good morning, my dear nieces."

The Earl of Wynburg had risen at their entry and now stood before them. He was a big man, easily as tall as Devon yet much wider. He had a remarkable pair of bushy brows and intelligent brown eyes and a smile that seemed to fill his whole face. He did not appear a bad man, as her father had once described him. But then appearances, Eden knew, could be deceptive.

"Welcome, my dears."

Eden kissed one weathered cheek as was expected of her.

"You can have no idea how long we have waited to see you all here. Come, sit, and let us eat our first meal as a family."

Shooting her brothers a questioning look at her uncle's exuberant greeting, Eden took her seat. Dev just shrugged and Cam ignored her in favor of eating.

Her brothers were staying in the smaller residence next door that their uncle owned, and Eden knew this was because neither was comfortable living in such close confines with Lord and Lady Wynburg.

"Fill your plates, girls, and then after breakfast the young ones will go and gather their bonnets and coats for our journey to the shops while your uncle and I have a chat with you elder nieces and nephews," Lady Wynburg said.

The Sinclairs ate with exuberance like they did everything else, and as this particular array of food was far superior to any they had previously experienced, they fell on it with, if not savage intent, then a healthy dose of enthusiasm.

"Warwick, your head does not need to be that close to your plate."

"Yes, Dev."

"Close your mouth, Somer."

"But, Essie, my nose is closed," the little girl said.

"Closed?" the Countess questioned the table at large.

"Somer sometimes gets a bit—ah—"

"Congested," Cam said, coming to Essie's aid.

"Ah, I see, well we will have to see what we can do about that." Lady Wynburg smiled at the little girl.

The meal progressed with their aunt and uncle asking questions, to which the elder Sinclairs were not overly forthcoming but answered with politeness.

"And have you left Oak's Knoll in the hands of someone?

Perhaps I could have one of my men check on it for you—"

"We were able to retain two servants, Uncle, they are caring for the house in our absence," Dev said, his tone curt.

"Ah yes, Bertie and Josiah Hemple. Wonderful men, your aunt and I were pleased that they were there to care for you."

"Our parents also cared for us, my Lord. It is the rest of our family who have stayed away from us!" Cam snapped.

"Cam, be quiet."

A heavy, uncomfortable silence followed Dev's words. Even the younger Sinclairs were unusually subdued, their eyes looking at the adults as they tried to grasp why there was suddenly a great deal of tension in the room.

Eden looked at her uncle, who was staring at Dev and Cam with a sad look in his eyes. Climbing to his feet he signaled for Pennyroll to come forward.

"Take the children to collect their outer clothing please, Pennyroll, and I will call for them when we are ready for our outing."

"We will look after our siblings," Dev said, also rising.

"I will accompany them, Dev," Eden added, preparing to follow.

"I would like to speak to you all, please." The Earl did not raise his voice yet his intent was clear to everyone in the room. He wanted to talk with them and he wanted to do so now. Eden suddenly saw the powerful peer in the man before them. His jovial facade had fallen away to be replaced by a determined man.

Eden, Essie, and Cam all looked to their elder brother, who in turn was glaring at their uncle. He gave a jerky nod and then forced a smile onto his face as he urged his younger brother and sisters from the room with the promise of coming to find them soon.

Eden's father had never liked the Earl and Countess of

Wynburg, and he had nurtured these feelings in his children, especially Dev, who had bore the brunt of their father's confidences. It seemed now all that hatred was about to come to a head. Eden jammed her earplugs in tighter and hoped there was not too much yelling, as her ears would never take it. She also hoped they would not pack up and leave London today, as the little ones would never cope with another long journey so soon.

They silently filed from the room behind their aunt and uncle, following until they reached another room into which they were shepherded. Each of the Sinclairs took a seat before the large desk while the Earl sat behind it with the Countess standing at his back. This was a sign of solidarity and Eden's throat felt suddenly dry. What was their uncle about to tell them? Whatever it was she knew they would not like it.

"Firstly I will address the matter of our abandonment in your eyes," the Earl said. "Your father kept your aunt and me away from you from the day he married your mother. We were allowed no contact with you and every time we tried to visit he picked you all up and left before we arrived. Any gifts we sent were returned unopened."

"You lie!"

"Sit down, Cam." Eden watched Dev place a hand on his brother's arm, urging him back into his seat.

"We have only your word on this, my lord, and you must understand that we loved our parents. Therefore, to ask us to believe what you say is impossible."

Eden nodded at Dev's words.

"Show them the letters, Sally," the Earl said as he looked up at his wife. "It must be done, love. They need to hear this or we shall never be able to move on with them in our lives."

The Sinclairs watched the Countess open a drawer in her husband's desk and remove a pile of letters tied in a lemon ribbon.

"Read the first out loud, Sally, and then the one at the birth of Eden, the rest they can read themselves later."

Eden felt a terrible unease settle over the siblings as their aunt nodded and opened the first piece of paper and began to read out loud.

"My darling sister, I hardly know how to begin this letter I am forced to write to you. Firstly, please know that I love my husband very much and you have no need to fear he will mistreat me. Sally, when you came for a visit yesterday I was so excited to see you. Having been married for only a few months, I had so much to tell you and I do miss our talks so."

The Earl handed a handkerchief to his wife as she sniffed; Eden watched the gesture and was filled with trepidation. What did that letter contain that was so dire?

"I had no idea that my darling Thomas would treat you so terribly, Sally. He was rude and ill-mannered and I told him so after you left. But, Sister, I fear he has a great jealousy for you and Elijah, and he has told me that under no circumstances are you to return to Oak's Knoll again. Of course I argued with him and perhaps in time he may relent, yet in this I must honor his wishes for now. Please try to understand, my dearest. Thomas is a good man yet he is prone to fits of temper. I will write soon and hope he has changed his mind."

The Sinclairs watched their aunt fold the letter in half before placing it on the desk. She then reached for another. Eden did not look at her brothers, instead, reaching to her left she took Cam's hand in her own, and then to the right she took Essie's, who in turn was gripping Dev's. They would face this together—whatever this was. She felt the tension travel through her, strengthened by their heightened senses.

"I will read the letter we wrote to your father just after your birth, Eden, and then I will read the reply from your father," their aunt said.

"I feel ill," Cam whispered. Eden squeezed his hand hard.

"You have made your wishes regarding the Countess and me explicit over the years, but I implore you to reconsider for the sake of your children. Having lost our only child we merely wish to offer love to your family. My darling Sally struggles greatly with the loss of both her beloved son and sister in her life. Please, I beseech you, let us visit if only to get to know our nieces and nephews, and for Sally to seek solace in the arms of her sister."

Eden watched as the tears began to roll down their aunt's cheeks.

"I-I cannot c-continue, Elijah."

Dear God, Papa, what you did to me was bad enough, but how could you have done this to all of us? She watched the Earl stand and hug his wife, then lower her into the chair he had vacated and take up the position at her back, with another letter now in his hand. He began to read in a deep, clear voice.

"You will never see your nieces and nephews, Wynburg. They are mine and you cannot have them, and as for your wife, I'm sure if you buy her a new bauble that will suffice. Now leave us alone, we want neither your money nor your time. If I see you on my property, I will shoot you, and I will aim to kill."

Closing the letter, their uncle looked at each of them in turn. Eden knew their expressions were the same. Shock and despair gripped the four eldest Sinclairs.

"I need to see that letter," Dev got to his feet, and held out his hand. He then looked at the page the Earl passed him. Eden saw the moment he realized the truth.

"Is it be true, Dev?" Essie asked.

"Yes, it is our father's handwriting."

Dev lowered the letter to the desk and stumbled back to his seat. "Why have you told us this?" his words were harsh, as if forced from his throat.

"Your mother wrote to us before she died and said that we must tell you the reasons we had not visited if your father died before we did. She believed you would be left without money and need our help, but that your father's words may have poisoned you against your aunt and me."

"How often did you try to visit us?" Essie questioned, her words wavering as she attempted to regain control.

"Every year once Devon was born, until the day your father threatened me with a shotgun."

Cam released his sisters' hands and leaped to his feet. With clenched fists he prowled to the window and looked down at the street below. Cam had always been the most demonstrative of the Sinclairs, his emotions on show for everyone to see, and she feared he would take this news very badly. He turned then and glared at the Earl.

"How could he have left us to struggle like that? The past few years have been hell, but most especially on Dev. He resigned his commission to care for us, for God's sake!"

"I sent your mother money when times were really bad, Cam. I also sent Bertie and Josiah to you, and it was through them I kept in touch with what was going on in your lives," the Earl said, going to stand before him. "I did not tell you these things to make you hate your father, I told them to you because I want you to accept what we are offering you all. Your father loved you, never forget that."

Cam snorted but remained silent.

"Why have you waited to tell us this?" Eden questioned.

The Earl looked from Eden to his wife; the Countess gave him a little nod.

"Sally has been very ill since your mother passed away. The doctors told me I would lose her if I did not take her to a warmer climate, thus we traveled to Italy and there we stayed until she returned to health. We did not learn of your father's death until we returned to London, and it was then we immediately started writing to you. Had you not returned our last letter, we had made plans to travel to Oak's Knoll to see you."

"What did you want to offer us?"

Dev's words were cold and she knew he was suffering as much as his siblings with their aunt and uncle's revelations. Perhaps more, as he was the one who had struggled to put food on their table.

"Is now the time for this discussion, when you have all received such a shock?" the Earl queried.

Each of the siblings nodded; they wanted all their shocks in one sitting.

"Very well." Once again he went to stand behind his wife. "We would like to provide dowries for your sisters, Devon, and to loan you enough money to aid you in your investments."

"What do you know of my investments?"

"I made it my business to be aware of how your family has fared over the years. I am also aware that the few investments you could raise capital for have succeeded, and it is through this that you have survived."

"My God," Dev said, looking stunned. "It was you who made sure we survived?"

Holding up his hand, the Earl of Wynburg said, "I merely invested in whatever you did, nothing more, Devonshire. Please do not think me foolish enough to throw money into something that would earn me no return."

"I-I do not need your help."

"Yet you will take it all the same, as it is not for you alone. We will discuss the money I will invest in you another time, but it will not come cheaply and I will expect a healthy return on my investments."

Dev just stared at their uncle, for once at a loss for words.

"Cam, we will also have a discussion in private regarding your future, but for now I want you all to know that you may stay with us for as long as you wish. If London becomes too stifling then we have several other estates that lie empty, and they are at your disposal if you so wish it."

"Oak's Knoll is our home," Cam said, anger still evident in his voice.

"As it shall always be," their aunt soothed. "But enough for now I think, Elijah," she added, regaining her feet. "Now we are to go shopping. Ladies, please gather your bonnets and the twins, and we shall leave in a few minutes."

Eden squeezed Dev's shoulder as she passed, then quietly followed Essie from the room. Once their aunt had left them to collect her things, the sisters gave in to their tears, hugging each other as they cried over their father's betrayal.

"It hurts." Eden said.

"Can you believe it of our father?"

Yes! Eden cried silently. *I know what he was capable of.* "I once heard mother and father arguing over our aunt and uncle, and father was saying horrid things. So yes, as much as I wish it wasn't so, I can believe it."

"Why did you never speak to me of these concerns you had?"

"They were my concerns, not yours, Essie."

"And yet I am your sister and we have always shared everything."

Not everything, Eden thought. She couldn't tell Essie the truth, not ever. "I did not want to worry you," she added lamely.

"What are you not telling me, Eden?"

"Nothing. Now hurry, Dev has just told me that I am to go straight to my room and not listen to the conversation he and Cam are having with our uncle."

Essie took Eden's hand and gave it a squeeze and then

tugged her up the stairs. Minutes later Eden had another set of earplugs firmly in place.

"Perhaps I should just listen to make sure no one is yelling?"

"No, now hurry with your bonnet, I want to see London."

"I don't." Eden shuddered.

CHAPTER NINE

James watched as Buttles, his butler, led his sister into the room.

"How did you sleep, Samantha?"

"Very well, thank you." She settled herself in the chair across from him.

"And do you like eggs for breakfast?" She shook her head. "Perhaps toast then?" Again silence, with only a head shake. Facing a bayonet was proving easier than trying to have a conversation with his sister, he thought grimly, looking at the top of her head. What did one talk to young girl children about anyway? He could hardly discuss stocks and bonds or horses. It was then he heard Devonshire Sinclair's voice in his head. *"Miss Somerset and Miss Dorset will have crumpets and jam for their morning repast."* He had said those words at the inn when they were seated awaiting their morning meal, and while he was not overly fond of the oldest Sinclair, he had to admit the man was very comfortable with children. James wondered if Samantha would like that. Christ did they even have crumpets and jam in the house?

"I believe Lady Samantha will have crumpets and jam for her morning repast, Buttles," James said in his most pompous voice. Samantha made a snuffling sound, which could have been a giggle but he wasn't sure, and then nodded. Victory!

"And shall I have Mrs. Gotheram procure a companion for

Lady Samantha, your Grace?"

Of course she needed a companion, James thought, pinching the bridge of his nose, why the hell hadn't he thought of that.

"Yes please, Buttles."

"Mrs. Gotheram has also assured me that the nursery is in need of a thorough cleaning. I have set the maids to work this morning, but she fears it will also need completely refurnishing, your Grace."

Thank God for his housekeeper. James felt his head begin to throb. "Do whatever you and Mrs. Gotheram believe is necessary, Buttles, thank you," James said, hoping his butler would now clear off so he could finish his breakfast before he lost his appetite completely.

"Mrs. Gotheram has also asked me to enquire if you would visit the nursery, your Grace, at ten o'clock this morning to discuss the requirements for Lady Samantha."

Looking at the large clock that stood before him, James noted it was nine thirty. Half an hour to eat and read the morning paper. Could he read the paper with his sister sitting silently across from him? Dear Lord, another ritual it seemed would have to go by the wayside whilst breakfasting with her.

"We will visit the nursery as soon as my sister has eaten, Buttles," James said, hoping that now he would actually leave the room and stop firing questions at him.

Samantha's breakfast arrived shortly thereafter and James was relieved that she tucked in straight away. She ate like she did everything, silently and neatly. Small movements that gave no one reason to either look at or censure her. James felt ill watching her, because he had done just the same when he was a small boy. She stiffened as a drop of jam fell onto the white tablecloth beside her plate. He watched as she shot him a quick look, her eyes wide and terrified, her fingers curling into themselves so they could not be whacked hard with whatever implement of torture was handy. Their father would have punished her had he been present. James, however, was not like his father and never would be.

"J-James I did not mean to—"

James reached across the table and picked the spoon out of the jam pot and turned it over so a large dollop fell onto the cloth between them.

"There, it seems we are both clumsy today, Samantha." James then picked up his knife and fork and proceeded to finish his breakfast, which now tasted like ashes in his mouth. Samantha looked first at him and then at the large dollop of jam he had dropped on the cloth, then picking up her crumpet, she gave a little smile and began to eat once again.

"Thank you, James."

Her words were tentative, but she had spoken without him prompting, and in that moment he felt they had made progress.

"Are you ready to inspect your rooms, Samantha?" he asked twenty minutes later.

"Yes," she said, wiping her mouth.

James assisted Samantha from her chair. Remembering how the Sinclairs had constantly seemed attached to each other, he held out his hand. Samantha took it, and they made their way down the long hallway to the stairs. It felt so precious clasped in his, precious and vulnerable. Looking around him as they walked, he noticed how dark and austere his home was.

"We need to redecorate this house, Samantha."

"Yes, it is very dark, James."

And you hate the dark just like I did, he realized. Because their father had not wanted to spend money on candles or lamps, therefore they had lived in darkness.

"You will never have to live in the dark again, Samantha, I promise you."

James kept up a steady stream of words as they made their way to the nursery, which was not easy, as talking had never been his strong suit, yet Samantha appeared to listen and occasionally nodded or murmured.

Eden had told him to exercise patience when dealing with his sister and it had been advice that went against his nature, as he was a man who took action and expected results. However, James was determined to forge a relationship with Samantha, so he would be patience itself.

The nursery had two huge windows that looked over the gardens at the rear of the property. There was a main room with two smaller ones leading off it. The walls were a drab gray and the curtains equally as drab. Looking at his sister, he thought that perhaps the curtains were made of exactly the same fabric as her dress. Should young girls dress in such dull colors?

"I think you need some new clothes, Samantha."

"Yes, please."

Well that seemed comprehensive enough. Now how did one go about buying young girl clothes, James wondered.

"Your Grace, Lady Samantha."

"Mrs. Gotheram." James acknowledged his housekeeper as she entered the nursery behind them. Short and stout, she had been with him since he was bundled from Raven Castle and sent to London at age ten. It had been she who was waiting for him when he came home from school and she who had helped him through his darkest moments. James had spent many hours with this woman in his youth.

"We will need all new furnishings and entertainments for Lady Samantha, your Grace."

"Of course, please get whatever you think is necessary."

"And what of other things, Your Grace?"

"Other things, Mrs. Gotheram?" James said, feeling totally at sea, as he had no idea what the "other things" were. What sort of brother was he?

"She'll need things to occupy her time, your Grace. Books and such. Because I am sure there will be plenty of times when you are not here and then Lady Samantha will be on her own."

Mrs. Gotheram always made her agitation known by the line of her lips, drawn straight and tucked inside each other.

"Ah-ah perhaps Samantha and I will see to the other things then."

When had he ever opened his mouth before thinking? *Yesterday, when you promised Miss Somer a trip to Astley's*, James reminded himself.

"Excellent, your Grace, I knew you would take to the task of looking after your wee sister once you had some guidance," Mrs. Gotheram said, patting Samantha's cheek as she bustled past. "Now about the colors in here, do you have any particular favorites, my dear?"

Samantha looked at James, who shrugged, and then to the window where a weak sun was trying to break through the clouds.

"Sunshine yellow."

Remembering the darkness of Raven Castle, James immediately understood his sister's need to live in the light.

"Excellent choice, Samantha, and now we will leave Mrs. Gotheram and go shopping."

"She is a very nice woman," James said as they left the nursery. "You have nothing to fear from her," he added as his sister pressed closer to his leg. At least she wasn't pulling away from him.

"Really?"

"Really," he affirmed, taking her hand in his once more. He liked the feeling of it tucked inside his and realized it was something he could get used to. Funny, he'd never really understood the need for personal contact, but he was beginning to.

They left the house once Samantha had pulled on her bonnet and gloves, both equally as drab and ugly as her dress. Once in the carriage, they headed out through the busy London streets, with James pointing out sights for his sister along the way. She sat very still listening and watching, her hands in her lap, placed one on top of the other.

James wondered if you could hate a man more every day, especially as he was dead. Sending his father several curses for what he had done to Samantha, he vowed again to do whatever he needed to make her understand there was good in the world, in him, and that he would never harm her.

When the carriage stopped, he got out and lifted her down beside him.

"This is a store that has some of the things I believe we need, Samantha." At least he hoped it did. Buttles had told him it was the place to start. Taking her hand in his once more, he entered and found his butler had been correct. It appeared to have row upon row of books; surely some of them would be suitable for a young girl.

"There are a great many books, James." Samantha's eyes were wide as she looked from side to side, taking it all in.

"Yes, there certainly are." The smell was musty and yet spoke of many hours of wonderful reading adventures hidden between the pages before them. James remembered the first day he had entered a bookshop and purchased whatever he wanted. The sense of freedom had made his knees weak.

"Good morning."

"Good morning." James nodded to the proprietor as he approached.

"We have a large amount of books suitable for children upstairs, as well as other toys that the young lady would like to see, I'm sure."

"Excellent, thank you. That is where we shall head then."

They climbed the stairs with Samantha leading the way, her little legs hampered by her thick skirts and the sturdy boots on her feet.

"Oh," she said when they reached the top. If possible there was the same amount of books as downstairs. "May I go and look, please?"

"Of course," James said, heading toward the first shelf himself. "Take as much time as you need, Samantha." He soon found himself as engrossed in the collection before him as his sister.

"Can we add this book to the collection, Samantha?" James said, holding up the tales of Robinson Crusoe some time later. The tutor his father had sent him had never allowed him to read anything like this, but he had heard other boys discussing it at school.

"Yes." She nodded, her face a picture of concentration as she once again turned to the book of fables she was studying. "Can I have this one, James?"

"Of course," he said, taking the large book with bright-colored fairies flying all over the cover from her. He may not be able to go back and make the last few years easier for her, but he would bloody well try to make the rest better.

Samantha had lost some of her reserve toward him as the minutes ticked by, and was now showing him one book after the other; in fact their pile was growing with every one she viewed.

"Can I look over there now, James?" Samantha pointed to another room. She seemed eager and he wondered what she had seen to cause such excitement.

After organizing for their purchases to be delivered, James followed his sister. He was surprised at how much he'd enjoyed accompanying her to the store. He found her on her knees before a large dollhouse; the front was open and she was studying the inside intently. Crouching beside her, he looked inside.

"There is a small table and chairs and a bed too," Samantha whispered reverently, as if she did not want to wake the tiny people who slept inside.

"This is a nice doll," James said, picking up one that lay beside the house. It had black ringlets, green eyes, and a dress of bright pink with ruffles.

"She is very beautiful, just like Eden and Essex, don't you think, James?"

"Hmmm" was all he could manage by way of agreement. Eden intruded far too much on his thoughts without his sister reminding him of her beauty.

It was testament to just how far their relationship had come in such a short time that he felt only slightly awkward discussing dolls with his little sister.

"James."

"Yes, Samantha."

He knew what she wanted; he could see the longing in her eyes as she looked down at the doll now in her hands. But he wanted her to ask him if she could have it. He wanted her to feel comfortable with him.

"C-can I have her?"

"Yes, but you must give her a pretty name to match her face."

"Eden," Samantha whispered.

"Ah… no," James said, feeling his necktie tighten and restrict his breathing. "I think she should have her own name, don't you? Not someone else's."

Samantha looked at the doll then back at him and nodded.

"Thank you, James."

"You're welcome."

She struggled to her feet, clasping the doll to her chest. Her eyes were level with his now, and then she bent at the waist and kissed his cheek.

"It is the most wonderful gift in the world."

"No," James rasped, lifting a hand to cup her cheek. "You are the most wonderful gift in the world."

Her smile lit her entire face.

"Samantha!"

James heard the squeal from behind him and knew it was a Sinclair. Regaining his feet, he inhaled, pushing the emotion that choked him aside. Bracing himself he then turned. The twins were running toward Samantha, squealing loudly, and Eden was following slowly behind. The little girls soon joined Samantha on the floor and were immediately lost in the world of dolls while their sister had stopped several feet away looking everywhere but at him.

"Have you come to purchase books, or dolls?" James said, hoping to draw her gaze.

"Neither. My sisters grew tired of watching the dress fittings, so I brought them here until Essie and my aunt are finished."

"And have you all settled in?"

"Yes, thank you."

Her words were polite and distant, which was what he had wanted. James closed the distance between them, forcing her to retreat or look at him; he knew she would choose the latter. She had been crying, he could see the pallor of her cheeks and redness in her eyes. Someone had upset her and he could do nothing to control the rage that flooded his body.

"Who has made you cry?" His hand wrapped around her wrist as she turned to leave. "Tell me, Eden."

"Release me at once."

"Not until you tell me who has made you cry."

"I am no concern of yours, Duke. I have family who look after my welfare."

"They do not appear to be doing a very good job," James whispered. There was so much sadness in the gray depths of her eyes that his stomach churned.

"No good can come of this, James, so please release me, and keep your distance."

"Eden, come and see these dolls!"

Wrenching free, she hurried to her sisters. He watched as she hugged Samantha. His sister did not respond, but also did not pull away.

"They are beautiful, my loves."

"Look at this one, James."

James moved to stand before Dorset Sinclair and took the doll he was handed while his mind grappled with the fact that Eden had been crying. Surely he was not the cause? Had she lain awake last night thinking of their kisses?

"It is time for your fittings now, girls," Eden said minutes later. Once again she looked everywhere but at him.

"We are to have new clothes, Samantha," Dorrie said, taking the doll back from James and replacing it reluctantly on the shelf.

"Would we be asking too much to join your fitting, ladies?" he said quickly before he gave himself time to think. James had not the first idea how to go about procuring his sister new clothes. "Samantha is in need of new clothing also and as we are yet to secure a companion for her, the task, I am afraid, is left to me—a man."

Eden muttered something that he did not catch, but thought it better he hadn't, if the look on her face was any indication.

"If you wish, Duke, we will take care of Samantha's needs and return her home to you in a while. There really is no need for you to accompany us."

"His name is James, Eden."

He didn't smile as her teeth snapped together at Somer's words, but at least her eyes now held fire instead of sadness.

"If it will not be too much of an inconvenience, I would be most grateful for your assistance, Eden."

James had a task that he needed to see to, and this would give him the opportunity to do so.

"Thank you, James," Samantha whispered. Her little face had lost the pinched look of a few days ago and he thought she looked happier. Perhaps some of it was the Sinclairs' presence, but he also believed their blossoming relationship was helping.

"I have a few errands to run, Samantha, and then I will return home."

"In that case, we shall keep Samantha with us until you collect her, if you wish?"

"Very well, and thank you, Eden. I shall call at the Wynburg residence later today."

After a round of curtseying they left, and James wondered again who had made Eden cry and how he could find out.

***

He stepped from his carriage before a small brick-fronted building, tucked discreetly down a narrow lane. Taking the four front steps in two strides, James knocked twice on the white door. Seconds later he was ushered into a parlor that held a desk, two chairs, and a large cabinet. Rather than sit in one of the two upright chairs he walked slowly around the room.

Devonshire Sinclair had given James Mr. Spriggot's name yesterday, telling him the man was one of the best private detectives in the business. James had not questioned the eldest Sinclair on how he knew this, he had merely nodded and taken the card. Sinclair may irritate him with his knowing looks and continual teasing, but he was an honorable man and he had saved James's life, therefore he was trustworthy.

"Your Grace," a small thin man said, walking into the room. "I am Mr. Spriggot."

James shook the offered hand before lowering himself into a seat; the man circled the desk and did the same.

"How may I be of service to you this day?"

James could understand why Spriggot was so good at his work, as he had an appearance that was easily forgettable. Small, thin, and with a face that held little if no expression, the man would blend easily in any crowd. His eyes however were another matter entirely; the dark depths were alive with curiosity.

"Someone is trying to kill me, Mr. Spriggot, and as I have no wish for them to succeed, I would like to employ your services to ensure that does not eventuate."

Rather than appear startled as most people would in learning that someone was trying to eradicate one of the more powerful peers of the realm, Mr. Spriggot's brow furrowed in thought.

"I have come to you as I wish the investigation to be undertaken with the utmost privacy, and was assured you were the man for this."

"I will do what I can, your Grace. Now then," he picked up a quill, dipped it in the ink, and looked up at James, "I shall need all the details you have, and I would ask for half my fee up front if you please."

The man had obviously dealt with several members of society in his time, James thought, pulling some notes from his pocket. Many aristocrats believed they did not need to pay as others did for the services rendered to them. He should be affronted but wasn't; in fact he respected the man for daring to ask him for money.

"Excellent, now please begin to relate the facts in a slow and concise manner and I will make notes."

James did as he asked, telling him about the attempt made on his life.

"An extremely brave lady to have taken such a risk, your Grace, if I may say so."

"Yes, I will forever be in her debt."

Mr. Spriggot scratched a few more notes before lifting his head once more to look at James.

"Can you tell me anything about the men, your Grace?"

"I cannot. However, the woman who rescued me said one of the men was called Syd, and that they referred to the man who wanted me dead as 'his lordship.'"

"You have obviously given thought to who may want you dead, your Grace. Heirs, business dealings gone wrong?"

"I do not have business dealings go wrong, Mr. Spriggot, and my heir at this point in time is my cousin, but I have no reason to believe it is he. Last I heard he was in America building a vast fortune. There are of course other family members here in London, but they are not due to inherit should I die."

Mr. Spriggot questioned James thoroughly until he believed he had all the facts he needed.

"I shall begin my investigations at once, your Grace."

"I should be grateful," James said, getting to his feet.

"May I also enquire how you came to know my name, as I usually only work with clients who have used my services before, your Grace."

"Lord Sinclair gave me your name, sir."

Nodding, the small man smiled, although it was not a gesture that warmed his face, just the smallest baring of his teeth and then it was gone.

"A very shrewd man, if you don't mind me saying so, your Grace. I have a great deal of respect for Lord Sinclair."

James wanted to ask what services Sinclair had used Spriggot for, yet he remained silent. The information was not his to know. Nodding good-bye, he left the establishment and climbed into his carriage to start the journey back to the Wynburg townhouse, where he would collect Samantha and once again see Eden.

Who had made her cry?

"You have to stop this, James, she is not now, nor will she ever be part of your life." Feeling better for this bracing talk, he sat back and watched London roll by his window.

CHAPTER TEN

"Take the carriage back to the stables please, Nolan. Lady Samantha and I will walk back to the house."

James walked up the steps to the Wynburg townhouse with the sound of his carriage rolling away. His knock was answered instantly and he was ushered inside seconds later.

"If you will follow me, your Grace, the family are expecting you."

He had been inside the Earl and Countess's home only once before for a ball. It was plush and grand on a scale he had rarely seen, yet he still felt the warmth reach out and wrap around him as he followed the straight back of the butler down a hall and up several flights of stairs. He smelled the fresh sweet scent of flowers and beeswax. Visions of his youth filtered through his head and James tried to remember if Raven Castle had ever had flowers dotted in vases or bright splashes of color upon the walls, but all he could see was darkness and the heavy weight of silence.

"The Duke of Raven."

James entered the room after the butler had announced him and came to a halt just inside the door.

"Raven, you are just in time." Lady Wynburg hurried forward and took his hand. "Come and take a seat as the show is about to begin."

James allowed her to tow him to a seat, simply because he was incapable of speech or movement himself.

"Doesn't Samantha look sweet?"

He managed to nod at the countess's words as he looked at his sister. She stood wrapped in gold satin, a small felt hat on her head. She looked at him, her eyes wide with uncertainty and fear. *Dear Lord, she thinks I will put a stop to whatever it is I have walked into.* Clearing his throat, he somehow formed a smile, and watched the anxiety fall from her face.

"Are we ready, ladies and gentlemen?"

Eden spoke from behind the piano and James dragged his eyes from Samantha and wished he hadn't. She sat under a window in a pale lemon dress that the sun had turned to a soft glow. He was relieved that all he could see of her was her neck and shoulder, although she had such a graceful neck and he longed to place his lips right at the base and kiss the soft skin. Muttering something vile beneath his breath, he crossed his legs and forced himself to focus on the children, not the lush temptress playing the piano.

Somer, Dorrie, and Samantha all stood together dressed in various costumes, waiting for Eden to begin playing. Essie stood to one side and began clapping as the music started. The Earl and Countess were obviously the audience and by the tears in the latter's eyes and the way she clutched her husband's hand, James realized this was a moment she was cherishing.

He had believed the relationship between the Sinclairs and their aunt and uncle was not a comfortable one, as none of them had seemed particularly happy about coming to London, but the emotion in this room suggested otherwise. What had happened to change things?

James watched as the little girls began a series of dance movements as Eden began to play the piano. Samantha was obviously not as accomplished as the twins, having probably only learned the steps today, yet she had a youthful grace that given time and instruction would blossom. He felt a fierce pull of emotion as she stumbled then righted herself, and identified it as a need to protect her. James tried to make sense of the emotions he felt when he looked at her.

She was his blood. His to care for and love, if he chose to do so. Could he risk loving her? As he sat there watching his sister he realized that there was no choice but to do so. She was a part of him now and his belief that he could keep his distance from this little girl was foolish. He'd thought himself a solitary person, but the thought of not having Samantha in his life made his previous existence now seem bleak.

He knew he had cousins, and one in particular he had once been close with. She had been younger than he, but he remembered that he'd cared for her, because she like he was raised by a monster, but like everything good in his life, his father had eventually driven her away too.

He had vague memories of people calling at Raven Castle and being turned away until finally they had just given up and left him to fend for himself with the beast that the civilized world had called the Duke of Raven. Yet he and Samantha had both survived and now they would begin to heal; he and his sister, together.

"Bravo, bravo!" The Earl roared as the trio finished.

"Now Eden can sing for us!" Dorrie cried as she Samantha and Somer went to have their costumes removed by Essie.

"Oh no, I don't think that's—"

"Please, Eden, I have yet to hear you sing, and your mother told me once of the beauty in your voice," Lady Wynburg begged her niece.

James knew she didn't want to play in front of him, yet she was torn as her aunt urged her on. Her teeth bit into the plump softness of her bottom lip as she tried to come up with the words to refuse.

"It would be an honor to hear you sing, Eden."

She threw him a look as he spoke, and he could not read her expression from where he sat, but thought perhaps it would not be pleasant.

"Did you see me dance, James?"

Dragging his gaze from Eden, James looked into the sparkling eyes of his sister. "Indeed I did, and am sure they will be asking you to perform at Covent Garden any day now."

Her little snuffle made his heart swell, as did the hand she patted on his knee. She then sat in the chair beside him.

"I am to have a pink dress," she whispered before clasping her hands neatly in her lap.

"Pink is an odd color for a girl, surely?"

She did not answer him, but James saw the smile curl her lips and was happy with that. Looking to the stage as the music began, he watched Eden open her mouth to sing the first note. He was not enamored of this woman—he refused to allow it.

Her voice reached all corners of the room, and in seconds James could not drag his eyes from her. She was an enchantress, weaving some sort of spell around him, and he wanted to throw her over his shoulder and run for the hills, where she would be his alone.

"Eden has a beautiful voice, James."

Nodding, he squeezed Samantha's hand while his eyes remained on Eden. He had no idea how long he sat there watching her, the delicate arch of her brow, the high cheekbones and small stubborn chin. Her voice was pure, each note she hit perfect, and it wrapped around him, rolled through him and left him feeling raw and exposed.

For pity's sake man, gain control. You are a duke, not some simpering, wet behind the ears boy.

"I had no idea you had the voice of an angel," the Earl of Wynburg said as Eden sang the last note.

"Thank you, Uncle, but I am sure you exaggerate."

"He doesn't," James said, when he had himself under control. "I have rarely heard better."

"Thank you."

She accepted his words as she rose from the piano, then moved to the opposite side of the room.

"And now it is supper time and I think we will put off Astley's until another night if you do not mind, Raven, as the children are still weary from their journey," Lord Wynburg said.

"Of course," James said, bowing, unaware that he had decided that tonight was the night they would attend. Finding Somer, he saw her frown.

"We shall go, Somer, but I think it best to wait until everyone has settled."

Her sigh was loud. "All right, but please make it soon, James."

"I promise," he said solemnly.

"I have promised Samantha that she may stay for tea, James, which means you will also stay."

He wondered how he could extricate himself without appearing rude.

"I'm sure the duke has more important things to do, Aunt—"

"Nonsense, Eden dear." Lady Wynburg smiled. "Surely he can spare us a moment of his time to share our table. Is that not right, James?"

It seemed like he, Eden wanted distance between them.

"Please, James."

Samantha tugged his hand, excited at the thought of taking tea with her new friends. Did she really want to eat with the Sinclairs? he thought, remembering the loud and exuberant meals he had shared with them on their journey to London.

"Give in, Raven," the Earl said in his booming voice, "they'll win anyway, they always do."

"Well then, that's settled," Lady Wynburg said, putting an end to any further attempts at evasion by James. "Come along, everything should be ready for us."

James knew when he was beaten and so gave in gracefully. "If you are sure, my lady," he said, placing a hand on Samantha's shoulder. "My sister does tend to eat a great deal. I hope there will be enough for everyone."

The little girls giggled, as he'd hoped they would. Eden did not make a sound, instead walking from the room, and he could tell by the set of her shoulders that she was as happy as he at Lady Wynburg's invitation.

Tea was informal with the family all sprawled in chairs. Eden dragged the twins to a couch and beckoned Samantha to join them too. The Duke sat across from her, his long legs stretched out before him.

She'd watched James with Samantha earlier, and there was no doubting they were more comfortable together. While she may feel frustrated, angry, and several other strong words about the Duke, Eden was glad the siblings, who had obviously always been alone, had finally found each other.

"Cherry cake!" Somer squealed, bouncing back out of her seat as the maid started distributing plates loaded with food.

"Did I hear the words cherry cake?"

Eden watched Cam walk into the room. The smile on his lips did not reach his eyes and she knew their father's betrayal still cut him deeply. She feared for him, because unlike the others in her family, he would take longer to deal with what they had learned. Growing up, he was the one who forgave last and remembered any slight or grievance longest. Plus there was the matter of his excessive drinking habits and overindulgence in any vice he could find. Now he was once again in London, she feared that would only escalate given his state of mind.

"James," he said, bowing to the Duke who had risen to do the same. "I see you too have heard of my aunt's legendary supper table."

"She was very persuasive," James said, returning to his seat and plate of food.

He looked surprisingly comfortable with the small teacup in one hand and a piece of cake in the other and Eden felt the slow thud of her heartbeat rise as she tried to observe him without him realizing it.

He wore a waistcoat of charcoal and a matching jacket that pulled tight as he bent to replace his cup on its saucer. His necktie was neatly folded, but not as outrageously as Cam's often was. She saw the outline of his muscular thighs through buff breeches tucked into hessians. Why him? What was it about this man that made her heart race? She'd convinced herself her preoccupation with him was because of the history between their families, but was fooling only herself. This man produced feelings inside Eden she'd never experienced before.

"Where are Dev and Uncle?" Dorrie said around a mouthful of cake.

"In a meeting, I believe," Cam said, taking a second piece of cake and balancing it beside the first on his plate before finding himself a seat.

"How have you found your first day back in London, Cambridge?"

"It has been enlightening, James, thank you."

Eden hadn't realized she was holding her breath until she released it. Cam often spoke without thought and when he was feeling cornered or angry he was volatile. She had feared he would alert the Duke in some way to their discussions this morning and she had no wish for him to know that anything was wrong with the Sinclair family, especially since he'd questioned her on why she had been crying.

"How so?" the Duke inquired.

"It is always enlightening to learn one's parent is not quite what one—"

"Cam!"

Both Eden and Essie stopped him. Thankfully their younger siblings had heard nothing as they were in conversation with their aunt and uncle, who also seemed oblivious to the undercurrents in the room, but it would not take long before they did so, if Cam continued.

"Believed whilst growing up," Cam added, finishing his sentence as if his sisters had not spoken.

Eden watched the Duke look first at Cam then to Essie and Eden.

"I'm sure your childhood was more pleasant than mine, Sinclair."

She knew that he didn't say the words to garner sympathy, they were just a statement of fact, and her heart ached for the boy he had been.

"You know nothing of our childhood, Raven," Cam snarled. At least he was aware that their little sisters were in the room because he was speaking softly.

Eden glared at her brother. "That is enough, Cam."

"Don't tell me that is enough, Eden. I am an adult and able to speak my mind without you two shrews interfering," her brother hissed, his face twisted with malice.

"Adult?" Eden scoffed. "Perhaps if you behaved like one occasionally we would not be forced to censure you constantly."

Cam regained his feet, glared at his sisters, and in seconds had stormed from the room. Essie started to rise but Eden motioned her back down with a shake of her head.

"You cannot help him, Essie, leave him be."

Eden felt the Duke's eyes on her, but refused to look his way, knowing they would be full of questions she could not answer.

"Samantha told me she is to have a pink dress, Essex. I cannot thank you and Eden enough for coming to my aid. I fear I would have failed miserably had my sister's clothing choices been left to me."

Eden was relieved when the Duke changed the subject; she did not wish to discuss Cam's petulant behavior with him.

"We are more than happy to help you anytime," Essie replied.

Soon they were discussing what else Samantha would need, and to his credit the Duke appeared to be listening and even asked a few questions. He was changing, Eden realized. He was becoming a big brother and the thought was a pleasing one, even if she wanted to shake him at the same time for making her realize the joy in a simple kiss.

She was relieved when he finally rose and signaled to Samantha they were to leave.

"Thank you once again for your help with Samantha."

He bowed to Essie and then Eden. She did not meet his eyes as he looked at her, and she inhaled her first deep breath when he had left the room.

***

Life for the Sinclairs changed dramatically living under the roof of their aunt and uncle. Since the day they had discovered their father's perfidy, everyone but Cam had worked hard at strengthening the bond with their aunt and uncle.

Essie and Eden spent most mornings shopping and being fitted for their new clothes and the afternoons were put aside for dance instruction and learning what would be required upon entering society. Dev was often called upon to be a partner, as was their uncle; of Cam however there was no sign.

"I have not seen Cam for four days, Dev," Eden said as he waltzed her around her aunt and uncle's ballroom.

"I cannot talk here," Dev said, easing them to a halt as the music finished, "but there is something I must tell both you and Essie about Cam."

"Well, my dears, I do believe you are both coming along very well. By the time of your first social gathering you shall be quite proficient in all aspects."

"Thank you, Aunt, and if you are finished with us for the day Dev wishes to take Essie and me for a drive in the park."

"Lovely, of course, my dear, and I shall go and see how the children are fearing."

"Come, Essie." Eden grabbed her sister's arm. "Dev, we shall meet you in the carriage shortly."

Hurrying to their rooms, she told Essie what Dev had said, and in minutes both had pulled on their bonnets and gloves and were running back down the stairs and out the front door to join Dev in the carriage. No one spoke until it had rolled out the drive.

"Tell us what has happened to Cam, Dev?" Eden asked.

"He is going out every evening to drink and gamble. I have no idea how he is paying for it and fear he must owe someone a vast amount of money."

Eden felt her stomach clench at the devastated look on her brother's face.

"He feels betrayed and hurt by what father did to us and is attempting to numb the pain by drinking himself into a stupor every night. He stumbles home as the sun rises, then falls into bed to sleep until he is ready to rise, bathe, eat, and start the entire process once more."

"Dear Lord, that selfish idiot!" Eden snapped. "We are all suffering yet it is always he that must make a production out of everything."

"I can't get through to him, and I fear if we don't stop him he will not live to see the end of the year."

Eden and Essie looked at Dev as he slumped back on the seat. He was exhausted, his eyes bloodshot and defeated, and the pallor of his cheeks suggested his sleep had been little better than his errant younger brother's. Both sisters had hoped that once they arrived in London and were under their aunt and uncle's roof Dev would feel less burdened by his family. They wanted him to fall in love, laugh, and enjoy life now the responsibility had been lifted from his shoulders. Cam, however, made that difficult. Damn their brother and his selfish ways.

"Do you go out at night and try to find him, Dev? Is this why you look so tired?" Eden asked.

"I shadow him as best I can, but if he sees me he flies into a rage." Dev ran a tired hand over his face. "I knocked him unconscious one night and carried him to the carriage then home, but I fear I cannot do that every night."

"You should have told us, Dev!" Essie cried.

"And what could you have done except worry?"

"Should we come and talk with him to see if we can make him see sense?"

"Yes, Eden is right, perhaps we can get through to him. We will come over this evening and tell him that Warwick, Dorrie, and Somer keep asking after him," Essie added.

"He didn't come home last night. I will go out and find him soon and when I get him home I will call for you both," Dev said.

He was weary to his bones, Eden could see it as he slumped back on the carriage seat and closed his eyes.

"Is there no one you can ask to help look, Dev? Perhaps I could come and just sit in the carriage, I would be able to hear Cam's voice and—"

"Absolutely not, I forbid it, Eden," Dev said, still with his eyes closed. "This is not our village, this is London, and it is not safe for a young woman to frequent the places I am forced to, even if you remain in the carriage."

"All right, Dev," Eden placated him. Her brother's words did not send her into a missish fit of vapors as they would many; she understood about London. Their brothers had lectured her and Essie about the dangers awaiting them in London before leaving Oak's Knoll. She knew what waited for a person after dark in the wrong parts of town.

"But what about our uncle, can he not help?"

"No, he has done enough for us already, and after the way our father treated him I have no wish to drag him through this as well. This is something I must fix as swiftly as I can before our brother's journey to self-destruction is complete. Cam is in a very bad place at the moment and I want no one but us dealing with him."

"Can you see it, Dev, what is destroying him?"

Shaking his head, Dev opened his eyes and looked at Essie. "All I see is black, Ess, dark and angry. Even when he was bad before I could see the orange that filled him, but now I see only darkness. Our father's betrayal has toppled him over the edge and I am fearful we will never have our brother back."

The sisters each took one of their brother's hands then let him sleep as the carriage rolled slowly around the park.

"This will not end well, Eden, I feel it," Essie whispered when she was sure Dev slept.

"I do too." Eden nodded. She would do what she could to help her brothers, no matter the cost.

CHAPTER ELEVEN

James stared out the carriage window at the night sky as it carried him home. He saw flashes of light as he passed a lamp, and heard the occasional burst of voices. The night was cool, but he still travelled with the window down, enjoying the air on his face.

His evening had not gone to plan, and for the life of him he could not work out why. He'd seen his sister to bed and then gone out to his club to have a meal, as he often did when in town. The season did not start in earnest for two weeks, but there were still plenty of people around. James had shared his meal with Lords Gideon and Halverstorm, two men with whom he could loosely lay claim to friendship. Both had gone to Eton with him and then fought alongside him during the campaign. They understood him as much as anyone ever had, or perhaps the correct phrase was as much as he allowed anyone to.

The problem was he kept thinking about Samantha and Eden. Was his sister settled in bed? Did she miss him? Was she scared? He should not have left her so soon after arriving in London. James knew this was how a parent must feel leaving their child for the first time. And then there was the beautiful Miss Eden Sinclair.

Would she be betrothed by season's end? How could she

not be? Someone with her beauty and spirit would be sought after from her first foray into society. He hated the ugly twist of pain in his gut at the thought, and acknowledged it as jealousy. She was not the woman for him, she was far too passionate and would demand his attention. No, when he wed, it would be to a gentle, well-bred lady who was happy to do what gentle women did. Read, stitch, and raise his children.

Propping his boots on the opposite seat, he contemplated the darkness as he drew nearer to his home and Samantha. In the past he had neither liked nor disliked returning home. It had been a place where he slept, ate, and dressed, but now his sister lived there and for her sake he would make it into a home. Yawning, he leaned to look out the window to see how much further he had to travel. It would not do to fall asleep so close to home.

He saw two figures walking quickly down the road, and suddenly the hair at his nape rose. Getting to his feet, he leaned out and looked to where they now were. They were women, both about the same height. Why the hell did that bother him? Women should not be walking at such an hour, but there was no law against it.

"Stop the coach, Jonah!"

Leaping from the vehicle, he told his driver to wait as he ran back down the street. James wasn't sure why he was approaching them, but he knew he must. They turned, hearing his footsteps, then picking up their skirts, both women started to flee. James didn't know what alerted him, but in seconds he knew he was closing in on the Sinclair sisters.

"Eden, stop!"

She looked over her shoulder as he shouted and stopped running when she realized who was pursuing her. James was upon them seconds later. He watched her step in front of Essie as if to protect her from him, which annoyed him as he'd never hurt either of these women—or any woman, for that matter.

"What the bloody hell are you doing out here alone at this time of night!"

"How dare you speak in such a manner to us!"

She would never back down from him, James knew, and the irrational part of his nature relished her spirit.

"I will not let you take another step, Eden, therefore it is in your best interests to tell me why you are standing alone and unprotected on a London street at such an hour."

"What we do is n-none of your concern, Duke." She was terrified, he realized. Her eyes were wide, face pale and when Essie stepped to her side James noted her expression was the same.

"We are not moving until you tell me what I want to know." To show his intent he widened his stance and folded his arms, looking deliberately intimidating.

"We are taking in some air," she said quickly. "Our room is stuffy and Essie has a headache, therefore we thought a stroll would clear it."

"At midnight?"

"As you see."

"With no escort?"

"We have each other."

James let an uncomfortable silence settle between them before he said, "You are lying to me, Eden, and I will stand here as long as it takes for you to tell me the truth."

"Tell him, Eden, perhaps he can help us. We have nothing to lose."

"No. Dev said no one but family must know."

James did not speak, just waited and watched. Eden looked at him then looked away. He could tell she was shaking; her hands were trembling as she pulled her cloak tighter around her body. What the hell was going on and where were their bloody brothers?

135

"I know what he said, but in all honesty, Eden, James looks about as moveable as the house we just left, and I for one have no wish to stand here all evening."

Good girl, James thought. At least one of the sisters was still thinking clearly.

Eden stayed silent as she looked at her sister, and then let out a loud, weighty sigh before once again facing James. "My uncle gave us some news, and it has upset my brother Cambridge. He has not been himself."

She shivered after delivering these words, so he said, "Come, we will finish the conversation in my carriage." James took her arm and that of her sister. They put up little resistance as he bundled them inside his carriage. Once seated, he turned up the small lamp and removed two blankets from beneath the seats. The air had a chill, and he did not know how long they had been out in it, or if their shivers were driven by fear, but he handed one to Essex and the other to Eden.

"Now continue."

"Before I say anything, you must promise not to tell my aunt and uncle that you saw us out here tonight, and you must also promise not to tell them what we discuss."

James held Eden's gaze and then gave a curt nod.

"Dev told us yesterday that Cam has been out every night, drinking, gambling, and—"

"I understand," James said, waving her on.

"Dev has spent his nights trying to find him. One night he was forced to knock Cam senseless and bring him home unconscious. Unfortunately, it did not scramble what little intelligence he has into rational thought, and Cam proceeded to leave the house again the following evening."

"Eden," Essie said softly, "he is our brother."

"He is a fool, Essie, and you know it. Irresponsible and childish and now he has put Dev in danger. I shall never forgive him for that if Dev is hurt in any way."

"Why is he behaving this way?"

It was Essie who answered him.

"We were given some distressing news upon our arrival in London, James. It concerned our father, and I fear Cam took it harder than Dev, Eden, and me."

"I could kill him," Eden growled.

James wanted to reach across the carriage and grab her. He wanted her seated on his lap, his arms around her. She was frightened yet still fighting it. This woman would never show weakness, he realized, at least not to him.

"That still does not explain why you two are walking the streets at midnight."

"I overheard two footmen discussing my brothers," Eden said reluctantly. "They said they feared Cam was playing a smoky game and that soon he would be in too deep and Dev would not be able to help him out."

"Do you know where they have gone?" James said, wondering where she had been to overhear the footmen.

He watched her hands twist in the blanket she had laid over her knees; it was the only outward sign of her agitation.

"Easy, Eden." He grabbed her hands to hold them still. "Tell me what you know."

"Bastil's."

James knew the place by reputation; he had never been there personally. Bastil's had taken many a young man's fortunes, and some had gone on to take their lives. It was a place frequented by those who were desperate, and those who preyed on the weak.

"I will take you home and then go and find your brothers."

"No! We will come with you," Eden said, pulling her hands free.

"Be reasonable, Eden, Bastil's is not a place for either you or your sister."

"We will wait in the carriage, then, but I will not return home without my brothers."

She raised that bloody determined chin of hers and James knew if he did return her to the Wynburg home she would only slip out again.

"All right, but you will stay in the carriage, do you understand?"

Both ladies nodded. He held Eden's eyes the longest, knowing that if anyone was to defy him it would be her.

After giving his driver the change of direction, James turned down the lamp once more and sat back in his seat. If Cam had got in deep at Bastil's then he could possibly buy him out, yet he knew the eldest Sinclair would not handle his interference easily. The man would just have to swallow his pride, however, if that was the course that needed to be taken. James wondered if before the night was out he would actually have found a way to repay some of the debt he owed the Sinclairs.

Eden sat silently clasping her sister's hand across from him. Her eyes flitted from him to outside the carriage window then back to him again. Now that she was safe, the tension in his body was beginning to ease. Infernal woman, he wasn't meant to feel like this, and especially not for her. Between Eden and Samantha, they had exposed things inside him he'd just as soon remained locked away.

When the carriage began to slow, Eden appeared to pull something out of her ear, and she rushed to open the door and stick her head outside.

"Close that door!" James roared, reaching for her.

"Please, James, let her do this, she has—um—she will know if either of our brothers are inside." Essie stumbled to a halt after these strange words.

What the hell was that supposed to mean? Before he could grab Eden, she was back in her seat with the door closed once more.

SENSING DANGER

"They are inside, James."

"And how do you know that?"

"I just do," she said, looking nervous.

James wasn't sure what the hell was going on, and now was not the time to delve deeper, so he put that question aside for another day.

"Under no circumstance are you to leave this carriage, ladies. If you do you risk not only your own life but the lives of myself and your brothers, do I make myself clear?"

"Yes, James," Essie whispered. Eden nodded but said nothing.

"I'll have your word, Eden," James said.

"I will stay in the carriage." She didn't look happy about the promise, but he believed she would not break her word.

Stepping from the carriage, he told his driver to make sure neither of the women inside left, and that if they did he was to pull the gun from beneath his seat and point it at them.

"I heard that!"

"As you were meant to," James said, loud enough for Eden to hear. This was not a time for levity, but he found himself smiling just the same. The woman made him feel alive, and he would not examine that thought at this moment either.

Schooling his features into those of a bored nobleman seeking entertainment after a long night of drinking and revelry, he wandered into Bastil's, then through the rooms. Filled with the scent of spirits, tobacco, and whores wearing cheap perfume, they made him feel ill. A man could get anything for his baser needs here.

"Would you like a tumble, my lovely?"

Waving his hand vaguely, James did not stop as the woman leaned into his body, thrusting her breasts into his chest. He merely pushed her aside and kept walking. He noted several faces he knew; some surprised him, others did not, and then he heard Cam's voice.

"I don't need you to look after me!"

Moving into the next room, James saw Devon Sinclair holding his brother by the arm. Before him stood a table at which Cam had obviously been playing, and losing, by the look of the few chips left in front of him. Four men had moved to face Devon, all angry that their play had been interrupted. Three he knew vaguely. One he was unfortunate enough to call cousin.

"Gentlemen, it seems you will have to excuse us, as my friend wishes to retire from the game," James said, moving to stand in front of the Sinclair brothers.

"He owes me money, lots of it, and I want an assurance that I'll get it!"

James bared his lips briefly in a semblance of a smile, as he impaled the man before him with a steely glare.

"Lord Baraclough, how surprised I am to see you here. Surely not your usual haunt, but yes—of course I remember now," James said, with a small forced cough.

"What! I-I, h-how dare you!" Baraclough spluttered as he turned red. The man had been found cheating at one of the more respectable clubs and barred from it and several others. Word had spread quickly, until he was not welcomed anywhere in polite society.

"Cousin, I had not expected to ever see you play the role of cavalry."

"Shut up, Nicholas," James said in a hard tone as he looked at the man who could be his brother. Not as tall, but their coloring was identical. They were kin, but as close as strangers.

"You have no right to tell me anything, Raven. Sinclair owes us money—"

"God's blood, Nicholas, if you don't shut up I will make you!"

It seemed his cousin was not as stupid as he had originally thought because he sat back in his seat and closed his mouth.

"Now, how much does Sinclair owe you, all of you," James added, looking at each of the men before him. He heard Devon groan as the men told James what was owed. The amount was substantial.

"Go, Sinclair, take your brother and leave here now," James said, turning briefly to face Devon. He saw the lines of exhaustion and despair on his face. This was a man who had been pushed too hard and was ready to break.

"It would be wrong of our family to let you handle this matter, Raven."

James pulled out his trump card. "Probably, but as your sisters await you in my carriage, I think it best you go to them before they come and find you."

"Good God, you brought them with you?"

"They came looking for you and Cam and I intercepted them," James said, watching Sinclair pick up his brother and throw him over his shoulder.

"This family will be the death of me," Devonshire Sinclair growled as he stalked from the room.

James pulled cards from his inside pocket and handed one to each of the men, excluding his cousin, who knew exactly where to find him. "My man will deal with you all. Present yourselves at his address tomorrow and this matter will be settled. It will then not be discussed again," he said, meeting each of the men's eyes. When he was sure they took his meaning, he turned on his heel and followed the Sinclair brothers from the room.

Cam was putting up a fight as his brother and sisters attempted to get him into the carriage. They were creating a stir, and very soon all would realize that Eden and Essie were here, outside Bastil's at such an hour.

"Get in the carriage, Eden," James said as he wrenched Cam from his brother and then planted his fist into his jaw. He then gathered him up and threw him onto the carriage floor.

"After you," he said to Devon, and then climbed in behind him.

"He will wake soon, Miss Sinclair," James said as Essie ran her hands over her unconscious brother, who lay sprawled at their feet. "It was a light tap, nothing lasting, I promise you."

She looked uncertain but nodded.

"Thank you," Devon said, and James knew how much the words cost the eldest Sinclair. Like him, pride was something both men had in abundance.

"I believe the ledger is nearly clean," James said.

"I am unsure what transpired in Bastil's, but we will repay you if money was exchanged."

"Of course." James nodded. Sinclair's pride would allow nothing less. "You should tell your aunt and uncle, they are stronger than you believe," he said, looking across the carriage at Eden. Tears trickled down her cheeks as she looked at her big brother. The love she felt for him was written on every beautiful inch of her face, and James wondered what it would feel like to have that kind of devotion from such a woman.

"We have relied on ourselves for so long that I am unsure how to do as you say," Dev said, his words gruff as emotion and fatigue threatened to overwhelm him.

"I understand what you say, Devon, as it is the same for me, but lately I have realized that being an island is extremely taxing upon a person."

Devon managed a grunt of acknowledgment. James then watched Eden hold out a hand to her eldest brother and him grip it tight. She kicked Cam in the leg hard. He heard her mutter, "fool" and he wanted to smile, but swallowed it. The gesture was so very much her; if she was angry then everyone knew about it. James wondered when he had begun to understand her so well.

The hour was late as the carriage stopped outside the second Wynburg residence. James stepped down and then turned to pick up Cam.

"I will carry him." Devon moved to take his brother.

"Sinclair, you are swaying on your feet from exhaustion and while it would not hurt this young whelp to be dropped on his head, it would not do for anyone to see us at this hour."

Devon gave one short nod followed by a huge yawn, then helped his sisters from the carriage. They made it undetected into the house where the butler waited.

"Essie, you lead your brother to his bed and Eden and I will put Cam into his."

It was a testament to Devon's exhaustion that he allowed his sister to take him to the stairs and slowly followed her up.

"What is your name?" James questioned the butler.

"Randal, Your Grace."

"Please furnish us with directions to this Mr. Sinclair's rooms, Randal, and then have one of your largest footmen follow."

"At once, your Grace," Randal said. After giving directions, he then bowed and retreated into the bowels of the house to follow James's orders.

"Lead the way," James said, nodding to Eden.

The journey was not long, one flight and one hallway and they had arrived. Eden swung the door open and walked inside. The room was immaculate, which forced a small laugh from her lips.

"What?" James said, throwing Cam onto the bed. Eden did not appear unhappy when her brother's head connected with the headboard.

"Cam's room at Oak's Knoll never looked this tidy."

"Come, we will remove his boots and coat, the rest can wait until tomorrow."

"Will he be all right?" Eden whispered as she began to pull her brother's arm from the sleeve.

"Yes, I promise you he will."

"H-he is not a bad man. He just makes mistakes."

James dropped the last boot onto the floor as she spoke. "I know that, Eden."

"I am scared for him," she whispered, her voice thick with tears as she looked down at the face of her brother.

In two strides James had her in his arms. Wrapping them tightly around her he tucked her head under his chin and held her while she cried. Hot tears seeped through his shirt as the events of the night caught up with her.

"It will work out, Eden, your aunt and uncle are good people and whatever demons are driving your brother, with the love of your family he will get through this. And if not, then I'll beat it out of him."

Lifting her head from his chest she smiled up at him through her tears. Such beguiling eyes, they made him want to promise her anything she desired.

"No more tears, Eden," he whispered.

"How can we ever thank you?" Their faces were so close her soft breath brushed his lips.

"I think you have that wrong, madam. It is I who owe you. Twice your family has saved my life. It will take me a lifetime to repay such a debt."

"History would suggest there will be more to come." She attempted to smile but failed.

"It is my fondest wish that you are wrong." James knew he should walk away but he was powerless to do so. Her brother lay snoring beside them and any second her siblings could appear, but he could do nothing to stop lowering his head.

"No, James, not again." She shook her head.

"Yes, James, again," he prompted, and was rewarded with

her sweet sigh as she leaned into him.

"This is wrong."

"I know." When his lips met hers his body shuddered. James had been waiting for this moment since their last kiss, wanting to have her in his arms again, desperate to taste her soft lips. Slipping a hand inside her cloak he stroked the length of her spine, wanting more of her, needing to feel her body beneath his fingers. He deepened the kiss, his tongue slipping past her defenses to duel with hers. Tracing the edge of her bodice, he then stroked her neck. Her skin felt like warm silk. They both groaned at the contact, her fingers starting a journey of their own, up his shoulders to tangle in his hair.

A groan from the bed made them stop. Eden stumbled backward out of his arms.

"Eden, we must go." Essex Sinclair appeared in the doorway.

"Yes." She walked past him. "Good evening and thank you, James."

"I shall walk you to your door."

"There is no need, it is but a few feet." Eden did not look at him as she spoke.

"There is a footman waiting for us, James," her sister added.

He would follow and watch until they were inside, but he did not tell them that. "Very well, good night, ladies."

After Eden had gone, James stood for several minutes reliving the feel of her in his arms. She was a complication in his life, a huge complication that he had no clear answer how to deal with.

Giving the bed a last glance, he checked Cambridge Sinclair, who was still lying in the exact position he had put him. James walked from the room. After instructing the footmen to keep a watch on Cambridge, and that under no circumstances was the man to leave the house, he climbed into his carriage and headed home.

145

Perhaps when the season started and he was surrounded by other women his need for Eden Sinclair would ease. *And you're a fool if you believe that.* One thing was certain; he could not be alone with her after tonight. She was too tempting and she was a lady, therefore she deserved his respect. If anyone had seen them tonight he would be marrying her in the morning, and that thought should terrify him a lot more than it did.

***

"My head hurts."

James walked into Cambridge Sinclair's room the following morning as he grumbled those words to a servant who was removing a tray. Closing the door behind the maid, he then locked it and walked to the bed. Of the elder Sinclair there was no sign, which James was grateful for. He had a few words to say to the man who had caused his family so much grief the previous evening.

"What do you want?" Cambridge Sinclair snarled as he struggled into an upright position where he leaned against the headboard. His breath was raspy and his skin sweaty. All signs of a man experiencing a ripping sore head after a night spent imbibing.

"Last night I found your two elder sisters walking down the street—alone, Cambridge. When I realized it was them, I stopped my carriage and asked what had possessed them to take such a reckless jaunt in the dark, alone, where any scoundrel could pick them up and do unspeakable things to them. Do you know what their answer was, Cambridge?"

He shook his head but his eyes told a different story. He knew exactly why his sisters had done what they had.

"They were trying to find you and your elder brother," James said, reining in his temper as it began to simmer once again. Anything could have happened to those two last night.

Any unscrupulous lowlife could have harmed them. The thought made his blood boil.

"Devon had been following you for many nights, making sure you stayed safe from harm, but you were making his task extremely difficult, and so they had decided to assist him."

"Go to hell!" Cam snapped. "You have nothing to do with our lives, unless it is to thank us for saving yours."

"Not this time, Cambridge. This time you cost me a great deal and your family more."

"Wh-what do you mean?"

He was sweating profusely, a large hank of dirty hair had fallen over his eyes, and he looked about fifteen years old.

"According to your sisters, your brother has not slept or eaten for nights in his pursuit of you. Your younger siblings are wondering why you do not visit them, and Essie and Eden are caught between tears and anger at your selfishness. They are all lying to your aunt and uncle to keep your reputation safe."

"You don't understand." Cambridge threw James a sullen look.

"You, sir, need to grow up," James said quietly. "You have a family who love you, a brother who would lay his life down for you, and yet you treat them in such a cavalier manner."

"You don't understand," Cambridge said again, but this time his words held little strength.

"I understand that you feel betrayed in some way by your father and yet he allowed you to live under his roof, in a home that may not have always had money, yet it always had love. Do you know what it is like to live without love, Cambridge?"

He was honest and shook his head, and then winced as the action made it hurt.

"My father banned me from my own home at ten years of age. I lived between schools and servants, but if I am ever lucky enough to live with the love you have, I would never treat those who give it to me with so little respect."

James watched the belligerence leave Cam's face, to be replaced by shame.

"I-I, oh God, what have I done?"

James did not move as Cam buried his face in his hands. He stood quietly until he was once again in control, and then he finished what he had come to say.

"You owe me a vast amount of money, Cambridge, as last night I cleared your gambling debts."

"Mother of God," he groaned again.

"I am aware you do not have the resources to pay them back, and I will not allow you to borrow the money, therefore you will repay it by working for me. I will expect you at my front door at precisely nine o'clock tomorrow morning—and Cambridge, do not be late," James said as he walked toward the door.

CHAPTER TWELVE

"There are thousands of people looking at us, Dev."

"You exaggerate, there are only hundreds and they are just curious about what you look like, Eden. Once they see you are whey-faced with the body of a dumpling they will lose interest."

"Whey-faced!" Eden hissed, her nails biting into the sleeve of her big brother's jacket as he guided her down the stairs.

The Sinclair sisters were attending their first social event, Lady Dalton's musical evening. Their aunt had assured them it would be a small gathering for their first foray into society.

"A few people, Aunt said," Eden muttered, glaring at her aunt and uncle who were ahead of them.

"She has lived in society for years, Eden, this is probably a few people to her, and compared to some events I have attended, this is a small gathering."

Looking over the sea of faces Eden studied the room. Huge candelabras stood on cabinets and in alcoves, and more candles hung suspended in chandeliers from the ceiling. The guests glittered and sparkled, dressed in a myriad of colors, and waiters dashed about dispensing drinks. The sight was in fact everything Eden had thought it would be and so much more.

"I am here with you, and as you can see Cam has Essie, love, now relax." Dev patted her gloved hand where it clenched his sleeve.

"Cam looks good, doesn't he, Dev?"

"Very good. In fact I'm stunned at the changes in him, and I'm sure in some way the Duke is behind it. Yet Cam will not tell me anything."

Eden refused to acknowledge the flutter in her chest at the mention of the Duke.

"Why do you think that?"

"Because no one has approached me for money and Cam had none, but gambled heavily. There is also the matter of Cam spending a great deal of his time at the Duke's house."

"Does he, I had not realized. What do you think he is doing there?"

Two weeks had passed since that horrible night, and she had seen very little of James—which she was pleased about, Eden reminded herself yet again.

"My guess is paying off his debts."

Eden wondered if he was correct. Had James paid their brother's debts, and if so why? Was it to his mind recompense for her and Dev saving his life?

"Don't think about it now, Eden, tonight is for you and Essie."

"Are we dressed appropriately, Dev?"

"Yes, you look beautiful. Although had I my way your neckline would be several inches higher and the material of your dress would be thick brocade. Are you wearing a corset under that flimsy material?"

"Should you be mentioning my unmentionables, brother? You look very handsome too, by the way." Eden scanned the crowd as they followed Essie and Cam, although who she searched for was a mystery as the only people she knew were family.

"Christ!"

"What?" Eden questioned as Dev cursed beside her.

"Good God what the hell is that odd woman wearing now!"

"What woman?"

"Miss Lilliana Braithwaite."

Eden followed her brother's gaze to where a fair-haired lady stood. From the large, floral arrangement topped with a cluster of grapes, perched in her hair, to the hideously ill shaped orange dress, she did indeed appear odd.

"She's a bloody, brainless twit."

"Dev!" Eden looked around them; thankfully no one stood close enough to hear her brother's outburst. His eyes were focused on Miss Braithwaite with furious intensity, brows lowered, his scowl menacing.

"What?"

"I cannot believe you are cursing in public, where anyone can overhear you." Eden waved her hand around. "It is not like you."

"Sorry," he mumbled. "Just stay away from her, Eden."

"Why?"

Dev sighed. "Why can you just not accept my words?"

"You know me better than that."

"She's—she's just strange, Eden. Please stay away from her."

"But surely there must be a reason for your reaction?"

He threw the woman a dark look. "I had the displeasure of dancing with her once. She spent the entire time explaining the migration habits of a Red-Necked Grebe. I was so bored I'm sure I nodded off standing up. Then when I told her I had heard enough, she called me an unintelligent clod."

Eden placed a hand on her chest in mock horror. "Never tell me she didn't spend the entire dance flattering your ego?"

"Eden," Dev warned.

"You being the epitome of male elegance, and a highly regarded and upstanding member of society."

"Have you quite finished?"

Eden smiled. "I believe so."

"This season," he muttered, "is going to be testing on my nerves."

"Poor delicate man that you are."

"Shrew," he said beneath his breath, knowing quite well she would hear it.

Eden patted his arm but remained silent. She threw Miss Lilliana Braithwaite a last look as he led her away. She would make sure she was introduced, because anyone who made her big brother react so violently deserved closer inspection, and then she would decide for herself the character of the woman.

"Smile and simper, sister."

"Must I?"

"It is the done thing."

"Says who?"

"All the silliest debutantes do it."

"I have no wish to be known as silly."

Dev smiled, and she saw the brother he had been before responsibilities had weighed him down.

"Too late."

He grunted as she elbowed him in the ribs.

Eden was introduced to the hostess, Lady Dalton, who to her mind appeared a silly type of woman. She seemed to giggle a great deal and bat her eyelashes at Dev, but for all that she was polite, and took the time to introduce Eden and Essie to some of the guests.

Soon they were taking their seats and the first person to perform took her seat behind the piano. Thirty minutes later Eden was stifling a groan as the woman hit yet another wrong note.

"Push them in further!"

"I'm trying!" Eden snapped to Cam, struggling to force her earplugs deeper as the girl singing hit a high note and failed, and the sound nearly pierced her eardrums. The problem was Eden could pick out every wrong note and missed key and that made her a terrible critic.

"Oooh, that was two wrong notes," she whispered to Dev.

"Stop it," he hissed back.

Most of the Sinclair family, barring Warwick who played a creditable flute, refrained from playing a musical instrument or singing as Eden was forced to leave the house when they practiced, because she couldn't help constantly trying to correct them.

"Thank you, Miss Blackford-Smyth, such a wonderful voice," Lady Dalton said, clapping loudly as around her everyone sighed with relief. "And now we have a surprise for you all."

Eden sat up straighter; she loved surprises as long as they were good ones. Turning slightly in her seat, she studied the guests, and it was then she saw the Duke. Their gazes collided and the look they shared was brief but had her body prickling all over. Looking forward once more, she refused to glance his way again.

"I thought you said he was not coming?"

"Who?" Cam whispered back.

"The Duke."

Cam shrugged. "He wasn't but something obviously changed his mind. Perhaps there is a woman here he sees as his future duchess."

Eden did not like the kick of jealousy she felt at her brother's words.

"Imagine marrying such a man," Essie said.

"You could do worse," Cam added. "He has power and money, and owns several estates, and I believe is considered quite a catch."

"And what of love and happiness?"

Cam made several scoffing noises at Essie's comments. "There is no place in many marriages for such things, sister. Often it is merely a transaction between two families and nothing more."

"How sad."

"You will all marry for love."

Cam, Eden, and Essie all looked at Dev in surprise.

"I will not watch any of you unhappy. I would rather you simply stayed at home for the remainder of your lives than live such a life."

Eden could tell this was a serious matter for him because the muscles in his jaw were bunched.

"Not entirely practical, brother, yet a lovely sentiment," Cam said. "However, these two could get us out of the poorhouse should they marry well. In fact one of them should wed the Duke, that would certainly see us right and perhaps diluting the Raven blood would remove this bloody curse that hangs over us."

Eden didn't react, outwardly appearing calm as she took in those seated nearby. "Very mercenary of you, Cam, to want us sold to the highest bidder."

"Neither of you will wed the Duke," Dev said. "I shudder to think what such a liaison will do to the senses of your progeny. We are also no longer in the poorhouse, strengthening my point that you will marry for love. Now be quiet, as our hostess is about to speak."

"I have been reliably informed by a certain duke," Lady Dalton said loudly.

Eden wondered how many dukes were in the room. Surely not many, in fact possibly only hers. *He is not yours, Eden.*

"There is only one," Dev whispered, anticipating her question.

"That Miss Eden Sinclair, one of our newest debutantes, can

sing and play the piano tolerably well."

Eden sat up straighter. Surely the woman had not just singled her out?

"Please say this is not happening." Eden could feel the color draining from her cheeks as Lady Dalton continued.

"Please offer Miss Eden Sinclair your encouragement for filling in on such short notice, and urge her to come and entertain us."

Dear God!

"Would I be hanged for stabbing a duke, Dev?"

"Yes," he gritted. "But I'll beat him to a pulp for you."

"He's not a bad fellow, Dev, probably thinks he's doing Eden a favor helping her launch into society."

"I am not a ship, Cam!"

"Shall we say frigate, then?"

"Cam, you are not helping!" Dev snapped. "Now calm down, Eden. Just get up there and do what you do best."

"I'm going to stab you as well," Eden hissed at Cam.

"You'd have to catch me first, and we both know I'm quicker."

"Give me your earplugs." Dev held out his hand.

She was never really sure why, but Eden could not sing or play with them in, so she reluctantly pulled them out and slipped them to Dev, who put them in the pocket of his coat.

"How's the noise?"

"My head is already starting to hurt," Eden whispered. She wore earplugs to go about everyday life simply because her hearing was far more acute than that of a normal person. Of all the Sinclairs she had the worst gift, in her opinion. The others may dispute that, but not Eden. If she went without them into a room filled with noise and people she suffered terribly, and the eventual result was a severe headache.

"Come on, I'll be your page turner." Dev stood and held out

his arm. He looked grim and the glare he shot the Duke suggested he would have words with the man when the time presented itself.

Eden rose from her seat and placed her fingers on her brother's arm. She heard the murmurs and whispers as she and Dev walked to the piano. Some thought her presumptuous to be performing at her first social event, others were rustling their programs in boredom. She winced at a loud cough. One man whispered to another that she was a pretty filly.

This could be a disaster. What if she sat shocked and unmoving with no words coming from her mouth? At least one thing would come from this evening, and that was she now had reason to loathe the Duke, and that was far better than the other feelings he created inside her.

James inhaled slowly as Eden rose from her seat. Her dress was cream, with a sheer overdress of rose. It draped and fell around her lovely body, and to his mind she looked sinfully beautiful. The bodice was demure, yet not enough to please him, and left her neck and shoulders bare but for the smallest capped sleeves. The skirts fell in soft folds down her lovely body to stop inches above the ground, exposing a froth of lace beneath. James had thought her exquisite dressed in the clothes she wore in the country, but now she was breathtaking. Each sweet curve and line was exposed to every male present, and the ones he could see were certainly noticing the delectable Miss Eden Sinclair.

He hadn't thought about that when he'd overheard Lady Dalton say one of her performers had pulled out. Offering Eden's name had been instinctive. He'd never heard a voice like hers before, and wanted to do so again. As he watched Viscount Lindsay sit straighter in his seat when Eden stepped up to the piano, he realized he'd made a mistake. He'd singled her out, and now every man present knew who she was.

That should be a good thing, James, he reminded himself. Because once she was married, he would never be able to kiss her again. On this depressing thought he returned his attention to the performance that was about to begin.

Candles surrounded the small platform, casting a soft glow over the siblings. Dev stood to her right. His eyes lifted briefly and he found James, and that look told him all he needed to know. It seemed Lord Sinclair was not happy with him for singling his sister out. He stared back, not intimidated by a few dark looks. He'd cut his eye teeth on those from his father.

He watched as Eden glanced through the music before her. She winced as someone laughed loudly and he wondered if she was unwell. She then nodded to her brother and began playing, and he could think of nothing else.

James loved music, it was the only thing his father had forced him to do that he'd actually received pleasure from. Eden was brilliant, each note pitch perfect as her fingers flew over the piano keys. He dragged his eyes from her to look around the room. No one moved, indeed no one appeared to breathe as she sang. Hers was indeed the voice of an angel. When she ended the applause was loud and genuine.

"More!"

"More!"

He watched Eden briefly shut her eyes as the audience called for more. Her brother leaned closer, his stance protective, and James studied her face. Was she pale? He was sure she'd just flinched again. Could she be in some kind of pain?

They made a handsome sight, the two siblings. Devon was tall and broad, his black locks cropped short, dressed in a dark evening jacket, white shirt, and necktie. He was the perfect foil for his sister's beauty.

James wondered again what drew him to her. Her beauty, yes, but many had that. It was the innocence she carried;

untainted by society, she was open and honest and that was rare in his world. There was also her courage. To have done what she had, diving into the water to save him, had taken an act of incredible and selfless bravery, and he would never forget that.

Much too soon she drew the song to an end and the applause was equally as loud, however this time she did not play another. Rising, she sank into a very correct curtsey, then taking her brother's arm she slowly returned to her seat. Both siblings avoided looking his way.

"Well!" Lady Dalton said. "I think after that performance everyone else will be sadly lacking, therefore refreshments are available for those who wish to partake, and then the dancing shall begin."

James regained his feet.

"I want a word with you, Raven."

He'd known it would not be long before a Sinclair approached him. The dark avenging eldest of the clan glared at James, and he wondered briefly what it would be like to have someone care about you as much as this man obviously did for his siblings.

"What appears to be the problem, Sinclair?"

"Never again single one of my sisters out the way you did tonight. They are new to society, and have no wish to be thrust to the forefront before they are ready." The words were spoken softly, but the intent was there. Devonshire Sinclair was angry.

"Sinclair, your sisters are beautiful. They'll be in the forefront without even trying."

They both turned to watch Essex and Eden, who were being introduced by Lady Dalton to a group of people. The men looked extremely happy, the women did not.

"Be that as it may, it is not your place to do what you did. Eden is—she is different."

"In what way?" James studied Devon. He looked suddenly uncomfortable.

"It matters not in what way, only that she does not like crowds or noise, and most especially has no wish to perform as she did tonight."

"Society is not the place for her then, Sinclair, as it's filled with both noise and crowds. Furthermore, she plays and sings better than anyone I know, and it would be a crime not to share that." James was being honest, she did. The fact that he liked to watch her sing and play did not enter the conversation.

"What my sisters do is my concern alone. Never again take the liberties you did tonight."

"I am a duke, Sinclair, don't forget that fact." James felt his temper rise at the man's tone.

"And that is supposed to intimidate me? My sister and I saved your life, Raven, and history suggests so did several of my ancestors for yours, so I think it is safe to say I will probably never forget you until I draw my last breath."

If he were a dog, James knew his hackles would be rising.

"Your title means very little to me, Raven, other than the fact that it's probably because of it that my siblings and I are diff—"

Sinclair's words stopped abruptly, and James had a feeling he thought he'd said too much. "Different?"

"It matters not, just don't take liberties with my sister again. I hope we are clear, Raven."

Oh, I'd like to take liberties with her.

Looking at the clenched jaw before him, James was pleased he'd managed to keep that thought in his head.

He understood Sinclair's words completely, but that didn't mean he liked them. People did not speak to him that way—in fact, only the Sinclairs appeared to believe they had that right.

"Was that a threat?"

"Take it as you wish, but considering you once said you are indebted to us, one would think you had every wish to please us."

"I do owe your family a great deal, but that does not mean I will stand aside weakly and let you challenge me in such a way." James controlled his anger. He'd learned long ago that losing his temper achieved nothing.

"Challenge," Sinclair scoffed. "Me, a lowly baron, challenge a mighty duke."

James was not used to being mocked either, unless, of course, he was near a Sinclair.

"What is going on between you and Cam?"

The change in subject was swift, as most of this family's conversations were. Parry, thrust, and then repeat. James adjusted.

"That is between your brother and me."

"Did you pay his debts? If so, I wish for a tally, and will see them repaid."

"That is between your brother and me," James said again.

"I have no wish to be indebted to you, Raven, or owe you gratitude."

"It's not a comfortable feeling, is it."

"Bastard."

"Now, now, we both know I cannot lay claim to such a title." James found a smile. "A word of caution if I may, Sinclair."

"What?" he snarled.

"If you spend the entire season fighting what you see as slights to your sisters, may I suggest you sharpen your swords and ensure your dueling pistol is loaded."

"That was a poor attempt at humor, Raven."

"Yet an accurate one," James said. "Your sisters are intelligent and do not suffer fools. They will survive well in this nest of vipers if you let them."

James withstood the look the man threw at him before stalking away. Shaking his head, he watched Devon join his sisters. They were a family of passions. They loved wholeheartedly, protected each other fiercely, and laughed freely, and if he could name the strongest emotion they often produced in him, other than frustration, it would be jealousy.

CHAPTER THIRTEEN

"Good evening, James."

"Lilliana." James acknowledged the woman coming toward him. His eyes settling briefly on the purple turban wrapped around her head, before he looked into her eyes. Cold and unfriendly.

Neither stopped, simply nodded and moved on, and he felt something heavy settle in his chest for what had once been between them, but he pushed it aside. Miss Lilliana Braithwaite was no longer his concern; his father had made sure of that.

"Miss Sinclair." He bowed to Essex when he reached her side. "Are you enjoying the evening?"

"I am, thank you, Duke. It has been most enlightening."

Her words were accompanied by a sweet smile, and James wondered why his heart did not thud a bit harder seeing it. Essex was definitely more even-tempered than Eden, and would likely not go out of her way to jab at him repeatedly with pointed verbal barbs whenever they met.

"If I may take this time to thank you, James."

"For what, Essex?" He leaned closer as she had done, obviously wanting to keep her words unheard by anyone but them.

"For saving my brother."

"I am unsure as to what you are speaking of, and to my knowledge the opposite is indeed true."

"Yes of course, I understand you see Dev and Eden's actions that way, but what I was speaking of was Cam. He is a different person for your interference, and it is this I wish to thank you for. None of his siblings had been able to reach him before the night you stepped in."

James watched as she had a quick look around, and he guessed she was searching for her siblings. They constantly seemed to be checking on each other, he'd noticed.

"I have done very little for your brother, Essex. Cam is a good man, and merely lost his way. I simply helped redirect him."

"Even so, please accept our gratitude. I must also add to that, Dev is now much happier and getting enough sleep, therefore we are not on the receiving end of his lectures."

"I wish I were as lucky," he drawled.

Her laugh was sweet.

"My eldest brother is the very best of men, James, but a trifle overbearing where we are concerned. Still, he also is grateful, yet would never mention that fact."

"I noticed that also."

"We have always been close, but especially more so since our parents' deaths."

"Your brother's dedication to his family is to be commended, Essex. However, I would rather you not tell him I said that."

James looked to where the eldest Sinclair stood. He was conversing with several men, but while doing so his eyes were also searching the room, coming to rest on Essex and then Cam. He frowned and mouthed something, but James could not see what from this distance, or indeed who it was to.

"My sister is most like him, and yet she has not learned his control yet."

"Eden?" James queried as he looked for her.

"Yes. Unlike me, Eden is filled with passion and fire. The man who steps into her life will need to understand that. I fear if he tries to control her the results will be disastrous."

James did not like the knowing look in Essex's eyes as she studied him.

"Marriage is not something to be entered lightly," James said when he could come up with nothing else. Suddenly his throat felt tight at the thought of Eden married.

"And yet a happy state if one gets it right."

The silence that settled between them should not be comfortable after that statement, yet strangely was. James was almost reluctant to excuse himself from the only comfortable member of the Sinclair clan, but he wanted to find Eden.

"Please excuse me, Essex." James bowed and left her side.

Looking over heads, he found Eden skirting the edges of the room alone. He intercepted her by taking a more direct route and meeting her head-on.

"Are you looking for someone, Eden? Perhaps I can help."

He thought her eyes were narrowed in anger, but on closer inspection he saw the gray depths were filled with pain. Her face was pinched, lips in a thin line.

"No, I believe you have done quite enough for one evening, thank you. Please excuse me."

Her words were polite, yet he knew had they been alone she would not have been so restrained.

"Eden, are you unwell?"

"No."

She said the word softly before turning her back on him and walking away, leaving James standing there watching her.

She walked through guests, nodding and smiling, and then reached the doors that led outside. Her hand went to the handle; when it did not yield, she moved to the next one.

What the hell is she doing? James moved closer.

She looked first left and then right before pushing open the door and slipping through. Looking around, for once he could find no Sinclair nearby. He should ignore her, walk away and talk with one of the other young ladies, who would be polite and seek to flatter him—and he would be bored in seconds. Besides, someone had to stop her walking about outside. Anyone could be out there; in fact, she may be in danger even now. Moving to the same door, James opened it and stepped through.

Striding along the stone terrace he breathed deeply, enjoying the cool evening air after being closed in with so many perfumed bodies. Where was she? Walking to the edge he looked below and saw a flash of pink. What was she doing in the gardens alone? Had no one told her that young ladies did not leave social gatherings unescorted? She was not in Crunston Cliff now.

James ran down the steps and followed Eden into the gardens. Torchlight lit the shell path and he followed it to where he knew a fountain stood. The sound of his boots on the stone must have alerted her, yet she did not turn as he approached. Instead she stood facing the fountain looking at the cascading water.

"It was foolish of you to come out here alone, Eden." Her shoulders stiffened. "Anyone could have seen you and you could have been compromised, in fact, being out here with me would not bode well for you if anyone chanced upon us."

Still she didn't speak and James felt the last moorings of his temper loosen. Bloody *Sinclairs*, he thought, stomping to where she stood. He was done with their insulting behavior.

In seconds he was behind her his hands reaching for her.

"I am a bloody duke, you little shrew, and as such I deserve your respect, therefore I demand you look at me when I am addressing you!" Wrapping his fingers around her upper arm, he turned her. She stumbled. James caught her.

"Eden?"

She was in agony, her face white, teeth clenched, the sudden movement causing her more pain.

"Tell me how I can help you?"

"My head aches," she whispered, clenching her eyes shut. "I need Dev."

"Does Devon have some medicine for you? Is that why you need him?"

"No, he can take me home."

He lifted her into his arms and walked to the closest seat, where he lowered her gently.

"Do not touch me."

"I only want to help you, Eden, not ravage you."

"Yet I have no wish for you to do so."

James could hear her pain in the short clipped bursts of air she expelled. He moved to stand behind her, then placing his hands on her temples he began to massage them.

"Don't—"

"Sssh, let me help you. Trust me just this once, Eden."

"What are you doing?"

"These pins cannot be helping your headache." James pulled them from her hair, placing each in his pocket before moving on to the next. "Good God, there are at least a dozen here, and half of those digging in to your scalp."

"It takes a great deal of work to secure, and you really should not be—"

"Yes, I should." James removed the last one, then teased the mass of curls free so it hung over the back of the seat like a river of dark silk.

"Someone could see us."

Her moan was low and long as James pressed his fingers to her temples.

"We are hidden here, no one will see us, so relax and let me help you," James soothed as his hands worked slowly over her head. "Slow breaths. That's it, good girl."

Around them the night sounds receded, and the gentle flow of the fountain soothed. Her hair was thick and soft beneath his fingers, and he fought the urge to sift them through it.

"It eases."

He heard the surprise in her words.

"How did you learn to do that?"

"When I was young I used to suffer from headaches and the housekeeper often did this to me."

"Thank you, I feel much better. However, had you not singled me out, I would not have been in this predicament."

"You should be thanking me, ungrateful woman. I just ensured your season will be a success."

Her sigh was soft. "I have no wish to be a success, I want to go home."

"Surely not. Every young woman wants wealth, status, and a handsome husband, all of which are at your fingertips."

"So my aunt tells me."

"The prospect of marriage does not please you then?" James had no right to feel happy about that fact.

"I have never been good at being told what to do, and I believe that is a husband's job."

"And that is meant to surprise me? Your brother is not my favorite person, but he has my respect for the task of managing you all."

"Yes, he has patience I have yet to cultivate. In fact, I sometimes wonder how he does it."

"He loves you," James said, knowing it was the truth. They may be a family that would send him to bedlam were he to spend too much time with them, but James knew that each of the Sinclairs would lay down his life for the other, especially the eldest.

"He is the very best of men," she said, mirroring her sister's earlier words, "and my life would have been vastly different were he not in it."

"Yet you had parents." James sat beside her, enjoying the solitude they had. For once they were just talking, not arguing, kissing, or saving lives. The seething mass of emotion that lay between them, for a few brief moments, seemed to have eased.

"Dev was the one who cared for me the most."

James thought about that as he stared out at the night sky. With so many siblings he imagined it was not easy to find time with a parent, time to be cuddled or kissed. Not that he'd had either, but he understood not all families were like his.

"I really must get back, as Dev has been calling me."

"Really? I heard nothing."

She did not answer him, and he wondered about the communication abilities this family seemed to have. It was almost as if they knew what the others were thinking without words.

"You will not be able to go back into the party, Eden, your hair is down, and as much as I would like to be able to assist you, I cannot play lady's maid." James took one of her curls and ran it through his fingers. It felt wonderful against his skin.

"Then why did you take it down?"

"Because it was not aiding your headache."

"I should thank you for that then."

"Yes, you should."

"Thank you."

He laughed. "Come now, surely you can put a bit more into it."

"Thank you, sir."

"Again," James said, enjoying himself.

"Thank you, most noble and kind sir."

"Duke."

SENSING DANGER

"Thank you, most noble and kind duke."

She looked at him, her eyes clearer, yet pain still lingered. He ran his eyes over the delicate arch of her brows, down the small, straight line of her nose, and came to a stop at the sweet bow of her upper lip.

"You really are beautiful."

"That did not sound like a compliment."

"Miss Eden Sinclair," James said in his haughtiest tone. "Allow me to say your beauty eclipses all others."

She giggled.

"I can see you have said such things before."

"Often, but rarely have I meant them."

"James—"

"Come." James got to his feet, cutting off her words before she said something to irritate him. "I will escort you to my carriage and then I will go and tell your brother what has happened."

"I do not want to inconvenience you any further, and now I can think clearly once again, I have decided I am still angry with you, especially as you are the reason my head hurts."

"Be quiet, Eden. For tonight we will call a truce and tomorrow you can begin anew with a scathing attack on my perfidious actions this evening."

"Oh, yes, well as to that—" She faced him.

He kissed her, just one gentle brush of his lips.

"Oh dear. I do wish you would not do that."

"So do I, but when you are near I'm afraid it just happens," James said honestly.

"Then we shall have to keep our distance, as we really do not like each other, and if we were caught—"

"The consequences would please neither of us," he finished for her.

"Precisely," she said, and James ignored the niggling voices inside his head that denied her words. He was surprised when she took the hand he held out to her.

"Where are we going? Surely if I do not return there will be questions?"

"You are not that important yet, madam."

She let him lead her along paths, over cobbles, and soon they were at the front of the house. Walking with her down the row of carriages, he located his and lifted her inside and onto a seat.

"Now wait here and I shall return shortly, after I have located your brother."

"He will be angry with you."

"We have already conversed on the matter, and yes he was angry, but I am not easily intimidated, especially by a Sinclair."

James pulled a blanket from beneath the seat and wrapped it around her. She rested her head and closed her eyes. Still pale, but at least her face was no longer tight with pain.

"I'm sorry if it was my actions that caused you pain, Eden, it was not my intention."

"I know."

He left her then, although he wanted to stay to ensure she was safe. In the morning his behavior would seem out of character and he would worry about that, but right now he had more important things to do. He found the eldest Sinclair prowling through the crowd. His face darkened as he saw James approach.

"I'm still angry with you, Raven, and should punch you in the nose, but right now I need to find Eden."

"You could try," James said, smiling. It would not do for the people around them to know the two men were passing anything other than pleasantries.

"She, Eden, does not like to be placed in situations she has no control over."

"No one likes that, Sinclair, however it seems my actions

have caused her pain and for that I apologize." James watched a flicker of unease flash across Devon Sinclair's face. "I found your sister outside, she said her head was sore and that she needed to locate you."

"Where is she, I will go to her at once!" James held up his hand as Devon tried to brush by him.

"She is safe from harm in my carriage. Her headache has eased but she still needs to go home."

"I will take her," Devon said, stalking past James.

James followed a few feet behind, nodding his farewells to people as he went. Sinclair, however, ignored everyone, his intent to reach his sister his only goal. Once outside James caught up with him.

"I should have known when I did not find her. Eden always goes outside when her head is sore."

"Does it happen often?"

"Not for some time, but tonight…." His words fell away. "It matters not."

These people had more secrets than he, James thought, following Devon. He wondered which would be the easiest Sinclair to coerce them from. Because one thing James realized was that he wanted to know more about these people who were entwined in his and Samantha's lives.

"I am all right, Dev, don't fuss," Eden said as her brother entered the carriage.

"I'm sorry, Eden. I should have given them to you as soon as you finished singing. You have had so few headaches over the last few years I had forgotten what noise does to you."

"It's not your fault, please, Dev. I should have remembered too. But my headache has gone now, and I just want to sleep."

What were they talking about? James wondered, moving into the doorway. What had Devon not given his sister?

"I shall get the others and we will leave at once."

171

"No, please just come home when they are ready. Aunt and Uncle left early as Aunt was feeling unwell, so they will be there by now, and the Duke will drop me off, then I will simply fall into bed and sleep the night away. You know what I'm like after a turn."

The siblings were whispering to each other, so James moved closer.

"It is not right for you to be alone in this carriage with the duke, Eden. At least let me get Essie."

"And ruin her night? No, I do not wish that. I will not be seen, and you know the Duke will cause me no harm. I shall simply slip inside the house quietly and go straight to my room."

"All right, but we will follow as soon as I gather everyone together. I will have Essie check on you before she retires, and I will call upon you in the morning."

James looked in the door as Devon placed a gentle kiss on his sister's forehead. The gesture held both love and affection and James called himself every kind of fool for the jealousy he felt at their obvious bond. Stepping aside, he made room for Sinclair to climb out of the carriage, and was impaled with a hard stare.

"Do not speak in a loud voice and make sure to place her in the hands of her maid before you leave."

"Of course," James said immediately.

"She is fragile after one of her turns and—"

"I can see she is weakened, Devon, there is no need for this."

"Yet you have never cared for anyone but yourself, Raven, therefore I reserve the right to tell you how to care for one of my own, as I have been doing since her birth."

James did not show how much the words affected him. He more than anyone was aware of his solitary existence before Samantha entered his life.

"Dev, don't be mean. The Duke has done nothing wrong,

and in fact believed he was doing me a favor by suggesting I play." Eden's words were softly spoken yet both men heard them.

Devon exhaled loudly then stuck out his hand.

"Forgive me, Raven, I had no right to speak to you thus. My sister is right, please accept my apologies. I fear that I am overly protective—or so my family tell me—where they are concerned, and most especially with Eden."

James took the hand, surprised at the apology.

"You people have more mood swings than changes of clothes."

"We are volatile, Raven; some say that is the sign of a healthy mind."

"I would like to meet the person who says that."

Devon snorted. "Forgive me if my earlier words were insulting."

"Pay it no mind, Sinclair; I am beginning to realize what having a family entails."

Devonshire Sinclair gave him a rueful smile. "Yes, and in time your little sister will test you constantly as do mine."

"I heard that."

"As you were meant to, sister. Please let no one see you, James, as my sister's reputation is at stake."

"Of course." James climbed into the carriage as Devon walked away. He took the seat opposite Eden and soon they were on their way.

"How does your head feel?"

"Better, thank you." She had not opened her eyes. "And please allow me to thank you for whatever it is you have done for Cam."

"You and Devon have a very strong bond, don't you?" James ignored her words in favor of his own.

"He was the only one I felt safe with."

Her words were whispered and James could see she was struggling to stay awake.

"Safe from what?"

"Him."

"Who?"

She chose not to answer and James did not push her. Leaning back into the shadows as the carriage rolled through London toward their homes, he watched as she struggled to keep her eyes open. Her lashes fluttered several times before finally succumbing. He could see only the tiny sleeves of her dress and the long white gloves; the rest of her was covered with a blanket.

He mulled over her words. What or who could possibly have threatened her, especially growing up in such a large family surrounded by loving parents and siblings? James could come up with nothing so he pushed the thought to the back of his head, like several other things that he would find out about this complex family.

There was something peaceful about sitting in a carriage with her, probably because she wasn't attacking him. However even now she was not completely relaxed; her hands were clenched and a small frown marred her brow. She flinched as someone shouted outside the carriage window and he wondered how she had heard it in her sleep. He fought the impulse to take the seat next to her and pull her into his arms. They had declared a truce for the evening and James was sure that did not include him taking advantage of her while she slept. And of course there was the promise he had made to her brother to keep her safe. So he just sat and watched her, the gentle curve of her cheeks, the tumbled curls, and the small circle her mouth formed as she slept, until finally the carriage stopped outside the Wynburg residence. James didn't bother to wake Eden, instead he lifted her into his arms and stepped from the carriage.

"Have Miss Eden's maid summoned at once," James told the Wynburg butler as the door opened.

"Your Grace, is the young miss unwell?"

"Lower you voice," James whispered. Eden twitched but remained asleep. "Direct me to Miss Eden's rooms."

"Of course, please follow me, and shall I summon a doctor?"

"No, she just needs her maid and rest."

Pulling her closer, James climbed the stairs. Eden turned her face into his chest but didn't wake. She had the longest eyelashes; they fanned over her pale cheeks. Lifting his head, James directed himself to stop staring at her or he could miss a step.

"This way please, your Grace." Pennyroll opened a door after they had traversed the length of the hallway.

"Dear Lord! What has happened?"

A maid hurried forward as James lowered Eden to the bed and then stepped back, taking one last lingering look.

"She suffered a headache tonight. I offered my carriage to bring her home; her family will follow shortly."

Bobbing a curtsey, the maid looked at James expectantly.

"Right… I'll—I'll leave you to assist her."

Nodding to the maid, James followed the butler back through the silent house, down the stairs and out to his carriage. Staring at the toes of his polished shoes, he tried to find the rational side of his nature. The cold unemotional side that would have felt nothing carrying a woman and hugging a small girl child. *But you would never have done those things before*, James reminded himself. Pinching the bridge of his nose, he realized that life as he knew it was changing, and the small kernel of warmth uncurling inside his chest told him that perhaps it was not a bad thing.

CHAPTER FOURTEEN

"My feet have blisters on blisters." Eden sighed as she slumped into the chair beside her sister. "I fear I am about to fall flat on my face and start snoring right here in the Tittmore ballroom."

"Well, you do insist on rising early to go riding, dear, therefore you have only yourself to blame for your tiredness."

Life for the elder Sinclair siblings had become extremely busy now the season had started in earnest. Most days were spent paying morning calls or shopping. Driving or walking in the park, or entertaining Somer, Dorrie, and Warwick. Dev and Cam were busy, the former with his uncle learning things about business and increasing the family coffers.

"Are you not tired, Essie?" Eden looked at her sister, but could see nothing but a sweet smile.

"I am of course, but…."

"But?"

"I met a man, Eden." The smile that accompanied the words was dazzling.

"And what is this man's name?"

"Lord Laurent."

"The Frenchman?"

Essie nodded.

"Are you blushing?" Eden leaned closer and saw the color

filling her sister's cheeks.

"Of course not. It is just a trifle stuffy in Lady Tittmore's ballroom with so many people in attendance."

"Trifle stuffy." Eden rolled her eyes. "You sound as if you have been in society for years when you say words like that."

"Don't be snooty because you are out of sorts."

"Am I? Out of sorts, I mean?"

Her sister continued to study the dancers.

"It appears that way."

"What gave me away, because I have been trying very hard to be the perfect debutante."

Essie nudged Eden gently. Unlike her, Essie did most things gently.

"Your smile is not wide and never reaches your eyes. You have yet to raise your voice, or for that matter deliver something devilishly cutting to one of your brothers that will make them snarl. Then there is the small matter of a large duke."

"I told Cam he was beef-witted just this morning!"

"I noticed you did not mention the Duke?"

Eden waved her hand about, for no other reason than it looked dismissive.

"He is of no consequence."

"Now who sounds like a society miss?"

"I have no wish to discuss him further. However, I wish to discuss a certain Frenchman who has garnered your interest."

"Oh, Eden. He is kind and sweet-natured, and yes, handsome, there is also the small matter of his wonderful accent."

Eden released her breath when Essie took the conversational lure she had dangled.

"Actually, I agree with you. The few times we have danced he seems very nice, but he is far too sweet-natured to be of interest to me."

To her detriment, she liked aloof dukes, who occasionally betrayed their true nature by carrying a sleeping woman into her house.

"Many men are paying you attention, Eden. If not the Duke, then surely there is one who interests you?"

"Why do you keep mentioning the Duke?" Eden let her exasperation show.

"Because I have never seen you react with any man the way you do with him."

Glaring at her siblings had never worked.

"I have no interest in any duke, and I have no wish to discuss the matter further."

"I believe someone mentioned the word duke?"

Eden looked into the eyes of the Duke of Raven and prayed he had heard nothing more than his title spill from her lips.

"James, how wonderful to see you," Essie said with a great deal of enthusiasm, which hopefully hid the color flaming Eden's cheeks.

Eden had not seen him since the musical evening, which considering what had transpired that night, was a very good thing. Still, she had thought of him constantly.

His evening jacket was black, and his waistcoat the same with a thin silver stripe, necktie perfectly tied with a small gold pin through the folds. Lord, he was a good-looking man.

"Miss Sinclair, may I have this dance?"

Lord Laurent, the handsome fair-haired Frenchman, appeared beside James, and Essie got to her feet so quickly she nearly tumbled into the man.

"I should love to dance, my lord."

"Will you dance with me also, Eden?"

She looked at the arm James held out to her, and thought seriously about refusing, but instead found herself getting to her feet.

Of course it was a waltz, Eden thought as James placed a hand on her back and took her fingers in his. It seemed her theory that time and distance would lessen the impact this man had on her was false.

"Is all well with Samantha, James? The twins ask after her constantly."

She had wanted to ask Cam where James was, yet did not want to sound like she cared. Now, however, she had the perfect opportunity to find out why he had not attended any social gatherings for two weeks.

"Did you miss me, Eden?"

"Absolutely not. Samantha, however, I missed dearly."

Eden thought it wrong a man could be so ridiculously handsome when he did something as simple as smile.

"I must thank you for carrying me from the carriage the night of the musical. When I get a headache I tend to fall into a deep sleep."

"Do you know what brings on the headaches?"

He led her around other couples, and she followed each step. Eden had partnered many men since entering society, yet James was by far the most natural. He had an elegance that suggested he, like she, loved music.

"I have no idea," she said, unable to tell him the truth. She could never tell anyone that, as the results would be dire.

"As to your question regarding Samantha, I have been a nurse the past few weeks. My sister has been unwell, but is nearly back to full health."

"Oh dear, I hope it is nothing too serious?"

"She has had a fever and sore throat, but seems improved today, hence my appearance here."

"And as you have yet to hire a companion, you and your staff must have been rushed off your feet, James. You should have sent word, my sister and I would have nursed Samantha."

"I am more than capable of nursing my sister, thank you, Eden."

"I have no doubts, James, but we also understand how tiring that can be, having three small siblings in our family," Eden said.

His sigh came from the soles of his large feet.

"In truth there were times I wondered if I was doing the right thing. Samantha clung to me, hot and sweaty with fever; she would not let me leave her side."

"How wonderful that she turned to you, James, and not away."

His smile confirmed her words.

"Yes, it was a wonderful thing. But I must admit the fear that she would not get well was not something I would care to live through again."

But you will, Eden thought silently. *Again and again.*

"I spoon-fed her fluid; washed her," he added, "and she treated me as a pillow and lay spent in my arms for hours while I read to her. I would not trade one minute for all the gold in the world," he added softly.

Eden had wanted to distance herself from this man, yet even as she thought it he somehow pulled her closer. The changes in him were weakening her resolve. He seemed so much more real to her now. The harsh, cold man she'd pulled from that water was being erased.

"The bond my sister and I share grows stronger every day, and I believe she has all the burgeoning traits of a minx who will in time twist her big brother in circles as I attempt to curtail her high spirits."

"And are you like Dev, who can move through each day with little sleep, or like me, and turn into a virago?"

"I learned to exist on little sleep in the army."

"Of course." Eden remembered Dev telling her about James

and how he led his troops.

"Can I ask if there has been any further news on who was responsible for the attempt on your life?" She had to ask, as that too had been plaguing her, worry that whoever had tried would soon try once again, and there would not be a Sinclair handy to save him.

"Nothing so far, and before you ask, yes I am being careful."

"Excellent. One can only hope that whoever is responsible has died, or is suffering from a wasting disease that renders him incapable of speech and movement."

His laugh was loud enough to startle the couple beside them.

James had missed her, there was no getting around that fact. Actually, he'd strangely missed all the Sinclairs, although that knowledge would have to be pulled from him with a horse and plough, but Eden the most. They made him feel alive, and had shown him what family life could be if people actually cared for each other.

He'd hated the bite of jealousy he had felt when Cam had informed him earlier today that his sisters were proving a success in society. That each danced constantly and had several admirers.

Coming tonight had been something he'd had to do or go mad. It was getting harder and harder to ignore this need inside him for Eden. He'd sought her out instantly upon his arrival. Dressed in ivory silk, it was a simple gown, unadorned by frills and bows that caressed her body and rippled as she walked. He'd dreamt of her, thought of her when he had a moment to think, and tried to rationalize his need for her. Still he had no answers. He either had to distance himself from her, or hope this, whatever this was, eased given time.

Looking down, he noted the small pink shell of her ear. A tendril of hair lifted as they turned and he saw something inside.

Some sort of obstruction.

"Do they stop your headaches?"

"Pardon?" She looked startled by his words.

"What you have in your ear, does it stop your head from hurting?"

She lowered her lashes and James realized she was uncomfortable with his questions.

"Is Samantha fully recovered?"

"Almost, and you did not answer my question."

"Question?" She was being deliberately vague, and if there was one thing he knew about this woman, it was that she never forgot anything, and had never been vague a day in her life.

The music finished just as he was about to question her further.

"Thank you, if you will take me back to Essie, please, James."

"Of course."

More questions with no answers, James thought. She did not look his way as he led her to where her sister stood, now surrounded by both ladies and gentlemen.

"Miss Eden, come and lend my argument some weight. Mr. Johnson has vowed that a Gunther's lemon ice surpasses a strawberry one."

Idiots! James thought, scowling as Eden swept the small party a wide smile. Each of the men stood a little straighter, one ran his eyes over her lovely breasts, and he could feel the heat of anger slowly flushing his body. When had he last experienced jealousy? Several weeks ago when he had seen men looking at her at the musical. Hell, he was in trouble.

"Oh, an orange ice surely surpasses them all," Eden said, joining the inane conversation.

"Yes, of course you are correct, Miss Eden. How can we have forgotten orange!"

"Excuse me," James said, offering the group a bow before leaving. He did so before he said or did something that would raise the eyebrows of society. Dukes did not fight in public, nor did they throw women over their shoulders. Making his way through some of the guests, he headed for the doors that would take him to his carriage.

He needed a drink and male companionship, so he made for his club. After giving orders to his driver, he sat back in his carriage. Having been inside with his sister for the last few days, he had not caught up on the latest news, therefore he would have a nightcap and there would be someone at his club willing to fill him in on what had been happening.

James wasn't a gossip, but he had several investments that he kept abreast of, and often what he needed to know was not to be found in the newspapers.

"I will not be overlong, Jonah," he said to his driver after climbing from his carriage a short while later.

He found a group of men he knew gathered around the fire. Signaling for a brandy, he joined their ranks.

"I have just placed a bet that the younger will wed before the elder, especially now that the Earl is putting some blunt behind them. Makes the package all the tastier if you ask me."

"Raven would know," Lord Percival said, looking at James as he joined the group.

"Know what?" James said, hoping he had misunderstood the conversation, but the unease inside him suggested he had not.

"There are bets being placed as to which of the two beautiful Sinclair sisters will wed first. Personally, my money's on the younger one; the body of a siren and sweet-tempered as well. What more could a man ask for?"

James choked on his brandy and accepted the thump on the back by the man to his right. He wasn't sure which comment infuriated him more, that Eden had the body of a siren, which of course she did but no one but he was allowed to notice that fact, or that she was sweet-tempered. Eden? Good lord, the woman was a virago when riled.

"As the Sinclair family are friends to both my sister and me, it would not be polite of me to comment further."

Silence greeted these words. James smiled into his brandy goblet. He had probably shocked them, using words like friends and then informing them that he had a sister. Most people had believed him incapable of emotion or involvement. The cold calculating Duke was what they called him. Yet James was no longer sure the title fitted him, and he wanted people to know he had a sister. He loved Samantha and would protect her with his last breath; she belonged to him now. His to cherish, and he would do so to the best of his ability.

"Sister? We had no idea you had a sister, Raven."

"She is six, Percival, and lives with me here in London."

"Yes, yes, I'm sure your sister is a gem, Raven," Viscount Bitterly boomed. "But about the sisters, man. Surely you can give us the inside running. Is the youngest worth pursuing? She'd be bloody comfortable in my bed, but what about as a mother to my children?"

James felt rage travelling through his body with alarming speed.

"Tupping her will be a pleasure," someone else said.

"Wynburg's money will come in handy too. Not to mention a man of his position and power at your back."

He listened as they talked about Essie and Eden as if they were nothing more than empty-headed vessels, deserving of no respect. God, had he ever been like that?

"A word of warning," he managed to get out calmly. His voice was not loud, but carried enough that he had everyone's attention. "A disparaging or insulting word against the Sinclair family I will take as an insult to me. Therefore, I suggest you think carefully before you speak in my company again."

Disgusted with their comments and their company, James stormed from the building. The foul mood he had arrived in was now significantly darker.

"God's blood, was it too much to ask for a drink and idle conversation," he muttered. Crossing the street, he then started down it, to where his carriage awaited.

"Your Grace, please, come quick, a man is hurt over here!"

Spinning on his heel, James looked to where a man stood waving madly at him from the entry to some stables.

"Who is injured?" James said, not moving.

"'Tis a man, your Grace!"

"We've established it's a man, yet I am asking you who he is."

"He is injured and needs your help, your Grace! Please come quickly."

James's body tensed as the man moved toward him. Bracing his legs, he waited.

"How do you know I am a duke?"

"I know who you are."

James watched the man's expression change from anxious to cunning. He knew the game was up and that James was no fool to follow him down the lane where he could be dragged into an empty stable. He just had time to raise his fists as he saw another coming at him from the right. His carriage was still some distance away and Jonah was probably sleeping. He yelled anyway but had little hope of waking his driver. The man slept deeply.

"Get him before he runs!"

Run? James was insulted, he had never run from a fight in his life. He took the full impact of the man as he ran at him, fists flailing, legs pumping. Grunting, he swung his arm and heard a satisfying thunk as it connected with a jaw. The other was closer now and the few seconds it took him to look his way was enough to earn him a fist to the chin. His head spun, eyes temporarily closed. Shaking his head to clear it, he then started fighting with everything he had. Two against one was never good odds but he'd had worse.

"May I offer my assistance, Raven?"

James grunted as the Frenchman Lord Laurent joined the fray. The man could fight, not the prissy boxing type, but brawling just like he could. Swinging his leg in an arc he caught one of them in the thigh and the man hit the ground with a thud. The other followed seconds later courtesy of Lord Laurent. James watched the men groggily regain their feet and run off into the shadows; too tired to follow, James braced his hands on his knees and sucked in deep lungfuls of smoke-laden London air. When his breathing had calmed he rose and looked at the Frenchman.

"I am unsure what has you here at such an opportune moment, but thank you, Laurent."

"Think nothing of it," the man said. "Always said Englishmen could not fight worth a damn, and I have just confirmed it."

"I hope you are not including me in that statement?"

"No indeed," Lord Laurent took the hand James held out to him. "You fight like a Frenchman."

James looked around them. "I think it best we leave here. If you have no transport, Laurent, please allow me to take you home."

"I would be most grateful for a lift to the Grillion's Hotel in Albemarle Street," Lord Laurent said, wiping the blood from his lips with a white square of linen.

It only took a matter of minutes and they arrived at his carriage.

"The Grillion, Jonah," James told his driver.

For long minutes the only sound in the carriage as it rolled through the streets was harsh breathing. James studied the Frenchman who had come to his aid. Not as tall as he, the man was also of a lighter build, and yet he had handled himself well.

"Thank you."

"I did not arrive for the first punch, Raven, and yet it seemed to me those men wanted more than just your purse."

Looking into the steady gaze of the man across from him, James wondered how much to tell him. Surely the fact that his nose was bloodied on James's behalf suggested he was someone he could trust. Yet trust was not something James had in plentiful supply, having been betrayed more than once in his life. Still, perhaps it was time to try once more.

"That was the second attempt on my life in the past month, Laurent, and I fear I am no closer to finding who is so intent on sending me to my maker."

"My name is Louis. I would be honored if you would use it."

Louis, Lord Laurent, James thought, fighting a smile.

"When you hear my middle name is Lyon, you will sympathize with me and understand that my mother was fond of alliteration."

This time he could do little to hold back his snort. "My name is James, Louis."

"So who is on the list of suspects, James?"

Releasing a breath, James looked out the carriage window. Only the faint light from the gas lamps lit the streets, leaving eerie shadows and crevices for some of the more nefarious members of society to frequent.

"I have an heir, but he is off travelling the world and enjoying himself. There are other family members, but none who would gain by my death. Business interests perhaps? But I cannot think of any who would wish me dead. There must be others, men I have unwittingly insulted or—"

"Even I, who have not been in London over long, have heard of your chilly exterior and rapier-sharp tongue," Louis drawled.

"I was exactly as you say." James shrugged.

"Was? May I ask after the change in your manner, James? Although on such a short acquaintance I understand if the question is too personal."

It probably was too personal and James would usually have bristled and delivered a sharp set down at such a question. But he was different now, for better or worse, and he did seem to feel emotions that previously had been a stranger to him. He also knew the sources of these changes, yet was only willing to supply one of them.

"My sister."

"I have heard they are wonderful, yet exasperating creatures, sisters." Louis smiled then winced as the cut on his lip gave a vicious tug.

"Do you have any siblings, Louis?"

The sadness that passed over the Frenchman's face made James wish he had not asked the question.

"Alas, I have no family alive, James."

He did not ask, but wondered if like many, Louis had lost family during the French revolution.

"Do you fence, Louis?" James said as the carriage stopped before the Grillion.

"Oui, James. I am a Frenchman. Therefore, I am superior to you, the staid Englishman."

James laughed at the arrogance.

"I would be happy to set you on your backside a time or two," Louis added.

"Perhaps tomorrow afternoon then?"

"Excellent. Shall we say Angelo's at 2:00 p.m.?"

"I shall look forward to it," James said, "and thank you once again."

"My pleasure, and if I may be bold, James. I would not advise you to go anywhere unaccompanied until this matter is settled."

James shook the hand offered. "Thank you, yes I shall show caution."

He watched Louis leave with a last raise of his hand, and then sat back as Jonah headed the horses for home. He had to find out who wanted him dead. Before Samantha, he would not have cared; life to James had never held much meaning, but now he had a sister who needed him and a woman he wanted more with every dawning day. Not that he would ever follow through with that.

CHAPTER FIFTEEN

"Shall we walk, Eden, as it is not too far?"

"Yes, Somer, both you and Dorrie should gather your outer clothing and I will call Essie and we will be off at once."

The Sinclair sisters stepped out into a beautiful sunny day minutes later. They planned to walk to the Duke of Raven's house to pay a call on Samantha. Eden had told the twins about the little girl's illness over breakfast that morning, and they had been insistent upon visiting. Eden had sent word, and the reply was in Samantha's handwriting and stated that she would love to see them.

Essie carried the small posy of flowers they had made for Samantha.

"I am getting used to the noise and bustle and even beginning to like it here, Somer," Dorrie said, skipping beside her twin.

Eden smiled at Essie over the heads of her sisters. It was good they were beginning to like it here. She knew much of her siblings' happiness was because of their aunt and uncle and the love they so obviously lavished on their nieces and nephews.

"Which house is it, Eden?"

"The big one there," Eden pointed to a large gray building.

"It's even bigger than our uncle's," Dorrie whispered in awe.

A tall black fence ran along the front of the property. The sisters walked through the gates and looked up at the somber stone facade.

"Come along," Eden said, urging the small party toward the front doors. Essie knocked and they stepped back to wait.

"We are the Sinclair sisters, come to visit with Lady Samantha," Dorrie said when the door opened.

The butler did not appear surprised at being addressed by a young girl, and stepped to one side to allow them to enter.

Eden glimpsed a large staircase, dark walls and tiled floors, and then they entered a small parlor.

"If you will please wait in here, I will see if Lady Samantha is receiving this morning."

"She is receiving, because we sent her a note and she replied," Somer said.

"Well then, if you will just wait here, I shall tell her you have called."

Dreary and uninviting were the best words to describe the room. Dark brown brocade hung at the windows and the walls were paneled halfway with dark wood and the rest papered in deep burgundy. The furnishings were, if she was being flattering, ugly, and no one made a move to sit, instead walking toward the window where the light provided some relief in the drab room.

"It is not a very welcoming room."

"Sssh, Somer, it would not do for someone to hear you," Essie whispered.

"But don't you think Somer's right though, Essie?" Dorrie added. "The room is unwelcoming. Not even a small vase sits upon a table; a few flowers would surely help with the gloom."

The twins' thoughts mirrored Eden's but she did not comment further. *Surely living in such a depressing house cannot be healthy for the spirits?* Eden wondered how James had coped living in such a place as a child.

"Indeed you are both correct, it is a very unpleasant room, yet it is not for us to comment on how others live. Now let us remove our things so we are ready to visit with Samantha," Eden said.

When the butler opened the door the Sinclair sisters were more than happy to follow him. They walked up the wide curved staircase. Hunting scenes hung from the walls, mingled with ancestors whose eyes glared down upon them. Eden squeezed the little hand that slipped into hers, offering reassurance. The butler led them down hallways and up more stairs until the sisters had completely lost their bearings. Finally they stopped before a door. Opening it, he ushered them inside and into an explosion of light and color.

"Oh my," the twins whispered.

Eden and her sisters stood just inside the door and stared. Light from the large windows touched the buttercup-colored walls, and the room appeared to glow. Chairs and sofas covered in bright colors with large squishy pillows dotted the room, and silks and pictures hung from the walls. Shelves spilled with books and toys, and a huge vase filled with bright blooms sat on a cabinet.

"Dorrie, Somer!"

This squeal came from the floor before the fire. Eden watched as Samantha climbed to her feet and hurried toward them. She could see dark circles beneath the girl's eyes and her skin was pale, however the wide smile on her lips was enough to dispel her fear that Samantha was not recovering. Dressed in pale blue, her hair tied in a large, floppy matching satin bow, she looked as every young girl should.

"Hello, Eden, do you like my room?"

"Indeed I do, Samantha, and who could not, it is surely the most beautiful room I have ever been in."

Samantha seemed delighted with the compliment and was more than happy to accept Eden and Essie's hugs and kisses.

"Your dress too is lovely, Samantha."

"It is one of the dresses you chose, and James and I decorated the room."

Eden swallowed the lump in her throat at the prospect of James and Samantha together decorating the room. It seemed the bond between the siblings had indeed strengthened.

Samantha loved her flowers, and soon the little girls were sitting before a large dollhouse, playing as if they had been friends for many years.

Essie and Eden sat before the windows in two comfortable chairs, more than happy to let the girls play until they tired.

"Did you enjoy last night, Eden?"

"Of course."

"Liar."

Eden puffed out a breath. "I am not lying to you. I enjoyed parts of last night, it is just…." Eden could not find the words to express what she felt.

"The men seem shallow when compared with the men of our family and the women are little better," Essie finished in a dry voice. "Lord Laurent is excluded from that statement, of course."

Her sister was falling in love, she realized.

"Is he to stay here in England, Essie?"

"Yes, he has nothing to go back to, and is looking to purchase a house here in England."

"How sad that he has no family."

"I have not questioned him on the subject as it is obviously a painful one for him," Essie said.

Eden grabbed her sister's hands. "I pray it works out for you, Essie."

"It will," she smiled. "Will you talk about your feelings for the Duke with me now? Last night you dismissed the subject when I broached it."

"There is nothing to discuss, Essie. We are not suited, and I would never be the wife he wished for."

"Believe that if you wish, and I shall say no more."

"There is no more to say," Eden said in a firm voice. When had she betrayed her interest in the Duke?

"I found Miss Bartrum's gown far too excessive for one so young, and those plumes nearly took poor Mr. Hadleigh's eyes out when they danced."

Eden laughed as her sister intended, glad to change the subject. Taking out one of her earplugs, she rubbed her ear. They sometimes began to hurt after a while if she pushed them in too far. Listening to the hum of voices in various areas of the house, she sorted through each. The rattle of plates, the bang of pots was obviously from the kitchens. She heard James's voice and then another.

"Cam is here."

"Are you sure?" Essie questioned, looking around as if he stood behind them.

"Yes," Eden said, climbing to her feet. "Wait here." She waved her sister back. "We shall finally see what he and the Duke are up to."

"Do not antagonize him."

She lifted a hand at her sister's words and left the room. Following Cam's voice, Eden soon stood before another door. Pushing her earplug back in, she tapped before entering.

Unlike the rest of the house, this was a room worthy of spending time. The ceiling was high, with the farthest wall holding floor-to-ceiling windows that, like Samantha's room, made it seem as if she were stepping into the sunlight. Books lined two walls, high enough that a ladder would be needed to reach the top ones. The furnishings were of rich deep reds and blues with woven patterned rugs scattering the polished wooden floors. It was alive with a feast of color and light, and Eden knew that this was the room James spent all his time in.

"This one is extraordinary, and seems to be a map of an island somewhere in the Caribbean, and this one—"

Both heads swiveled as Eden shut the door.

"What the hell are you doing here?"

"I believe that was going to be my question, brother dear." Eden looked from Cam to the Duke and back again. They were bent over a large desk upon which was spread a big piece of parchment. Both were in shirtsleeves and waistcoats. James smiled, Cam scowled.

"I asked first."

"Oh please, like a Sinclair has ever cared who asks first. It's who gets the answer first that matters," Eden scoffed. "Besides, we are intrigued as to what it is you do here with the Duke for hours."

James folded his arms and leaned back against the desk. He loved watching Eden when she was sparring with her siblings; it was a game all parties seemed to relish, no matter the outcome or the original topic, as usually they covered many over the course of the debate.

She looked like a sweet piece of confectionary today waiting to be devoured, dressed in pale lemon muslin with blond lace trim. Her hair was simply styled and her beautiful face alive. He wanted to lay her upon his desk and ravish her.

"I am to be cursed with you even here," Cam growled. "Christ, am I allowed no peace!"

"Do not curse in your sister's presence, Cam." James felt he needed to say something.

"Peace!" Eden screeched, ignoring him and forcing both men to wince. "Peace is it, you insufferable ingrate. You, who do not live with the children, crave peace. Oh and I was to know you were here, was I? We came to visit with Samantha, not follow you, you self-important puffed-up—"

"Now, children," James chided softly, knowing it would annoy the hell out of them. Smiling, he wondered when he had begun to understand the rules to their games.

"Oh Lord, Eden. I'm so sorry, I was supposed to tell you she had been sick," Cam said, anger fleeing as quickly as it had come.

"It is all right, brother, the Duke told us last night and Dorrie and Somer were insistent upon seeing Samantha. Had they found out any earlier they would more than likely have caught whatever was ailing her."

From rage to empathy in seconds, James thought, shaking his head. It was exhausting just watching them. He could only imagine how tiring it would be to live with the Sinclairs.

Cam was now hugging his sister tight and kissing her cheek. They were a very demonstrative lot, always touching and kissing each other. James's skin tingled just at the thought of all that close contact with another person. Close contact with Eden however, now that was a different matter entirely.

"Good morning, Eden."

"Oh, forgive me, James," Eden said, dropping into a curtsey. "Good morning to you."

"Think nothing of it. I can see how important it is to be on your guard when faced with a Sinclair sibling."

"What happened to your face?"

James braced himself as she moved closer, one hand lifted to touch his jaw and then at the last minute, almost as if she realized what she was about to do, it fell to her side and she retreated.

"'Tis nothing, just an accident."

"That was caused by a fist, James, and not nothing. I know

what they look like, as my brothers have upon occasion come home with just such a mark."

"Some men tried to jump him outside his club."

Glaring at Cam, James raised his hand as Eden began to speak.

"I am unharmed and a friend came to my aid," James said, surprised at how comfortable he felt saying the word friend.

"You cannot go about London unescorted, James, surely you see that? Someone is trying to dispatch you to the afterlife and you seem hell-bent on allowing it to happen!" Eden snapped.

James sent Cam a look as if to say "help," however the younger man just raised his hands and smiled.

"While I do not make a habit of agreeing with any member of my family and most especially not Eden," Cam said, rolling his eyes as Eden poked out her tongue. "In this I fear she is correct. It was folly to gad about unprotected. Perhaps in future may I suggest you take one of your protectors with you."

"Dukes do not gad anywhere, Sinclair," James said, "and I do not need a protector."

"Cam is right, you must take more care, James."

"I need a drink," James growled, his earlier good mood having fled with the start of the discussion about his death. The thump he had taken to the side of the head last night had been throbbing steadily all morning, and now Eden's haranguing had made it worse. Stalking to the table, James reached for the decanter. Pulling out the stopper and tipped a large amount into a glass.

"You took more than a punch to your jaw, didn't you?" Eden said, as she and Cam followed him. "Your movements would suggest your ribs are also sore."

"Don't fuss, Eden, I am well."

Cam laughed. "You sounded just like Dev and me then."

James grunted something no one but he understood, and then raised his glass to his lips.

"What is it, Cam?"

James watched as Cam sniffed loudly at his sister's query.

"Don't drink that!"

James was so surprised at the roared demand he lowered the glass instantly.

"Get Essie!" Cam said, taking the glass from his hands.

"What's happening?" James said as Eden picked up her skirts and ran from the room. "What the hell is going on, Cam?" he demanded.

"If you will wait for an explanation until my sisters arrive, James, I wish to be sure I have my facts right."

Eden's brother had lost all trace of his usual jovial demeanor; his eyes were narrowed as he stared at the glass he still held in his hand.

Several tense minutes later he heard the thud of feet approaching at a run.

"What is it, Cam?" Essie hurried into the room with Eden on her heels.

"This drink contains poison, Ess, but I need you to confirm it."

"What!" James roared. "Are you sure?"

"Yes," Cam said softly, and that one word told James that whatever was in that glass was intended to kill him. He watched Essex Sinclair take the glass in her hands and dip her handkerchief in the liquid. She then allowed one drop to fall on the tip of her finger, which she rubbed on her teeth.

"No! Surely it will harm you?" James tried to stop the woman.

Eden placed a hand on his arm. "It will not harm her, James. Such a small amount will have no impact on Essie, but she will determine what the poison is."

James stood silently at Eden's side, watching the Sinclairs. How had Cam known there was poison in his glass, and how did Essex know from one drop what that poison was?

"Belladonna."

"Are you sure?" James could not take it in. How had someone entered his house and poisoned his brandy?

"We will take the decanter and glass, James, and dispose of them," Cam said, nodding to Essie to follow him. "We shall return shortly to discuss what should be done next."

As Eden prepared to follow her siblings he gripped her arm, halting her.

"I think not," James said, hauling her back to his side.

"I-I must return to our sisters."

"They will be well cared for with Jane, Samantha's maid, watching over them."

"I must go to Cam and Essex, they may need my help."

James could feel the tension inside her.

"A glass and a decanter will not tax their strength, Eden, and I have a few questions for you, which you *will* answer."

James pulled her with him deeper into the room, until they stood before the windows.

"It is a wonderful room, James. H-have you read all these books?" Eden was looking around, determined to distract him. "I love reading—in fact, if I may I will have a look around—"

"Be quiet, Eden."

She did, biting her lip. Her eyes shot to the door, hoping no doubt for her siblings to return and save her. Something clenched in his chest as he looked at the top of her head and suddenly all the questions he had wanted to ask were replaced with a desperate need to touch her. He took hold of a curl, rolling the satin between his fingers.

"Look at me," James tugged the curl. She lifted her head and he saw the longing that he knew she would read in his eyes too.

One more tug and he had her in his arms, his lips upon hers, her body pressed to his. This kiss was fierce, a clash of mouths and teeth as they fought for more. He swallowed the soft noises she made and pulled her closer; it wasn't enough. He wanted her skin in his hand and the layers of clothing between them removed.

"Eden, God, what you do to me." He shuddered as he dragged his lips from hers to run them down her neck.

She smelled like the most alluring flower in any garden, arousing him further. Sliding one hand up her waist he stroked her ribs then cupped her breast, dipping his finger inside her bodice and tracing the edge.

"Oh, James."

Her throaty cry nearly undid him completely. He grabbed a handful of her skirts, but as he lifted them, the one small rational thought he still retained told him to stop or be prepared for the consequences when her siblings returned. Claiming her lips in one last savage kiss, he then eased back. Stepping away from her, he fought for composure.

"James."

God, it was only one word, but the throaty purr nearly had him reaching for her again. Instead he started asking questions.

"How did your brother know there was poison in my glass?" Still in the grip of a fierce lust for the woman before him, the words came out harsher than he intended.

"Pardon?" She blinked.

"Your brother, how did he know there was poison in my glass unless it was he who put it there?"

"No!" She gasped, stumbling back a step. "Cam would never hurt you, or anyone, surely you cannot believe otherwise."

He didn't, actually. The thought had never entered his head before today, yet now he had said the words he would use them to get answers to the questions that niggled at him about the

Sinclair family. They were a closemouthed lot and would protect each other to the death. James needed some leverage to get the answers he sought and it seemed he had found it.

"Essie also knew it was poison after one taste, surely that is too much of a coincidence?"

"No, we—my family, we protect you, have protected you?" She was shaking her head and stumbling toward the door.

It hurt his chest to see the fear replacing passion in her eyes, but he could not back down now. He and his sister were close with this family, no matter how he had tried to deny it. Therefore, he had to know Samantha was safe in their company.

"I-I must go, my brother is calling me."

"I hear nothing, Eden."

She shot a look at the door. "Please, I beg of you do not question me further."

"It was definitely belladonna, James," Essie said, entering the room with her brother on her heels.

"Eden?" Cam questioned as he noticed his sister's distress. "Why is she upset, Raven?"

James wanted to be the one to comfort her. Running a hand through his hair, he bit back a frustrated sigh. He could not afford to back down now if he wanted answers, but seeing her distress was like a knife to the chest.

"How did you know there was poison in my glass, Cam?"

James watched the three Sinclair siblings grow still, each eyeing him warily. Essex moved to Cam's other side, and he lifted his arm and pulled her close. It was a telling gesture that told James they felt threatened by his questions and were seeking strength in each other.

"Are you accusing me of something, Raven?"

Cam seemed to grow several inches before James's eyes, and looked more like his elder brother with every second that passed—right down to the furious glint in his green eyes.

"You had no way of knowing what was in that glass, Cam, unless you had either tasted it or put it there. The same must be said of Essex, for that matter."

"You will not accuse my sister!"

Lifting his hands in a gesture meant to reassure as Cam roared at him, James shrugged. He hated questioning them like this because he knew instinctively they were innocent; had they not saved his life already several times? Yet he also knew there was something strange going on, and he wanted to know what. He looked at Eden, but she would not meet his eyes. Instead she huddled close to her brother.

"Then tell me how you both knew what was in that glass?"

The Sinclairs looked at each other for several seconds and then as if by silent vote Cam spoke.

"We must first speak with Devon before answering your questions. Therefore, I would ask that you wait until this evening for your answers."

Nodding, James realized it would be unfair of him to pursue the matter. Devon was the eldest and therefore their leader, if they needed his consent before speaking then he would wait, but the suspense would near kill him. There was little doubt that what he was to learn was something of great importance to this family.

"I suggest we then adjourn to the nursery to take tea with our sisters."

They did not refuse him as he had thought they would, instead it was a solemn group that trooped up to the nursery, yet when the door opened everyone was all smiles. Soon cakes were devoured by James and the little girls; the others, including Cam, who could devour an entire cake in one sitting, merely nibbled theirs.

Eden took great pains to hide her distress from her sisters. It was a testament to how closely he watched her that he could

SENSING DANGER

see the tension in her body. Her gestures had lost their elegance and her smile its brilliance, and James contemplated retracting his accusations. He had hurt her, and that to his mind was unforgivable. Yet something stopped him.

"Have you given Dorrie and Somer their dolls, Samantha?"

"No! Oh why did I not remember we had purchased them, James?"

"Don't do this to us."

He heard Eden's words as Samantha ran to a cupboard.

"Do what?" He looked into her lovely gray eyes. "Tell me something that will make me understand."

She shook her head and looked away, and James wondered if he had just achieved what he had once believed he wanted: to distance himself from this woman indefinitely.

CHAPTER SIXTEEN

Dear Lord, she felt sick. The tea Eden had swallowed was trying to make a reappearance, and her hands felt clammy. How would they deal with this situation? What would Dev say when he heard what the Duke suspected? Her eyes followed Samantha as she ran to a cupboard. Flinging the door open, she pulled two boxes from inside.

"James and I brought you these, Dorrie and Somer!"

Why had he done this to her? Surely she could not have been wrong about him, wrong about his character? She wanted to believe in her heart that James did not truly think them capable of the deeds he was accusing them of, but if not then why was he pursuing this? It was terrifying; the risk of exposure would have them run out of London and into hiding if their secrets got out. How could this have happened after what they had shared? How could he have kissed and caressed her as if she were precious and then turned on her? It was everything she had always feared. Everything her father had told her would one day come true. Did he really believe they were capable of murder?

"We can't allow you to purchase our sisters such extravagant gifts, Raven. We will of course reimburse you," Cam said in a quiet voice as the three little girls began to laugh and jump around the room in excitement.

"This is from Samantha, Cambridge, not me. I merely supplied the funds," James said in the same tone. "Your sisters are her first friends and she wished to celebrate the moment with matching dolls, as she also has one."

Eden knew it would be churlish for Cam to refuse, yet for her also, the gesture did now not sit easily, as it would not with Dev. Especially considering the accusations the Duke had just thrown at them.

"After what you have just accused us of, I think you would understand our reluctance," Essie said, her tone cold.

"That does not concern them," the Duke said, looking at the little girls. "And I merely—"

"I disagree." Eden cut off his words. "It affects all of us."

With a curt nod Cam then rose, and Eden knew only relief. She could not keep up this pleasant pretense for a second longer.

"Well, sisters, if you are ready, we will return as our aunt and uncle will have missed us. Please thank the Duke for his kind gifts, girls."

Somer and Dorrie were used to expressing themselves with gestures, having been raised in a loud boisterous family who cuddled and kissed regularly. Eden watched as Somer grabbed James's hand and pulled his head down to her level. She then planted a loud smacking kiss on one cheek while Dorrie did the same on the other.

Eden would have laughed at his expression had she not been sick to her stomach. His cheeks heightened with color as he straightened, clearly uncomfortable. However, he thanked the twins politely and told them to return soon.

Farewells were said, Somer securing a promise from James that he would take them to Astley's next week. Cam did not shake James's hand and Eden and Essie walked away from him without a backward glance.

As she was walking down the stairs to the front entrance with her family, she heard Samantha talking to her brother.

"I am not sure I would like quite as many siblings as the Sinclairs, James."

"Indeed, peace and privacy would be rare, I think."

"But there is something about the Sinclairs, they sort of—"

"Encompass you," the Duke said.

"Yes," Samantha agreed. "I like it."

From the Duke there was no reply.

The silence hung heavily over them as they walked from the Duke's house. Eden sent Dorrie and Somer to run ahead of them, as she knew they had much to discuss. Dev would be angry when they told him, but what would he suggest they do?

"I do not want him to know about our gifts."

"None of us want that, Eden, but I can see no way out of this. The man is persistent and knows something is not right. We cannot chance that he will accuse us of attempted murder," Essie said.

"I don't believe it would come to that," Cam added. His hands were thrust in his pockets and his eyes were on the path before him. "The man I have come to know is fair, and he would not accuse us without solid evidence. Plus there is the small matter of what lies between us, and the fact you have already saved his life."

"Solid evidence," Eden said. "He either believes we are freaks or that we are murderers, there is no other option. For him to believe one we must lie about the other, and neither option is appealing, brother."

As they were at the Wynburg residence moments later, no one spoke again, and Eden knew the next few hours would pass on leaden feet until they had a chance to speak with Dev in private.

***

"Can we trust him with the truth, Dev?"

"I fear we have little choice, Essie," the eldest Sinclair said, looking out the carriage window.

Eden and her siblings had told Devon every word of their encounter with the Duke of Raven, tumbling over each other in their anxiety to get the story straight. He had calmed them and told them it would be all right, as the Duke, for all his stuffiness, was a fair man. But Eden had seen the worry in his eyes.

The four siblings had decided to drive around the streets while they worked through what they would tell the Duke.

They had no wish for their aunt, uncle, or younger siblings to overhear the conversation, so after the evening meal they had put the children to bed and told their aunt they were visiting the Duke to view his library. Lord and Lady Wynburg hadn't questioned them, although the Earl had lifted one bushy eyebrow, as his own library was fairly extensive and they had not yet exhausted that. Cam had muttered something about treasure maps and the Sinclairs had said their good-byes and fled the room.

"He could have us locked up or deported, couldn't he?"

"He is an honorable man, Essie," Devon said, and Eden hoped he was right. "If I know nothing else about him I know that his men would have followed him to the ends of the earth, and that makes me trust him," Dev added. "And let us not forget the fact that we have saved his life; that must surely count for a great deal."

"But our secret, Dev. It is such a terrifying thought that someone other than us know of it. What if he chose to use it against us, after all our parents did to make sure that never happened?" Essie said, the anguish in her voice felt by them all.

Father used it against me, Eden wanted to say, yet she remained silent.

"We have no other choice; if he pursues the matter of the poison then he must be told the truth," Dev said, the strain showing on his face. "We are agreed then?"

"Aye."

"Aye."

"Aye," Eden whispered last.

"I will keep us safe," Dev vowed, but Eden was not sure anyone could do so once their secret was out.

The rest of the journey was completed in silence as each of the siblings came to terms that the night may bring an end to their secrets.

Eden felt unsteady when she stepped from the carriage and walked up to the front door. The door she had walked through with her giggling sisters not many hours before. The butler opened it to Cam's hard knock. Discarding their outer clothing, they followed him to where the Duke awaited them in his study.

James watched the small somber procession file into the room, eldest to youngest.

"Raven," Devonshire Sinclair said, speaking first, the others remained silent. Eden did not glance his way, instead moving to the sofa farthest from where he stood. Gone was the passionate woman he had kissed earlier. This one was coiled in on herself, her arms wrapped round her waist as she huddled in the seat. It was as if someone had extinguished the light inside her.

"Sinclair," James said in the same cool clipped tones. There had always been reserve between he and Lord Sinclair; it had now intensified.

Three of the siblings sat and Devonshire remained standing. James elected to stand also.

"My sisters and brother have told me what happened today and of your accusations. First let me say I am deeply offended that you would believe this of my family when weeks ago my sister saved you from certain death, as did I two years ago, and it appears Cambridge did this very day."

James did not flinch. He knew the words were just, yet this had been a means to an end, and now that end was about to declare its hand. Nodding, he remained silent.

"I would like to ask you before I continue if there is any way you will let the matter drop and take it no further, thus letting my family leave here this night with their secrets still their own."

James watched a muscle in Sinclair's jaw tick as he clamped his teeth together. The silence in the room became stifling as everyone waited for him to speak, and cad that he was, he simply held the eldest Sinclair's gaze for several seconds before silently shaking his head.

"It seems my original belief that you were a man of honor was well short of the mark, Raven."

"I understand your need to protect your family, Sinclair, but be warned that I will not tolerate another slur upon my honor," James said, feeling his temper tweak, even if it appeared to be just in the eyes of the man before him.

"If you were honorable you would not be forcing my family to reveal something that shakes the very foundation they live upon."

He didn't speak, just held Devon's gaze.

"So be it," Sinclair muttered, running a hand through his already ruffled hair. "But before I continue I must have your word that what is spoken in here tonight can never leave this room. If it did it would cause me and my siblings great and unimaginable harm. In this I am resolute, Raven. And I must trust that you will hold true to your word once given."

What the hell were they about to tell him?

"You have my word, which I assure you is my bond."

Nodding, Devon then looked to where his siblings sat. They in turn nodded.

"It will be hard for you to understand or believe, Raven, but I would ask you to wait until I finish before questioning what you see or hear."

James nodded, his eyes focused on Devonshire Sinclair. He could feel the tension in the room, taste it and touch it, so palpable it nearly choked him.

Devon began in an even tone, almost as if he read aloud from the newspaper.

"You are aware of the pact between our families, and that we were chosen to protect the Ravens, your ancestors, by King Edward III?"

"I am."

"What you don't know is that we discovered at a young age that we have heightened senses. Mine is sight, Eden's is hearing, Cam's is smell, and Essie's is taste."

James had thought of many scenarios—this, however, was not one of them. Did they honestly expect him to believe this tale?

"I can see the skepticism in your face, Raven, and frankly whether you believe us or not is of no great concern to me. Yet you have accused my family of a serious crime, therefore I must show you that I speak the truth, as I have no wish for any of us to end our days in a jail cell."

"I would not send you to jail, Sinclair."

"Your earlier words led my siblings to believe otherwise."

James remained silent, as he had threatened them and the guilt settled heavily on his shoulders.

"Eden, love, go outside the room."

James watched Eden rise and approach her brother.

"I have promised to keep you safe, Eden. Have faith in your big brother."

She nodded solemnly and then took the plugs out of her ears and handed them to Devon. Without looking his way, she walked to the door opened it, passed through, and closed it behind her.

"I would ask you to walk to the end of the room, Raven. Once there, face the wall and say something that only you will hear, but sound must leave your lips."

Every hair on James's body rose as he looked into the solemn eyes of the remaining Sinclairs. Could they be speaking the truth? Suddenly everything that had niggled at him filtered through his head. The ability of the siblings to hear those men intent on robbing their carriages on the journey to London. Eden hearing things James had not. Cam sniffing the poison and Essie tasting it.

"If you wish answers, then you must do as I ask," Sinclair said when James didn't react to his order.

Moving to the rear of the room as requested, he softly spoke. He then returned to Devon, who called Eden back into the room. Once again she did not look at him, her body tense, face fearful.

"Recite the words, Eden."

James watched her hesitate.

"'Tis all right, love, say the words," Devon said, bending to brush a kiss on her forehead. "I will keep you safe."

James wanted to tell her to stop; her obvious distress was making his stomach ache. She was so unlike the woman who had stormed into his library earlier this day. The spirit had left her eyes and they appeared subdued, beaten.

"Eden, I—"

"When forty winters shall besiege thy brow, / And dig deep trenches in thy beauty's field, / Thy youth's proud livery so gazed on now, / Will be a tattered weed of small worth held."

Eden recited the Shakespeare poem word perfect yet her voice held no inflection. Emotionless and precise, she finished then once again fell silent.

"Go and sit beside Cam now, love," Dev said, handing Eden her earplugs.

His head still reeling, James watched her push them back into her ears, then reclaim her seat. Cam wrapped her in his arms and hugged her hard.

Was it true, could she have heard him? Yet surely the facts spoke for themselves. She would have had no idea that he would quote Shakespeare. God, he couldn't take it in, was it possible?

"Cam, what can you smell?"

"Whoever does the laundry uses lavender in the wash and the Duke uses a scent combined with lemon and sandalwood. Before we arrived, he had coffee with honey tarts followed by a brandy. In the kitchens the cook has mutton cooking and is baking a fruitcake."

James fell into the seat opposite the sofa the three Sinclairs occupied. He wanted to clap his hands over his ears as Devonshire Sinclair cleared his throat and began to speak.

"The spine on that book on the highest shelf closest to the wall reads, *The Pilgrim's Progress From This World, To That Which Is To Come, First Edition 1678*."

James knew that book was at least thirty feet away and on the top shelf, which he needed a ladder to reach. He also knew it was *The Pilgrim's Progress*, just as he knew every book on his shelves and where it was located.

"Call for tea and biscuits or cakes, Raven, and Essie will tell you what the ingredient in everything is," Devon said.

"Enough." No one moved as James spoke quietly. "I knew there was something about you all, yet never did I see this coming. It must be both a burden and a pleasure to have such talents."

Eden finally looked at him, and he couldn't be sure, but thought there was relief in her eyes. Had she believed he would expose her, that he was the kind of man to do such a thing to people who had saved his life? The answer was yes, she had, and the thought was not a pleasing one, but no less than he deserved.

"We have lived with it for a long time, Raven, it is merely a part of who we are." Cam said the words in a solemn tone. "We believe our heightened senses are a result of our ancestors' duty to your family."

James tried to make sense of what he had learned.

"You believe your heightened senses are a direct result of what happened in 1335?"

The elder Sinclair nodded. "We can find no other reason."

"And are there others?"

"Others?" Cam questioned.

"Others with heightened senses."

Devon laughed, but it held no humor. "We believe there were other Sinclairs, yes. But as you can understand, this is not something one brings up in general conversation, Raven, because if we did, we would be locked up. But for all that, we would be arrogant to believe we were the only ones gifted in such a way."

"Gifted," Cam scoffed. "Cursed, more like."

"I would advise you not to give the matter too much thought, as all you end with is a sore head," Dev said, ignoring his brother. "What we have told you is the truth, and besides us, you are now the only one who knows. You will understand how unsettling that is for my family. You now have the power to cause great and unimaginable harm to us should you choose to do so."

"I have given you my word, Sinclair. All of you," James said, looking at each of the siblings. Eden did not meet his eyes. "You have saved my life on three occasions now, and your ancestors many more for mine. I promise you that your secret is safe in my hands."

"Thank you," Essex Sinclair said, and he heard the relief in her words.

"And is there more to these senses?"

"Aye," Devon sighed. "They have developed in different ways over the years."

James saw he was uncomfortable, but he wanted to know all the details now he knew the truth.

"Different ways?"

"Do you need to know everything?" Eden was finally speaking to him, or perhaps growling was the more accurate term.

"I would like to know more, purely because I am interested. If that is a problem—"

"As he knows the worst of it, we may as well enlighten him." Essie shrugged.

Eden said nothing further, instead lowering her eyes to the floor once more.

"When we are together our senses are stronger, and when we touch, even more so. Eden can sometimes hear an unspoken word before it is said," Devon added. "Cam can smell fear or distress, Essie can taste it and I can see long distances, Raven, and I also have the ability to see—ah—colors."

James was intrigued; he watched Devon look away and knew he was reluctant to discuss his own senses.

"Colors?"

"I don't suppose you'd just take my word for it?"

"You know me better than that, Sinclair. However, my interest is genuine and not intended to harm any of you."

Devon's sigh was louder this time. "Everyone has a color. Essie is pink, Cam is orange, Eden is blue, and I am green. The colors grow stronger as you age. When a person is ill or near death they weaken. There is more, but I will not bore you with the details, and I do not use this vision often, as everything becomes vivid and it can be uncomfortable depending on the situation."

"Good God," James said slowly. "Living in your family must have been a mixture of heaven and hell. There would have been nowhere to hide."

Surprised laughter filled the room at his words.

"It was certainly never dull," Cam drawled.

"And your parents?" James looked at Eden, but she still would not meet his eyes.

"Our father could see, but it was not strong," Essie answered him.

"I never believed you capable of harming me, you know," James needed to say the words out loud. To ensure this strange yet amazing family understood they had nothing to fear from him, and most especially that Eden believed him.

"Then why—" She finally looked at him, and he saw the fear. Unlike the others, it still had her in its grip.

"I knew you were hiding something from me, Eden, and as you seemed to have been elected my protectors I wanted to understand what that something was. I apologize if I have hurt you in any way."

"I will kill you if you use this against any member of my family," Devon said, not ready to forgive him.

Reluctantly James turned from Eden to the eldest Sinclair. "The debt I owe you is large enough to ensure my silence even if I were not a man of my word."

"Annoys the hell out of you doesn't it, Raven, being indebted to us?"

"I can find several stronger words to express my unease at the notion. But now if you will all excuse me for a moment, I will order refreshments, as I know Cam cannot go more than an hour without them."

James left the family alone to talk about what had transpired, and reassure themselves that he would keep their secrets safe.

CHAPTER SEVENTEEN

Eden looked at the closed door. Could it be true, would he really keep their secret safe?

"I believe he will keep his word," Essie said, as if reading her thoughts.

"It is unlike you to trust on such a short acquaintance, Essie."

"I know, Dev, but he is a good man, I can feel it. What color is he?"

Eden watched as her elder brother began to pace the room. He had definite ideas about the colors of people and how this affected their personalities. He also believed his siblings should marry only their color match, but as yet he'd had no reason to enforce this.

"Dev?" Essie prompted.

"Blue."

They did not look at her but Eden knew they wanted to. He was a match to her in color but little else. Especially now, after revealing what a strange person she was. He had given the appearance of understanding about their gifts, and yes she believed James capable of keeping his word. However, she knew that he would not want to associate with them in the future, and the twins would be kept away from his sister. Her father had told her often that she would end up locked away if anyone learned what they were capable of, because people like her and her siblings were fit only for a circus.

Restless, Eden regained her feet and made her excuses, saying she needed a moment to herself. Her skin felt tight and panic had worn her nerves down. Closing the door behind her, she unclenched her fingers and removed an earplug to scratch her ear, and it was then she heard the cry. Samantha was calling out in her sleep. Pleased lamplight lit her way she hurried to the little girl's rooms. Opening the door, Eden left it that way so soft light showed her the small body tucked into the big bed.

"Sssh now, Samantha." She stroked her hair.

"James?"

"It's Eden, sweetheart, don't be afraid."

"Eden? Why are you here?"

"We are paying your brother a call to see his maps."

"I was dreaming."

The raspy little whisper tore at Eden's heart. Climbing onto the bed, she lifted Samantha and resettled her on her lap.

"Bad dreams?"

"Y-yes."

"Do you remember what they were about, because sometimes it helps to discuss them."

"Eden?"

"Yes, Samantha."

"My father was a bad man."

"My father was a bad man too, so we have that in common."

"Really?"

"Really, Samantha, and it is all right to be angry with them. In fact I think it helps if you are. Sometimes I yell at my father even though he is no longer able to hear me. But the most important thing to remember is our fathers can no longer harm us, because we have others who will always love and protect us."

"James loves me, he said so."

"Of course he does, and he will always be there for you, sweetheart. Big brothers are very special people, Samantha; they take their responsibilities seriously, especially when it means protecting their little sisters."

Samantha's giggle made Eden smile. Her fears had been chased away, and Eden wished hers could be so easily erased.

"Why did your father not love you, Eden?"

Eden felt the paralyzing fear of her youth. Breathing deeply, she forced it away; he could hurt her no more.

"Because he made me be someone I did not want to be, Samantha."

"I hated my father, Eden. He was not a nice man."

"Well, as we both hated our fathers we shall be able to talk about it together," Eden said. "We shall yell at them sometimes, and very soon you will hardly think about yours and I shall forget mine."

"I would like that."

Samantha yawned, so Eden settled her back on the bed and kissed her head.

"Sleep now, and I shall stay until you are asleep."

"Thank you."

Eden did not have to wait long until the little girl's breathing grew into a steady rhythm. Quietly she left the room, closing the door softly behind her.

James was leaning on the wall, his eyes serious as she started toward him.

"She was restless, and I heard her call out, so I came to see if she was all right."

"Thank you, I was just about to check on her when I heard your voice." He pushed off the wall to block her path as she drew near. "I know how she suffered at the hands of my father, yet I could do nothing to stop it."

"Because you did not know of her existence."

"I didn't even know my father had remarried." The words were cold and emotionless.

"I'm sorry," Eden whispered. She knew how a parent could destroy a child.

"Do you know that he used to beat me for writing with the wrong hand. He broke two fingers once, and tied my left hand behind my back for days."

"I'm so sorry, James." She felt helpless.

"He caught me playing in the village with some of the children when I was ten. He had seen me as he drove by in his carriage. I was called to his office and beaten. He said, 'No son of mine will associate with village children. They are beneath us. Now begone from this house and learn to be a Raven.'"

"Oh, James."

His gaze went to his sister's bedroom door. "I cannot bring myself to ask what he did to her, yet know I must."

"I think it would help her to talk about it."

He looked down at her then and she saw the turmoil in the brown depths. His words had been calm, yet the pain was still there. His father had wounded him deeply.

"What did he make you do?"

"Who?" Eden tried to step around him but he shadowed her, his hand reaching for one of hers.

"What did your father make you do, Eden?"

"It matters not."

"It matters to me, and as I have just unburdened myself, surely you can do the same."

"No." Eden shook her head and tried to withdraw her hand. He enclosed it in his larger one. "What matters is that you keep your word and do not expose us for the freaks you now know we are." She had needed to say the words to understand how he truly felt about her. His abhorrence for what she was would go a long way toward extinguishing the flames of her attraction for him.

"You think I believe you a freak because you have heightened senses?"

Eden nodded.

"Don't be foolish, Eden. Knowing what you are makes you special, and I do not think of you and your siblings as freaks. In fact, I'm insulted that you would even suggest it."

"I don't believe you. Now let me pass."

"I'm telling you the truth, why is that so hard for you to believe?" He slipped his fingers up her arm, slowly pulling her closer.

"Because he said people would turn away from us."

"Your father said that?"

Closing her eyes, she tried to shut out her father's face, the horrid twisted smile he would give her when he wanted to make her do his bidding.

"I don't want to talk about this and wish to return to my family."

"What did your father make you do, Eden?"

She didn't want to cry. She had shed so many silent, solitary tears over her father that she would allow him no more.

"I had believed tonight's revelations would force you to see me in a different light. That you would have no wish to see me again."

"It would take a great deal more than knowing of your gift to stop me wanting you, Eden. In fact, I'm not sure anything will do that. Now tell me what your father did to you."

"He made me go with him and listen to people talking so he could blackmail them, and I loathed him from the first day he forced me to do his bidding until the day he drew his last breath."

James swore beneath his breath, and Eden liked hearing his anger on her behalf.

"And this is why you are closer to Devon than any of the others. He was your father," James whispered, understanding what her siblings had not. "Yet I doubt you have ever told him why you turned to him, have you?"

"My father said if I told anyone he would hurt them."

"Did he use the others at all?"

His hands moved to her shoulders and then she was resting against his chest. Lord, he was warm. Eden closed her eyes as she absorbed his strength.

"No, it was only me he took with him on his 'outings,' as he called them, and my siblings believed it was because he favored me, when in fact the truth was far different."

"And it hurt because you did not want to go."

"Yes."

"You told me I must talk with Samantha about our father, and you must do the same, Eden. Tell Devon. He needs to know what his father did to you."

"It would hurt him too much."

"I believe Devon, more than the others, would understand what your father was capable of. It was, after all, he who had to pick up the pieces your father left behind."

Was that true, would Dev understand? For years she had longed to tell him.

"My father told me that if people found out about us we would be hanged or locked away." There, she'd said it, given voice to her biggest fears.

"No one is locking anyone away, Eden." She felt his lips in her hair. "You need never fear exposure, I promise you. Your secret is safe with me."

Did he really mean it? Placing her hands on his chest, she looked into his eyes.

"I have given you my word, can you not trust me?"

"Yes." She could, Eden realized. He would keep their secrets safe. The relief would have dropped her to her knees had he not been holding her.

"Tell your brother because I think his reaction will surprise you."

"I will think about it, and thank you for understanding." Before she allowed herself time to think Eden climbed to her toes and placed her lips on his. The kiss was soft and sweet. Drawing back, she then walked away.

"We were just formulating a plan, Raven, for your safety," Devonshire Sinclair said as James returned to his study.

He'd taken a few minutes to compose himself after his conversation with Eden. He'd never told anyone about his father, and she had not spoken of hers, and the revelations had shaken him more than he'd allowed her to see.

His anger at hearing how her father had treated her had far eclipsed the emotion he felt remembering how he had suffered. Was that telling? He very much believed it was. But in what way? Were his feelings stronger for Eden that he had thought? No, James did not think so. In fact he knew he was not capable of loving anyone... well, except Samantha. He loved his little sister now, very much.

Taking the cup Essie handed him, James dropped in two spoonfuls of sugar and tried to focus on the eldest Sinclair. Eden, he noted, sat once again beside the fire staring contemplatively into its depths.

"A plan?"

"Cam will have to move in here. My uncle will need to be told, of course, and perhaps we could bring a runner into the household. Your staff will need to be questioned on the brandy's origins, and then—"

"Cam, move in here?" James had heard very little after that. Eden's snort of laughter made him feel better. If she was laughing, surely that meant she was feeling better.

"This, madam, is not funny. I have no wish to have your brother living with me."

"He can use his senses to protect you until we know who is behind the attempts on your life."

James took a large swallow of tea. A Sinclair living in his house? He'd rather wear a hair shirt.

"If it were only you, Raven, then of course I would not even consider moving into this gloomy mausoleum," Cam added, winking at his sisters. "However, Samantha's welfare must also be taken into account."

"I have yet to get it redecorated," James said defensively. He knew the house was exactly as Cam had described. When it had been just him it had not seemed to matter; after all, he had spent the majority of his time in this room, which was decorated to his tastes. "And I am able to care for my sister, thank you very much."

"My aunt is very good with colors and decorations, James," Essie chipped in from the sofa. "I will ask her to come and visit with you. You can then discuss your needs and she will see to it they are carried out."

"Ah— I think I would rather—"

"Not scared of a little old lady are you, Raven?" Devon slapped him on the back.

Before he could comment further, the siblings had risen and were taking their leave.

"Cam will return in the morning, Raven. Shall I organize for a runner?" Devon questioned him. His earlier animosity appeared to have eased.

"I don't believe I agreed to his staying."

"Of course you did." This time Cam slapped him on the back. "Quiet as a mouse, James. You won't know I'm here."

"You cannot enter a room without raising your voice,"

James felt compelled to say.

"Already you know him so well," Devon drawled.

"And I shall organize the runner, Sinclair."

"As you wish, Raven, but I suggest you do so this very night."

James stared blankly around his parlor after the Sinclairs had left. What the hell had he just agreed to? Lady Wynburg was going to decorate his house and Cam was to move in. Shaking his head, James wondered when he had lost control of the evening, and more importantly, his life. He could do nothing to stop the smile at the memory of Eden resting on his chest. It was time to acknowledge the fact that he wanted her in his life.

He wanted her, yet knew he could not take a gently bred woman to bed without consequences. Did he care about her gift? No. Having her in his life would be beneficial to Samantha and he could make love to her whenever he chose to. He cared for her as much as he was able to care for another person, and surely that would be enough? However, he could not think of marriage with someone set on killing him. Then again, marrying Eden would ensure Samantha was safe if they were successful. Thoughts churning, he went to bed. His last thought as his lids finally grew heavy several hours later, was that surely Eden was practical enough not to expect a love match.

CHAPTER EIGHTEEN

"I will escort you, Miss Sinclair."

Eden shot her uncle's groom a frustrated look. She was used to riding alone, yet here in London she was forced to have a constant companion.

"I am meeting my brother in the park, Cooper, therefore I am sure I can—"

"I will just see you there then, Miss Eden."

Eden looked at the determined jaw of the groom.

"My aunt and uncle told you to do this, didn't they?" Cooper merely smiled and fell in behind her as they made their way through the quiet streets of London.

Waking at dawn, Eden had pulled on her riding habit and left the house. After a night spent dreaming of James and her father, she had woken weary and worried, yet determined to talk with Dev. James had been right in this, he did deserve to know, and it would be good to have someone else aware of what she had suffered. Yawning, Eden guided her horse around a cart where enticing smells filled the air.

"What are you selling, sir?" she asked the vendor.

The man lifted his craggy eyebrows, then rubbed the end of his red nose and said, "Pies, my lady."

"I am a mere miss, sir. Cooper," Eden turned to speak to

her groom, "Do you want a pie?"

"I—ah…."

Cooper appeared to be struck mute by her question, so Eden decided for him.

"I find I am hungry and I know my brother will be. Therefore I think, kind sir, we will take three." She dug around in the pocket of her habit for some of the coins she always carried, because Dev insisted upon it. Supposedly if she ever got into trouble they would buy her out of it.

"Meat or fruit?" the man said, looking from Eden to the footman.

Eden looked at Cooper, who appeared to have swallowed his tongue, and said, "I will have fruit, however Cooper and my brother will have meat."

Minutes later, Eden carried Devon's wrapped pie on her lap while she ate hers.

"Must you ride behind me, Cooper? My neck hurts from twisting to see you."

The groom nudged his mount forward and fell in beside her, and they ate in companionable silence the rest of the way to the park. Popping the last piece of fruit-laden pastry into her mouth, Eden dusted off her hands then looked around for her brother.

"Can you see my brother, Cooper? The eldest one."

The groom immediately stood up in his stirrups to look for Devon.

"I see him up ahead, Miss Eden. Just at the end of that stretch."

Taking several deep breaths of crisp morning air, Eden filled her lungs and urged her horse forward. Dev was riding alone, steam rising from his horse's rump as she neared. She loved him, therefore she was biased, but surely he was the most handsome man ever to ride a horse. Eden ruthlessly squashed the image of a certain handsome duke that had popped into her head.

"I had thought to let you sleep in this morning, sister. Last night was very taxing on everyone."

"I like to ride," Eden accepted his kiss before handing him the pie.

"What have you done?" Devon said, unwrapping the offering and taking a large bite.

"Why do I have to have done something to bring my brother a pie?" Eden stalled, because now that the time had come to tell him she was no longer sure it was the right decision.

"What's the matter, Eden?"

She didn't speak for several seconds, her eyes looking forward, focused intently on something in the distance.

"Talk to me, love, we have no secrets between us," Dev said, stroking one of her cheeks.

"Dev…."

"Yes?"

"Let's walk," Eden urged her mount forward, and he fell in beside her. "Did you ever wonder why I turned to you instead of our father, Dev?"

"Yes, but I never minded, you know that, Eden. I was honored to have you look to me for love and support."

Eden bit her lip as emotion threatened to choke her. She had to tell him before she could not.

"I love you too, Dev, so much."

Swallowing the last of his pie, he then held out a hand. Eden took it, gripping it hard and then slowly, haltingly, she began to tell him what their father had done to her. His breath hissed and he snarled but remained silent until she had finished.

"My God, that bastard!"

"He never hurt me, Dev, he just—"

"Made your life a living hell from which you had no escape.

Christ, Eden, you should have told me, and if not me then Mother!"

She looked at him then. His eyes were narrowed, jaw clenched.

"I could not, he said he would punish whoever I told, and that the family would suffer. He always spoke of what would happen if our senses were exposed. How we would be ridiculed, treated like circus acts or worse."

Surprise had Eden gasping as Dev lifted her out of her saddle and settled her before him. His big body shook as he held her close. Her hat went flying as he buried his face in her hair.

"Forgive me, Eden."

His words were hoarse, his breathing harsh. Wrapping her arms around his shoulders, she held him as tight as she could.

"It was not your fault, Dev. I did not tell you to punish you, I—I told you because I no longer wanted to carry this burden myself. I am sorry if my selfishness has hurt you."

James saw Devon and Eden as he rode into the park. They stood in the middle of a stretch of grass with only a groom beside them. Quickly he moved to their side and signaled for the groom to take Eden's horse's reins. Murmuring a few instructions, he managed to guide them all beneath some trees where they would be sheltered from prying eyes. Devon's shoulders were shaking but he was making no sound, unlike his sister who was crying loud, heart-wrenching sobs. It was obvious from their distress that she had taken his advice and told her brother what their father had made her do.

"You could never be selfish, Eden," Devon finally said, easing his head back to look at his sister. "Were he not dead, I would kill him for what he has done to you."

Eden sniffed loudly, and James wanted to take her from her

brother's arms and comfort her himself.

"Please, Dev, I do not want you to be angry. I just need to feel at peace. This fear and anger—dear God, it has been destroying me. I have listened to you all talk of him with love and laughter, yet I could feel none of it."

James agreed with the eldest Sinclair at that moment. He'd kill the bastard who sired her himself were he alive.

"Here, Eden."

The siblings looked at James in surprise, neither having heard him arrive. It was Devon who took the handkerchief and wiped his sister's eyes.

"James told me to tell you this, Dev. We talked last night, after I found Samantha crying."

"I came upon your sister talking to mine, Sinclair, and overheard her discussing her own father." James took up the explanation as his eyes lingered on Eden's face.

Her riding habit was soft dove gray with black braid marching in a line down the front. Her hat was missing and her hair bundled into a loose knot on her head. Even with red-rimmed eyes and pale cheeks she was stunning, and his belief that she was the woman for him strengthened. Surely they could live a comfortable life once he had satisfied this need for her.

You are gentleman not an animal, James, he reminded himself.

"Dev, we cannot tell the others."

James focused on the conversation Eden was having with her brother once more.

"No, I think it best we keep this to ourselves."

"Should I not have told you?"

"No love, Raven was right in urging you to tell me. In the last few years before his death, I became aware of the man our father was, and I am only sorry that I was unable to protect you from him."

Eden grabbed her brother's lapels in a fierce grip, and James thought again about the prospect of having this woman as his wife. Surely he could tame her given time?

"No one knew because he wished it that way. Even Mother, who was closest to him, did not know."

"She always took the peaceful road, Eden, try not to resent her for that," Devon said.

"I don't. I loved her so much, Dev. Yet sometimes I was angry that she did not stop him."

With a final kiss, Devon placed her back on her horse. "I need to ride hard, Eden. Will you see her back, Raven?"

"Of course." James nodded. The man looked as if the Devil himself sat firmly on his shoulder. He needed time to digest what his sister had told him.

They watched him ride away, Eden biting her lip and sniffing, James contemplating what to say to someone who was obviously hurting deeply. He had never been good with words or emotions, but he was learning. Samantha was seeing to his education.

"I have been thinking, Eden, and believe the best option for everyone is for us to wed." The words had come out so quickly it seemed to take her a moment to grasp their meaning.

"What!" When she did, she spun to look at him, nearly unseating herself. His hand shot out to steady her.

"You get on well with Samantha, and if you marry me I will tell no one about…." James waved his hand toward her ears, stumbling to a halt when he saw her expression.

He suddenly had a feeling of impending doom. Had he worded his intent wrongly? It was hard to say, as he could read nothing in her face. The grief of moments before had fallen away to be replaced by a cool facade. Should he have delayed this conversation for a better moment?

"Eden—"

"How kind of you to offer for my hand with the intent that

I would be a suitable companion for your sister. Let us also not forget the threat that should I not concede then you will no longer keep our secrets safe, when just last night you promised you would do that without proviso."

"No, that's not what I meant. I—"

"It can mean nothing else," she interrupted him.

"I would provide for you and any children we may have. You would want for nothing," James plowed on, determined to state his case now he had made the decision to do so.

"And what of love?"

James tweaked his necktie, as it was suddenly restricting his breathing.

"Of course if you love me I will—"

"If I love you? How dare you! You bloody arrogant, conceited— How dare you offer for me in such a clod-handed manner."

"Most women would be honored to have a proposal from me!" James flared, stung by her words. He was a duke, for God's sake!

"Eden, I am not capable of love, I need you to understand that." James attempted to explain the man he was. He had bungled the entire proposal, he knew that now. Just looking at Eden's raised chin told him he would be best to retreat and regroup, but he had never been the type to do either.

"I would never marry a man who wed me only to stop others from knowing what a freak I was," Eden hissed. "A man who is not capable of love yet will accept the emotion in his wife. A m-man—"

Hell, she was crying again.

"A man who is merely marrying me to care for his s-sister."

"Eden, you are deliberately misinterpreting my words."

"Am I, Duke? Then tell me if you could ever love me?"

Why could he not find the right words to say.

"Your sister has my pity, Duke. Because she needs love, and it seems you are incapable of giving her what she most needs."

"I love my sister!"

Shut up, you foolish man. James could have bitten off his tongue.

She looked at him for long drawn-out seconds before saying, "So it is just me you are incapable of loving then."

Eden summoned her groom, who was loitering a few feet away trying to appear indifferent to their conversation. Urging her horse into a gallop, she rode away from him. He followed seconds later, trailing behind them until they reached the Wynburg residence. When she was inside the gates, he headed for his own house, wondering how the hell he had got everything so wrong.

Handing his horse to the groom, James stomped inside thinking about Eden. He would have to apologize, but wasn't sure she would accept it. God, woman were complex creatures. His life had been simple and uncomplicated before the Sinclairs had ventured into it. It had also been empty, he reminded himself.

"Your Grace, Mr. Sinclair is now in residence." Buttles appeared before him.

"Good God, already?"

"It would appear Mr. Sinclair is an early riser, your Grace. As is a Mr. Brown, who is keeping him company in the green parlor," he added, taking James's coat and hat.

"And that is all I need for my day to deteriorate further," James muttered, making his way to the green parlor. Inside he found a large neatly dressed man with blunt features and a bald head talking to Cam. Both rose as he entered.

"James, come and meet Mr. Brown, he is a representative from the Bow Street Runners. He received your summons."

"Mr. Brown," James said, pushing thoughts of Eden aside.

He would return to them later when her brother was not nearby. "I had not expected to hear from Bow Street at such an early hour."

"You are a duke, if I may speak frankly, your Grace. My superior does not like to tarry when summoned by a man of your station."

At least someone respected his title.

"Mr. Sinclair has been telling me of the attempts on your life, including the suspected poisoning last night here in your home."

"How thoughtful of him," James drawled, sinking into a seat. He was rarely tired, yet it seemed to be a constant state after an encounter with a Sinclair, and the day had only just begun.

"I believe you have employed the services of one Mr. Spriggot, and with your permission I will have a chat with him about his progress before I settle myself in here, your Grace?"

Pinching the bridge of his nose, James wondered why he was surprised that he was now to be burdened with a Sinclair and a runner. His life had always been orderly and controlled, yet now it was anything but. In fact, it was like a runaway carriage, which he could only partly blame on the Sinclairs no matter how much he wished otherwise.

"And in what capacity will you live here, Mr. Brown?"

"A footman, your Grace. Mr. Sinclair and I have come up with an excellent cover for my appearance in your household."

"This should be good."

Cam merely smiled at James's words.

"If you will inform the staff you have employed me as a favor, as I served under you during a campaign?" Mr. Brown said, looking very pleased with his story. Beside him Cam nodded, endorsing the idea. "I may seem a bit on the rough side if an explanation is not offered."

"James?"

Looking at the door, James saw his sister's head appear.

"Good morning, Samantha." He held out a hand. The gesture was natural to him now, and when she hurried forward to place her fingers in his it went some way to easing the turmoil his meeting with Eden had created inside him.

"I'd like you to meet Mr. Brown. He fought beside me during a campaign, and is in need of a position now he has returned to London. He is to be one of our new footmen."

He had told her nothing of the attempts on his life and had no plans to. Hopefully he would find whoever was responsible before they succeeded.

"How do you do, Mr. Brown," Samantha said, as if she were introduced to the staff every day. However, James wanted Samantha to be aware of Mr. Brown. If there was any trouble and he and Cam were not there, it would be Mr. Brown she could turn to now he had linked himself to the man.

"Are you having tea, James?"

Laughing for the first time that day, James tweaked one of her curls. "I am yet to have breakfast, minx, however I suppose I could manage tea, especially if cook puts some of those apple tarts you're partial to on the plate."

"Apple tarts!"

"Yes, Cam, they are the very best and seeing as you are now living here to help James with his library, you will get to eat them too," Samantha stated.

"Excuse me for a moment, Samantha, Cam; I will introduce Mr. Brown to Buttles." Rising from his seat, James left them discussing the merits of apple against cherry tarts. Finding his butler, he then made the introductions and left Mr. Brown in Buttles's care after ordering tea.

"So how was your ride, James?"

"Very good thank you, Samantha," he said, avoiding Cam's

eyes as he returned to his chair.

"Did you see my siblings? I believe they were riding this morning also."

"I did." James did not elaborate and felt Cam's eyes on him. He would go to his study soon, and there he would work through what must be done to get Eden to be his wife, because now he had made the decision it had become a burning need inside him to do so.

"So it is just me you are incapable of loving then."

Her words had settled uncomfortably inside his head. Could he love her, now he had already admitted loving Samantha? Surely if the emotion was inside him, then it could be shared?

Squeezing his eyes shut, James prayed the day deteriorated no further. If it did, he may just lock the door to his study and to hell with everyone beyond it.

CHAPTER NINETEEN

"We have many invitations, my darlings! Tonight we are attending the theatre and as you know tomorrow is the Simpkin ball, and of course next Friday we are… um."

Eden looked up from her toast as her aunt stuttered to a halt. She had not heard much of the conversation, but the stutter had drawn her attention.

"We agreed they would come to no harm with us all there, Sally."

"Are you sure, Elijah? They are such innocents," Lady Wynburg said, pleating her napkin.

"What are you both discussing?" Essex said. The twins were also looking at their aunt, Warwick was lost in a plate of food as usual.

"Your uncle has given you both permission to attend the Middleton-Smythe masquerade ball next Friday, and I am unsure such an event is suitable for two young ladies in their first season," Lady Wynburg said, glaring at her husband.

"A masquerade?" Essie murmured. "Why do you not wish us to attend, Aunt?"

"They are very smoky affairs. People think because they are covered by masks and costumes they are at liberty to behave in an inappropriate manner."

"Not always, Sally, and I fail to see how too much can happen in a ballroom filled with people. So they may dance too close to a man or converse on subjects a little more outrageous than every other evening. Let them have fun." The Earl gave his wife a smile that spoke of his feelings for her. "If I remember correctly, you fell madly in love with me at just such an evening—"

"Elijah!" Lady Wynburg gasped.

This was true love, Eden thought, and she would accept nothing less. Her heart ached just thinking of James's proposal. Until that moment she had not realized that she loved him, yet the pain she had felt at his cold words had been swift and fierce, forcing her to realize how deep her feelings went for him. But she would not marry him if he could not return those feelings, in that she was adamant.

"Is it a fancy dress with masks, Aunt?"

"Yes, Essie dear, and we will go shopping today to get your outfits. Your brothers too must be appropriately dressed."

"And I will take these three terrors to the park and we shall have to have an ice from Gunthers on the return journey, for I will be quite fatigued by then."

Squeals of delight greeted Lord Wynburg's words, followed by kisses and hugs from everyone except Warwick, who was still steadily consuming his food.

"Are you sure, Uncle? I do not want you to be overburdened by these three. Perhaps I should accompany you?"

One large hand covered Eden's as she finished speaking. "Devon is coming with me, Eden. He has things he wishes to discuss."

"Do I hear my name?"

"Dev!" Dorrie and Somer squealed, launching themselves at him.

Putting one under each arm, he spun them round several

times before lowering them back into their seats. He then ruffled his little brother's hair before kissing his aunt and Essie. Cupping Eden's face, he placed a gentle kiss on her forehead.

"I am well, Eden, don't fret," he whispered so only she could hear.

Nodding, she lifted her teacup and sipped. Cam arrived minutes later to the same greeting from the girls, and soon he too was seated with a large plate of food before him.

"I understand you have been staying with the Duke for the past week, Cam. To help him catalogue his maps? Surely you could do that from next door; after all, it is not as if he lives streets away."

"I am sure he has his reasons, Sally. Now, I must just run a few things past Devon. You three terrors go and gather your things, we will leave shortly," Lord Wynburg said.

Dev had not told Aunt Sally, only their uncle, about the threat to the Duke's life, and he had offered his assistance in any capacity should it be required.

"And we must also leave, ladies," Lady Wynburg added.

Eden was collecting her bonnet when she heard a knock on her door. Opening it, she found Dev outside.

"May I talk to you, Eden?"

"Of course." Standing to one side, she motioned for him to enter, closing it behind him.

"Cam and I rode with Raven this morning, you however were noticeably absent."

"I wanted to sleep late." What she had wanted, in fact, was to avoid seeing James. But she would not tell her brother that.

"He asked after you... several times actually. In fact he seemed disturbed that you were not riding."

Eden said nothing to this.

"What lies between you and the Duke, Eden?"

"I—Why would you asked me that?" As her knees felt

suddenly weak, Eden sat on the bed. She had expected him to question her further about their father, not the Duke.

"Just answer the question," her brother said, impaling her with a steady look.

"No, I bloody will not!"

Dev smiled. "I am pleased society has not managed to chisel away all your hoydenish tendencies."

"I have no wish to continue this discussion."

"Yet you will."

"No." Eden shook her head. "And you have no right to ask me to."

"As your guardian I have every right."

The bed dipped as he settled beside her.

"Listen carefully now, love. Because as a man who has lived in society and among these people I have knowledge of how men like Raven work."

"He is not a piece of farming equipment."

"He is, however, not a man to toy with, Eden. Men of our breed are not malleable fools like most of the male populace who fawn upon your every word. He is a man who understands the power he holds in this country. A man of considerable wealth and one who is linked to our family, for better or worse."

"There is no need for this, Dev, I assure you."

Ignoring her, he continued. "My original dislike of the Duke stemmed from his obvious interest in you, Eden, no matter how much he fought to hide it. But should you and he come to an agreement, then I would not stand in your way, as I have never doubted his honor. Although I question his ability to make you happy."

Eden tamped down the little spark of hope at her brother's words.

"He is incapable of love, Dev. So you can rest easy that there will ever be anything between us."

"And how do you know this?"

"I just do, so leave it alone if you please."

"Has he hurt you in some way?"

"He was honest," Eden said, refusing to acknowledge the pain James had inflicted on her.

Dev took her hand in his.

"He seems to care for Samantha a great deal."

"Yes, she is the only one he loves."

"He told you that?"

She nodded. Why did it hurt so much to know he could not love her? Surely he had given her no reason to believe he ever could.

Except those kisses, Eden thought. They were from a man who should be able to love.

"He was raised without love, Eden; that cannot have been easy."

"No, it cannot, and perhaps that is why he will never love a woman, only his sister. Maybe he has the capacity to only care for one person?"

"Do you love him?"

"It matters not what I feel for him, only that he can never care for me. Therefore, this conversation is meaningless."

Something in her tone must have stopped further enquiry. "Very well, but should you wish to discuss this further, then please come and speak with me."

"I will. Now I have a question for you, brother."

He nodded for her to continue.

"Why do you dislike Miss Braithwaite so vehemently, when in fact she is no different from many, and politer than some?"

Dev's teeth snapped together as his face drew into a grim mask.

"I told you to stay away from her."

"You did, but of course Essie and I have not. Therefore,

perhaps you should enlighten me as to why you have formed such a dislike for the woman?"

"I have told you why, and cannot believe you have gone against my wishes in this matter."

"We have merely conversed with her in a social setting, nothing more," Eden said, glad the conversation had moved from her to him.

"Good, ensure you keep it that way."

Eden had never seen her brother so visibly upset by a woman before. It was intriguing, and she really needed to talk further with Miss Braithwaite to ascertain why. Yes, the woman had hideous fashion sense, and appeared to behave in silly manner when in society. However, after observing her closely, Eden was almost certain there was more to her.

"Are you all right, Dev? I mean after what I told you about our father."

"Yes. What you said shocked me, but in truth I should have realized what he was capable of."

"I hate him."

"As you have every right to, love, but to heal you must at least try to forgive him."

"Such a wise man you are, brother."

"Experienced more than wise, sister."

"And now I need to go, because I can hear Essie calling for me, as the carriage is waiting." She kissed Dev's cheek. "Don't worry about me, I shall be just fine, and there will be a handsome prince out there somewhere whom I shall tumble madly in love with."

"Perhaps," he said, getting to his feet and pulling her up beside him. "Or perhaps you have already found him."

On these ominous words he led her from the room.

CHAPTER TWENTY

Fourteen days after his disastrous attempt at securing Eden's hand in marriage, James lay on his back staring at the canopy above his bed. Having just opened his eyes, one would think he would be rested; alas, that was not the case. His sleep had been filled with restless dreams and visions of that raven-haired witch.

He had attended every event and social gathering the Sinclairs were also attending, and still James had not managed to get Eden alone. She was always otherwise engaged when he asked her to dance. She was polite in her attempts to rebuff him, he'd give the little witch that. *"Oh forgive me, Duke, I have promised this dance to another,"* or *"I am afraid I must refuse, Duke, my hem is torn and I must fix it at once."* He was sure she'd had more torn hems or flounces in one season than other women had in three.

"Your bath is drawn, your Grace," his manservant called from the foot of the bed.

"Thank you, Brenton."

He was tired but the minute he closed his eyes his sleep was filled with dreams of a highly sensual nature involving Eden. Beneath him, on top of him, in each vision she would look at him, her gray eyes filled with the need that rampaged through his body.

She had men dangling after her, and that blithering, brainless twit Lord Cowley on a string. Picking up his pillow he gave it a good thump then hurled it across the room, narrowly missing his manservant, who retrieved it and replaced it at the bottom of his bed without blinking.

What the hell was the matter with him? No woman had ever made him behave like this. He was a Duke, for Christ's sake, he commanded and ordered and he was never ignored. Damn her!

"No more," he said, rolling out of bed. "I will stand for this no more. Tonight she will talk to me."

Thirty minutes later he was washed and dressed and on his way downstairs. The problem was he was jealous, and the emotion was as foreign to him as many others. Muttering under his breath, he headed for his breakfast parlor, maybe a full stomach would ease his anger.

"Did the cow poo really make your feet warm then?"

Walking into his breakfast room, he looked at Cam who was talking with his sister… correction, teaching his sister bad habits, he realized as Samantha picked up her saucer and drank from it.

"Yes, we would follow the cows around then quickly take off our shoes and—"

"Yes, thank you, Cambridge, I believe we have the general idea," James said, glowering at the younger man then at his sister until she giggled.

"Coffee please, Buttles," James said, filling his plate and then taking a seat at the table. The problem with having a Sinclair in the house was that they didn't do anything quietly. In the days since Cam had arrived, he had learned everything about him and his siblings. If a thought came into Cambridge Sinclair's head it came out his mouth seconds later.

"Jane and I are going to visit Somer and Dorrie this morning, James."

"That will be nice," James smiled at his sister. Her brown

eyes sparkled; no longer world weary and sad, they glowed as every young girl's should. Her cheeks were a healthy pink and anyone looking at her would not guess the life she had been forced to live with their sadistic father. His personal life may be turning into a carriage wreck but at least his relationship with his sister was flourishing.

"Would you like me to come with you? We could bring along the tales of Robinson Crusoe?"

"No thank you, James, we are going to play with our dolls today," Samantha said, getting off her chair.

"And are you happy with Jane?" he said, doing the same.

"Oh yes, she is a wonderful companion, James."

At least he could make one of the ladies in his life happy, he thought, bending to give her a kiss on the cheek. She in turn wrapped her arms around his neck and hugged him hard.

"Buttles will call the carriage for you, and please make sure you have warm clothing on before you leave. Is Lucinda going with you?" Lucinda was her new doll.

"Yes, and it is warm outside today, James, so I will not need a coat."

"All right, but—"

"James." Samantha looked up at him with her hands braced on her hips. "I promise to stay warm and act politely, you really have no need to worry."

He swallowed his smile and nodded.

"Very well, I shall fuss no more."

She kissed him again and ran from the room, and he stood looking at the door while the lump in his throat subsided.

"She is a lovely young lady, James. It seems you are both comfortable with each other now."

"Yes she is, and we are," James said, reseating himself. He picked up his fork and was soon swallowing a mouthful of kidneys.

"Funny things, sisters."

James grunted, not terribly keen to get into this conversation, especially as one of the sisters concerned was driving him to the brink of madness.

"Take Eden, for example. She has been acting very strange of late. Bit my head off last night for no apparent reason that I can see."

Looking at Cam, James could have sworn his intent was nothing more than idle chitchat, and yet….

"She said that I was just like all the other men she had recently met, besides her sainted Devon, of course. Totally without either compassion or emotion, and unable to form a rational thought that anyone would care to listen to, which I found quite harsh considering I was dancing with her. I mean, if not from a sense of duty why would I be partnering my own sister, who can blister me with one look, rather than some docile sweet-natured debutante?"

James grunted again, although this time he was feeling a little more in harmony with the world, knowing Eden was not quite as happy as she appeared.

"Of course, you're the problem," Cam added, destroying James's newfound sense of well-being with those five simple words.

"What?"

"Why the hell don't you just apologize and then we can all have some peace. The woman's a veritable fountain of ill humor and it is us, her family, who are suffering."

"How do you know I have something to apologize for?" James said, indignant. He had done nothing wrong.

Cam merely raised an eyebrow and continued eating.

"She is a shrew," James snapped, then realizing who he was talking to, he apologized.

Waving his fork around, Cam said, "Think nothing of it. I

totally agree with you. However, she is my shrew, therefore I will not have her hurt."

And just like that Devon made an appearance in his younger brother. The protector was back, ready to do battle if needed. Sighing, James picked up his cup. All he wanted was to eat his breakfast in peace; was it too much to ask?

"What did you say to her?"

None of your bloody business, James thought. "I told her I was incapable of love," he muttered seconds later.

"That seems a rather serious conversation, James. One hopes it was preceded by an offer of marriage," Cam said, impaling him with an icy look.

"Of course it was! Do I look like the sort of man to talk of such things in a random fashion?" James growled, and then realizing he had just declared his hand to Eden's brother he picked up his coffee and gulped it, burning the inside of his mouth. Several vile curses spilled from his lips as he struggled to breathe.

"And Eden turned you down?" Cam said, apparently now enjoying himself hugely, if the smile on his face was any indication.

"Yes," James rasped.

"What did you say to her?"

Why not? he thought. His life was fast becoming an open book, so why not cut open a few more pages.

"I explained that by marrying me she would ensure my silence about your family's peculiarities, and that she was good with Samantha, and that I would provide well for her."

It was now Cam's turn to choke, only like everything else he did, he did not hold back. James watched as he coughed several drops of tea onto the tablecloth.

"What?" James said, not liking the mixture of humor and pity in the man's eyes.

"There is little doubt you have a way with words, James." This was apparently amusing, as Cam started crowing with laughter once more. "L-lord, 'tis a wonder she left you with all your l-limbs intact," he managed to stutter out.

James was rapidly regretting the impulse of confiding in Cambridge. It must be because he was tired. Disgusted, he took another small sip of his coffee and waited for his companion to stop laughing.

"F-forgive m-me, I did not mean to laugh at you."

"Obviously," James drawled.

"You have to understand, James."

"For Christ's sake, man, just spit it out."

"The thing is, James, Devon has pummeled into each of us that we must marry for love first and comfort second."

Hence Eden's reaction.

"It may seem odd when one considers the man my eldest brother portrays himself to be. But he cares deeply for each of us, and once told us that to see us in an unhappy marriage would be a torture he could never bear. Therefore we promised him. When you offered for Eden in such a cold, unemotional manner, she would have been deeply disappointed and, I believe, deeply hurt, hence her current behavior."

James nodded. She would have been hurt if she cared for him. Did she care for him? The thought should not please him quite as much as it did.

"Do you attend the masquerade this evening, James?"

"Dear God, no!" James shuddered. He loathed masquerades. He could never identify anyone, and could end up talking to his worst enemy—if he knew who that was, of course. When had life become so complicated? He laid the blame firmly at the door of the Sinclairs; it seemed the easiest option.

"Eden attends, and from what I gather her costume is of the revealing variety."

"What the hell does that mean?"

"I shall just head to town and get us a couple of costumes, James, and then you will be able to find out firsthand."

"I hate masquerades," James grumbled.

"Your Grace, a Mr. Spriggot has arrived and is asking to see you."

"Thank you, Buttles. Have Mr. Brown serve Mr. Spriggot tea and I will be down shortly," he directed his butler. "I would like you to come to this meeting, Cam, if you have the time."

"Of course. Could you tell your cook to use less cinnamon in the buns; Samantha has a small allergy to it."

It was a testament to how his life had changed and how he had accepted the peculiarities of the Sinclairs that James merely nodded at Cam's suggestion and made a mental note to speak to Mrs. Gotheram.

Mr. Spriggot looked his usual bland innocuous self, his head wrapped and pomaded with several carefully placed strands of hair. He stood as James and Cam walked into the parlor.

"Your Grace, I have just been making the acquaintance of Mr. Brown, an excellent addition to your household, if I may be so bold. He has given me the details of the poisoning —very nasty business."

Waving the man back into his seat, James and Cam took theirs.

"Yes, it was a close thing. What news do you have for us, Mr. Spriggot?"

"I believe I have a lead on the men who attempted to murder you. Both are from a small village not far from your home, your Grace. Hired thugs, I am afraid, who I doubt have any links to whoever hired them."

James had thought this would be the case.

"I have eliminated your father's two brothers and their wives, and several cousins. I have yet to track down your heir, but as you stated you do not believe he is involved, I am not overly concerned about him."

James nodded. The man was thorough, which was what he was paying him to be.

"I am afraid the next news I have for you, your Grace, is of a more disturbing nature that you may wish to hear in private," Mr. Spriggot said, looking James in the eye.

"I will have the tea replenished, your Grace," Mr. Brown said, rising to leave the room. Buttles walked in as the Bow Street Runner walked out.

"Your Grace, Lord Sinclair has arrived," Buttles said.

"Of course he has," James said, looking at the ceiling. "Send him in then, Buttles; it seems my life is to be an open book."

"You get used to it, James." Cam slapped him on the back.

Devonshire Sinclair strode into the room, instantly filling up the remaining spaces.

"Raven, pardon the intrusion," Dev said, looking anything but repentant.

"Think nothing of it, Sinclair. Mr. Spriggot here was about to share with us a startling secret he has unearthed, and as removing you both would be a herculean effort that I do not have the strength for this morning, take a seat."

Devon shook hands with the investigator, then seated himself beside his brother. James wasn't sure why he wanted them there; perhaps because these men were responsible for his safety, even if he did not wish them to be.

"Speak, sir, these men are bent on the same purpose as I, to find whoever is trying to kill me, and I would trust them to keep their silence." *As I will keep mine*, he added to himself.

"Through my investigations, your Grace, I fear I have made some discoveries of an alarming nature in concern with your father."

"Everything about my father was alarming, Mr. Spriggot. He

was a vile, evil-tempered man who cared only for himself. I am sure nothing you say will shock me."

Mr. Spriggot looked uncomfortable. "As you are aware, your father had two wives, the first your mother and the second, Lady Samantha's mother. But you may not be aware that your father also took many mistresses, your Grace, and it appears that two of those mistresses had five children between them."

"And where are these mistresses and children, Mr. Spriggot?" Devon questioned when James failed to speak.

Dear Christ, James thought. Why had he not considered this possibility?

"Three are in France with their mother and two are here in England. Their mother has passed on."

"What relevance do these revelations have to the investigation and the attempts on the Duke's life?" Cam questioned.

"Miss Tolly, the late Duke's second mistress, died a very slow and painful death of a wasting disease that affected her lungs. Her son and daughter nursed her and when they ran out of money for food they approached the late Duke for support. He turned them away. The townspeople I spoke with told me the Tolly family was left homeless and on the streets. The mother did not last much longer without care."

"My father abandoned them?" James said, his voice hoarse.

"It appears that way, your Grace. The family traveled from town to town living on the goodwill of the people until their mother died. I have tracked them to Dover but the trail ran cold after that."

James felt sick. His palms were sweating, his breathing shallow. Climbing to his feet, he paced to the windows. *If I could lay my hands on you, sire, I would tear you apart.* How could one man be so evil?

"And you believe that these Tollys could be behind the

attempts on the Duke's life?"

James listened as Cam and Devon questioned Mr. Spriggot on his behalf.

He and Samantha had half brothers and sisters. The thought shocked him more than it should. He knew what his father had been, yet not once had he considered that he may have sired more children.

"I can neither confirm nor deny that, Lord Sinclair. Yet I believe it must be a possibility until it can be discounted."

"Of course. Please do what you must, Mr. Spriggot, and report to the Duke with any findings," Devon said. James watched him rise and usher the investigator from the room.

"I shall head into town, James, and get our costumes," Cam said, getting to his feet when his brother returned. He walked forward and gripped James's shoulder before leaving the room.

Minutes passed and slowly James managed to haul in a steady, calming breath. Only then did Devon begin to speak.

"When Eden told me what our father had done to her, I knew I had failed in the one thing I had vowed since she first turned to me as a babe. I had failed to protect her, and no words could have comforted me at that time. To realize that the man I had known as my father was in fact a monster who mistreated my sister was a revelation that rocked the foundations I walked upon. For men like us who live with order and control, caring for those we love is entrenched within us, and when something happens to tilt our world it is very hard to readjust the balance."

James listened as Devon spoke, taking in each word while he sorted through the turmoil inside his head.

"Changes are happening, Raven, for better or worse, and I would offer my support if you should need it in any capacity."

James, who had turned to face the window, felt Devon draw closer. He laid a hand on James's shoulder as Cam had done.

"In death he can no longer cause harm, James. Do not allow

what he did in life to consume you. Give freedom to your rage and then find a way to fix the wrongs."

James exhaled as he heard the door closing softly behind Devon. Staggering sideways, he fell into the nearest chair.

CHAPTER TWENTY ONE

"Get back to your room and put on the rest of those dresses at once!" Devon thundered.

Eden simply rolled her eyes as she and Essie continued down the stairs to join the family before leaving for the masquerade.

"I am serious!"

"Oooh, they look like mermaids," Dorrie said, ignoring her scowling brother and touching the silky fabric of Eden's skirts.

"I mean it!" Dev added loudly.

"Don't be so stodgy, Dev, they look like sea princesses," Somer said, walking behind Essie as she stepped off the bottom stair. "Your hair falls to your waist and it shimmers. What did your maid put in it?"

"Small pearls," Eden said, pulling a strand forward and bending to show her sisters how it had been attached.

"For God's sake, do not bend over like that when in company!"

"Devon, darling, relax. Your sisters are quite adequately covered and more so than many," Lady Wynburg said, taking the tense arm of her nephew.

Eden looked at her brother. He was handsome dressed as a pirate in fitted black breeches and a flowing white shirt.

"Adequately covered? I think not."

Essie giggled as Eden poked out her tongue.

"At least put on your cloaks before you get sick," he added as he removed his sword and handed it to Warwick, who inspected it thoroughly.

"I want one just like this," the young boy breathed, holding it reverently.

"And one day you shall." Eden rubbed his head.

Lord Wynburg walked into the room dressed as Henry the Eighth, the outfit suiting his large frame. His wife was dressed as one of his many wives, although Eden was uncertain which one.

"Now you three go to bed and we will tell you all about the masquerade in the morning," Lord Wynburg said, planting loud smacking kisses on the twins' cheeks. Warwick he merely kissed on the top of his head, which the boy seemed happy with.

After many hugs and kisses and well wishes they were soon in the carriages and on their way. Devon, Eden, and Essie in one and the Earl and Countess in the other, as the latter had suggested they would leave early to attend another gathering.

Eden hoped James did not attend tonight. Each evening she had forced herself to smile and laugh and pretend she was happy when in fact she was miserable. What luck to fall in love with a man who could not love her back? A man with deep emotional scars from a father who had not loved him. She had avoided him as best she could, and yet for some reason he insisted on asking her to dance. Solemn faced, he would make his request, and each time she would tell him she was promised to another. He would then bow and walk away, but not before she saw the flash of anger in his eyes. What had he to be angry about? It was he who had hurt her.

"We are here, Eden."

Surprised, she looked at the hand Dev held out to her. She

had not even felt the carriage stop.

"I would ask you to treat the Duke fairly tonight, Eden. The man has suffered a shock today that would in any other man have him staying behind locked doors."

"What sort of shock?" Eden asked, hating the fear that pooled in the pit of her stomach.

"That is for him to tell you, not I."

"Perhaps had he treated me fairly I would do the same to him!" Eden snapped, and was instantly ashamed of her petulant behavior. The man had turned her into a shrew. She was subjected to one of her brother's steady looks, which made her toes curl inside her evening slippers.

"I am aware that something has happened between you and the Duke, yet as you will not tell me what, I ask only that if you encounter him you are polite."

Eden nodded stiffly but said nothing further. They followed several other guests through the front doors, where they handed over their cloaks and then joined the line to greet their hosts.

She should not have come. Her humors were foul and the dress that in the privacy of her bedroom had looked lovely now suddenly felt gaudy, exposing far too much of her body. Pulling her hair forward, she hid her chest.

The ballroom was a riot of color. Flowers and silk streamers hung from the walls and a huge fountain cascaded water high upon a dais. Everyone wore masks. Eden saw a shepherdess and a gypsy and many Henry the Eighths.

"Good Lord," Dev whispered.

"Is it too much for you to see?" Eden questioned, taking his arm. Sometimes an explosion of color could affect him, even blinding him momentarily. It would be many times worse if he were to use his other sight.

"I will be all right once I become accustomed to it," he said, slowly making his way down the stairs.

"Cam will spend the whole night sniffing," Eden whispered, "and Essie will want to taste every delicious morsel."

"Ahhh gluttony," Essie sighed, "my gravest sin."

"Incoming from the left," Dev drawled making Eden and Essie's heads turn in that direction. "Behave yourselves, sisters, I see a Cleopatra in need of a dance partner."

As Dev left, the Frenchman arrived with eyes only for Eden's sister.

"Lord Laurent." Essie sank into a curtsey, her smile wide as she rose.

"Miss Sinclair, will you allow me to say I have never seen a more beautiful mermaid."

"My sister is also a mermaid, my lord."

Eden watched color flood the Frenchman's cheeks beneath his black mask. Dressed as a naval officer, he certainly looked the part.

"Please excuse me, Miss Eden. I did not mean to offend you."

"No offence taken, Lord Laurent. Indeed, I agree with you completely, my sister is the most beautiful mermaid I have ever seen."

Essie blushed, her eyes fixed on the man at her side.

Eden liked him. He had easy manners but more importantly, he seemed enamored of her sister, which showed he had exquisite taste. Plus, Essie had told her that Lord Laurent was intending to live in England, and not return to France, which pleased her. If he and Essie did wed, then she would not lose her sister. Happy that Essie was in good hands, Eden accepted the invitation to dance with a Roman gladiator. At least if she was busy, she would not continually be looking for a certain duke.

James had arrived at the masquerade late after urging Cam out the door and assuring him he would attend. He had then spent a calming few hours with his little sister, who had assured him in his current outfit he would make every maiden swoon, which lifted his spirits considerably. He enjoyed her chatter and soothing company, desperate for any distraction to drive away the thought that somewhere in the world they had sisters and brothers who may need him—or at the least his money.

He had talked to a few people but he was not good company, and in fact contemplated leaving, but as that thought entered his head he saw Eden. His breath lodged in his chest as he took in the vision she presented.

She was some kind of sea creature, a mermaid he guessed. The bodice was blue and beneath it a sheath in the same color, over which was a gossamer overlay. Her hair was loose and sparkled as it caught the light. Matching ribbons were wound through her long curls and his hands itched to touch them, trail his fingers through the silk. Every time she dipped or curtseyed her breasts pushed against the bodice, and he wanted to plant his fist in the face of anyone who dared look—anyone, that is, but him.

He wanted to do more than just look. James ached to cup the flesh and taste her. His temper was boiling, his body hard, and he was feeling savage after days of torment. The leash he always had on his temper had slipped and the polite facade of the Duke of Raven cracked wide open.

Enough! he thought, pushing off the wall. He cut through the guests until he reached Eden as the music finished.

"Miss Sinclair, I beg of you, just one more dance."

"Alas, my gladiator, I fear we have already danced overmuch," Eden said gently.

"Eden, you will not dance with him."

The voice came from over her shoulder and she knew instantly to whom it belonged. For the first time that night she felt alive; her skin prickled and her fingers tingled. Turning, she found the Duke of Raven looking at her over the heads of several people. He was still some distance away, but she had heard his words clearly. People parted as he walked and she saw he was dressed entirely in black, from mask to his gleaming boots. Breeches molded his thighs, a flowing shirt was laced at the neck, and she could see his skin through the V at his collar.

"I-I…." Her throat felt suddenly dry as James advanced on her. Eden had the urge to run, but where would she run to? People crowded her in on all sides.

"I beg you, Miss Eden, just one more dance."

"She is dancing with me."

James reached them and stood before her.

"Excuse me, sir, Miss Eden and I were conversing," the gladiator said.

Eden was sure she did not want to dance with James. The look in his dark eyes was dangerous, and she knew it spelled trouble for her.

"She is dancing with me."

Before she could retreat, his fingers had clasped around hers.

"I-I am promised to another," Eden said, hating how breathless she sounded as he led her away.

"No, you are promised to me."

"I could never be with a man who cannot love me," she whispered furiously.

He didn't speak again, instead pulling her indecently close until their thighs were touching and her breasts crushed against his chest. She felt the anger in him, every muscle taut, and her body reacted traitorously.

"Please, James, I am asking you to release me," Eden said, uncaring that her voice shook.

"No."

The dance was both pleasure and pain. Pleasure to be held

in the arms of the man she loved, and pain because he could not love her back. His jaw remained clenched, his eyes on her face. Eden was not brave enough to return the look, so she concentrated on the laces of his shirt.

When the music finished, she turned to flee but James clamped his fingers around her arm and began walking. She had little option but to follow or make a scene. He moved slowly through the crowd, towing her behind him until they had reached a door that he opened and tugged her through.

"Release me!"

Ignoring her, he set off down a hall in long strides, his pace now faster. Eden was forced to trot to keep up with him. Using her other hand she tried to pry her wrist free but he refused to release her.

"James, let me go!"

He turned right and she lost her balance, so he hauled her to his side and half carried her up a set of stairs, then he began to test doors, opening and closing them until he found the one he wanted. Flinging it wide, he picked Eden up and carried her over the threshold. He lowered her to her feet and turned to shut and lock the door behind them.

The open curtains allowed the moonlight to flood the room and Eden stumbled backward until her bottom hit something solid—a desk. James followed, his eyes intent through the small holes in his mask.

"Wh-what do you want from me?"

He pulled off his gloves then wrenched off the mask, and threw them to the floor as he kept walking until his body touched hers.

"Take out your earplugs," he rasped. "I want you to hear everything clearly."

"I do... I will," she said, but he held out a hand. She did as he asked, and watched as he tucked them into his pocket.

Lifting his hands, he removed her mask and then cupped her face, tilting it so he could see her clearly. "I need you, Eden."

Four simple words that undid her completely. The emotion in them was raw and true and she felt her resistance flee. Their lips met and he took her mouth in a hard, searing kiss. As one stopped, another started, and Eden met him head-on. Their teeth clashed, tongues melded, and it was not enough, not nearly enough.

"I have watched you for days." He spoke the words against her lips. "Watched and wanted you until you filled my every waking thought, and when I sought relief in sleep, you tortured me in a web of sensual dreams."

Eden moaned as James trailed heated kisses down her neck. He grabbed handfuls of her skirt, raising it up her legs until he could wrap his hand around her thigh, the heat of his touch almost too hot to bear. Her hands fisted in his hair, tugging his curls, stroking his neck. Innocent she may be, but intuition and blind need were directing her. Throwing her head back, she sighed as his lips touched the curves of her breasts rising above the bodice of her dress. He was a master of torture, each stroke or lick sending a pool of heat between her legs. She felt his fingers pull the lacings of her dress free, and he then eased it from her shoulders, letting it fall to the floor in a soft pool of silken fabric at her feet.

"I know not what madness you have created inside me, my sweet siren, but only you can soothe it."

James eased her chemise slowly up her body, his hands caressing the flesh they encountered on the way. Eden shivered as he slipped it over her head and threw it aside.

"Trust me, sweetheart, and know I would never hurt you."

"I want to," Eden whispered, knowing that only the truth could be spoken now. "But I'm scared, James."

"Trust me," he said again. "And forgive me for the idiot I have been."

His eyes held hers and she saw he meant every word. Only when she nodded did he look at her body.

"In my dreams you were beautiful, but this…." Eden heard the emotion thicken his voice. "You are so much more that words fail me."

She could manage no words either as his hand cupped her breast.

"Yes, love, just feel."

Heat slammed into Eden as James lowered his head and ran his tongue up her breast, teasing the aching flesh before taking the hard bead of her nipple into his mouth. She was awash with pleasure.

"It is so much," she whispered, trying to find words.

He lifted her onto the desk and stepped between her thighs, and suddenly she was exposed to him.

"Christ, Eden, you're beautiful." She felt the heat from his eyes as they ran over her body.

He kissed her again. This time it was slow and heated, a torturous pleasure that sent liquid heat through her veins. She felt his fingers touch her breasts before trailing down her waist to run through the curls only she had ever touched.

"Trust me," he whispered again as his hand moved lower to stroke the damp petals between her legs, soft caresses that drove a whimper to her lips.

"Just feel, Eden."

James kissed her lush breasts again, laving her nipples as she arched into his mouth. He swept a finger over the tight bud between her thighs. She arched forward in shock as he circled it slowly. Her moans made his passions soar, yet he wanted this for her, needed her climax before he took her. She was innocent, he reminded himself, trying to pull back, determined not to terrify her with the fierce passions that urged him on.

Slipping a finger inside her sheath, he began to stroke her.

He watched her eyes, watched for any sign she was not right there with him, but the gray depths were glazed with sensual heat.

"So beautiful," James said, easing his fingers from her. He quite literally wanted to feast on the body before him. Soft, pale skin, long silken limbs. Blood thundered through him, his body hard with need. Pushing a cloud of dark curls over her shoulder, he took her mouth once more. Kissing Eden was unlike anything he had ever experienced. Before, it had been brief and a means to an end, but with her, it was as if his soul stirred.

He felt her fingers on his clothes, pulling the shirt from his breeches.

"I want to see you, James. I need to touch you as you have me."

She slipped her hands beneath the hem and caressed him, her wicked fingers stroking his stomach.

"Sweet Christ, Eden," James rasped, pulling free. "Your touch is like a brand on my skin." Quickly he removed his clothes and returned to her. Gritting his teeth, he let her touch him once more. She started with his shoulders and then moved to his chest. When she placed a soft kiss on the V at the base of his neck, James could do nothing to stop the shudder that rolled through him.

She continued to kiss his neck and chest while her hands moved lower. He moaned, long and deep, as she touched his arousal, her wicked fingers circling the top and then moving lower. When she wrapped a hand about him he was sure he would find his release. Gritting his teeth, he let her continue for three heartbeats before removing her hand.

Easing her backward on the desk, James thought he would always remember how she looked right here and now. Spread before him, her body aroused, eyelids lowered, hair everywhere.

Her breasts were full, nipples tight.

"There will be pain, sweetheart."

"I know, but I want this with you, James. I am not afraid."

He stroked her body, slowly arousing her further until she was again arching toward him. Aching to be fulfilled, James eased forward, slowly entering her tight wet sheath. His arousal pulsed with the need to drive in hard, but he would not hurt her. Teeth clenched, he tried to hold back. Her hands went to his cheeks, cupping his face. Her eyes held his as he slowly pushed through her innocence.

"I love you, James!" The words were a cry as he sheathed himself deep inside her.

"Eden, I—"

"Sssh, I want no promises from you. I give you my love freely, and ask for nothing in return."

"You humble me." James braced his hands on either side of her head, looking deep into her eyes. Her smile was the sweetest he had ever seen.

"Hold still, sweetheart, let your body adjust." She was tight and hot and his body was tense as he fought the urge to pull out and thrust hard inside her again.

"The pain is easing." Eden touched the ridge of his clenched jaw.

"Are you sure?" He could feel his release, yet would not succumb until Eden had found hers. Cupping her breasts, he caressed the tips.

"Oh, James."

James watched as her breath grew rapid, fingers now digging in to the desk she lay on. She was so close. He thrust into her again and again, and then she cried out his name. One thrust more and he found his release. The sensation shuddered through his entire body as wave upon wave of ecstasy crashed over him. James slumped forward on top of her, completely spent.

"Oh my."

He found the strength to suck in several lungfuls of air before bracing himself over her once more. Her eyes were closed and a blissful smile tilted her ravaged lips. She looked like a fallen angel, his fallen angel. Looking around the room, he found a daybed, and lifting her into his arms, he staggered backward and collapsed in a tangle of limbs on it. Laying her on top of him, James closed his eyes. What the hell had just happened?

"Eden, please be my wife."

"Yes."

"I know I am a stiff, uncompromising man, but—"

"I said yes, James."

He was stunned. She had said yes and he had not even used the arguments he had spent days marshalling. Cupping the back of her head, he held her close as the realization that she would be his wife settled inside him. He felt something for her, there was no doubt about that. This jealousy was not normal, and neither was the fierce need that came over him whenever he saw her. He just wasn't sure what name to give the emotions yet.

"I will try to be the husband you want, Eden, but in all honesty I will not be the easiest of men. I-I have never lived with people. Never had to think about their needs, and I am not a malleable person." James needed her to understand what she would be stepping into if she did wed him. *When*, he added silently.

"James, I live with Cam and Dev. Do you honestly believe your surly temper can upset me?"

"I did not mention a surly temper, but yes, I take your meaning. Living with those two cannot have been easy."

"I love you, James, a strong unwavering once-in-a-lifetime love, and I ask nothing in return from you that I know you are not ready to give."

Her words caused warmth to spread through his body. Samantha had begun to reach all those cold places inside him, and something told James that Eden would be the one to finish the job.

"All these feelings are so new to me, Eden. My father once told me that there was no place in a man's life for love or emotion, and as such he beat them out of me whenever I displayed any."

Eden pushed herself upright to look down at him, her eyes filled with anger for his father. James did not like sympathy, but anger he could cope with.

"It is my fondest wish, James, that our fathers are settled in the bowels of hell for eternity."

He found a smile at her words. She would always be there to make him smile, and the thought had it widening.

"'Tis all right now, my sweet. The memories no longer hurt me. Samantha has begun to heal me, and you—well, the minute I met you every other thought was driven from my head."

Cupping the back of her head, he pulled her down for a kiss. Soft and sweet, their lips clung.

"But there is more I must tell you. Today, the private investigator I had employed to find who attempted to kill me told me that I have half brothers and sisters—five of them, to be precise."

"I can imagine that was quite a shock."

"Somewhat, but to be honest I am unsure why I had not come to this conclusion myself. I knew what my father was, the thought should have crossed my mind."

"Perhaps, and then perhaps not, but what matters is that I am sure you wish to locate them."

How could she understand him so well already?

"I do, but the investigator also believes that it is possible that one of them is intent on harming me." James told Eden what he knew, and that her brothers were also party to the information.

"Well then." She rubbed his chest. "We shall deal with what arises, but be assured you shall have us there at your side as you do."

James felt that fierce jolt of emotion once more as he looked at her. "If I marry you then I get them also?"

"I'm afraid so." She laughed.

James gave a weighty sigh. "If I must, I must. And now, my sweet, we must dress and return before your brothers hunt me down and find me ravishing you once more."

"I wish I could stay in this room with you for the remainder of the evening. I hate these things, all that simpering and gushing." Eden shuddered.

"I like it no more than you, and promise that when we are wed we shall accept only a select few engagements. I will not marry you until I have found who is trying to kill me, Eden, it would be unfair to place you at risk. For now we must keep our engagement in the family."

James felt the tension that suddenly filled her body. "Please take care, James, I-I do not want to live without you."

He looked at her solemn face. She really did love him.

"I have so much to live for now, my sweet, therefore, I promise to take care. Plus, I have the Sinclairs to protect me."

"It shall be my life's work," she said as he lifted her off his body, and he liked the sound of her words.

They dressed and tidied each other. He tied her mask and she his. He laced her gown, his hands straying to her breasts, but she slapped them away and reached for her slippers.

"Come, Duke, we must return."

"Promise me you will not torment me by dancing with every man present in that dress. It will drive me to distraction" he said handing back her earplugs.

"Promise," Eden said, kissing his cheek.

"Why do I not believe you?" James shook his head as he followed her from the room.

He sent her in to the ballroom first, and followed several minutes later. The first person James encountered was Louis.

"That is a very convincing costume, James. I could almost see you holding up a coach."

"Stand and deliver," James muttered, looking around for Eden.

"Your sea nymph is currently dancing with her surly elder brother." Louis studied him. "By the look on your face, Raven, I would say the rift between you and Miss Eden Sinclair is repaired."

"I could wipe that smile from your face, Laurent."

"You could, however my debonair looks are what attracts women to me and to damage them would harm my prospects irreparably."

James snorted, then muttered a few unflattering words in French.

"Tsk tsk, such language, and from a Duke no less."

"I thought you had already set your sights on someone, Laurent, and believe that someone has the surname Sinclair also?"

"Perhaps," was all he said before he went to find his next partner.

Shaking his head, James threw a last lingering look at Eden before doing the same. It was going to be a long evening.

CHAPTER TWENTY TWO

"Eden, the Duke has arrived and you are to come to Uncle's office as soon as you are dressed."

"Go away," Eden groaned, burying her head beneath the pillow. "I have barely been asleep."

"Did you not hear me!" her sister shrieked. Wrenching the curtains open and flooding the room with light, Essie then stormed to the bed and pulled off the bedcovers. "The Duke is downstairs talking to Dev and you are to join them soon."

"What!" Eden screeched, leaping out of bed. "Here, now? So soon? I had thought he would wait until—never mind, quick, help me wash and dress."

"Has he offered marriage, Eden?" Essie had gone very still, her hands clutching one of Eden's shifts to her chest.

"Yes, and I have accepted." Eden hugged her close.

"But you said he was the last person you would marry just days ago and now—"

"I love him, Essie, so very much."

"Really?"

Eden nodded.

They both burst into tears, remembering the talks they had shared long into the night at Oak's Knoll—talks of marrying for love and nothing less. They had promised Dev this, and Eden would honor that promise by marrying James, the man she loved.

"Come, you must wash and hurry downstairs then, as I am sure Dev will not be as happy about the Duke's request as you are."

"I can hear the murmur of Dev's voice, but not James's." Eden tried to pick out her fiancé's words. "It is quite strange, Essie, but since I realized my feelings for him, I do not seem able to hear him like I do others."

"Really? That is unusual, don't you think?"

"Very, but now is not the time to think about that."

Eden was soon dressed with the help of Essie and her maid. She then ran from the room and down the stairs.

Standing outside her uncle's office, Eden placed a hand over her heart to ease the thudding in her chest. She knocked on the door and then entered.

James sat on one side of the desk, looking handsome in a dove-gray jacket and darker gray trousers. Dev sat on the other; they were scowling at each other. They stood as she walked forward.

"Good morning, James, Devon," she said, offering a tentative smile.

"The Duke has asked for your hand in marriage, Eden. I have neither accepted nor declined the offer, wishing to speak with you first."

"James, may I speak to my brother alone for a few minutes, please," she said. He looked at her for a few seconds then smiled, a soft tender smile that was for her alone and made her toes curl inside her slippers.

"Call for me when you are finished," he said, taking one of her hands and kissing the back, and then ignoring the loud growl from Devon, he walked from the room, closing it softly behind him.

"I know I told you I respected him, and that you were to be nice to him last night as he has had a trying time, Eden, but I also remember our discussion of a few days ago. He hurt you, and you said he was incapable of love. What has changed to make me think seriously about his proposal?"

Eden walked around the desk to stand beside her brother's chair. Taking his hand in hers, she gripped it tight.

"The problem for me has always been that no man can match or better you in my eyes. None had your honor or loyalty; none made me feel safe like you did. I didn't expect devotion, Dev, but I wanted to be someone's princess, which is how you always made me feel."

He didn't speak, just watched her as she continued, his green eyes intent.

"It took me until last night to see that James could be that man. Like me, he harbors deep secrets that have scarred him. He portrays himself as a cold and aloof man who has hidden himself behind an emotionless façade, yet that is not the real James, Dev. He is a man capable of seeing me as his princess, and I love him very much."

"God! Eden, really?" Dev groaned. "The man has a reputation to fear and is cold as an iced-over lake most days."

"A bit like you, Dev?"

His smile was wry.

"He is a protector, also like you. He loves Samantha and in time I believe he will love me."

"If he doesn't I'll rip his head from his shoulders."

Laughing, Eden kissed his cheek and hugged him hard. "You, however, I have always loved and will do so till I draw my last breath. My savior, my friend and companion, the man I have always adored."

"I love you too, little sister, and I needed to know that you would be safe when you left my care. It seems you have found a man to provide that. It may take time for me to adjust, but if you believe he is the one, then I shall not stand in your way."

The siblings held each other for a while and then Eden said she would go and find James.

"At least he has your colors," Dev said as she reached the door. "Essie has made me promise not to look at Laurent's, and that worries me."

"I am impressed you are obeying her."

"I have not seen the man anywhere but at a social event, or I would not be. You know how much changing into my other sight can hurt me when there is all that color about."

"Perhaps it is not as important as you believe it to be, Dev?"

"Perhaps."

Eden smiled and blew her brother a kiss then left, quietly closing it behind her. She found James looking out a window, shoulders hunched as if he were contemplating something disagreeable.

"James."

Turning, he held out a hand as Eden walked toward him.

"You look beautiful this morning." The words were gruff and sounded unromantic, and yet they made her heart sing.

"Dev wants to talk with you."

"Are we to go another round then?"

Eden moved in to his body as he faced her. Rising to her toes, she grabbed a handful of his hair and tugged his head down until their lips met. His arms circled her, holding her close, only releasing her when she had been thoroughly kissed.

"All will be well now, I promise. My brother is just protective of me, and had not understood my feelings for you," she whispered against his lips.

"Tell me again."

"I love you."

"Thank God I had not imagined those words."

Eden stood back and lifted one of his hands. Opening it, she kissed his palm before closing it.

"I will always love you."

Closing the distance between them once more, he kissed her hard before walking away.

***

James could not turn around without falling over a Sinclair. It seemed that now he was to be one of them they were more determined than ever to protect him. Cam sniffed every drink and piece of food he and Samantha ate. If he was uncertain, Essie would be called in to taste test. Dev insisted on looking his staff over, checking their colors to see if any of them displayed the darkness that he termed evil. James endured it and soon began to accept that if he wanted Eden then her family came with her. It was also obvious that they meant a great deal to her, and loath as he was to admit it to anyone, they were beginning to mean a great deal to him as well.

"Eat your own food!"

"Ah, the lord of the manor has arrived," Dev said, waving his knife at James as he walked into his dining room. "Mr. Spriggot is due to arrive shortly, James," he added around a mouthful of ham, "therefore I thought it important to be present."

"And is Mr. Spriggot due in the dining room?"

Sarcasm was obviously too subtle for the Sinclairs as they both stared at James as if he were a trifle spare in the attic, and then looked carefully around the room.

"I do not believe so, James. However, should you wish to discuss business in here, Dev and I will be more than agreeable," Cam said.

Of course they were deliberately baiting him. He knew it, they knew it, and still he took the lure with both feet, both hands, and anything else he had at the ready.

"Of course we are not going to conduct the interview in here, you numbskull!"

"Tut tut, Duke. I hope you will not display your temper in such a way in front of my sister. I will not have her tender sensibilities wounded."

"Go to hell!" James snarled, stalking to the sideboard. "And take your big brother with you."

"A trifle testy this afternoon, Sinclair?" Dev said. "And please remember that we are not easily offended by insults. In fact, my family cut their eye teeth insulting each other."

James was not a man who sulked, snarled, or insulted without serious provocation. Therefore he was instantly ashamed by his behavior. Filling his plate, he sat before the Sinclair men.

"Please forgive my outburst, I am merely concerned by the pace at which this investigation is running. Before, when I was alone," he waved his hand around vaguely, "I would not have cared either way—"

"If you lived or died?" Cam queried softly.

James loaded his fork and stuffed it into his mouth. The beef suddenly tasted like straw. He was not a man for confidences like these Sinclairs were, and was uncomfortable with two sets of green eyes focused on him with unwavering intensity. Swallowing, he took a mouthful of coffee.

"Not everyone has a childhood filled with love and laughter, Cam."

"I understand that, James, and am sorry yours was not."

"But now you have a family in Samantha and Eden and us, for better or worse, and you have no wish to be dispatched and would like whoever is intent on just that to be found?" Dev added, filling the silence.

"Yes."

Silence settled around them, and James was surprised how comfortable it felt.

"I gather you know Lord Laurent well, James. Can you give me any information about the man, as it appears he has an interest in my other sister?"

James thought about Dev's words while he swallowed his mouthful.

"I know he is a viscount, and has no family. I'm unsure what happened to them, but wondered if they were lost during the revolution."

Dev nodded, but remained silent.

"He is a good man, and came to my aid when I was being attacked, as you know. He is a skilled fencer, and from what he tells me, is intent on settling in England."

"What of his financial situation?"

"He seems comfortable. At present he is staying at the Grillion, but has had a trip to the country to view an estate he is thinking of purchasing."

"What I have seen of him I like," Dev admitted. "But as you know I am protective of my sisters. Therefore, I want to be sure that he will be good to Essie should he offer for her."

"A Frenchman," Cam said. "Not sure how I feel about one of them joining the family.

Have you checked his colors?"

"Essie made me promise I would not. She says she has no wish to know what color Laurent is."

"But this makes you uncomfortable?" James asked.

Dev did not look happy. "Very, as it is no secret I believe my siblings should wed only their color match."

James knew he and Eden were a match.

"I have given my word, so will stick to it, but only as long as I remain comfortable with what lies between them."

James had an understanding of this man now. He followed

along with his family's wishes until he felt it necessary to intervene, then he did so without hesitation.

"I would be grateful if you hear anything further about Laurent, you let me know."

"Of course."

"I suggest you eat up, James. As your butler is about to open that door, and announce the arrival of one Mr. Spriggot," Dev added.

James didn't turn. He knew the door was closed. Lifting an eyebrow, he stared at Dev.

"Your butler is a very bright shade of orange, James; in fact," Dev added, his face the picture of innocence, which told James what he was about to say was far from it, "he'd make a perfect match for Cam."

James gave a bark of laughter while Cam howled with rage and lobbed a forkful of carrots at his brother.

"Miss Sinclair has arrived, your Grace, and Mr. Spriggot. Mr. Brown is serving him tea while Miss Sinclair is—"

"Here!" Eden said, squeezing past his butler and into the room.

James felt her smile through his entire body as he rose to his feet. It lit her face; her eyes sparkled and her cheeks were flushed, and he wanted to take her to bed and ravish every inch of her. Dressed in soft peppermint with fine rose and cream stripes, she looked angelic and far too disturbing for his peace of mind. His eyes settled on the little row of buttons marching up the front of her bodice. He could have those open in seconds.

"Hello, James," Eden said, standing on her toes and kissing his cheek. A hint of her floral scent drifted over him and then it was gone.

"Brothers," she said, nodding to her siblings.

"Sister," they said, doing the same yet not rising to their feet.

"Such gentlemanly behavior," James said.

"If we stood every time one of our sisters came into the room we'd be exhausted by lunch," Cam said, wiping the gravy from his plate with a piece of bread.

"I met a very interesting man on the walk here."

"I have told you not to walk here, Eden, it is too dangerous."

She patted his arm. "It is only a few feet, and my maid was with me."

"It takes only one step for someone to harm you, and I am adamant in this. If you do not obey me then I will set a guard on your aunt's door, and every time you leave the house he will follow you."

"We shall keep Mr. Spriggot company until you are free, James," Cam said, quickly climbing to his feet and almost running out the door, closely followed by his brother.

"Your brothers are cowards."

"Undoubtedly, however we digress." She placed a hand on his chest to regain his attention. "It is not me they are after, James. Surely there is no need for me to take so many precautions."

"And if whoever wants me dead sees you walking down the road unescorted and gets the idea that in kidnapping you they would get to me, do you not think they would take that opportunity?"

"But no one knows we are betrothed, James, so I fail to see the danger."

She thought she had him there; he could see the triumphant little smirk on her face.

"Eden, someone would just have to see me within two feet of you to know what is between us," James drawled, taking a step closer.

"Really?"

"Really."

His arms slipped around her waist.

"Every time I look at you I want you," he growled, kissing her neck.

"Let's marry then. Now." Eden sighed.

James undid a few buttons and parted her dress, then tugged down her chemise, exposing her breasts.

"S-someone could come in."

Lifting her high, James buried his face between her breasts, then lowering her down his body he pushed her against the door. Pulling out one of her earplugs, he said, "You'll hear them if they do."

"I-I can't hear when I'm with you."

She shuddered as his tongue swiped a long hot lick down her breast.

"Really?"

Nodding, she clenched her eyes shut. "Oh dear, I-I had not wanted to tell you that."

"No,"—his breath made her shiver as it blew over her damp flesh—"I'm glad you did."

"You seem to d-destroy my concentration when you touch me. I would have to really focus to hear anything."

James could do nothing to stop the slow smile spreading across his face.

"Of course that may change with familiarity," she added quickly.

"No it won't, because you love me. Therefore I will always destroy your concentration." James once again focused on what he had uncovered, running his tongue down the sweet-scented valley between her breasts.

"We—we should—Mr. Spriggot—"

"Can wait," James mumbled. He had never done anything like this, taken the risk of exposure, or behaved in such a reckless manner, but this was Eden, and she destroyed his control.

"But—"

"It's impolite of me to talk with my mouth full, therefore, shut up," he added before taking her nipple into his mouth. Wonderfully responsive, Eden arched toward him, her fingers biting in to his shoulders.

"No, love, don't undo my clothes, yours will take us long enough to fix," James said, stopping her wandering hands. Clasping them in one of his, he lifted them above her head and continued his wicked torture.

"Wh-what are you doing?" Eden gasped as he released her wrists and dropped to his knees before her.

"Hold your skirts, Eden." James bunched them and urged her to take them in her hands.

"James!" Her furious whisper as he licked the soft petals between her thighs urged him on. Nudging her legs apart, he ran his tongue along the damp cleft and felt her shudder. She tasted wonderful, his woman.

"James—this is h-highly improper."

"Sssh," he breathed against her, tasting and teasing her, feeling her body tense with each lick. Her breath quickened as he tormented the small hard bead.

James could not wait for the day she would be in his bed. His wonderfully responsive little fiancée would love everything he taught her. Climbing to his feet, he looked at her dazed expression then opened his breeches and lifted her.

"Wrap your legs around me, Eden."

Still dazed, Eden obeyed the ragged command and then moaned as he braced her against the door before thrusting inside her. She made him feel primitive, like a man who could conquer whatever he chose. Her fingers dug in to his shoulders, her face now buried in his neck, and seconds later, just as he found his release, she joined him. It had been hard and fast and his heart thudded as if he had ridden hard for hours.

Eden slumped on his shoulder as his forehead hit the door. Breathless, they held each other for several minutes until he slowly lowered her to the floor.

"We have to find the man who wants me dead, because next time I take you it will be in a bloody bed," James said, pulling up her chemise and then starting on the buttons. "And I will take my time worshipping your beautiful body."

"Yes," she whispered, spent. Moments later they were once again presentable, although the lingering heat in their eyes told a different story.

"Will you visit with Samantha while I see Mr. Spriggot?"

"But I would rather know what is happening."

"I will tell you everything if you let me go in there alone," James said. "And while I don't care what your brothers think of me I know you do, therefore they will see us together and know instantly what we have been doing and—"

"All right, I understand, but I want to know what is said," Eden said, turning to leave. James spun her back and kissed her, then held out her earplug.

"Try not to eavesdrop, my sweet."

Eden just snorted and flounced away. James took a moment to enjoy the view then made his way to his study, where he hoped someone would tell him what he wanted to hear.

CHAPTER TWENTY THREE

That evening they were to attend a ball at the house of the Earl and Countess of Vallan, and as usual there were hundreds of people in attendance.

"'Tis an awful crush," the hostess said, looking gleeful as the Sinclairs greeted her.

"I should have some nose plugs made," Cam griped as the scents started to reach him.

"There is Lord Laurent, Eden. I have promised him my first dance," Essie whispered.

"He is a wonderful man, Essie, I am glad you like him and he likes you."

"Oh well—"

"He can't keep his eyes off you," Eden said, turning toward the Frenchman as he detached from the group he was talking with and came toward them. Essie was positively glowing by the time he arrived; in fact, Eden had never seen her sister looking more beautiful.

"May I have the honor of this dance, Miss Sinclair?"

"Of course, my lord." Essie placed her hand on his arm and then let him lead her to the dance floor.

Eden and Cam watched their sister walk away on the arm of Lord Laurent.

"I cannot believe Mr. Spriggot has no news about who is intent on harming James, Cam."

"Spriggot believes he is on to something, and should have more news within the next day or two. He is just waiting the return of his man to London. Until then, we will keep your beloved safe, sister."

"Lord, I hope so." Eden hated the thought that out there somewhere, someone wanted to kill the man she loved.

"Put your worries aside for now, Eden, as Crawley is about to ask you to dance, and I am going to find the delectable Miss Beadle."

Eden accepted Mr. Crawley's request to dance, and as she took her place she looked for James. He was in the line opposite, dancing with the Duchess of Abernathy. Eden narrowed her eyes at him, but he merely smiled back.

"What has you smiling in such a secretive manner, Duke?" Eden heard the Duchess say as she moved closer.

"I have a sunny nature, Duchess, nothing more than that."

Eden giggled, which he heard, because his lips twitched. She shot him a look and he pointed to her ears. On the return to where she started, she eased one ear plug out slightly. Just enough so she could hear him, but not enough to give her a headache.

"You look beautiful tonight, my love."

Eden smiled.

"However, that bodice is a trifle low. Crawley just tripped over his feet as you bent over."

Eden heard James's words and then gave her partner a slow smile.

"Eden," James growled.

Eden batted her eyelashes, which had Mr. Crawley stumbling once more.

"You will desist, woman!"

Oh this was fun, Eden thought, ruffling the usually unflappable Duke of Raven.

"When I get you alone, I will make you pay for the torment I am currently enduring."

Eden decided she had teased James enough just as she heard the Duchess of Abernathy speak.

"I will be blunt, Duke. I am without a bed companion at the moment and I have heard of your prowess in that area, therefore I have my heart set on you taking the place of my last lover."

Eden intercepted the warning look James sent her, however, it did nothing to calm the rage currently bubbling inside her.

"I think not, Duchess. I have no wish to be your latest bed companion."

"Come now, Duke. We high-ranking peers must stick together, surely. Lying with those beneath us cannot be healthy."

"Eden."

Ignoring the warning in James's voice as the dance carried her closer to him, Eden deliberately stomped on the back of the Duchess's dress. Unaware, the lady moved and the fabric ripped.

"Oh dear, please forgive me, Duchess. How clumsy," Eden cooed as she looked at the rent she had torn in the hem. She ignored the coughing fit James appeared to be having.

"Imbecile! Do you know how much this dress cost? Why, the fabric was imported from France!"

Eden just smiled, albeit through her teeth, and continued on with her partner.

"Country chit!" she heard the Duchess snap. "That girl is a heathen, as are her family."

"Be warned that the Sinclair family are very important to me, Duchess, and I will not tolerate another word against any of them."

James's words made Eden feel warm all over; the Duchess, however, did not look pleased.

As soon as the dance ended James returned the furious Duchess of Abernathy to her friends and made a hasty departure before she attempted once again to get him into her bed. He shuddered thinking of bedding that viper.

He swallowed the swell of laughter over Eden's behavior. There would be nothing easy about having her as his wife. She would love passionately and demand a great deal of him, and where before the thought had terrified him, now he could not wait.

Every part of him was aware of her. No more apathy or cold indifference. He was alive now, and wanted to stay that way. Waiting a few minutes, he sipped champagne, and then when he saw Eden return to Essie he made his move. He wanted to hold her and to do that, he would need to dance with her—at least until he could get her alone.

He smiled and bowed as he moved through the crowd, exchanging a few greetings on the way here and there. He was only a few feet from her when a hand gripped his shoulder. Spinning, he found Devonshire Sinclair looking at him intently. His eyes were wide, pupils large black dots, and James felt the tension in him.

"What's wrong?"

"Who were you with?"

"Pardon?"

"A few minutes ago, who were you talking to?"

"I danced with the Duchess of Abernathy, and then I drank a glass of champagne while Eden danced once again with another man that is not me, and now I am making my way to her side so that does not happen anymore this evening."

"Someone evil was close to you, black with traces of deep

red, menacing and evil." Devon's eyes had changed color, nearly black now, and his face was clenched and pale.

"How did you see that from across the room? There must have been hundreds of people between us?"

Around them people talked and laughed, yet James was focused solely on Dev. The man was not his usual calm self, something had disturbed him greatly.

"Are you in pain, Dev?"

"There were too many colors, and it was hard for me to take them all in."

"Then why did you?" James moved to the man's side, unsure what to do next.

"I had a feeling—a premonition that something was not right. I changed vision and found you, and then saw the color nearby. When I changed back and located you once more, you were alone."

"But surely there are others with my color."

"Not exactly the same, no one is."

"How do you know the person meant to harm me?"

"The color. Black is bad, and the red when mixed with it. Very bad coloring. I've only ever seen it twice. Once when I saw them taking a murderer to be hanged."

"The other?"

Dev dropped his eyes briefly before once again looking at James.

"Your father. Our paths crossed briefly one day in Crunston Cliff."

"Can you see him now, this man?" James said softly. He was not surprised his father had been colored in such a way, but he was surprised that the mention of him did not disturb as once it would have done.

Dev looked around them and shook his head. "I can't go back into my other vision again. I would probably end up unconscious at your feet."

"I am to dance with Eden but after that I think we should all leave," James said, suddenly needing to get everyone he cared about out of the ballroom.

Dev gave a curt nod. "I will find the others. Dance and then out, Raven, no risks."

This time it was James's turn to nod as they parted. He cleaved a way through the people until he reached Eden. Touching her arm, he did not speak but led her to the floor. He felt a small measure of peace as she fitted into his arms; his heart stopped thumping and his body slowly unclenched.

"What has happened, James?"

He didn't bother denying it. "Dev thought he saw someone close to me who was bent on harming me."

Biting her lip, she moved closer to James. Curling her fingers into his jacket, she held him close.

"I'm here, love, no one is going to hurt you or me," James whispered, his hand stroking her back. He saw the fear in her eyes, felt the sudden tension in her body, and hated that it was he who had put it there.

"I am scared for you, James. Promise me you will take no risks to find this person who wants you dead. Promise me, please."

"All right, I promise," he said, kissing her brow. "Now let me hold you close, Eden, and then when the dance finishes we must leave. Dev is gathering the others as we speak."

Nodding, Eden pressed close and let him guide her up and down the room with the other couples. As the music drew to a close, he whispered to her, "I want you to say loudly that you have a headache, and of course I will escort you out."

"Duke, I am afraid I feel most unwell," she said as the music finished. "I fear I am about to faint," she added, laying the back of her hand on her forehead like the heroine from a torrid novel.

"My dear Miss Eden, allow me to see you to your carriage at

once," James said, taking her arm.

"Oh my head!" she wailed.

"Don't overdo it, love."

She sniffed a few times but said nothing further.

They walked slowly up the stairs amidst murmurs and words of sympathy until they reached the top. Eden stumbled and James placed his arm around her waist.

"I am going to need my wits about me to wed you," he said under his breath. "Your acting is most convincing."

Eden did not speak as they made their way to the entrance, and then stepped out into the cool evening air. The carriages had already been called, and Dev, Cam, and Essie were waiting for them outside.

"Come, Cam, Essie, and I will take the second carriage, you and Eden take the first. Thankfully our aunt and uncle have already left."

Soon they had begun the journey home. Eden sat pressed against James.

"Eden, it will be all right, I promise you."

"How can you promise me that? We do not know who he is, this man determined on taking you from me."

Lifting her onto his lap, he found a blanket and covered them both. Holding her close, he pressed her head to his chest.

"What did you do to stop thinking about your father? When he made you do things you didn't want to do, how did you escape?" James tugged a curl free and wrapped it around his finger.

"I thought about riding along the cliffs of our home. Flying, free from him and his demands. It was just me and my horse and he could not take that from me." She slipped her hand beneath his jacket to rest on his heart. "What did you do to escape your life?"

James lifted her chin and placed a soft kiss on her lips.

"I climbed to the highest turret of the castle. I would stand there looking out over water and the village. I would see the tops of trees, and the winding road that to my mind led to freedom, and imagine how one day I would walk or ride it to escape him."

"I hate your father for forcing a small helpless boy from his home to live in a world filled with adults who offered him no love and affection, but I am also relieved that when he did, you were not subjected to his vile, perfidious actions for a second longer."

He kissed her again, their lips clinging almost in desperation.

"James, we are going to live a long happy life filled with love and laughter, and more affection than you can cope with," she said, cupping his cheek. "We will give our children everything our parents did not, and then we will teach them to ride along the beach and climb trees—but we will be right there with them, my love, watching their every step."

Blinking, James was surprised to feel the sting of tears. Eden's eyes were so full of love and emotion, her words wrapping around him like a warm blanket and forming pictures of a future he had only imagined, and it was then he knew.

"God I love you, Eden." He shuddered, burying his head in her neck. The words felt so right. "I have never said those words to anyone but Samantha before, but I need to say them now. Need you to understand what you have come to mean to me. I'm a fool for not realizing sooner."

"I do understand, my love, and I will treasure them and you always."

They clung to each other until the carriage pulled up outside his house. Kissing her once more, he then stepped down and helped her down behind him, as she would need to join her siblings in their carriage for the short journey to the Wynburg residence. The three Sinclair siblings were waiting for them before his front door.

"Cam will stay close and alert Mr. Brown of tonight's events before you go to bed," Dev said. "We will have a meeting after the picnic tomorrow and plan a strategy to flush this bastard out and get rid of him once and for all."

"Picnic?" James said, latching on to that one word and not the fact that Devon was organizing a meeting without first asking him. He must be mellowing.

"Unfortunately it is unavoidable, James. It is the twins' birthday tomorrow. They requested a picnic, and of course invited both you and Samantha," Essie said.

"And I am just hearing about this now?"

"I had thought Samantha would have told you," Eden said.

"She probably did," he admitted. "I have been preoccupied."

"Which is entirely understandable." Her hand brushed his, and it felt natural for James to open it and let her fingers slip between his. Even here, with her siblings looking on.

"We have managed to convince them to go to the park at the end of the street. It is small and we should be safe there. Aunt and Uncle have organized staff to go early and set everything up. We shall all arrive at eleven o'clock."

James nodded at Devon's words. "Then of course we shall be there." Reluctantly he released Eden's hand after a final squeeze.

"I cannot thank you enough for everything you have done for me and Samantha." He looked at Essie, Cam, and Dev. "I understand the Sinclair-Raven history, and that it spans many years, yet I know that this goes beyond that," James said, shaking the Sinclair brothers' hands before he bent to kiss Essie's cheek.

"We care for our own," Dev said before he and his sisters climbed back into their carriage and drove away, leaving Cam at his side.

James said the words, "I love you," and hoped Eden heard

as the carriage took her away from him. He felt raw and exposed now that he had allowed himself to truly see what he felt for Eden and her family.

"Come, James, a nightcap and a chat with Mr. Brown before we retire, I think," Cam said, urging him into the house. James followed, his thoughts on the love he and Eden would lavish upon their children. Hope began to spread through his body. Hope for the future that had once been so bleak. A future he would share with her and their families.

CHAPTER TWENTY FOUR

"And do you think Dorrie and Somer will be happy with those necklaces, Samantha?" She wore buttercup yellow today with matching ribbons in her hair, and looked like every young child should—happy.

"Oh yes, James."

His sister's eyes sparkled with excitement as she walked beside him swinging his hand. It was natural and felt right and he wondered how the hell he had existed without her and the Sinclairs in his life. Especially Eden, his love.

"I wonder if they will have cherry cakes. They are Cam's favorite you know, James."

"Yes, they are, Samantha, and I expressly requested that my aunt's cook make them, because I know they are a favorite of yours also." Cam loped beside them with his long-legged stride.

The day had seemed unusually bright and sunny to James from the first moment he had opened his eyes. Letting people inside his heart had not resulted in the pain he had once thought it would; in fact, the opposite had happened. He felt lighter and unburdened.

They entered the park and walked along the path.

"Oh look, James!"

At his sister's squeal of excitement James followed her gaze and found the Sinclairs. They had set up the picnic beside a pond and under a large tree, which would offer shade from the sun when it reached its peak in the middle of the day. A long table was laid with a bright blue cloth and loaded with food and drink.

The twins were dressed in blue, pink, and white. Seeing them approach, their little legs started running. Releasing his hand, Samantha did the same.

"Ahhh," Cam sniffed the air. "The smell of food."

James smiled as he found Eden. She was sitting on a blanket with a book in her hand and Warwick pressed to her side.

"Hello, my love."

Her chin rose at his words, and the smile she gave him made his heart thud.

"Have mercy, Raven, I am due to eat, and that look you and my sister are sharing is making me nauseous."

"Go away, Cam," James said, making his way to where she sat and dropping down before her.

"Hello, Warwick," he said with his eyes on Eden. Beneath the shade of the tree with dappled sunlight all around her, she looked almost magical.

"We have just finished reading the adventures of Captain Vesely, James, and now I am going to eat."

The boy got to his feet and without a backward glance ran to the food-laden table.

"I dreamt of you." James said cupping her cheek. "And woke up wanting you."

"Soon," she whispered, and he closed the distance and brushed his lips over hers in a brief kiss. "I love you, James."

"And I you, Eden."

He wanted to hold her, lay her down on the blanket and cradle her close, but of course he could not.

"Come." James got to his feet and held out his hand. It was

not done to be overly demonstrative with one's fiancée, especially in public, and yet these were the Sinclairs. Very little was proper and correct with them, so he retained her hand as they walked.

"Happy birthday, Dorrie, Somer."

"Oh, James," they said in unison, holding up the necklaces Samantha had selected for them. "These are beautiful."

They threw themselves at him and he caught them because they were his family now too, and besides, he rather thought he enjoyed being hugged.

They ate as the family teased and annoyed each other. He joined in when he could think of something to say, but for the most was content to watch. Samantha sat between he and Eden, and were it not for the man intent on killing him, James could say he was the happiest he had ever been in his life.

A game of hide-and-seek was decided upon once their food had settled.

"But you will not go far, and use the trees closest," James cautioned the children and adults. "No one is to move out of shouting range, and I want the children in pairs."

There were a few grumbles but surprisingly no one challenged him. It was decided that Lord and Lady Wynburg would stay by the tree and watch proceedings to check for any cheating.

"Of which there will be a great deal," Eden told him. "We can't do anything without cheating," she added.

"I have much to learn it seems."

"I shall teach you." She gave him a secret smile.

"Watch and learn, James. I am something of a legend at this," Cam said, as he jogged by with Warwick.

"What you have is an overinflated ego," Eden said.

Lord Wynburg counted, Dev was to find them, and the rest of the party hurried to find places to hide. The three little girls were allowed to hide together, but only because Eden said she would be able to hear them wherever they wandered, simply because the twins had never worked out how to keep their voices down. James, Essie, and Eden were to hide alone.

"How does one chose a hiding place I wonder?"

Eden smiled as James spoke to himself, or perhaps her. He knew she had taken out her earplugs as the game began, believing it important to keep track of where everyone was. She hadn't added that she liked to cheat if given the opportunity to do so.

Slipping behind some bushes, Eden forced herself inside one, ignoring the leaves and branches catching in her hair. Appearances were given no consideration when competing with family members. She settled in the middle and then listened. Warwick was grumbling that Cam was being too fussy, and any old tree would do. Dev was counting, their aunt and uncle chuckling over the goings-on. Essie was close, because she was humming softly. The little girls were giggling, but were some distance away.

She heard Dev stop counting and declare his intentions loudly, that he was coming to find them. Listening as the voices hushed, Eden tensed as she heard a scream. Forcing her way from the bushes took seconds, but once free she listened again, and this time heard the twins running, their voices raised in fear.

"Come quickly!" Eden cried as she picked up her skirts and ran in their direction. It was a matter of seconds before she rounded a tree and found them, legs pumping, hair flowing behind them. Dorrie and Somer were crying, their distress obvious. Eden's heart chilled as she realized Samantha was not with them.

"A man, Eden!"

James arrived first, followed by the others.

"Where is Samantha!" he bellowed.

"The man, he grabbed her and ran, we t-tried to stop him!"

"Which way?" Dev bent to haul his sisters close.

"That w-way," Somer managed to get out before bursting into loud sobs.

"Go to Aunt and Uncle, tell them what has happened, then insist they return to the house, Warwick."

The boy nodded at Dev's words, then taking his sisters' hands, he started running.

"Everyone quiet!" Eden held up her hand as she started running in the direction her little sister had indicated. She felt James at her side. Dev charged forward, using his sight to search for Samantha's colors. When they reached the gate, he held out his hands. The siblings quickly took hold, forming a small circle.

"Focus," she whispered.

She felt the strength of her siblings flow through her as she sorted through the sounds around them. Carriage wheels, the clop of hooves, voices rising over other sounds. James breathed heavily behind her, and then she heard it, the soft whimper that belonged to Samantha.

"Left, there," she said.

"I can see her," Dev added. "Quickly!"

They were all running once more. James, Dev, and Cam were faster, with she and Essie at the rear.

Dev held up his hand as they reached another street, and the siblings all grabbed hands once more. Cam sniffed loudly, and Essie closed her eyes.

"She was carried passed here, I smell the cherry cake she tucked in her pocket before the game," Cam whispered

"I taste fear," Essie added.

Eden lowered her head and focused. She could no longer hear Samantha, but the voice of a man. He was directing someone to drive fast.

"The carriage, it is coming this way and Samantha is inside!" Eden cried.

The three men, and Eden, pulled out their pistols. All lined the road, holding them before them. The driver saw them and yelled at them to move, but no one did.

"Stop or I shoot!" James roared.

Eden watched a head come out the window; seeing them, it ducked back inside. The carriage door then opened, and Samantha was held out, dangling from a pair of hands.

"No!" James ran forward with Eden on his heels. As the carriage drew near, the hands dropped the little girl, and Eden watched in horror as James dived forward, arms outstretched. The breath seized in her throat as he reached for his sister; catching her, he fell, turning so he took the impact with Samantha clasped in his arms.

"Eden move!"

Dev's words galvanized her. She leapt off the road as the carriage sped by. Landing on her feet, she kept running until she reached James and Samantha.

"Dear God, please tell me you are unhurt!" She dropped to her knees. Samantha lay sprawled on her brother's chest, his arms wrapped around her like two bands of iron.

"James, talk to me." Eden's words were desperate.

"I am unharmed." His words were cold and clipped, anger evident in each.

"Eden, that m-man wanted to hurt me."

Samantha's tear-drenched face lifted to look at Eden.

"Oh, you poor little girl." She stroked a trembling shoulder. "But do you remember what I told you once, about big brothers?"

Samantha looked down at James, who did not look inclined to release her, or indeed move from his current position in the gutter.

"That b-big brothers are very special people, because they t-take their responsibilities very seriously. Especially when it comes protecting their little sisters."

"That's right, and didn't your big brother do exceptionally well today?"

"Oh yes." The little girl managed a shaky smile. "He is the b-best big brother."

James sat upright, cradling her. He then kissed the top of her head. "Are you all right, Samantha?" Each word sounded like it was wrenched from his chest.

"Yes, I am not hurt, but that man scared me."

"He will not do so again, love."

Eden saw the rage in her fiancé's eyes as he looked over Samantha's head.

"Come, you cannot sit in the street all day, Raven. To your feet, so we can check you are uninjured."

James handed Samantha to Eden and took the hand Dev held out to him. He then silently took his sister back, and the child wrapped her arms around his neck and lowered her head to his shoulder.

"Are you hurt, James?" Eden did not like the ice-cold look in his eyes.

"No."

Gone was the happy, smiling man who had approached her at the picnic, replaced by the cold and unapproachable Duke.

"Come, we need to get back to your house, Raven."

Dev's words galvanized them and soon they were in the park once again.

"The carriage was not about to stop, so we jumped clear," Eden heard Cam tell James. "It had no markings and was black all over. The driver had his hat pulled low, but I would recognize him should I encounter him again."

"Can you tell us what happened, Samantha?"

"I don't think that now—"

"Yes, James, now is the best time, her memory is fresh," Dev insisted.

Eden walked at James's side as Samantha haltingly told her story. It seemed the man had come up behind her, picked her up, thrown her over his shoulder and started running. She had heard the twins screaming, but they could do nothing to stop him, even though she hammered on his back.

James soothed her as she talked, running a large hand up and down her spine.

"When we reached the carriage, he opened the door and threw me onto a seat. I bounced, and then we were moving."

"Did the man say anything to you?"

"Nothing, Cam. He just said to the driver to hurry."

"Did you see his face?"

Samantha shook her head. "I never looked at him until we were inside the carriage, and when I did, the lower half was covered."

"Could you smell anything unusual," Cam said. "Anything at all, Samantha?"

"Manure." She wrinkled her nose. "The man smelt of m-manure."

"Enough." James said the word softly, but they all heard the threat. He did not want his sister upset any further. "Once again I am in your debt," he added. "Thank you for coming to my sister's aid today."

As no one knew how to respond they remained silent. The family had gone; when they reached the picnic area only the servants were there, cleaning up. James continued walking, striding ahead with Samantha, and Eden could not match his long stride.

"Let him alone now, love. He is hurting and angry, he needs time to deal with all that emotion, as he is not a man used to it."

"But I am to be wed to that man, Dev, and as such he should talk to me, surely? Or am I to live my life 'giving him time?'"

The Sinclairs walked behind the Ravens, keeping them near the entire journey back. Once they reached James's town house, Eden ignored her brothers' efforts to stop her and hurried to reach him before he entered his house.

"James, shall I stay? Would you like me to help you with Samantha?"

He turned at her words, his eyes cold and distant.

"No, go home, Eden."

"James, I am to be your wife, I want to—"

He glared. "I am aware of who you are, but at this moment, my sister takes precedence over everyone else in my life."

"But I want to comfort her also." Eden felt as if the ground were moving beneath her feet. She could not reach him, his intent only to push her away.

"She is my sister," he snapped. "I do not need or want a Sinclair to help us."

Eden stepped back at the fury in his words.

"Eden, that came out wrong, I did—"

She saw the moment clarity returned to his brown eyes, but she did not stop, instead turned from him to follow her family out the gates.

CHAPTER TWENTY FIVE

Eden had slept badly. She was now sitting in her bedroom watching people pass by on the street below. Her thoughts were of course settled on James, and how he had turned away from her yesterday. *"I do not need or want a Sinclair to help us."* Lord that had hurt.

Of course she had understood what he was dealing with; the intense reaction to nearly losing the sister he had only just learned to love had shaken him badly. But Eden had wanted him to turn to her in his pain. She was to be his wife. Was this to be their future together? Whenever something challenged the foundations of his life, was he to turn away from her?

Eden knew she could be a demanding person, but then who would not learn to be when they had been raised one of so many. She had understood early that to be heard she had to speak the loudest, had to ask the questions until she received the right answers. She also knew she could not live with a man who would not allow her into his life, a man who refused to share his burdens.

She had heard her brothers leave the house early, and knew they had gone to have a meeting with James about what must be done to find the man who intended on harming the Raven family. She was not included, supposedly because she was a woman whose opinion was of no consequence. The woman, she thought, who was to become a Raven.

With distance and hindsight, Eden realized she had not handled yesterday's situation well. James was a novice at dealing with strong emotion, and she the exact opposite. She knew her faults, and patience had never been something she'd cultivated, so she had pushed him, instead of giving him time.

"Enter," she called in answer to the knock on her door.

"I have brought us tea, and then you must change, as Lord Laurent is taking us driving in the park."

In direct contrast to Eden, Essie looked refreshed and happy. Her green eyes sparkled, and she knew that love was the reason.

"Of course I should love to accompany you." The distraction would do her good.

Essie lowered the tray to a small table, then pulled her chair close to Eden's.

"You love James, and he you, Eden."

"I know that, and I know I should not have pushed him yesterday. But I am to be his wife, Essie. I do not want him to pull away from me every time a situation arises that challenges him."

She took the hand her sister held out to her.

"You are the most loving, passionate person I know, Eden. You give so much of yourself without a care of how it affects you. I have faith that you and James will come to understand each other, and in time he will not turn away from you when he is gripped by strong emotions."

"Are you sure, Essie?"

"Very. The man loves you to distraction, and if that alone is not enough, then Dev will beat him into submission."

"I hope you are right," Eden sighed. "Not about Dev beating him up, but the first part."

"I know I am right. Now enough of this moping. It is a beautiful day, and I wish to go driving with Lord Laurent." Essie regained her feet and headed for the door. "So ready yourself, and put on your prettiest dress, as I may direct him to drive by James's house in the hopes he is standing at his window."

Eden laughed as her sister wanted her too, although they both knew her heart was not in it. She then called for Grace and got herself ready.

***

"You look beautiful today, ladies."

"Thank you, kind, sir," Essie smiled across the carriage to where Lord Laurent sat. The look in his eyes confirmed everything Eden already believed. The man was in love with her sister.

Looking out the window, Eden let the couple talk while her thoughts returned to James. She would send him a note upon her return home, and ask that he pay her a call. She loved him, and with love came compromise, so she would make the first move to breech the gap yesterday's events had placed between them.

"Are you to attend the Langley Ball, this evening, my lord?"

"I am afraid I have other plans, Miss Essex."

Eden knew Essie had a new dress to wear tonight, and that she had chosen it expressly to please Lord Laurent.

"I shall miss you, my lord."

"And I you."

Eden managed to swallow her sigh. It was not easy feeling low and listening to two people so obviously in love.

You are pathetic Eden Sinclair!

They had been driving a while, when she noticed they were not heading toward the park. In fact the streets were not familiar to her at all.

"Lord Laurent, I believe your driver has taken a wrong turn."

Unease suddenly gripped Eden as the smile fell from his lips at her words.

"All will be explained in due course," he said bending to retrieve something from under the seat, and as he straightened, in his hand was a pistol.

"Louis!" Essie cried. "What are you doing?"

"My name is not Louis.

Before their eyes, the man they had always known as Lord Laurent changed. His face, which before had seemed open and honest, was now twisted into a menacing mask.

"Explain yourself, sir!" Eden demanded.

"It is quite simple, Eden. I am going to kill you and your betrothed is going to watch you die before his eyes."

"No, Louis. Please stop this foolery, you are scaring me!"

His eyes passed over Essie as if she were nothing to him.

"Louis, we love each other!"

"I don't love you, Miss Sinclair. You were simply a means to an end. Do not call me Louis again."

"No!"

Eden reached for her sister as she cried out.

"You were a foolish woman to believe my lies. Foolish and gullible."

Rage had Eden lashing out with her foot. She connected with his hand, sending the pistol flying, and momentarily distracting him.

"Open the door, Essie!"

She managed to fling it open seconds, later, and Eden was right behind her.

"Jump!"

Essie did not hesitate, leaping from the carriage. Just as Eden prepared to follow hands hauled her back inside, and the door was slammed shut.

"I think not, Miss Sinclair."

He grabbed her, wrestling her beneath him onto the seat.

"Time for you to sleep now."

She struggled as a cloth was placed over her nose and mouth, but the fumes made her head swim, and slowly she closed her eyes and slumped to the floor.

***

"Hello, James."

"Hello, Samantha," James said, looking over his paper as his sister skipped in. "You appear to have recovered from your ordeal yesterday."

"I was scared briefly while that horrid man had me, but I kept telling myself over and over that you would not let him harm me—and you did not. Therefore, I am scared no longer."

The resilience of youth, James thought. He wished for his sister's ability to push aside yesterday's incident. The memory of her being taken from him was still vivid in his head.

"Dev and Cam have just visited with me and are now taking tea in the breakfast room."

"Now there's a surprise," James muttered, rubbing his chest. He suddenly felt a tight pain there, a stabbing as if someone were sticking pins into him.

"They told me that they were my new brothers and that if at any time I needed you but could not find you, then I was to go to them and they would help me."

"Did they?" he said, folding the paper slowly and precisely. It gave him a warm feeling knowing that if something happened to him the Sinclair men would step in and protect his little sister. He also knew they would love her as if she were theirs.

Hadn't they shown that love yesterday, when they had used their senses and hunted her down? James realized he had not thanked them near enough for what they had done for him and

Samantha. Instead he had abused their sister, the woman he loved, and turned her away.

"Yes, and they said they also get to tease me like they do their siblings and that I can tease them back."

"Excellent, we will put our heads together to find something for you to tease them about after my meeting with them," James said, standing because his chest was now burning.

"James, you were not very nice to Eden yesterday, and as I like her and want her to live with us, I want you to apologize."

"I was scared, Samantha." James dropped to his haunches before her. "I reacted badly and pushed Eden away."

"You love her very much, don't you?"

"I do. So much that I'm worried that once again I have ruined everything."

Samantha placed a hand on his shoulder and looked deep into his eyes.

"She loves you, so she will forgive you. But I think you should buy her something nice just to be sure."

"When did you grow up?"

"Cam taught me."

"Now that is a frightening thought." Standing, he kissed the top of her head and led her from the room. Handing her over to her companion, he then changed direction and headed to where Cam and Dev awaited him.

Before he could reach them, James heard the thunder of feet. Looking up, he noted Dev in the lead with Cam hot on his heels; both wore fierce expressions, and James was instantly on alert.

"What?" he demanded when they reached him.

"Someone is in trouble!" Dev said, stepping around him and running to the front doors.

"Who?" James said, falling in behind Cam.

"Don't know, but we both felt it."

"Eden!" he said, overtaking Cam and shooting out of his front door behind Dev. "It's Eden!" he roared, coming level with the eldest Sinclair.

"How do you know?" Dev wheezed, still sprinting.

"Ch-chest… stabbing pains."

Neither spoke again, arriving at the Wynburg house minutes later.

"P-Pennyroll, get everyone here at once!"

If the butler was surprised by the three men, all bent double and gasping for air in the entrance way of his master's home, he did not show it. Closing the front door he said, "Lord and Lady Wynburg are visiting Admiral Eales at the present time, Lord Sinclair."

Somer, Dorrie, and Warwick stopped further conversation as they appeared at the top of the stairs. James saw the worry on their faces, and felt the pain in his chest increase.

He had turned away from Eden yesterday, simply because he had always dealt with anything challenging by himself. The fear of Samantha's abduction had been unbearable, so he had shut down, and hadn't known how to reach out and ask for help from the woman he loved. Rubbing his chest, he tried to ease the pain that seemed to be burning a hole straight through him.

"Where is Eden, Pennyroll?"

"Lord Laurent called this morning to take Miss Sinclair and Miss Eden driving, your Grace."

"Then surely they are safe?" Cam said.

"Essie is coming, Dev."

All eyes turned to Warwick as he spoke. It was Cam who dropped to his knees before the boy.

"How do you know Essie is coming, Warwick? Where is she?"

The young boy looked at his sisters, they in turn nodded and then he spoke.

"She's close, I can hear her yelling."

James was suddenly aware that the Sinclairs had gone very still; even the little ones were silent and looking at their feet. The eldest was the first to move. Wrenching open the front door, Devon went to find his sister.

"How do you know she is yelling, Warwick?" Cam said slowly.

"I can hear her."

"No!"

"It's true, Cam, he can hear," Somer said.

"Someone tell me what the hell is going on?" James demanded.

"How long have you been able to hear like Eden, Warwick?" Cam rasped.

"Our senses are not strong yet. But he can hear, I can taste, and Dorrie can smell," Somer whispered, her eyes filling with tears. "We didn't tell you because we didn't want you to be upset."

"Christ!" Cam groaned, grabbing all three of them and hugging them tight in his arms. The children burrowed into him, sniffling.

"Eden, Cam!" James roared. "Where is she and what the hell is going on?"

"I heard her talking to him—Lord Laurent—but I couldn't hear everything because Dorrie and Somer were singing. Just that he was taking Essie and Eden driving," Warwick said when his brother had released him to stand once again.

Behind them someone knocked on the open door and they all turned as one. Pennyroll stepped around the family to intercept whoever was there.

"A Mr. Spriggot is here, your Grace, and wanting to speak to you with some expediency," Pennyroll said, as if they had not all heard the man talking just two feet away.

"Let him in."

Mr. Spriggot stopped just inside the door, his face showing surprise at seeing such a gathering in the front entrance. Next through the door was an ashen faced Essie in the arms of her brother.

"What has happened, Essie?" Cam stepped to her side.

"L-Lord Laurent," she sobbed. "H-he is not who we think, Cam. He had a gun, and then Eden urged me to jump from the c-carriage, but she d-did not follow."

Dear god, not Eden. Please don't let her be hurt. The thought nearly dropped James to his knees.

"Lord Laurent!"

James spun to Mr. Spriggot, who had said the name in shocked tones, which could only be a bad thing.

"Speak, Mr. Spriggot. If my fiancée is in danger then we must move quickly."

"Lord Laurent is not his real identity, your Grace. His mother was Miss Tolly and she was your father's mistress—"

"I know who she was, Mr. Spriggot," James said, his mind whirling in circles. Louis was his half brother and he was going to harm Eden to get to him. What other reason would he have for hiding his identity?

"He said he would k-kill Eden while you watched, James." All eyes turned to Essie as she slumped into her brother's arms. Cam cradled her against his chest as if she were a small child.

"I'll kill him if he harms her!" James's words shook with rage and fear.

"Where would he take her, Spriggot?" Dev said urgently.

"I have located his sister, your Grace. She lives here in London. Perhaps she can shed some light on where her brother has taken your sister, Lord Sinclair."

"Get whatever you need to travel," James told the Sinclairs. "We leave as soon as I have the horses readied." He ran out the door.

He tried to focus as he sprinted back to his house. She would be safe until he got to her. He would not hurt her, not Louis; surely he had no reason to harm Eden, as it was James that he wanted. He tried not to think of the attempts on his life, the ruthless ability of a man to throw another bound hand and foot into the sea alive.

"Eden!" he whispered, praying that she could hear him, but knowing he was fooling himself. *Please don't take her from me.* He felt the emotionless man he had once been slide back into place. Could he live like that again? Be forced into the dark, when he now knew what it felt like to live in the light.

Throwing open his front door, he surprised his butler, who was moving an arrangement of flowers.

"Buttles! Have three of my best horses brought to Lord Wynburg's house at once!"

"Right away, your Grace."

He fired out several other orders about coats and hats then took the stairs two at a time to his office.

He pushed his knife into his boot, then armed himself with two pistols and supplies to fire them. Lastly he pulled a pouch of money from his desk.

"James, has something happened?" Samantha had entered behind him.

"Someone has taken Eden, Samantha, and I must go now and get her back."

He watched the old fears flit across her young face, and hated that it was he who had put them there. Pulling her into his arms he held her close

"We will return, sweetheart, but until then Jane will take you to stay with Warwick, Somer, and Dorrie, and I want you to stay with them and Lord and Lady Wynburg until I return," he said, releasing her.

"I love you, James. Promise that you and Eden will come home safe."

"I promise, and I love you too."

Samantha nodded and then ran from the room with James on her heels. Reaching the front entrance, he shrugged into his coat and hat, then took his gloves and went outside. Mr. Brown was mounted and leading James's horse; a groom held two others.

"I thought you could use my help, your Grace. I'm a fair shot."

"My thanks" was all James said as he swung into the saddle.

"Buttles, escort my sister and her companion to Lord and Lady Wynburg at once. I am unsure when I will return, and she will stay there until I do."

"At once, your Grace, and God be with you."

In minutes they were at the Wynburg residence, where Dev, Cam, and Essie waited for them outside. Essie was lifted by Dev to ride behind Cam, her face pale yet composed, a satchel on her back.

As a small somber group they rode through London. Slowly the houses lost their grandness and grew shabby, pressing closer together and stacked one on top of the other, until finally they stopped before a small building.

"This is the address Spriggot gave us," Mr. Brown said.

"Stay with Essie, Cam, you too, Mr. Brown. Devon and I will go and visit with Tolly's sister."

"She is your sister also, James," Dev said, knocking on the worn front door. The place was dismal and dark even though the sun still sat high in the sky.

"I am aware of that," James said, rubbing his chest. He watched the door open slowly. A young woman the same height as Eden looked up at them. She could only be Louis's sister; the blue eyes and blonde hair were identical. *And your sister*, James added.

"Can I help you?"

"Miss Tolly?"

"Yes." She nodded, looking anxious, her eyes flitting from

James to Dev then back again.

"We are looking for your brother, Miss Tolly," James said.

"I—I am afraid he is not here."

"I am the Duke of Raven, Miss Tolly. Your half brother."

Her fingers gripped the door, knuckles white as she stared at him. "I believe your brother has abducted my fiancée and I must find her. Please help us."

"Oh Louis, no!" Her moan was that of a wounded animal as she stumbled backward and fell to her knees, sobbing. James stepped forward and knelt beside her.

"Miss Tolly, please don't cry. We shall try to return your brother to you unharmed, but I must find my fiancée."

Tears streamed down her face as she looked up at him.

"H-he never recovered fr-from our mother's death, you see," she whispered. "The D-Duke would not help us and Louis could d-do nothing for her. It destroyed him, your Grace."

"Where would he go?"

"The church at Raven Castle," she whispered. "It was as close as he could get to the castle. He would go there at night when no one could see him, and sit and plot his r-revenge upon your family."

James did not wait to ask further questions. Lifting her to her feet, he held her shoulders between his hands, forcing her to look up at him.

"I am your brother, Miss Tolly,"

"Emily," she whispered.

"I realize our father gave you no reason to trust the word of a Raven, yet I would ask you to do just that, Emily. I will come for you upon my return, I promise," James added, placing a kiss on her forehead. Closing the door behind him as he left, James and Dev ran to their horses.

"Raven Castle!" Dev barked as they mounted, and they were soon on the road out of London.

CHAPTER TWENTY SIX

Eden woke feeling dizzy and nauseous. Her wrists and feet were bound and a piece of cloth was tied around her mouth, forcing it open. Her eyelids felt heavy as she opened them. She was lying on her side on the floor of a carriage that was travelling at speed. The curtains were drawn, but she knew that night had fallen, which suggested she had been asleep—drugged for some time. She was alone in the carriage. She could hear no one else breathing so Lord Laurent—or whoever he was—was either on horseback or sitting with the driver.

Struggling into a sitting position, she turned and wedged her feet against the opposite seat and pushed herself up and onto the seat at her back. She wriggled her wrists, but they were bound tight. Now she was awake, the gag was making her choke, and it was a struggle to inhale. Slumping sideways, Eden closed her eyes again. Her head was aching from whatever foul thing that man had made her breathe.

At least Essie had escaped, and Eden prayed she had not harmed herself when she jumped from the carriage. Did James and her family know she had been abducted yet? Had her sister made it back and told them? How would they find her? Fighting down the swell of panic, Eden knew she could not let it overwhelm her if she was to somehow get out of this situation.

Where was he taking her? Eden didn't know how long she lay there in the dark with thoughts tumbling through her head.

Her family would not stop until they found her, but what of James? No, he loved her, he would be distressed that she was missing. Eden may have been hurt by his behavior yesterday, but in this cold, dark carriage, she realized that it was he she wanted most. She needed the strength he gave her when he held her in his arms. She would not allow herself to doubt they would find her, for that path lead to fear and tears, and she could not go to that place yet.

Their senses would lead them to her, she just had to be strong and stay alive until they did.

When Eden woke the second time, the carriage had stopped. Her body ached but her head was now clear. Her eyes went to the open curtains, and she saw early morning mists out of the window.

"I have food and drink for you, Eden."

The man she had known as Lord Laurent stepped into the carriage and sat opposite her. In his hand was a wooden bowl. His eyes were narrowed, face taut, and she wondered how he had fooled them all for so long.

"I will feed you, as I do not trust you enough to release your bonds." He pulled the gag from her mouth.

Eden breathed deeply and then glared at him.

"I want nothing from you."

"That is your loss. It worries me not if you go hungry."

She watched him as one would a venomous animal.

"No questions, Eden? Have I at last found a woman who can hold her tongue?"

"If you have kidnapped me in the hopes of luring James to your side, then think again. Yesterday we argued after you attempted to take his sister from under his nose, and I doubt he will miss me overmuch."

"He loves you, so he will come."

"I will see you pay for what you have done to my sister." She hissed the words at him.

"Your sister is a gullible fool. How she could believe a man like I would love her is beyond belief."

Eden wanted to lunge at him, scratch his handsome face, and make him pay for the pain he had inflicted on those she loved.

"Are you not curious as to who I am, and why I want to kill your precious Duke?"

She saw it then, the madness that haunted his eyes.

"Why do you want to harm the man I love?" she whispered.

"Because of what he did to my family," he spat out. "My mother died writhing in agony because of that man."

"You are James's half brother," Eden realized.

"The Ravens are no kin of mine!" he roared. "They forfeited that right when the Duke turned us away when my mother needed help. I will have retribution for her death—I will," he vowed.

"James is not responsible for his father's actions. You would make an innocent man pay for a death he had no hand in?"

"He has lived a good life, now it is time for him to die. No other of his blood will be Duke. I will make sure of it."

His simmering hatred had robbed his mind of all but vengeance, and Eden knew she would never be able to reason with him.

"Y-you will not succeed."

"Of course I will succeed. Your beloved will ride to your side, and I will kill you before his eyes, and then him."

"N-no." She tried to lunge at him, but he simply pushed her back to the seat, and once again she felt her head spin as he placed a cloth over her face.

***

They rode through the night, with a change of horses at each stop. Mr. Brown organized food at each inn or posting house, they ate and drank while standing, and then mounted and rode hard once more.

James could think of nothing but Eden. The thought of never seeing her smile again, or touching her hair and hearing her laugh, was a physical pain inside him. His chest ached as if a hot poker were pressed against it.

"The innkeeper said a carriage and a man of Tolly's description came through here two hours ago," Mr. Brown said, stepping outside the inn's doors. His face wore fatigue, as did they all, his clothes covered in dust and dirt. Behind him came two servants, one carrying a tray with five large pieces of pie, and another with mugs of ale and one of tea.

"The castle is five hours from here; we should arrive as he does, if not just after," Dev said, shooting James a look.

Nodding, James took a piece of pie and the cup of tea and went to Essie, who had not complained once since the journey began many hours ago. She had sat behind Cam, stoic and composed when he knew inside that his half brother had shattered her heart into tiny pieces. She was slumped on a mounting block, her head lowered, shoulders hunched, fatigue and defeat in every line of her body. Her brothers had tried to protect her as best they could, tried to talk with her, and yet she had remained silent, like he, locked behind a wall of agony.

"Eat this, Essie," James said, handing her the plate. She shook her head and reached for the tea.

"I will have your brothers hold you and we will feed you this pie one bite at a time if you do not willingly eat it," he added in a firm voice. "You will do your sister no favors if you faint before we reach her. Should she need you, then you must be strong enough to help, Essie, and when I get my hands on that bastard who has her, I am sure you, like me, will have a few things to say to him."

The look she sent him was filled with anguish. Her eyes were bloodshot and she suddenly appeared much older than she had yesterday.

"Essie, you will survive this because you have family who love you, family who would give their life for yours. Take their strength and hold it around you and know that you are not alone."

"I'm so scared, James, scared that I let this man into my heart when he is so evil."

"He fooled us all, Essie."

"I am scared that such a man, one so desperate for revenge he took the steps he did to secure it, has my sister. I want her back now, need her here with me."

"I know, Essie," James said, reaching for her hand. "I know your fears, for they mirror my own. My last words to Eden were angry bitter ones that I had no right to speak. I hurt the woman I love deeply, Essie, yet I cannot think about that. Only that Eden needs our strength. She needs us to stand up and fight for her and what we have."

"What do we have, James?" she whispered as the tears once again fell down her pale cheeks.

"Family, Essie. Family and love, and after years of living without either I am not about to lose what I have only just found. So fight with me, Essie."

She squeezed his hand one last time then took the pie and started eating.

James rose and returned to the men, where he gulped down his ale and then started in on his pie.

"Thank you."

Mouth full of beef and pastry, both of which tasted like ashes, James turned to look at the eldest Sinclair.

"I spoke the truth."

"Perhaps," Dev said, tipping his tankard and downing the last mouthful. "Yet what you said was what she needed to hear. However, from Cam or I it would not have held the same meaning, and for that we are grateful."

Nodding, James remained silent and kept eating. Was Eden well? Was Tolly treating her badly? Was she scared or hurt? Had she cried out for him? God, it was torture not knowing.

His beautiful Eden was feisty and strong, yet today he knew she had felt fear. She would know her brothers would come for her, but after yesterday did she fear he would not? God, he hoped not.

I'm coming, my love.

"Mount up!"

James took the fresh horse and placed a foot in the stirrup at Dev's words. He felt no fatigue or pain as he swung into the saddle. His body had gone from ice to a slow burning rage as the miles passed. He would find Tolly and kill him. He felt no remorse for the act he was about to commit. Tolly had dared to harm Samantha yesterday, and now Eden. The two people he loved most in this world. Therefore, he would die, just as he had chosen to kill James. Brothers they may be, but there was nothing but a blood tie between them. Any friendship he had once believed they shared was long since left behind in the glittering ballrooms of London society.

The pace was relentless, if possible even more so now they neared their destination. They all had the same goal. Eden would be saved. James would allow himself to think of no other outcome, except perhaps of his own death. He would sacrifice himself for her if there was no other option. He felt no qualms about this.

Looking to his left, he saw the determination on the Sinclairs' faces. Even Mr. Brown, Joseph, as they had come to

316

know him over the miles they had ridden, was determined.

"The cliffs!"

James saw them rise before him as Cam called out. The rugged beauty of the rock face and whitecaps of the waters below failed to stir him as they usually did. He saw the gulls swooping and diving, seeking their prey, and memories of the night he had first met Eden rose inside him. From the start she had shown him the kind of person she was. The selfless woman who loved him.

Following the line of rock, they veered right and headed for the small town of Crunston Cliff. Thundering through, they acknowledged no one as people ran to see who rode through their village in haste. Passing Oak's Knoll, James spared a glance at the castle that loomed above them before drawing to a halt.

"We will ride to the first rise and then walk to the church, as I have no wish for Tolly to hear us arrive," James said.

The ride took just minutes and James dismounted and tethered his horse. The others followed. The hill formed two tiers—the first held the church and graveyard where his ancestors lay, and on the level above sat the castle. James knew she was near; the pain in his chest had increased. Pushing aside branches, he kept close to the mountain, slowly circling the hill to reach the church.

"Eden, love, I am here with your brothers. We are coming for you, be brave." James spoke as loud as he dared.

"She will have heard our horses, James." Devon Sinclair moved to his side. "In fact, if she has removed her earplugs she probably heard us riding up the mountain, unless Tolly was speaking."

They climbed and finally the church was before them. On their bellies they studied the small building.

"Joseph, stay at the back with Essie," Dev ordered. "Should Tolly escape, shoot him."

"Very well, my lord."

Crouching, James, Dev, and Cam moved closer. The three men held guns, all ready to use them without hesitation to ensure Eden's safe return.

The church sat near the edge. Built of stone, its foundations had formed part of this hill for hundreds of years. Ravens had been wed and buried here, children had been baptized, and until his father became Duke, villagers had also used it. James vowed they would do so again. Shafts of sunlight pushed through the clouds and touched the weathered honey-colored stone.

James wondered if the peace and beauty before him was about to be tarnished with his death.

His home loomed above like an elderly grandfather overseeing its grandchild. He had never hated this place, only the man who had lived in it.

"He is inside," Dev whispered from beside him. "I see him."

"Eden?"

"She is there. Her color is strong."

James's heart thudded in his chest as relief pumped through him.

"I'm here, love."

"Something does not smell right," Cam said, moving forward, his nose in the air. "Dev, grip my hand."

James watched the brothers, Dev's pupils huge and Cam with his head thrown back.

"I smell poison in there. Poison and fear."

"Why would he need poison?" Dev looked at his brother.

"My first thought is he wants to make sure my death is slow and painful," James said.

"We shall try not to let that happen," Dev gritted out.

"You two circle the outside. There is a small door at the rear that is always left open. I will go in through the front and distract him, as it is me he wants," James said calmly.

"It is highly dangerous for you to do so, yet I can come up with no other plan," Dev whispered. "If he tries to shoot, then for pity's sake duck. Keep him talking as long as you can, which will allow us time to get inside. I believe from their position they are at the altar, and as Eden is not moving I think he has her tied to something."

"Take no risks with Eden, I want her out of there before you save me." James needed the brothers to understand that she was their main concern.

"We will save you both, Raven," Cam looked fierce.

"She is more important than me," James said. "I—I must have your word that you get her to safety before you—"

"She is our sister, Raven, we are aware of her importance," Dev hissed. "Yet we are also aware of your importance to us and her. Therefore, brother, we will save you both."

James looked at Dev for long seconds, then with one curt nod he turned and walked toward the church. He was aware of the sound his boots made upon the narrow drive and then as they hit the stone floor at the entrance. Gripping the handle, he felt the strength of his ancestors flow through him, and wrenched it open.

"You have come, brother, how kind!"

Light from a round stained-glass window high in the wall at the back of the church lit the altar. James blinked to adjust his vision and searched for Eden. She was standing tied to the large cross beneath it. Tolly stood beside her. In one hand he held a vial of liquid, the other a gun.

"Let her go, Tolly, it is me you want."

"If only life were that simple, brother," the man said, chuckling.

"I am sorry your mother suffered because our father would not help her, Tolly. But Eden is not responsible for his deeds, just as I am not," James said, moving slowly forward.

"With you dead his precious untainted bloodline will be snuffed out, Raven, and only then will my vengeance be complete."

"Let Eden go."

"Ah, now there I am afraid I cannot oblige you, brother."

James wondered how he had been so fooled by the man. This madman before him now bore only a physical resemblance to the Lord Laurent he and society knew. Gone was the perpetual smile and charm, replaced by narrowed eyes behind which James could see madness.

"Your father told me when I went to beg him to help my mother that I was not fit for him to step on, and she was nothing but a whore who had spread her legs for any man. Therefore, how was he to know if indeed I was his son."

James clenched his fists. He had thought he could not hate his father more—it seemed that he was wrong.

"I was told that you were his heir, a fine specimen of untainted pure blood, and that his precious line would live long through your pure well-bred children."

"I am not my father, Tolly, as you very well know."

"Yet you will pay for his sins, brother, because he is not here to do so."

"Emily is worried about you," James said, looking at Eden. He saw the fear etched in every line of her body, and also the anger that matched his. She struggled to break her bonds. A gag kept her quiet and James struggled to see through the red haze of rage as he saw a streak of blood on her lip. Taking a deep breath, he pushed it down once more. He would not help her if he did remain focused.

"Stay still, my love, I will get you out of here safely." She must have heard his whispered words, because her struggles instantly ceased.

"Stay away from her. I will care for my sister!"

"I have no wish to harm your sister, Tolly. I wish only for Eden's safety," James said, moving steadily forward. "In fact, I would like to help both you and your sister, see that you are comfortable."

"I would not have needed to take your beloved had I succeeded in my attempts to take your sister, yet you and the bloody Sinclairs foiled that."

"My sister is a child, Tolly!"

"As was I when I approached your father."

"Let me help you and Emily. Let me give you money, a house, anything you want," James said, trying to remain calm.

"We need nothing from a Raven!" Tolly spat. "Now move forward slowly and kneel before your precious Miss Sinclair."

He did as he was asked. Slowly and steadily he walked until he stood before her.

"Be strong, my love," he whispered.

"Down!" Tolly screeched, using the butt of his gun to hit James in the back of the head.

He heard her groan, but he did not flinch, merely did as he was directed. The second hit made him grunt, and she fought furiously against her bonds.

"I'm all right, Eden. Stay calm, love."

"Do you know what is in this vial, Raven?" Tolly said, shaking it before James's eyes. "'Tis poison. Your last vision will be of your beloved as she drinks it. You will die knowing she will suffer an agonizing death while you lie bleeding at her feet."

"No!" James heard the rattle of the back door, and knew he had been wrong. It was locked. He struggled to stand, lurching toward the vial. The gun fired, and he felt a burning in his arm. It knocked him backward.

"Drink it now or I shoot him dead before your eyes!"

James reached his knees as Tolly wrenched the gag from her mouth.

"James, be still!" she cried as he got to his feet. He saw Tolly had another pistol now in his hand.

"Don't drink it, Eden, he will kill me anyway!" He kept his eyes on her, begging her to listen to him.

"Drink it or I shoot him dead, now, with you watching."

"No, Eden!" James lunged at her as she opened her mouth, but Tolly had already lifted the vial. He dove to the floor at her feet as the gun discharged, but this time he felt no pain, the shot had missed him.

The thud of feet told James the brothers had arrived. Tolly took a bullet in the chest, and the impact threw him backward, his body hitting the wall then slumping motionless to the floor, the vial shattering at his feet.

"The bastard locked the back door!" Cam roared. "Christ, he shot you!" He reached for James as Dev reached for his sister.

"Poison!" James rasped. "He made her drink poison," he said, staggering to his feet and reaching for Eden as Dev freed the last of her bonds.

"Essie!" Dev roared.

"Eden, God, love." James shuddered, crushing her against him.

"I-I had to take it," she whispered. "I could not live if you died."

"Nor can I! Damn you, Eden, you will not leave me!" James roared as he felt her body grow limp.

"L-love you," she whispered.

"It's white arsenic!" Cam yelled, sniffing the bottle. "A large dose!"

"James, stick your fingers down her throat!" Essie screamed, running into the church. "We need to purge her of the poison," she added, ignoring the lifeless form of the man she had loved to drop to her knees beside her sister.

Rolling Eden onto her side, Dev pried her mouth open and James stuck two fingers inside. She retched and retched, but it took several attempts before anything came out.

"Cam, take me to Oak's Knoll now. I will find the herbs we need to rid her system of the rest of it," Essie said, throwing her sister one last agonized look before she ran from the church. "Follow us, Dev, quickly!" she cried over her shoulder, and then she was gone.

Ignoring the fire burning through his arm, James picked Eden up and followed her siblings. She lay limp against him as he rode toward her home, no life in her body, no fire in her eyes. "Stay with me, Eden. Please, love, hold on."

One of the brothers who served the Sinclair family awaited them on the steps of Oak's Knoll, his face lined with worry as they rode up. Taking Eden from James, he ran into the house with James and Dev following. They placed her on a bed.

"How is her color, Dev?" Essie asked from her place beside the fire.

"Pale."

"What does that mean, pale?" James demanded.

"She is weak," Essie said, carrying a small cup to the bed. "Dev, open her mouth for me. James, hold her head."

Between them they managed to force down the contents of the cup by massaging her throat between sips. Her cough was weak, and her eyes were now only half open.

"Eden, love. Tell me what you feel?" Essie said.

"M-my h-hands," she whispered.

"Arsenic makes the hands and feet tingle." Essie wiped away a tear as she stood and looked down at her sister.

James was numb with fear as he watched Eden struggle to breathe. The pulse on her wrist seemed to grow weaker with every breath she drew.

"How long, Essie? How long before we know if it has worked?"

Essie grabbed her sister's other hand and kissed it.

"The poison shuts down her system. Her stomach will cramp and we shall know soon if—"

"She will live," James vowed.

No one spoke as they watched Eden silently struggle to breathe as she clung precariously to life.

"Can you not do something—your senses, surely they…?"

"None of us have the power to heal by touch, James," Essie said quietly. "It is the one sense we do not have."

"And now, your Grace, we shall see to your arm," Bertie said.

"My arm?"

"'Tis bleeding, your Grace. Miss Essex will make a paste and bandage it."

He let them tend him, yet he did not move from his place beside Eden.

"The bullet has gone straight through, James." Essie's words did not register with him as he watched his fiancée. James was sure her breathing was growing weaker. She was so still, all color had leeched from her face. Tangled and messed, her hair lay around her head in a dark cloud. Eden was never still; even when she was sitting, often her hands moved or her feet tapped. She was the fire to his ice. The one who was filled with life, the one who had taught him how to love.

"Now take this, your Grace, 'tis merely a warm drink to stop the infection, nothing more."

He took the drink Bertie handed him yet still his eyes stayed on Eden. At some stage over the next few hours someone pushed him into a chair beside her, but he still held her hand and looked at her face. He heard them murmuring, watched Essie touch her cheek and check her pulse. Dev looked at her, his eyes filled with grief, yet James wouldn't move. She would live, she had to live. If she died she would commit him to a life of hell.

"Her breathing has grown shallow."

James watched as Essie stood over Eden, checking her pulse. Behind her Cam and Dev, their faces solemn, watched over their sister.

"No," James said softly. "No, she is not leaving us." He climbed onto the bed and lifted Eden into his arms.

"All of you touch her. Your skin to hers. Now!" he roared, when they failed to move. "The power of this family can heal her. I believe in you all. Now hold her, damn you. Give her your love and strength."

Dev grabbed Eden's arm. Pushing up her sleeve, he wrapped both hands around it. Cam reached for a leg, clasping her ankle in his hands. Essie gripped Eden's other hand.

"Focus," James said quietly, and then he began to talk to Eden, urging her back from the hell she had slumped into.

"Do you remember when we talked of the places we would go in our heads when we were frightened or alone, Eden? You told me you rode along the cliffs, and I climbed the castle's highest turret." He listened to the small wheeze of her breath before he continued. "I can't go there anymore, love, because you are my happy place. My reason for waking, the reason I now exist. Yes, I have Samantha, but you, my love… you are my everything." Grabbing a handful of her curls, he wrapped them around his fist. "In the short time you have been in my life I have known such happiness. You have filled all the dark places in me, given me hope and shown me how to laugh. You meet me head-on, love, challenge and chastise me. I know now what it means to find that one true love and to lose you would be to spend the rest of my days wandering in purgatory, waiting to meet you again. Don't leave me, Eden," he said, burying his face in her hair and releasing the tears that burned behind his eyes. Cradling her against him, he rested on the pillows, his cheek pressed to her chilled one.

Please don't take her from me.

He felt it then, the surge of heat that travelled through her body, and then he felt nothing.

James woke as he moved his arm, causing a red-hot ember of pain to slice through him. Eden! Opening his eyes, he looked down to where she lay on his chest. Placing two fingers on her pulse he felt it, strong and steady. Touching her forehead, he noted it was warm but not hot.

"Eden!" he rasped, tilting her head up so he could look at her face in the firelight.

"What!" Dev struggled to his feet from his position near the fire. Essie followed; Cam kept snoring.

"She is breathing well, and her skin feels warm," James said, easing into a sitting position and then getting off the bed so he could get a better look at her.

"She's stirring," Dev whispered.

"Come on, love, open your eyes," James urged her.

They fluttered open and closed again, then they opened and she looked at him.

"James?"

"Yes," he rasped, kissing her cheek as her fingers slid into his.

"I heard your words but I could not speak, the p-poison, it was so hard to fight through—and then I felt so warm, as if warm water were travelling through my body."

"James made us all touch you," Essie said. "The heat came from all of us, Eden, even James."

"This time you saved me."

"I could not have lived without you." James bent over her, his face close. "You are my life."

"I love you, Duke."

"I love you," he whispered.

He then moved back, allowing her family to hug and kiss her.

"James, don't leave me," she whispered when they were finished. Her eyes were closing as he moved to her side once more.

"I'm here, love, where I will stay." He took her hand, slipping her fingers through his. She gave him the sweetest smile and then fell into a deep, healing sleep, and for the first time since she had been taken, he drew in a breath, knowing that she was here safe and well surrounded by the people who loved her.

CHAPTER TWENTY-SEVEN

"Does she look like him—Tolly?"

James drew his gaze from the dismal surroundings outside the carriage window to look at Eden. She sat opposite, dressed in a blue sprigged muslin dress with darker blue matching velvet pelisse buttoned up over her splendid breasts. Her bonnet was of the same fabric and hid her glorious hair, and he was pleased to note some color in her cheeks, although she was still too pale for his liking. Her eyes had smudges beneath, telling him that although she strenuously denied having trouble sleeping, in fact she was.

"Yes, very much so, love. But we will not hold that against her."

"She shall not pay for her father's sins," she said, waving one delicate gloved hand in front of her.

"Something like that," he muttered, grabbing her hand and tugging her across the seat to fall into his lap.

"James, your arm!"

"My arm is fine and you, madam, are too far away over there," he whispered against her neck. She wriggled as his breath tickled her skin, before settling against him with a sigh.

They had returned to London one week after arriving at Oak's Knoll with Eden unconscious in James's arms, and he relived that memory daily. He had nearly lost her, and that would never be allowed to happen again. He would ensure it.

"You should have on your sling."

"Slings are for ladies," James said in a mock growl.

"Two weeks." Eden sighed.

"And you will be my wife and share my bed."

"Yes," she said again in that soft tone that made his bones melt.

She had woken the day after regaining consciousness as if she had never been poisoned, determined to carry on as if the little matter of a near-death experience were nothing overly worrying. However, her body and James had thought differently. He had refused to let them leave for London that day, instead making her stay in bed and traveling three days later. Even then they had stopped often. She was still feeling the effects of the poison and tired easily, and James watched her closely, much to her annoyance.

"Essie is doing well. Don't you think?"

"Very well, but I imagine she is more like me than you, and therefore has the ability to hide her feelings."

"I am such an open book, then?"

"To me you are." He kissed the top of her nose.

He had apologized for his behavior the day before Tolly took her from him, and she had of course accepted, with the proviso it did not happen again.

"It's disturbing to love someone as much as I love you."

"Disturbing in a good way I hope?" James could never get enough of this woman. Touching a soft cheek, he traced the contour, mapping each curve.

"I love my family, but this is vastly different. With you it's almost painful, and when I thought Tolly would take you from me…." She closed her eyes. "Oh, James, the pain—"

James pressed a finger to her lips to silence her. "No one is taking me from you, as no one will take you from me. We are two halves of a whole, sweetheart. I'm afraid you must accept the fact that you are stuck with me from now until I haul in my final breath with you weeping at my bedside." He said the words to remove the fear from her eyes.

"Ha, I shall be counting your money!"

"No, you won't." He pulled her close for a long heated kiss. "Because you will be inconsolable."

"I will." She touched his cheek. "Don't leave me."

"Never," he vowed. "Because this disturbing, wonderful love we share will never die, my sweet."

They sat in silence for the remainder of the journey, Eden's cheek resting on his chest, his arms holding her close.

"The carriage is slowing, James, let me up."

Placing her on the seat beside him, James climbed from the carriage then reached for Eden's hand, and together they walked to his sister's front door. Images of his last journey here had his fingers tightening.

"I hear her footsteps."

James simply nodded, now used to her and the Sinclair way. He watched the door open, and his sister's pale face appear.

"Y-your Grace, my brother?"

"I am afraid your brother is dead, Emily," James said, stepping through the door as she stumbled backward. Eden beat him and slipped through to reach for his sister.

"It's all right, Emily, we are here now, you are not alone."

James watched Eden gather the woman in her arms.

"Edward is dead?"

"I am so very sorry, Emily, but yes he is, dear."

Eden guided Emily to a small chair, with James on their heels. It seemed to be the only room in the house and he saw a neatly made bed, small table, and washstand.

"Now," Eden added, lowering Emily into the chair. "I think

we shall just take you home with us. This is no place for a young lady to live, especially alone."

"Oh, I—"

"James, find something to carry her belongings in."

He didn't argue. Eden had the fire in her eyes and her back was straight with purpose. She had not asked him, but he would not have protested if she did because he agreed with her. This was no place for his sister to live. In minutes he had located what was needed and handed it to Eden.

"Now, Emily, what do you want to take with you when you leave here?"

Wide-eyed, Emily looked from James to Eden then around the room. "But, I cannot come with you—surely? It would not be right."

"I'm not sure why," Eden said calmly. "James is your brother, I am his betrothed, and you shall not be living with just him, there is your half sister, Samantha."

"I-I have a half sister?"

James saw the hope flicker through her wary eyes.

"You do, and she is in need of an elder female to watch over her until I move into the house."

James didn't think he was doing a bad job with Samantha, but kept that thought to himself.

"Come along now, Emily," Eden said. "It need be only temporary if that is your wish, but you cannot stay here alone, it is not safe."

Eden's words seemed to galvanize Emily into action. Regaining her feet, she proceeded to grab several things and place them in the bag Eden held open. He watched as she tilted her head to one side, studying four books laid one on top of the other. James had seen Samantha do just that when she was thinking.

"M-my mother use to read this to Edward and me when we were little." She took the book at the bottom.

Edward. His brother's name had been Edward.

"Excellent. Well then, you had better bring it because one day you may wish to read to your own children," Eden said, taking Emily's coat off the hook and wrapping it around her shoulders. Her bonnet was next.

James watched as Eden tied the worn ribbons beneath his sister's chin. Humbled that this amazing woman now belonged to him, he stood silently, letting her take charge.

"James will take care of the rest of the details, Emily. We shall leave now."

"I—I—"

"Don't look back, Emily, the future is forward and in that direction lies happiness and love."

"She's right," James said, taking his sister's other arm and nodding to where Eden stood. "She gave me both, Emily. Let us share some of that with you."

"All right," his sister said with a small wobbly smile as she climbed into the carriage, and not once did she look back.

***

The marriage of Miss Eden Sinclair to the Duke of Raven took place in the church at Raven Castle, much to the horror of the Countess of Wynburg, who had imagined a grander church with many many guests.

"We wish to replace the memories of what last took place in here with new ones, Aunt. Surely you can understand that?" Eden had explained to Lady Wynburg. And eventually she had, sending out invitations, organizing a banquet after the ceremony that would take place in the castle, and everything else that went along with a wedding.

The day was fine and the sun high as guests filled the small church to the rafters. James stood with Cam at the altar, waiting for Eden to arrive.

"I hope you are only minutes away, my love," he said, hoping Eden was close. "As I cannot endure to wait much longer."

The sound of chatter reached his ears, and then Dorrie, Somer, and Samantha appeared in the doorway of the church behind Warwick, who was the ring bearer. Cam chuckled as he watched his little brother's tongue stick out of his mouth as he concentrated on walking slowly down the aisle without dropping the pillow that held the rings.

"Look at those three, one would not guess the trouble they cause us," he said as they watched the little girls trail slowly behind, throwing petals on the floor.

James tore his eyes from the children as Eden appeared on the arm of her brother. He slowly let out the breath he had been holding as she stepped inside the church. She was dressed in ivory satin, the gown seeming to float around her as she walked. In her hand was a small bouquet of flowers with matching ribbons, and her face was hidden from him behind a lace veil. His chest felt so full of emotion it nearly choked him.

"James!"

Dragging his eyes from his betrothed, James looked down at his sister, who now stood before him, her face tilted back and the ring of flowers on her head in danger of falling to the floor.

"Eden looks like a princess!" she whispered loudly.

Righting the flowers, James agreed. "She does, Samantha. Do I look like a prince then?"

"Delusions of grandeur, James," Cam muttered, taking Samantha's hand and leading her back to where his little sisters now stood.

James smiled as Eden reached him. Behind her, Emily and Essie took their places with the children.

Dev lifted Eden's veil and then he saw her, his beautiful girl. Her brother kissed her cheek and then shook James's hand.

"I'll kill you if you hurt her, Raven."

"I would have it no other way, Sinclair."

The service was conducted without mishap, the children perfectly behaved except for a few grumbles and fidgets, and then the minister said, "You may kiss the bride."

And he did. It was a slow meeting of two souls. A kiss that sealed their love and the happiness yet to come. A kiss that spoke of their relief that finally they were bound together by more than love.

"Is it true?"

"Yes, and now we must live happily ever after," James breathed against her lips.

"There may be a few things to disturb that, Raven," Dev muttered, trying to part Warwick and Dorrie, who were doing battle over something. "But I applaud the concept."

He couldn't help it. James wrapped an arm around his new wife's waist and then threw back his head and laughed, right there in front of the guests. Happiness bubbled through him and for the first time in his life he gave vent to it.

"Is he all right?"

"Yes, darling," he heard Eden answer Samantha. "He is merely happy."

"I am," James wheezed. "I really am."

"Well I should bloody well hope so, as you just married me."

Eden was smiling at him, and James knew that this, what he felt now, would be with him forever.

THE END

Printed in Great Britain
by Amazon

38997581R00203